Professor Bernard Knight, CBE, became a Home Office Pathologist in 1965 and was appointed Professor of Forensic Pathology, University of Wales College of Medicine, in 1980. Now retired, he is able to devote more time to his writing career. The author of ten novels, a biography and numerous popular and academic non-fiction books, he has also written extensively for the BBC and ITV, both for dramas and documentaries.

THE POISONED CHALICE

December, 1194. The well-born ladies of Exeter are not having a good week. First, Christina Rifford, the daughter of a rich merchant, is raped. Then, Lady Adele de Courcy is found dead in one of the city's poorest areas. The common factor is Godfrey Fitzosbern, the local silversmith. But it is the duty of the county coroner, Sir John de Wolfe, to protect Godfrey until he can find proof of his guilt. John slowly begins to put the pieces together. But a final, brutal act of violence brings a new twist to his investigation before he finally arrives at the truth.

Books by Bernard Knight
Published by The House of Ulverscroft:

THE SANCTUARY SEEKER

BERNARD KNIGHT

THE POISONED CHALICE

A Crowner John Mystery

Complete and Unabridged

ULVERSCROFT
Leicester

First published in Great Britain in 1998 by
Pocket Books
London

First Large Print Edition
published 2000
by arrangement with
Simon & Schuster Limited
London

The moral right of the author has been asserted

British Library CIP Data

Knight, Bernard, *1931 –*
  The poisoned chalice.—Large print ed.—
  (A Crowner John mystery)
  Ulverscroft large print series: mystery
  1. Rape—England—Devon—Fiction
  2. Devon (England)—Fiction 3. Detective and
  mystery stories 4. Large type books
  I. Title
  823.9'14 [F]

  ISBN 0–7089–4284–9

Published by
F. A. Thorpe (Publishing)
Anstey, Leicestershire

Set by Words & Graphics Ltd.
Anstey, Leicestershire
Printed and bound in Great Britain by
T. J. International Ltd., Padstow, Cornwall

This book is printed on acid-free paper

Author's note

Any attempt to give modern English dialogue an 'olde worlde' flavour in historical novels is as inaccurate as it is futile. In the time and place of this story, late twelfth-century Devon, most people would have spoken early Middle English, which would be unintelligible to us at the present time. Many others would have spoken western Welsh, later called Cornish and the ruling classes would have spoken Norman-French. The language of the Church and virtually all official writing was Latin.

At this period, the legal system for the punishment of crime was in a state of flux, as because of the financial benefits for the King's treasury, the royal courts were competing with the old-established local courts. The legal reforms of Henry II ('Henry the Lawgiver') deteriorated under his sons Richard the Lionheart and John — in fact, the Magna Carta, a decade after our story, was in part intended to prevent abuses of the legal system.

Acknowledgements

The author would like to thank the following for historical advice, though reserving the blame for any misapprehension about the complexities of life and law in twelfth century Devon: Mrs Angela Doughty, Exeter Cathedral Archivist; the staff of Devon Record Office and of Exeter Central Library; Mr Stuart Blaylock, Exeter Archaeology; Rev Canon Mawson, Exeter Cathedral; Mr Thomas Watkin, Cardiff Law School, University of Wales; Professor Nicholas Orme, University of Exeter; and to Clare Ledingham, Editorial Director of Simon & Schuster, and Gillian Holmes for their unfailing interest and support.

'This even-handed justice commends the ingredients of the poisoned chalice to our own lips'

MACBETH, Act I, scene VII

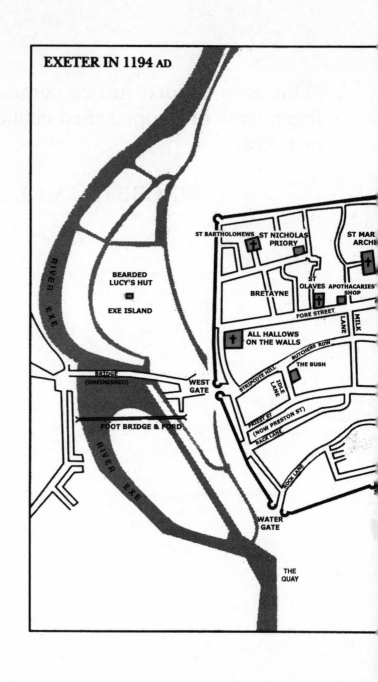

EXETER IN 1194 AD

ST BARTHOLOMEWS
ST NICHOLAS
PRIORY
ST MAR
ARCH

BEARDED
LUCY'S HUT

EXE ISLAND

ST
OLAVES APOTHACARIES
SHOP

BRETAYNE

FORE STREET

RIVER EXE

MILK
LANE

ALL HALLOWS
ON THE WALLS

BUTCHERS ROW

THE BUSH

BRIDGE
(UNFINISHED)

WEST
GATE

STRIPCOTE HILL

IDLE
LANE

FOOT BRIDGE & FORD

PRIEST ST
(NOW PRESTON ST)

RACK LANE

RIVER EXE

LOCK LANE

WATER
GATE

THE
QUAY

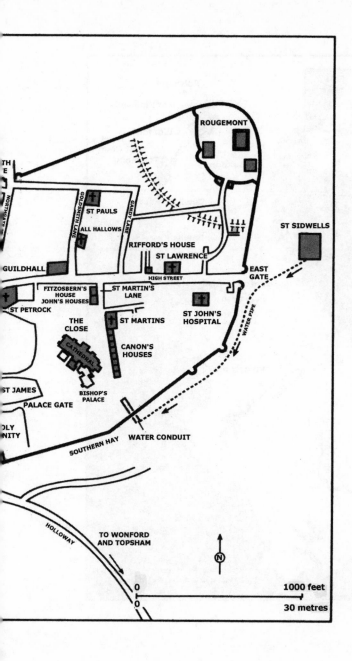

ROUGEMONT

NORTHGATE STREET

ST PAULS

GOLDSMITH LANE

GANDY LANE

ALL HALLOWS

RIFFORD'S HOUSE

ST LAWRENCE

ST SIDWELLS

GUILDHALL

HIGH STREET

EAST GATE

FITZOSBERN'S HOUSE
JOHN'S HOUSES

ST MARTIN'S LANE

ST PETROCK

WATER PIPE

THE CLOSE

ST MARTINS

ST JOHN'S HOSPITAL

CATHEDRAL

CANON'S HOUSES

ST JAMES

PALACE GATE

BISHOP'S PALACE

HOLY TRINITY

SOUTHERN HAY

WATER CONDUIT

HOLLOWAY

TO WONFORD AND TOPSHAM

N

0   1000 feet

0   30 metres

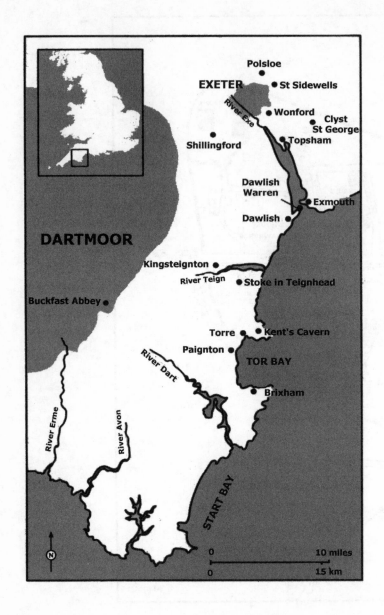

Glossary

ALB
A long garment, often elaborately embroidered, worn by priests under a shorter garment called the chasuble, q.v.

AMERCEMENT
The imposition of a fine for some breach of the law. The coroner would record the amercement, but usually it was not collected until after a decision by the visiting judges.

APPEAL
Unlike the modern legal meaning an appeal was an accusation by an aggrieved person, usually a close relative, against another for a felonious crime. Historically, it preceded (and competed with) the Crown's right to prosecute and demanded either financial compensation or trial by combat or the Ordeal.

ARCHDEACON
A senior priest, assistant to the Bishop. There were three in the diocese of

Devon and Cornwall, one responsible for Exeter.

ASSART
A new piece of arable land, cut from the forest to enlarge the cultivated area of a village.

AVENTAIL
A chainmail neck-covering, similar to a balaclava, attached to the edge of the helmet and tucked into the top of the hauberk.

BAILIFF
Overseer of a manor or estate, directing the farming and other work. He would have manor-reeves under him and in turn be responsible either to his lord or the steward or seneschal.

BALDRIC
A diagonal strap over the right shoulder of a Norman soldier to suspend his sword scabbard on the left hip.

BARBETTE
A fabric band over the head and under the chin, as part of a lady's attire.

BURGAGE
A house in a town, occupied by a burgess.

BURGESS
A freeman of substance in a town or borough, usually a merchant. A group of burgesses ran the town administration and elected two portreeves (later a mayor) as their leaders.

CANON
A priestly member of the chapter of a cathedral, also called a prebendary, as they derived an income from their prebend, a grant of land or pension. Exeter had twenty-four canons, most of whom lived near the cathedral. Many employed junior priests (vicars) to carry out their duties for them.

CHAPTER
The administrative body of a cathedral, composed of the canons (prebendaries) and the senior clergy. They met in the Chapter House, usually attached to the cathedral, so-called because a chapter of the gospels was read before each meeting.

CHASUBLE
A thigh-length garment, usually embroidered, with wide sleeves, worn by priests.

CONSTABLE

Has several meanings, but here refers to a senior military commander, often the custodian of a castle, otherwise called a castellan.

CORONER

Senior law officer in a county, second only to the sheriff. First appointed in September 1194, though there are a few mentions of coroners in earlier times. The name comes from the Latin *CUSTOS PLACITORUM CORONAE*, meaning 'Keeper of the Pleas of the Crown', as he recorded all serious crimes and legal events for the King's judges.

COVER-CHIEF

More correctly 'couvre-chef', a linen veil worn by women, held in place by a band or circlet around the forehead and hanging down over the back and bosom.

CRESPINES

Gilt nets on either side of the head, to hold hair.

CROFT

A small area of land around a village house (toft) for vegetables, a few livestock, used by the occupant (cottar) who was either a freeman or a bondsman (villein or serf).

CUIRASS
A breastplate or short tunic, originally of leather but later of metal, to protect the chest in combat.

EYRE
A sitting of the royal judges, introduced by Henry II in 1166, which moved around the countries in circuits. There were two types, the 'Justices in Eyre', the forerunner of the Assizes which was supposed to visit frequently to try cases — and the General Eyre, which arrived at long intervals to check on the administration of each county.

FIRST FINDER
The first person to discover a corpse or witness a crime, had to rouse the four nearest households and give chase. Failure to do so would result in an amercement (fine).

GORGET
Similar to a wimple, a band worn under a veil or hood, passing beneath the chin and

up to the temples: may also be a wide necklace, originating from armour.

HAUBERK
A chainmail tunic with long sleeves to protect the wearer from neck to knee.

HEAD-RAIL

Female head-covering, similar to cover-chief (q.v.).

HIDE
A measure of land, not always constant in different parts of the country, but usually between 30 and 80 acres. A hide was divided into four virgates.

HUE AND CRY

When a crime was witnessed or discovered, the First Finder (q.v.) had to knock up the nearest four households and if possible give chase to the suspect.

HUNDRED
A sub-division of a county, originally named from a hundred hides of land or a hundred families.

JURY

Unlike modern juries, the medieval jury were witnesses, local people who were obliged to gather to tell what they knew of a crime or dispute and to come to a decision on the verdict. The coroner's jury was supposed to comprise all the males over twelve years old from the four nearest villages, though this was often a practical impossibility.

KIRTLE

A woman's dress, worn to the ankles, with long sleeves, though fashions changed frequently. The kirtle was worn over the chemise, the only undergarment.

LEAT

A ditch cut to drain a marsh.

MANOR REEVE

A foreman appointed in each village by the lord of a manor to oversee the daily farm work. Although illiterate, like the vast majority of the population, he would keep a record of crop rotation, harvest yields, tithes, etc., by means of memory and notches on tallysticks.

MANTLE

A cloak, usually of square or semicircular shape, secured at the neck by a brooch-pin or ring. May have a hood for travelling.

MARK

A sum of money, though not an actual coin, as only pennies existed. A mark was two-thirds of a pound, i.e., thirteen shillings and fourpence (sixty-six decimal pence).

MIDDEN

A rubbish pit or dump, often used for sewage.

MURDRUM FINE

A fine or amercement levied on a village by the coroner when a person was found dead in suspicious circumstances and no killer could be produced, if the locals could not make 'presentment of Englishry' (q.v.).

ORDEAL

Though sometimes used to extract confessions, the Ordeal was an ancient ritual, abolished by the Vatican in 1215, where suspects were subjected to painful and often fatal ordeals, such as walking barefoot over nine red-hot ploughshares, picking a stone from a vat of boiling water, licking white-hot iron, etc. If they suffered no injury, they were judged innocent. Another ordeal was to be thrown bound into deep water: if they sank, they were innocent, if they floated, they were guilty and were hanged or mutilated!

PEINE FORTE ET DURE
'Hard and severe punishment' used for the extraction of confessions from suspects.

PORTREEVE
One of the senior burgesses in a town, elected by the others as a leader. There were usually two, later superseded by a mayor, the first mayor of Exeter being installed in 1208.

PREBENDARY
See 'Canon'.

PRECENTOR
A senior cleric in a cathedral, responsible for organising the services and singing, etc.

PRESENTMENT OF ENGLISHRY
Following the 1066 Conquest, many Normans were killed by aggrieved Saxons, so the law decreed that anyone

found dead from unnatural causes was Norman and the village was punished by a murdrum fine (*q.v.*) unless they could prove that the deceased was English or a foreigner. This was usually done by a male member of the family. This continued for several hundred years, as even though it became meaningless long after the Conquest, it was a good source of revenue.

REEVE
See 'Manor Reeve'.

SENESCHAL
The senior servant or steward to a lord.

SHERIFF
A 'shire-reeve', the King's representative in each county, responsible for law and order and the collection of taxes.

SUPER-TUNIC
Similar to a surcoat, but usually heavier: worn as a lighter alternative to a mantle (cloak).

SURCOAT
A garment worn over the tunic, usually shorter. It was also used to cover armour,

to protect from the sun and used for heraldic recognition devices.

TABARD
A male over-garment, open at the sides and laced at the waist.

TITHE

A tenth part of the harvest, demanded by the Church.

TUNIC
The main men's garment, pulled over the head to reach the knee or calf. A linen shirt may be worn underneath. For riding, the tunic would be slit at the sides or front and back.

UNDERCROFT
The ground floor of a fortified building. The entrance to the rest of the building was on the floor above, isolated from the undercroft, which might be partly below ground level. Removable wooden steps prevented attackers from reaching the main door.

VICAR
A priest employed by a more senior cleric,

such as a prebendary or canon, to carry out his religious duties. Often called a 'vicar-choral' from his participation in chanted services.

WIMPLE
A linen or silk cloth worn around a lady's neck to frame the face. The sides were pinned up above each ear and the lower edge tucked into the neckline of the kirtle or chemise.

Prologue

September 1194

The chamber was almost in darkness. The only light came through the slightly open door, from three tallow tapers burning in a candlestick in the next room. From the large bed came muffled whisperings and the sounds of increasing intimacy. A woman's gasps of half-reluctant delight alternated with the deeper murmurings of a man intent on extracting every ounce of pleasure for himself. He remained steadfastly in control, while she became progressively more abandoned, throwing her arms wildly above the fleeces that covered them, arching her back as she sobbed, and biting back cries of desperate delight.

The carved bedstead, itself a novelty in Exeter where most folk slept either on rushes or a mattress on the floor, began to creak rhythmically, then with increased vigour and pace. Suddenly there was a duet of strangled gasps, the sheepskins heaved in a final spasm and the creaking subsided.

After a moment or two of silence, a gentle

1

sobbing could be heard. 'This is so wrong,' she whispered. 'I must never come here again . . . never!'

The answering voice was deep and strong, with confidence verging on arrogance. 'You say that every time, Adele. But still you come. You need a man, a proper man.'

She sniffed back her tears. 'If we should ever be found out — oh God, what would we do?'

He grinned in the darkness. 'Well, I'll not tell anyone, if you won't!'

Then they were silent, each with their own thoughts in the guttering candlelight.

1

In which Crowner John attends a shipwreck

Silence also reigned in the narrow chamber set high in the gate-house of Rougemont Castle. It was broken only by the steady champing of Gwyn's jaws as he finished the last of the crusty bread and cheese left over from the trio's second breakfast. The other two members of the coroner's team were totally silent. Thomas, the clerk, was laboriously penning a copy of yesterday's inquest held on a forester crushed by a falling tree. The coroner himself was covertly studying the latest lesson set him by a cathedral canon, who was trying to teach him to read and write.

Sir John de Wolfe sat, silently mouthing the simple Latin phrases. With an elbow on the table, he held his hand casually across his mouth to hide the movements of his lips from the others. After twenty years as a soldier, he was sensitive about his efforts to become literate, in case it was thought effeminate. Thomas de Peyne, the unfrocked priest who

3

was his very literate clerk, knew of his master's ambition and was somewhat piqued that he himself had not been asked to be the tutor — though he appreciated the coroner's sensitivity about his inability to read his own documents. Gywn of Polruan knew little of this and cared less, as sensitivity was foreign to the nature of the red-haired Cornish giant, who acted as the coroner's officer and bodyguard.

This comfortable peace continued for a while, its background the mournful whine of the winter wind as it blew around Exeter Castle. There was the occasional slurping noise, as Gwyn washed down his food with rough Devon cider from their communal stone jar, ignoring the stringy curds that swirled from the bottom like seaweed in a rock pool.

As he concentrated on the neatly written vocabulary, the coroner's brow creased with the effort of making sense of these marks on the parchment. His clerk looked up covertly now and then to will his master to make a success of his studies.

The unfortunate Thomas was a born teacher and, had he known of it, would have agreed wholeheartedly with the quotation 'Far more than the calf wishes to suck, doth the cow wish to give suck'. His sly glances showed him a tall, lean man, who gave a potent impression of blackness. De Wolfe had thick, neck-length black hair, and though, unlike the usual Norman fashion, he had no beard or moustache, his long face was dark with stubble between his twice-weekly shaves. Bushy black eyebrows surmounted a hooked nose and deep-set eye sockets, from which a pair of hooded eyes looked out cynically on the world. The only relief to this hardness was provided by his rather full lips, which hinted at a sensuality that many women, both in Devon and much further afield, could happily confirm.

Black John, as he had sometimes been called in the Holy Land, enhanced his dark appearance by his choice of garments. He rarely wore anything but black or grey, and his tall, sinewy body with its slight stoop often looked like some great bird of prey. When his black cloak swung widely from his hunched shoulders, some men said he was like a huge crow — though others compared him more to a vulture.

The little clerk turned down his eyes again and was just reaching the end of his inquest record when their tranquillity was broken. He had barely scratched the final date on the parchment with his quill — 'the Second Day of December in the Year of Our Lord Eleven

Hundred and Ninety-four' — when footsteps and the clanking of a broadsword scabbard sounded on the narrow staircase coming up from the guard-room below.

Their tiny office, grudgingly allotted to them two months ago, was the most cramped and inconvenient chamber the sheriff could find in the whole of Rougemont, perched high in the gate-tower set in the inner curtain wall. Three heads turned to see who would appear in the doorway, a hole in the wall draped with rough hessian in a futile attempt to reduce the draughts. This sacking was pulled aside and a sergeant-at-arms appeared, dressed in the usual peacetime uniform of a basin-shaped metal helmet with a nose-guard, a long over-tunic with some chain-mail on the shoulders, and cross-gartering on the hose below the knees. His baldric, a leather strap slung across one shoulder, supported a large, clumsy sword that dangled from his left hip.

Gwyn climbed down from his stool, his towering height causing his tousled ginger hair almost to touch the ceiling beams. 'Gabriel, be damned! You're too late to eat, but there's some drink left.' Hospitably, he held out the stone jar to the sergeant, who took a deep draught after nodding a greeting to everyone.

Gabriel was one of the senior members of the castle garrison, a grizzled and scarred veteran of some of the same wars that John de Wolfe and Gwyn had fought in Normandy, Ireland and France although, unlike them, he had never been crusading to the Holy Land. He was an old friend and a covert antagonist of the sheriff, Richard de Revelle, who unfortunately was his ultimate lord and master, though Gabriel's immediate superior was Ralph Morin, the castle constable.

The coroner casually slid his Latin lesson under some other parchments and leaned back on his bench, his long arms planted on the table. 'What brings you here, Gabriel? Just a social visit to sample our cider?'

The sergeant touched the brim of his helmet in salute. He respected John de Wolfe both for his rank as a knight and for his military pedigree. Though his relations with the new coroner's team were relaxed, he took care not to be over-familiar with this tall, dark, hawkish man who, after the sheriff, was the most senior law officer in the county of Devon.

'No, Sir John, I bring a message from Sir Richard.'

The coroner groaned. Relations with his brother-in-law were more strained than usual, since the controversy last month over the murder in Widecombe.

The problem of jurisdiction over criminal deaths between sheriff and coroner was still unresolved and remained a bone of contention between them, so any message from Richard de Revelle was hardly likely to be good news. But John was to be surprised.

'The sheriff's compliments to you, Crowner, and he asks, will you please deal with three deaths reported from Torre?'

John's black eyebrows rose on his saturnine face, crinkling the old sword scar on his forehead. 'Good God! He's actually asking me to deal with them? What's the catch, Gabriel?'

The old soldier shrugged, his lined face wooden. He was not going to get involved in the well-known power struggle between Sir John and the sheriff, whatever his own personal sympathies.

'Don't know, sir, but he doesn't want to go down there himself. Far too busy, he says, with the Chief Justiciar coming to Exeter in a few days' time.'

Hubert Walter, the Justiciar and Archbishop of Canterbury, was virtually ruler of England now that King Richard had gone permanently back to France. He was to visit Exeter at the end of that week and one of his tasks would be to try to settle this

8

demarcation dispute between coroner and sheriff.

Thomas de Peyne, the crook-backed clerk, made the Sign of the Cross at the mention of the Archbishop — an obsessional habit he had developed since the mental trauma of being dismissed from the priesthood two years earlier. It was a counterpoint to Gwyn, who was prone to frequent and vigorous scratching of his crotch. 'What sort of deaths are these?' he demanded, in his squeaky voice, thinking ahead as to how much writing he would have to do on his sheepskin rolls.

Gabriel took off his helmet to run a horny hand through his greying hair. 'All I know is that a messenger came in from Torre an hour ago, saying that a hermit monk turned up there last night with a story of three corpses on the beach somewhere between Paignton and Torpoint. Drowned sailors, most likely. Doesn't sound very exciting.'

John snorted. 'Doubtless why my dear brother-in-law is content to leave them to me. No glory or fame for him in a few wet corpses. Any more details?'

'Only that this hermit fellow knows most about the matter. His name is Wulfstan and he lives in a cave near Torre. We've heard nothing about it from William de Brewere, the manor lord, or his bailiff.'

The coroner clucked his tongue in annoyance. 'We'll hear nothing from Lord William, he's always away on his political campaigning — the manors there are run by his son, the younger William.' He smacked a big hand on the table. 'How I'm supposed to carry out my royal warrant to keep the Pleas of the Crown with such scanty knowledge, God alone knows!'

Gwyn wiped a hand the size of a small ham across his wild moustache, which hung down each side of his mouth and chin like a red curtain. 'What are we supposed to do about this, Gabriel?'

'Sir Richard requests that the crowner find this monk and carry on from there. He devoted no more than a couple of heartbeats to the problem.'

De Wolfe rose, his grey-black figure hovering over the scatter of documents on his table. 'It's now about mid-morning. We can be there before nightfall, so let's go.' He took his heavy wolf-skin riding cloak from a wooden peg hammered between the stones of the wall and picked up his sheathed sword from the floor, then led the way to the stairs.

★　★　★

The winter dusk was falling as the trio trotted along the final mile of coastal track towards the village of Paignton. The coroner was on his massive grey stallion Bran, a pensioned-off warhorse with hairy feet. Just behind him was Gwyn on a big brown mare, while Thomas jogged along side-saddle on a small but wiry pony.

Until the previous week, the little clerk had ridden a semi-derelict mule, but during the de Bonneville case, when they had to ride long distances over Dartmoor, his master had become so exasperated by the beast's lack of speed that he had bought Thomas a cheap pony, using some of the money acquired from hanged felons.

The track wound close to the red cliffs and many combes that formed steep-sided bays along the coast south of the river Teign. To their left was the sea, grey and forbidding, with white foam caps whipped up by the bitter easterly wind across the whole expanse of water.

They now struck inland across the rocky prominence of Torpoint towards the lower, sandy coastline, which carried on around a wide bay, past Paignton to the fishing village of Brixham in the far distance. They were aiming for the hamlet of Torre, a small settlement a quarter of a mile inland from the beach at the northern end of Torbay.

'Where do we find this damned fellow?' growled Gwyn, pulling his coarse woollen cloak tighter around his neck to keep out the searching wind. He wore a round leather hood with ear-flaps tied under his chin. His bushy moustache helped to shelter his face, but his blue eyes watered and his nose ran in the cold breeze.

'He must live in that cavern near Torre — the cave where bones of old animals lie in the mud,' replied. John. 'I visited there as a boy, when I went with my father to buy sheep in Paignton.' He knew this part of Devon well, as he had been born and brought up at Stoke-in-Teignhead, a village between here and the estuary of the Teign, where his mother and brother still held a manor. In fact, they had called there for a quick meal on their journey today.

It was growing dark when they reached Torre, a straggle of huts and cottages belonging to one of the manors of William de Brewere. There was a ramshackle wooden church and a row of crofts, sheltering under the slope of rocky ground that formed the base of the great peninsula of Torpoint. A few hundred yards downhill was a row of fisherman's shacks near the beach, where stretches of coarse red sand lay between low rocky promontories. They reined up in the twilight and Gwyn dismounted to seek out the reeve, to claim a night's lodging. This meant a space on his earthen floor around the fire, where they could roll themselves into their cloaks to sleep — no hardship for old fighting men like Gwyn and his master, although the softer ex-cleric viewed the prospect with distaste.

The Cornishman lumbered back in his ragged brown cloak and climbed back on to his mare. 'The reeve was down at the beach, but I've told his drab of a daughter that we'll be back later to eat and sleep. She says the cave is something over a mile from here.'

'I know well enough where it is,' snapped John, wheeling Bran around and setting off up the hill.

Clouds were flying rapidly overhead, driven by the remnants of the south-easterly gale that had blown for three days. They picked their way in the fading daylight past strip fields, until they came to the scrubby virgin woods that covered the headland, except where the wind allowed only gorse and bracken to survive. Now a well-trodden path led through the gloom and John, who remembered the geography fairly well from his youth, was able to lead them to a small valley running down towards the sea on the eastern side of the headland. A glimmer of light led them to the foot of a low cliff, the face of which was rent by a rock shelter that hid access to deep caves in the hillside.[1]

As they approached through the scrubby undergrowth, Gwyn called out, in a voice like an angry bull, to attract the hermit's attention. The shout echoed against the cliff, then an answering cry came wavering back. A dark figure came stumbling down the slope from the cave.

'Are you Wulfstan, who knows about some corpses?' called the coroner.

The hermit, who in the fading light appeared as a frail, dishevelled old man, came up close to the grey stallion. 'Come up to my dwelling, out of this keen wind, and I'll tell you what I know.' He waved his staff at the cliff and hobbled off again.

They dismounted and tied their steeds to the bushes that grew on the muddy slope below the rock shelter, then trudged up behind the loping figure of Wulfstan. Just inside the cave mouth, the recluse had built a rough dry-stone wall, behind which he dwelt in utter squalor. Though John was far from particular about his own personal comfort, even he was glad that the gloom concealed

---

[1] Now called Kent's Cavern.

Wulfstan's living conditions, though the smell was suggestive enough.

A tallow dip flicked on the pile of flat rocks that served as a table, sufficient only to reveal the hermit's face as he squatted down nearby. This was almost hidden by unkempt hair and beard, all of a dirty brown streaked with grey. He wore a long, shapeless garment of rough wool, tied around the waist with a frayed rope, which smelt as if its last wash had been at about the time of Becket's martyrdom.

'Well, holy man, what's all this about?' Sir John was anxious to get out of this dirty hole as soon as possible.

'Dead men, Crowner. I saw three, but I'm sure there are more.' He pulled his fingers through his hair in a futile attempt to remove some of the tangles. 'I was at the beach near Torre yesterday morning, seeking shellfish in the pools, when I saw men from the village gathering planks from the tide-line. When I approached, others were burying three bodies just above the high-water mark.'

Wulfstan's voice was gentle and mellow, at variance with his wild and neglected appearance. The more sensitive Thomas wondered what had happened to him in the past to drive him into this miserable exile.

Gwyn's mind was on more immediate

matters. 'They were drowned men, then?'

'I think two of them were. It was obviously a shipwreck, from the profusion of wood and spars about the sands. But one had injuries on him that I thought were from a grievous assault.'

'Why so?' asked John.

'Blood was caked on his hair and there were wounds on his temple.'

De Peyne, always keen to show off his knowledge, interrupted the hermit. 'He may have struck his head on the rocks when pitched from the wreck or pounded by the surf.'

Wulfstan smiled. 'Then the water would have washed away the blood — but this was thick on his head, so he must have bled ashore, out of the water.'

The clerk, somewhat abashed, crossed himself for no particular reason.

'Why did you take the trouble to report this to these priests and not to the steward or bailiff, as you should?' asked the coroner, suspicious of any co-operation from the public.

The recluse looked troubled. 'Not only because of the wounds, brother, but those villagers of Torre are a bad lot. Yesterday they appeared even more shifty than usual and tried to get me off the beach as soon as I began to show an interest in what they were doing.'

'In what way?'

'I saw some casks hidden under bushes above the sand — and an ox-cart was taking away a load of planks covering something underneath. After they chased me away, my conscience troubled me over the dead men and I sought the advice of my brothers in God who are settled nearby. They took me seriously and sent a messenger to the sheriff.'

'Who are these brothers?' asked Thomas, his religious curiosity aroused. Though so ignominiously ejected from the clergy, he still hankered after his old life and pathetically sought out every ecclesiastical contact within his reach.

'They are a small party of White Canons, invited by Lord William to establish an abbey on ground that he is to give them above the beach. This is an advance party, living in wooden cells, but their Order, the Premonstratensians, hopes to build an abbey in a year or two on that spot.'

'Never heard of them!' said Gwyn gruffly. He had no fondness for priests or monks.

'They are followers of Saint Norbert, and are come to pray for the souls of old King Henry and his son, our present Richard Coeur de Lion.'

'He's not dead yet, thank Christ,' objected John.

Wulfstan again smiled his gentle smile. 'It comes to us all, my son. William de Brewere is being generous with his land for the sake of his own soul and to give thanks for the safe return of his son from durance in Germany.'

William the Younger had been one of the hostages sent as surety for the payment of the huge ransom of a hundred and fifty thousand marks for the release of King Richard, whose capture near Vienna still troubled John's conscience: he and Gwyn had been part of the royal bodyguard, yet had been unable to save him from seizure. But this was far from the problem now in hand.

Gwyn pulled off his leather helmet to scratch his ruddy thatch. 'You think they were pillaging the wreck of a vessel, then?'

Wulfstan nodded. 'Maybe not only pillaging it but getting rid of witnesses. I wouldn't put it past them to wreck a ship deliberately, with false beacons, though the weather was foul enough for a ship to founder anyway, on that lee shore with an easterly gale.'

'Have you any notion of what vessel it might have been?' asked the coroner.

The older man shook his head, and Thomas stood back hastily in case any lice were flung off in his direction. 'I saw nothing except shattered timbers on the sand.'

There seemed little more to learn from Wulfstan and, with some relief, the coroner led the way down to their horses. By this time the daylight had almost gone, and they rode slowly back along the track to the village, lit fitfully by a moon that constantly dodged in and out of the rapidly scudding clouds.

'The man seems definite about this, for all that he's an odd character,' Gwyn grunted, in his deep bass voice, his usual way of communicating.

'He is obviously at odds with the villagers — probably some old feud between them. But his story had a ring of truth,' replied John, his grey form almost invisible in the gloom.

Thomas, unwilling to be left out of the big men's discussion, piped up from the rear. 'The coroner's writ is doubly valid in this,' he offered.

'What are you on about, dwarf?' growled Gwyn. He pretended to despise the ex-priest, though he would have defended him to the death.

'A possible killing, and a definite wreck of the sea,' pointed out the clerk. 'Both well within the crowner's jurisdiction.'

'That had occurred to me already,' snapped de Wolfe sarcastically.

'Why are you charged with investigating wrecks, for Mary's sake?' demanded the Cornishman.

'All part of Hubert Walter's plan to revive the royal treasury. Too much money due to the King has been lost these past few years. Crooked sheriffs and manorial lords have all helped to impoverish the royal purse.'

'So why wrecks?'

'Everything washed up on the shores of the kingdom has traditionally belonged to the Crown.'

'Including the Royal Fish — the whale and the sturgeon,' chipped in the know-all Thomas.

'Damn the fish! It's these thieving villagers stealing everything from a wrecked ship, valuables that should have gone to the King's coffers. The sheriff said nothing about that, I notice, only about corpses that have no value.'

'Maybe he didn't know,' observed Gwyn reasonably.

Just then, the moon appeared through a wide gap in the clouds and they took the opportunity to speed up to a trot along the track. Here, so near the sea, the forest was thin and low, bent by the Channel winds that blew salt air across the land. Within minutes, they reached Torre again, a few glimmers of light escaping from the unglazed windows crudely shuttered against the keening wind.

'Too late to do anything now, with the daylight gone,' grumbled John. 'May as well settle for the night and make a start early in the morning.'

Gwyn led them along the double row of huts that was the village, the church and tithe barn the only larger buildings visible in the fleeting moonlight. Opposite the barn was a dwelling slightly larger than the rest, but with the same steep thatched roof, grass and moss growing from the old straw. There was no chimney and smoke drifted out from under the eaves.

The sound of their horses' hoofs brought Aelfric, the Saxon manor reeve, to his door. His youngest son was sent out to take the mounts to a shed at the back, where they were unharnessed, fed and watered. The arrival of a king's officer, however unwelcome, demanded automatic hospitality from the agent of the lord of the manor, even though the function of his new-fangled post of coroner was poorly understood.

The reeve had a vague idea, gleaned from the manor steward, that Justiciar Walter, in the name of the King, had revived the old Saxon office of coroner. In September, the General Eyre of judges in Kent had decreed that, in every county, three knights and a clerk be appointed to 'keep the Pleas of the Crown'. If he had had the education of Thomas, he would have known that in Latin this was *custos placitorum coronae*, from which sprang the title of 'coroner'. Keeping these Pleas meant recording all legal events, such as the imposition of fines, seizing of deodands, investigation of sudden and unnatural deaths, taking the confessions of sanctuary seekers, confiscation of the property of hanged felons, and a host of others that were required to be presented to the royal judges, who visited each county periodically to dispense what passed for justice.

Aelfric understood little of this. He was an older man than those who usually held the job of village headman. A widowed freeman, his house was run by a crippled daughter. His two sons cultivated his croft and gave the usual work-service to the manor.

It was the daughter who now brought the coroner's team a meal of broth and coarse bread, which they ate sitting around the fire in the centre of the earthen floor. There was no furniture in the room, but against the walls were heaps of dry bracken and straw covered with rough blankets, doing service as the family's beds.

'Thought a reeve could have risen to a table and a couple of stools,' muttered Gwyn, as he wolfed down the last of the soup from his warped wooden bowl.

Aelfric had gone out again, allegedly to check on the horses, and the woman had vanished into the lean-to shed attached to the back of the house, which served her as kitchen and dairy. A milking cow was tethered at the other end of the long room, behind a wattle screen that divided the living quarters from the stable, though it failed to divert the strong smell of fresh dung.

Sir John's business-like mind was on other things than his comfort. 'This miserable village is the nearest to the wreck, so they must be the ones involved,' he said. 'Thomas, you are the best at ferreting out secrets so get yourself outside when you've finished that crust and see what you can discover.'

The diminutive clerk, flattered at his master's faith in his ability as a spy, swallowed the last crumbs and slid out of the door. His narrow face and long nose were almost quivering at the prospect of doing something useful for the coroner. Though the other two usually treated him with impatient scorn, he felt a loyalty to Sir John born mainly of the gratitude he felt for his master having saved him from shame and destitution. Until two years ago, Thomas de Peyne, the youngest son of a minor knight in Hampshire, had been a teacher-priest at Winchester Cathedral, holding the living of a small parish nearby, which brought him in a regular stipend. Then he was disgraced and dismissed for an alleged indecent assault on one of his young female pupils. Though he steadfastly claimed that the girl had maliciously led him astray, he had been unfrocked and had lost his living and his lodgings. He had remained semi-destitute, eking out a bare existence by scribing letters for merchants, until John took him on as coroner's clerk. Humpbacked he might be, from old phthisis when a child, but a crafty intelligence and undoubted prowess with the written word compensated for his lack of good looks.

After Thomas had left, the drab daughter of the reeve silently limped in with a pitcher of her own brewed ale, together with some misshapen clay drinking pots. The coroner and his officer poured their beer and squatted near the fire, which smouldered in its clay-lined pit in the middle of the room. The only light came from the glowing logs, as the woman had blown out the wick that floated in a dish, to save her precious tallow.

'Where's this fellow gone?' muttered Gwyn suspiciously. 'It's a hell of a long time to see to a few horses.'

'I'm wondering if he's arranging for a few matters to be attended to down at the seashore.' John's black eyebrows came down in a frown as he contemplated the potential misdeeds of his countrymen.

'I could persuade him to answer a few questions when he comes back,' suggested the Cornish giant, hopefully raising his clenched fist. He had been with Sir John for many years, acting as his bodyguard: he was of too lowly origins for squiredom. Originally a fisherman from the far-western village of Polruan at the mouth of the Fowey river, he had taken service in various wars as a mercenary until John de Wolfe had taken him on.

De Wolfe, who possessed little sense of humour, shook his head at Gwyn's offer of violence. 'I'll just get his version of what happened. Then in the morning we'll see for ourselves — though they'll lie through their teeth if it suits them.'

When Aelfric came back some time later, the coroner told him curtly to give him the full story. Hunkering down near the fire, the reeve pulled a ragged sheepskin tighter around his shoulders to keep off some of the draught that whistled through the ill-fitting door and shutters. 'Three days now, God sent this gale to plague us,' he grumbled, pouring some of his daughter's beer into a pot. 'The night before last — Sunday that would be, as we went to the church that day — it blew like the end of the world was coming. And in the morning, we found wreckage and bodies on the beach.'

'How many bodies — and who found them?' demanded John.

'Three corpses, lying at the high-water mark among a scatter of planks and cordage that spread from the Livermead rocks up the beach. They were first seen by Oswald, a fisherman who lives in a hut down by the water's edge.'

'I'll need to speak to him, if he was the First Finder, he should have reported it straight away.'

Aelfric looked blankly at him, his loose-lipped mouth gaping to show yellow stumps of rotten teeth.

'Well, he did! He came and told me right away,' objected the old Saxon.

'And did you tell your lord or his steward at the manor?'

Under the new arrangements, any failure of individuals or the community to keep to the letter of the law, led to fines that helped to boost the king's sagging finances. One such failure was to neglect to follow the complex procedures about protecting a dead body until the coroner was notified and came to inspect it and hold an inquest.

'But here you are, Crowner. You were notified as soon as possible.'

'No thanks to you, reeve! We had to depend on the good offices of a hermit and the White Canons. That may yet cost you and your village a few marks.'

Aelfric groaned. 'We are poor here — it's bad ground for crops so close to the salt water. And the fishing is not so good as it is at Brixham, across the bay there.'

John ignored the familiar pleas of poverty. Everyone was poor in England since the Lionheart had squeezed them dry for the Crusade and his ransom — and now to pay for the French wars to regain land lost by his brother John while Richard was abroad.

'How did this hermit get involved?' asked Gwyn, putting another log on the fire.

'Wulfstan comes down to the beach to collect driftwood and to seek shellfish in the pools. He was there soon after Oswald found the dead 'uns and when we buried them in the sand. As he was there, we thought he may as well say a prayer over them to shrive them, even though he's not in Holy Orders.'

'Why not get your parish priest to do it? That's what he's there for.'

The reeve shifted uneasily in the gloom. 'He wasn't well that day, Crowner.'

'Drunk, you mean,' sneered Gwyn, who had a poor opinion of priests, including Thomas de Peyne.

'Burying the bodies before I could examine them is also a misdeed that attracts a fine,' observed the coroner sternly.

'We didn't know that, sir,' grumbled the reeve. 'And we couldn't let them lie on the beach where we found them. The tides are rising with the moon, for one thing. By today, they'd have been sucked out to sea again.'

John saw the logic of this, but said nothing.

'How do we know they drowned, then?' demanded Gwyn.

Aelfric looked at him as if he was a simple child. 'How else should wrecked sailors die?' he asked. 'And when we lifted them spurts of water came from their mouths.'

'That's no guide to drowning, man! Drop a dry corpse into a millpond and he'll fill with water. Did you see froth at their noses and mouths?'

The reeve nodded, glad of this leading question. 'Yes, one of them. A young fellow, little more than a youth.'

John interrupted them. 'Have you any idea

what vessel this might have been?'

Aelfric shook his head, the greasy grey hair swinging about his pinched face. 'There were planks and rigging all about — and a few broken casks. One of the planks had something carved upon it, but no one can read here except the priest — and I told you he was unwell.'

John's own illiteracy prevented him from commenting on the villager's inability to identify the ship. 'Any cargo washed up? Were any goods salvaged?'

The village headman held up his hands in the universal gesture of denial. 'Wreckage only, sir. There was a lot of dried fruit along the water's edge, but it was ruined by salt and sand, not even good enough for us to feed to the swine.'

'What about these casks?' demanded John.

The reeve took a deep swallow of his ale before answering. 'I've never seen wine barrels, Crowner, but I know our manor lord had one at Christmas two years ago. These bent staves could have been from shattered casks — though I have heard that this Frenchy fruit do get transported in barrels, too.'

There was little else that Aelfric could — or would — tell them, and soon they were sleeping on the piles of bracken, the reeve with his daughter and sons along one wall, Sir John and his officer along the other, furthest from the stench of the cow-byre.

Before he slept, the coroner's mind wandered over a variety of problems. He wondered if his clerk was worming out any better information than they had squeezed from the reeve. John respected the intelligence of the former priest, just as he envied his prowess with book and quill, but the soldier in him could not fail to feel derision for the puny body and craven timidity of the little clerk. He had taken him in at the express pleading of his friend John de Alecon, one of the few senior churchmen for whom he had any respect.

'He's my nephew, God forgive me,' the priest had said. 'My sister will never speak to me again if I let the damned fellow starve. He's a genius with pen and parchment, even if he's over-fond of putting his hand up young girls' skirts.'

The opportunity arose to hire someone who could read and write properly, rather than painfully scrawl a signature, it had seemed too good to miss. Now Thomas was on a stipend of twopence a day and had a pallet to sleep on in the servant's quarters of a canon's house in the cathedral Close.

The coroner's thoughts drifted on to the

perennial problem of his snobbish wife Matilda, sister to the sheriff. Married for sixteen years, he had achieved domestic harmony by being absent at the wars for most of that time. But since he had returned from the Holy Land last year, after accompanying Coeur de Lion on his ill-fated journey home, he had been stuck in Exeter with Matilda.

With faults on both sides, their relationship had gone steadily downhill: now they hardly spoke to each other except to exchange recriminations. Yet Matilda had energetically campaigned for John's appointment as coroner, using her family influence with her reluctant brother and his high ecclesiastical friends — although mainly to further her own social ambitions to be the wife of an important royal official.

John had been in two minds about taking the post, even though his strong military links with both the King and his soldier-Justiciar Hubert Walter made him a strong favourite for the job. However, as the coronership was officially elected by the burgesses of Exeter, influenced by the sheriff of Devon, Matilda made sure that her brother overcame his dislike of her husband sufficiently to support his appointment. De Revelle had himself only just been reinstated as sheriff, after being put out of office for months because of his links with Prince John's rebellion. The crafty young brother of King Richard had taken the opportunity of the Lionheart's incarceration in Austria, to try to seize the throne, but the attempt had been a dismal failure.

There should have been three coroners established in Devonshire, but in September only two could be found. This was partly due to the arduous nature of the post in such a large and wild area, especially as it was unpaid. In fact, the Justiciar had decreed that only knights with an income of at least twenty pounds a year could be coroners. The assumption was that if they were sufficiently well-off they would not need to milk the system, as did most sheriffs, by embezzling funds intended for the royal treasury.

The other knight was Robert Fitzrogo, who was meant to have jurisdiction over much of the rural area, especially in the north and west of the county while John covered Exeter and the more populous south. But within a fortnight of taking office, Fitzrogo had had a riding accident, and died, leaving John to deal with the whole of Devon.

Though Matilda had succeeded in getting her husband into the upper ranks of county society, she now complained that his duties kept him out of their house and her company on an almost permanent basis. John had soon discovered that he liked the work and, even more, that it kept him away from his wife almost as much as he had been when he was campaigning at the wars. It also gave him ample opportunity to visit his several mistresses, especially Nesta, the vivacious Welsh widow who kept the Bush tavern in Exeter.

His final rumination, before sleep overcame him in this odorous dwelling, was about the forthcoming visitation of the Chief Justiciar to Exeter within the next few days. He knew him well, as Hubert Walter had been Richard the Lionheart's second-in-command in Palestine and had been left in charge of the English army when the King sailed for home, with John as one of his escorts.

But Hubert's imminent visit to Exeter was in his capacity as head of the English Church: the King had made him Archbishop of Canterbury as a reward for both his military prowess and his genius as an administrator.

Now the Archbishop was overdue for a tour of his various dioceses so he was coming to visit Henry Marshall, Bishop of Exeter — and brother to William Marshall, the most powerful baron in the land. The occasion would outwardly be ecclesiastical, but politics would be high on the agenda, rather than the cure of souls in that part of the kingdom.

But before John could go over this in his mind for the hundredth time, sleep suddenly overcame him. He began to snore gently, dreaming of the soft arms and plump breasts of Nesta.

★ ★ ★

At about the time that Sir John was dreaming of his favourite mistress, his stunted clerk was forcing down drink that he did not want, in the hovel that housed the village priest.

In the short time that he had been with the coroner, Thomas had learned that one of the best sources of information about local intrigues was the local priest. These men were often poverty-stricken vicars frequently placed in village churches by absentee prebendaries who held the living and rarely if ever visited their parishes. They preferred to live comfortably in the cathedral cities, paying a pittance to barely literate priests to carry out their duties.

The coroner's clerk had made his way from the reeve's cottage to the church, crossing the muddy track that was the village street. The House of God in Torre was the second largest building, the tithe barn next to it being considerably bigger. Thomas could see the thatched church roof, with its plain wooden cross, silhouetted against a moonlit gap in the fast-moving clouds. As he came closer, he could see that against the rear wall was a lean-to hut, made of the same rough boards as the church itself. A dim flicker of light showed through the cracks of the shuttered window opening, which told him that the incumbent of this rude vicarage was at home.

Stumbling over rubbish strewn on the path, de Peyne groped his way to the door and banged on the boards. There was a lengthy silence and he knocked again. This time he heard mumbling inside, and unsteady footsteps brought the priest to his door. He opened it sufficiently to peep suspiciously through a crack: he was not used to visits from his flock after dark — or at any other time, given the scorn in which he was held.

Thomas had developed a routine for such occasions. He rapidly established his religious status by sententiously delivering a greeting-cum-blessing in good Latin and making the Sign of the Cross. The bewildered pastor, already more than slightly drunk, dragged open the door and mumbled some response that the clerk took to be an invitation to enter.

De Peyne pushed his way inside and looked around the room in the minimal light of the guttering candle, apparently the remains of one from the church altar. As with the reeve's dwelling, there was virtually no furniture, apart from an old milking stool, a slate slab on two stones for a table and a pile of straw covered in rags that served as a bed. The remains of a fire glowed in the central hearth, surrounded by a few dirty pots. The most prominent feature was a large jug near the stool and a mug half filled with red liquid.

Thomas began his patter to dampen any doubts the priest might have, claiming that he was the personal chaplain to the new coroner, who had come to investigate the deaths of the seamen washed up on the beach. The fuddled mind of the local parson was reassured that Thomas had not come to murder him or steal his non-existent possessions. He motioned him hospitably to the stool, pressed another grubby pot into his hand and poured a ruby fluid into it from the jug. Then he subsided with a thump to sit on the floor. 'Drink, brother and be welcome,' he said thickly.

Thomas had little need to wonder where the poverty-stricken priest would get a limitless supply of good French wine: the answer seemed obvious and already he felt a glow of achievement in his espionage operation for his master. He made a pretence of enthusiastic drinking, though he was not fond of liquor. When his host was not looking, he tipped most of his drink into the tangled rushes on the floor, to keep his head clear so that he could encourage the man to reveal the source of his supplies. The conversation was less productive. The priest, an emaciated wreck with yellow skin and bloodshot eyes, seemed mentally stunted. Whether this was from years incarcerated in a remote village or due to his chronic alcoholism was not clear. Thomas wondered which condition had led to the other — was he a drunk because he was stuck here, or had he been banished here because he was a drunk? Either way, the man seemed intent on slow suicide by alcohol as a means of escape.

Thomas tried to get details from him of the wreck and the drowned men, but the priest, whose name he never discovered, had been 'indisposed' on that day. He knew nothing of the matter and had not even been asked to say a few words of prayer over the corpses as they were buried under the sand. Asked if he knew anything of the identity of the ship, he muttered that the reeve had brought in a plank with words carved upon it, but he admitted that he could not read well enough to decipher it. Thomas was not surprised at the admitted illiteracy of a man in Holy Orders — although priests were supposed to be able to read and write, many could barely scratch their own name.

The man soon tired of de Peyne's questions and rose unsteadily from where he squatted on the floor, picking up his now empty jug. He tottered off to a hole in the rear wall, which led into a cupboard-like extension built on to the back of the hut. He stooped into this and leaned around the corner, clumsily fiddling with something out of sight. Thomas padded across the rushes behind him and peered around the corner of the alcove. He saw a small cask standing on end, probably the cleanest object in the hut. The top had been stove in and the priest was dipping his jug into the dark red contents.

Suddenly he became aware of the clerk at his shoulder and his hollow face split into a guilty grin. 'A gift from my parishioners.' He giggled, his shaking hand spilling some of the wine on to the floor. 'And plenty more where that came from!' he added, with a wink.

He shuffled out with his jug and, again, Thomas had to go through the charade of drinking with him.

The vicar's boast that more wine was hidden somewhere stimulated Thomas's new-found detective skills. As soon as he could he escaped and decided to investigate further.

Outside, in the cold darkness, he stood for a moment to consider where stolen goods might be hidden. The obvious place — almost too obvious — was the tithe barn, where a tenth of all the produce of the manor's efforts was kept for the Church.

The barn was next to the priest's hovel, looming above him, and Thomas felt his way carefully towards it: the moon was now temporarily hidden behind the clouds. The rough boards and wattle of the walls were under his hands as he felt his way towards the tall entrance, high enough to admit ox-carts piled with hay, corn and roots.

He found the bar that held the two shaky doors closed and lifted it out of its sockets. The whistle of the wind hid the creaking noise as he opened one door just far enough to slip through. It was pitch black inside and he had to feel his way forwards, hands held out in front of him. The oats had long ago gone to market and only hay and root crops remained for animal feed, although the villagers, often on the verge of starvation at the end of the winter, might well be driven to living on turnips by February.

When he reached the stack of hay piled above his head, the clerk felt blindly about him until, as if in answer to his unspoken prayer, the moon came out again. The walls of the barn were riddled with splits and gaps between the wattle panels, letting the pale lunar gleam light up the interior. Thomas's eyes were by now fully accustomed to the gloom and he dived at the sweet-smelling hay, plunging his hands deeply into it, moving rapidly from one place to another. At the side of the stack, against the wall, his fingers came upon something solid. He soon traced a line of casks and boxes, of differing shapes and sizes, tucked against the wall and thinly concealed with a scattering of hay. He counted at least a dozen, including some square wooden crates.

The moon still glinted and he ran to the mound of turnips, but it was impossible to feel underneath them without a great deal of labour in moving them.

Then the light failed as quickly as it had appeared and he had to give up his quest, well pleased with his discovery, which should increase his standing with the stern, critical coroner. He pulled the hay back over the casks to conceal his snooping, slipped out of the barn and picked his way back to the reeve's cottage.

2

In which Crowner John finds three corpses

At dawn next morning, the coroner's team was on the beach. After hot gruel and cold beer in the reeve's cottage, they had walked the short distance through the scrubby pasture to the sea, where a few flimsy fishermen's huts were built on the low bank above the high-water mark. Aelfric loped ahead, turning left at the edge of the beach to walk northwards towards the rise of ground that sloped up to the start of the rocky cliffs.

The worst of the gale was over, but there was still a strong south-easterly that blew scuds of foam off the white-capped waves that crashed and boomed partway down the beach. The tide was ebbing, leaving a smooth expanse of sand, unmarked by footprints.

As they walked, with half a dozen curious villagers trailing behind, the reeve bent down and scooped up a handful of sand from the high-tide mark, not far below the brown rocks that marked the upper margin of the beach. 'See? There is fruit all along here.' He held out his hand and John could see, among the shingle grains, some soggy raisins and a fig.

Mindful of what Thomas had covertly told him about the wine casks, he asked innocently, 'But no chests or casks from the cargo?'

Aelfric shook his head virtuously. 'Never a one, sir. Only broken staves and timber that will help a poor village like ours mend our houses and feed our fires this winter.'

Your poor village will be a damned sight poorer when I've finished amercing you, thought John grimly, but for now he held his tongue.

They reached a point a few hundred yards from the start of the low cliffs. Ahead of them on the left, the ground began to rise, ending in another line of cliffs that marched higher until it was broken by a small valley. The coastline on the further side of this combe was much higher and turned through a right-angle, so that more cliffs faced them, ending in the blunt promontory of Torpoint.

Aelfric stopped and beckoned to a couple of the village men. They carried wooden shovels and, without a word, went to the drier, shingly sand above the high-tide line where three crude crosses were standing, each just two sticks bound with cord.

John and Gwyn stood huddled in their

riding clothes, their backs to the gusting wind, as they watched the men digging. Within minutes they had scooped out two feet of sand and the first body began to appear. One of the peasants dropped his spade and knelt to scrape away more sand with his hands. As soon as a leg and an arm were visible, he and his companion heaved on them and slid the body up on to the surface. As they moved to do the same for the other two corpses, the coroner and his officer bent over the first to examine it.

Thomas hung back, busily crossing himself in the presence of death. Strangely, for a man steeped in the belief of resurrection and everlasting life thereafter, he was morbidly afraid of death, especially his own. Notwithstanding his damaged body, ravaged by old disease, he was greatly attached to life. His fertile imagination caused him a great deal of torment as he anticipated his own demise. Sometimes, especially since he had begun his work for the coroner, dealing daily with corpses, Thomas would stare at his own hand and imagine the flesh decaying and shrivelling in putrefaction as he lay in a wooden box under the damp soil. Now he tried to shake off these morbid thoughts as his companions went about their business with apparent indifference.

'A young man, looks about twenty,' observed Gwyn, wiping the sand from the cadaver's face.

The body was fresh, having kept well during two cold December days. The face was peaceful enough, eyes closed and the mouth relaxed. When John lifted a lid, the front of the eye was beginning to cloud over. The man was dressed in typical sailor's clothing of a tightly belted tunic over thick serge braies to the knees, below which the legs were bare, as were the calloused feet.

The coroner turned his attention to the mouth and turned down the lower lip to look at the teeth, still tightly clenched in rigor mortis.

Gwyn, the former fisherman, was better acquainted with drowning than John de Wolfe, whose considerable experience of death was mainly centred around battle casualties. He said, 'If you're looking for froth at the lips, it disperses soon after the body is taken from the water — the bubbles burst and dissolve away in a few hours.'

Having delivered this lecture, for he was usually a man of few words, Gwyn knelt, placed a massive palm on the dead man's chest and pressed forcibly downwards. The young sailor made his last sound on this earth as air was squeezed from his lungs — and with the macabre gasp came a gout of white foam from his nostrils, seeping down over his lips. The Cornishman stood up and dusted the sand from his hands. 'That sometimes works for a day or two, though you get more from bodies drowned in rivers or ponds than in this salt sea.' He sounded satisfied that, for once, he had outdone his master in knowledge of the ways of death.

The other two victims were rapidly unearthed and examined by the coroner and his henchman. One was that of a thin, grey-haired man, probably in his fifties, the other a fat fellow of indeterminate age, with a sodden thatch of yellow hair. He failed Gwyn's chest pressure test, but the older man produced a little blood-tinged spume from his mouth.

At John's command, his officer pulled off their belts and rolled the three corpses on to their faces. He lifted their tunics and undershirts to examine the back of each body, but nothing was to be seen, except the lividity of the skin, where gravity had caused the blood to run down after death.

'Often see them bright pink like that, when they've been in cold water.' The Cornish giant seemed unwilling to forsake his expertise on drowning.

The fronts of the corpses were now

examined, the breasts and bellies searched for injuries, but apart from a few scratches on the hands and shins, there seemed no signs of violence.

'Those grazes are from being dragged across the rocks by the surf — fair hammering in here it was,' confided Aelfric, helpfully.

John and Gwyn stood up and banged the ubiquitous sand from their hands and clothing. 'Drowned right enough, so what was that damned hermit on about?' muttered the coroner's officer.

'There's something amiss with the whole affair,' murmured John, out of hearing of the reeve. 'After Thomas's story last night, we have to get to the bottom of it.'

With the bodies now laid out side by side on the sand, Aelfric and his men looked anxiously at John de Wolfe. 'Now that you've seen the cadavers, Crowner, shall we bury them again?'

'No, indeed not! They have to be properly identified and presentment of Englishry made, if that's possible.'

The reeve looked blankly at the King's coroner. The words meant nothing to him.

John, who had never been a patient man, snapped an explanation. 'Under the new law, someone must prove to me that these dead men were Saxons. Otherwise it will be assumed that they were Normans and a murdrum fine imposed on your village.' He ignored the groan from Aelfric and carried on. 'Already you're in trouble and liable for amercement for burying the bodies before I had a chance to see them, and until we can put names to these corpses there is no hope of proving they are English or even West Welsh.'

The reeve looked at his men and rolled his eyes upwards in horror at the prospect of double fines when they eventually came before the Justices. 'But how can we tell who they are, sir? Just bodies washed up from the sea, nothing to do with our village at all!'

John shrugged — his job was merely to enforce the new laws, he felt no responsibility for their existence.

Gwyn, a commoner more in tune with the lowly inhabitants of Torre, felt a little more sympathy and tried to help. He looked around the beach, his shaggy red hair blowing wildly in the gale. 'Was there nothing to show what vessel this might have been? The dress of these men looks more local than that of Bretons or Frenchmen.'

Aelfric shouted something to one of the men, who scrambled up into the rough grass above the beach and returned with a

47

four-foot length of plank, freshly shattered at both ends.

'This has some marks on it, but no one here can read.' The villager held up the board and John studied it gravely, pretending that its message was profoundly significant to him, though in fact the words meant nothing — his tutor at the cathedral was teaching him only Latin grammar.

'Thomas, what do you make of this?' he demanded, as if offering the clerk the chance to confirm his opinion.

Thomas took a quick look at the incomplete lettering cut deeply into the oaken board, which had obviously been one of the bow planks of the vessel. It read ' . . . ARY OF THE S . . . ' and below this 'TOP . . . '
'It's part of the nameboard of the ship,' he said.

'So what's the name?' demanded John.

'It's not complete, the ends are missing, but I suspect it says *Mary of the Sea*, from Topsham.' This was a small port on the east bank of the River Exe, where it widened into the tidal estuary a few miles downstream from Exeter.

'I know the ship!' exclaimed Gwyn, who had an inborn interest in all things maritime. 'It's a vessel belonging to Joseph of Topsham, who runs quite a few boats across to Brittany and Normandy taking wool. He often brings back French victuals, such as wine and fruit.'

John nodded, for Joseph's vessels often took his own wool across the Channel for sale in France. The coroner had a part-share in a wool business with one of the Portreeves of Exeter. He had wisely invested most of the loot he had won in foreign wars in this business, which together with his share of the family lands at Stoke-in-Teignhead, brought him a comfortable income.

'So! We must get Joseph to identify these poor souls, if they were his seamen. Might anyone else know who they were?'

Thomas, whose nosy nature made him a mine of Exeter gossip, had a suggestion. 'With wine on board, then surely Eric Picot would be involved. He is the main importer into Exeter and supplies most of the nobility and the taverns. In fact, I think he might own a share in Joseph's ships.'

John turned to the reeve. 'Send a man to your manor bailiff to tell Lord William that the King's coroner requires him to dispatch a rider immediately to Exeter on the best horse he has. He is to tell the sheriff — or, if he is absent, the castle constable — that a message be given to Joseph of Topsham and Eric Picot at the Watergate. He is to tell them that their vessel *Mary of the Sea* has foundered in

Torbay and that all the crew and cargo are lost. They will have to come in a day or so to identify these bodies, but I will be back in Exeter tomorrow to talk to them.' It took several repetitions of this message to get it fixed in the head of the messenger.

When he had gone, the coroner turned again to Aelfric, prepared to deliver his hammer-blow about what was concealed in the tithe barn. But this pleasure was suddenly delayed, as Thomas was tugging at the edge of John's dark wolf-skin cloak.

The clerk's ever-roving eye, squinted though it was, had seen something further up the beach. 'Look up there, Crowner, near to where the rocks begin!' he hissed. John stared at where Thomas's sharp forefinger was pointing and saw a smooth semi-circle of tide-washed sand, where the spring tide earlier that morning, higher than the previous day, had pushed a line of seaweed and debris almost up to the rocks at the head of the beach. Within this area, three shallow depressions could be seen, where the weight of water had pulled out recently disturbed sand.

On previous days, with lower tides, these had been just above the high-water mark, but today the rising tide had swept over them. From one of these slight hollows protruded a white, bleached foot. De Wolfe nudged Gwyn and gestured towards it. With a loud bellow of surprise, the Cornishman strode towards the hollow, his ragged-edged brown cloak blowing out in the wind behind him. John and his clerk hurried close after him, across the shiny wet strand.

When he reached the dead limb, Gwyn bent down and, with a single tug, lifted a whole leg from the sand. He roared with the effort and tried to pull the rest of the body out of the grave, but the depth of sand over its trunk was too great.

John turned and yelled at Aelfric, immobile and aghast beside the first three corpses. 'Bring that shovel, reeve! And you've got some explaining to do.' He saw one of the other men running away as hard as he could in the direction of the village.

Reluctantly, the reeve and the other two came across the beach. Gwyn seized a spade from one and began to dig furiously. The coroner grabbed Aelfric by the collar of his grubby tunic and shook him. 'What's this, damn you? Did you know these were here?' While the reeve stammered out a string of denials, Gwyn had pulled the first body from the shallow pit and was rapidly exhuming the other two.

John, his tall, crow-like figure towering

above the reeve, shook the man again. 'Well?' he demanded.

'I know nothing, sir! These bodies must have drowned as well and been covered by the sand.'

The coroner rattled the man like a dog shaking a rat. 'A likely story! Did the tide place them side by side in a row, eh? Exactly in line and buried to the same depth?'

Aelfric made no attempt to answer but stood dejectedly when John released his grip.

By now, Gwyn had hauled the second body from the sand and was digging down into the third depression. The coroner went to help him and soon another three corpses lay side by side on the beach. This time, the findings were different. Though again the bodies were those of men in seafaring clothes, their faces were streaked with blood, thin and watery, leaking from clots matted in their hair.

'They must have been buried before this high tide, so that the dry sand has preserved the blood, as the hermit claimed,' said Gwyn.

'And the much higher tide today came up beyond yesterday's level, washing away the loose sand and exposing that foot,' John deduced, in a satisfied, though menacing, tone.

He pushed back the hair of the first corpse, who stared up at the clouded sky with softened eyeballs partly covered with sand. On the upper forehead, extending back into the fair hair, was a deep gash, exposing the skull beneath.

'Is that from a sword?' demanded Gwyn. John shook his head. 'Can't tell. Even a blow from a plank or an axe shaft can split the scalp like that.' After years on the battlefields of Ireland, France and the Holy Land, he considered himself an authority on wounds. 'But it's certainly not from the sea pounding him on the rocks, for look here.' He parted the bloody, sand-crusted hair on the crown of the head, to display two similar wounds, exactly parallel with the first. 'What rock strikes a head three times with the same strength and in the same direction, eh? And the surf not wash away the blood!'

He turned to the other bodies. The first one, another young man, had no blood in the hair, but down the side of the neck, from behind the left ear to the Adam's apple, was a sharply defined double line of bruising. Across the left cheek was a similar pair of parallel bruises, four inches long and over an inch apart. The last victim, a burly, brown-haired man, probably over thirty years of age, had two sharply defined black eyes. When John opened the swollen lids, the whites were heavily bloodshot. On feeling the head, shattered skull-bones crackled under the coroner's probing fingers and when he parted the sodden hair, he saw a great mass of swollen bruising on the top of the scalp. None of the corpses had any significant wounds on the rest of their bodies, apart from a few scratches.

John turned again to the terrified reeve. 'Very active rocks, these, eh, Aelfric? They just jumped up and struck these poor men only on their heads, then the sea buried them in nice regular graves, side by side?'

His sarcasm brought nothing but denial from the village headman. 'I tell you, sir, we know nothing of this!'

John showed his teeth in a snarl reminiscent of his animal namesake. 'Like you know nothing of the casks and boxes in your barn? And why did your man take to his heels just now?'

Aelfric had no answer, but continued to shake his head in desperate denial: this sounded like a hanging matter.

'Get these bodies taken up to the barn — my officer will go with you to see that your thefts from the wreck do not go astray,' ordered the coroner. 'In a day or so, when the ship-owner comes to identify his seamen, I will hold the inquest — and then decide what is to be done with you and your village.'

With that ominous warning, he strode back along the beach, intent on visiting the lord of the manor, to see if William de Brewere the Younger had any knowledge of this affair, before they rode back to Exeter.

3

In which Crowner John hears of a ravishment

Meanwhile, back in Exeter, the daughter of one of the town's Portreeves was becoming impatient with her old Aunt Bernice. Christina Rifford was a very beautiful young woman; at seventeen years old, she was as near perfection as any man could desire — and even the women of Exeter, many ridden with jealousy, found it hard to fault her looks or her innocent charm. Her face, framed by glossy black hair peeping from under her white linen coverchief, had a madonna-like calm, though her full lips and the occasional sidelong glance from her violet eyes caused the dames of the town to murmur that 'still waters run deep.'

So attractive was she, that many in Exeter marvelled at the fact that she was betrothed to Edgar, only son of Joseph of Topsham. Even his best friends could hardly claim that Edgar was the ideal match for Christina, who could have chosen almost any man in the West Country. A thin, gangling young man with a somewhat vague and moody manner, Edgar was learning the apothecary's trade under Nicholas of Bristol, who had his house and shop in Fore Street, the steep continuation of High Street down to the West Gate.

This Wednesday evening, Mistress Rifford was to collect a present for Christ Mass promised by her fiancé. Funded by an over-indulgent father, Edgar had offered her a bracelet and she had decided on one fashioned in heavy silver, custom-made for her slim wrist. The obvious place to seek it was from the Master of the Guild of Silversmiths, Godfrey Fitzosbern, who was the coroner's next-door neighbour in Martin's Lane.

Two weeks ago, Christina had spent a delightful hour in his workshop with her cousin Mary, deciding on the exact design that she preferred. Last week, they had returned to approve it but although Christina was delighted with the ornament, it proved a little too loose, falling down on to her small hand. Fitzosbern, eager to please the only daughter of Henry Rifford, offered to alter it and promised to have it ready by this evening.

In the late afternoon, however, Mary had sent a message by her serving-maid to say that she had a sudden fever and was unable to accompany her cousin to the silversmith.

Disappointed, Christina moped about the house for a couple of hours, to the irritation of her Aunt Bernice, who had kept house for her brother since his wife died five years before. Though Christina was very fond of her aunt, who was a kindly old soul, her constant fussing and over-protectiveness became more irksome as the girl grew older and more independent.

'It will have to wait until tomorrow, girl,' declared Bernice. 'Maybe Mary will be well enough then — and if not, I'll come with you myself. The bauble's not going to crumble away just because you're a day late in collecting it.'

But the headstrong beauty had other ideas and after their early evening meal, when her father had gone off to the Guildhall to chair a meeting of the Guild of Leather Merchants, Christina made her own plans. Aunt Bernice was dozing in the upstairs solar, sleepy from the effects of a large mutton chop and cabbage, as well as some 'medicinal' mead that she kept in a small stone bottle alongside her chair.

The well-to-do Riffords had a large town house near the East Gate, next door to the church of Saint Lawrence. Pulling on her heavy winter cloak, Christina slipped out of the side door into the lane and walked down it into the High Street. There were still plenty of people about, but most were head down against the keen east wind, hurrying home to reach their own hearths. A few hardy peddlers were still selling roast chestnuts, hot pies and new bread at the sides of the narrow streets, as she happily stepped out to fetch her new bracelet.

Crossing the High Street, she lifted the hem of her cloak and kirtle as she daintily tried to avoid the worst of the mire, then dived down Martin's Lane towards the cathedral Close. Her destination was the second narrow house on the right, the workshop and dwelling of Godfrey Fitzosbern. It was a tall timber building with a slate roof, almost identical to the one next along, which she knew was where Sir John de Wolfe lived.

She pushed open the heavy oak door, its riveted hinges creaking as she went into the shop. It was warm in there after the chill wind outside and she slipped back her hood and undid the shoulder-brooch that held her otter-skin cloak closed. The room was dimly lit by half a dozen tallow lamps set on shelves around the walls, but she knew the place quite well, after her previous visits. At the back sat Alfred, Fitzosbern's senior craftsman, working behind a cluttered table with hammer and punch, a horn lantern alongside him to give extra light. Christina smiled at him and he grinned back toothlessly. She blushed as she felt his eyes undressing her and quickly moved hers away, to rest on the other workman, leaning on a bench to the left of the door. He was a large young man, whose name she did not know, and was slowly buffing a silver goblet with a long strip of soft leather. He, too, gaped at her, and deliberately altered the stroke of his polishing, somehow giving it a suggestively erotic rhythm. No doubt the two men thought her a vision of beauty and desire to lighten the dull routine of their long day, but she felt distinctly uncomfortable under their blatantly lustful gaze. On previous visits, Fitzosbern had been present and they had had to keep the eyes down on their work — except when his back was turned.

'Is your master here? He's expecting me.'

Alfred, a haggard Saxon in early middle age, tore his eyes from the swell of her bosom peeping through the open cloak. 'He is indeed, mistress, and will be more than glad to see you, I'll swear.' In his thick Devon accent, he managed to imbue the simple words with lascivious meaning.

The younger man, dressed like Alfred in a long leather apron over his dull woollen tunic, ended his stropping to bang loudly on the wall behind him. 'Master Godfrey!' he yelled. 'The young lady is here for you.' He leered at her as if he had just announced the arrival of a new courtesan for the Caliph.

Christina was becoming accustomed to the ill-concealed lechery she attracted, although this made it none the less unwelcome. She turned to examine a shelf with silver jewellery on display, as a way of avoiding the eyes of the workmen and their murmurings.

A moment later, she heard a heavy tread beyond the curtain that screened the door at the back of the shop and the master silversmith entered. 'Mistress Rifford, a very good evening to you. I see that you are alone.'

For a few moments, they indulged in polite conversation, then Fitzosbern led her by the hand to a stool set against an empty table on the right of the room. He was a large man, powerful and fleshy but not yet running to fat. In a few years, he would begin to look coarse and dissipated, but now he was still good-looking with a dark, heavy kind of handsomeness. Big features, clean-shaven and with a mass of wavy hair, there was an animal intensity about him that many women had found irresistible — and some still did, even though he was almost forty and twice married. He dressed well, and as he moved behind the table, unrolled a velvet cloth before Christina, she noted that he wore a surcoat of finest yellow linen that came to mid-thigh, showing the bottom of a knee-length green tunic, the hem and neckline decorated with delicate embroidery. His fine woollen hose ended in shoes of the latest style, with long toes padded out with wool to form curled points.

Godfrey unwrapped the velvet and carefully lifted out her bracelet. He took two wax candles, an expensive luxury in place of the usual tallow dips, and lit them at the nearest flame so that a better light could dance on the bright silver of her new bauble. 'A beautiful thing, mistress, fit for a beautiful woman,' he said, in his low, strong voice, which caused a little shiver to run down her back. Unchaperoned, she felt both vulnerable and a little excited at the almost palpably sexual atmosphere that the three men generated in the dimly lit room.

She murmured her appreciation of the bracelet, for it was a very pretty thing, the bright new silver glittering in the candlelight.

'Here, let me try it for size.' Godfrey picked up her hand and held it in his large fingers for an unnecessarily long time while he slid the bracelet over her white fingers and set it in position on her wrist. Still he held on to her and, indeed, placed his other hand on her forearm, pushing back the floppy sleeve of her kirtle to support her arm just below the elbow, the better to admire the set of the ornament.

She trembled slightly at his touch, as no man — not even Edgar — had touched any part of her without some other woman being within sight.

'Perfect! Now that we've shortened it a trifle, it sits where it should, yet you can get your hand through without trouble.'

Christina's cheeks had coloured and she was glad of the gloom to hide her embarrassment. She was not sure how she felt about Godfrey Fitzosbern — he had a certain reputation among the gossips of the town, but there was no doubt that he was good-looking, even if he was almost old enough to be her father. His own wife, Mabel, was only a few years older than herself, though the whispers said that they disliked each other as much as John de Wolfe and his wife Matilda.

Christina drew her hand from his, slowly, so as not to give offence. 'It is very lovely, I like it very much,' she said softly.

Fitzosbern leaned forward to pat her cheek. 'You should thank Alfred and Garth there, as well. Though I made the design, theirs were the hands that fashioned it.'

Reluctantly, she turned and nodded to the two men, who had been watching her like hawks all the while.

Alfred touched a finger to his forelock. 'Always a pleasure to do you a service, mistress,' he said, in a voice redolent with double-meaning. 'And I'm sure Garth here feels the same.'

Fitzosbern, catching their tone, scowled at the men, who hurriedly dropped their eyes to the benches, tapping and buffing at the white metal that was their life. 'It's a cold night, mistress. Can I offer you a cup of hot wine before you go?' He motioned with his head towards the curtained door.

A flush ran up the girl's neck again. She was still unused to handling unwelcome invitations from masterful men. 'Thank you, sir, but I must go now.'

'Nonsense, Mistress Rifford! The evening is bitter outside, you need something to warm you. I'll not take no for an answer.' Fitzosbern came around the table and took her hand again. Almost pulling her, he steered Christina towards the inner doorway.

'I really should be leaving! I have to meet someone — at the cathedral.' She used the first location that came into her mind.

'I'll wrap this bracelet in a piece of silk and

put it in a small casket for you, while you sip some wine. Come through.' This time, Fitzosbern's arm slipped around her slim waist as he almost lifted her up the step into the room beyond. As she reluctantly passed through the doorway, she saw the gap-toothed leer of Alfred and the loose-lipped stare of Garth watching every move that their master made, jealous longing stamped on their faces.

The inner room was another workshop, now in darkness apart from the glow of a damped-down metal furnace. Wooden stairs at the back led up to the silversmith's living accommodation on the floor above. Reluctantly, but now committed too far to refuse, Christina allowed him to escort her upstairs. Here, a good fire burned in a hearth and more dips and candles gave a mellow light. At a long table, a glass flask of wine sat with some pottery cups. Godfrey released her waist with obvious reluctance and poured two generous measures of wine, then went to the fireplace and brought a kettle that was simmering on the hob. He added some hot water and held out a cup to her, touching his own to hers. 'Here's to a happy Yuletide to you, Christina — and may you enjoy your excellent present!' He gave her a broad wink and held up the bracelet.

The young woman sipped the wine reluctantly, not wishing to appear ungrateful for his hospitality but uneasy at the intimate overtones.

'Is your wife not at home this evening?' she asked, rather pointedly. 'I spoke to Mistress Mabel at service in St Lawrence only last Sunday.'

Fitzosbern's heavy features drew together slightly in a frown. 'She's out visiting some poor sick woman or some such thing,' he replied shortly, then changed the subject. 'Your man Edgar — that lucky fellow — told me to give you the bracelet when it was complete, but said that you should keep it unopened until he visits you with his father on the forenoon of Christ Mass.' Going to a shelf, he took a small wooden box and placed the bangle inside, wrapping it in the square of red silk that was already lining the casket. He gave it to her, and pressed Christina to have more wine, sit near the fire, before going out into the winter night.

This was too much for her and she shook her head decisively. 'I heard the cathedral bell just now, I must be there very soon.' Pushing the little box into a pocket inside her cloak, she improvised quickly on her excuses. 'I wish to pray at the shrine of St Mary for the success of my marriage. I am meeting my cousin Mary there,' she lied. Closing her cloak around her, she thanked Godfrey Fitzosbern for his kindness and for the excellent workmanship on the bracelet, then turned, walked resolutely downstairs and through the door into the workshop.

The silversmith followed her so closely that she could feel his heavy breath on her neck through her thin veil. He grasped her elbow, as if to help her down the step and kept it tight until she reached the street door. Once again, she was acutely aware of the intensity of the inspection that the two silver-workers focused on her, but her inborn good manners made her stumble out some parting words. Alfred chattered out a response she could not catch, while Garth merely made some sucking and blowing noises through his teeth.

Fitzosbern opened the heavy door and steered her through it, his arm tightening on her waist for a last squeeze as she escaped. Pulling her pointed hood up over her head, she thankfully scurried away down Martin's Lane, obliged to go towards the Close for her fictitious appointment.

★ ★ ★

John de Wolfe pushed open his own front door, which was never locked as someone was

67

always about the place. Matilda was usually to be found embroidering in her solar upstairs or gossiping with her friends around the fire in the hall. If she was out, then either Mary, the buxom cook-housekeeper, or the poisonous Lucille, his wife's handmaiden, were somewhere in the house or in the yard at the back, where the cooking, brewing and washing took place.

Tired from a day in the saddle, the coroner shrugged off his heavy black cloak and hung it on a peg in the vestibule. Ahead of him was a passage to the back yard, and on his right, an inner door to the hall, a gloomy vault that rose to the roof-timbers, the dark wooden walls hung with sombre banners and tapestries. He looked inside and saw a small fire burning in the large hearth, but the settle and chairs around it were empty. The long trestle table was bare of dishes, food or drink.

'A fine bloody welcome for a man after a long day's ride,' he muttered to himself, even though he was half relieved that his scowling wife was not there to berate him. He walked wearily through to the yard and found Mary sitting in the lean-to hut that was her kitchen and sleeping place. She was busy plucking a chicken by the light of the fire, his old hound Brutus wagging his tail at her feet. She jumped up in surprise, laying down the chicken and brushing feathers from her apron. 'Master John, I didn't hear you come in. We didn't expect you tonight.'

Mary was a good-looking woman in her late twenties, a strong and energetic worker with a no-nonsense outlook on life. The bastard daughter of a Saxon woman and a Norman squire, John had bedded her a few times in the past. They were genuinely fond of each other, but these days she kept him at arm's length, as she suspected that her arch-enemy Lucille was trying to betray her to John's wife. 'The mistress is out — she's gone down to St Olave's to some special Mass. There's nothing ready cooked, but I can get together some bread and cold meat for you.'

John sighed. 'No matter, Mary. My wife's soul must be more important to her than my stomach. She spends more time in that damned church than I do in taverns.'

Mary grinned at his self-pity and risked giving him a swift kiss on the cheek, with one eye on the open door in case Lucille was spying. Matilda's maid, a French refugee from the Vexin north of Paris, lived in a small shed under the outside staircase that went up from the yard to the solar. This was a room built out on timbers from the upper part of the hall, where John and his wife slept and where Matilda spent much of her time.

'I think I'll go down to the Bush for a bite to eat and a jar of ale,' he said.

Mary prodded him in the chest with a strong finger. 'Make sure that's all you get from Nesta tonight! The mistress is working up for one of her moods so be on your best behaviour when you get back.'

'Tell her I've had to go to the castle to see her damned brother, will you?'

As he retreated down the passage, she murmured under her breath, 'You're treading on very thin ice, Master John. One day you'll fall right through.'

★　★　★

Two quarts of beer and a leg of mutton later, John felt more at peace with the world. Having spent half his life on the back of a horse, the twenty-two miles back from Torre that day were soon forgotten as he sprawled in front of the roaring logs in the large room of the Bush. His long, hawkish face with the big hooked nose was relaxed for once and the arm that was not holding the big pot of ale was comfortably around the shoulders of the innkeeper.

Nesta was a vivacious Welsh woman, with red hair quite a few shades darker than

Gwyn's violently ginger thatch. Twenty-eight years old, she was the widow of a soldier from southern Wales, who had settled in Exeter to run a tavern, then prematurely died. Her round face, high forehead and snub nose were attractive enough, but a tiny waist and spectacular bosom made her the object of secret fantasies for half the men in Exeter. John had known her husband at the wars and had been a patron of the inn before he died. Afterwards, he had covertly given her money to help her continue the business. Her hard work and steely determination had made such a success of the venture that after four years it was the most popular tavern in the city.

It was an open secret that she was John de Wolfe's mistress, know to all including his wife, who used it to scold him during their frequent dog-fights.

This winter evening, with the unremitting wind still whistling outside, the inn was less busy than usual and only a few regulars were drinking in the big low room that filled the whole ground floor. Nesta had time to sit with him without interruption and he told her the story of his trip to Torbay. She always listened attentively, and made intelligent and often useful suggestions. More than once, her innate common sense had helped him to arrive at some decision.

'So you've got to ride back there for an inquest?' she asked, at the end of his tale.

'Joseph of Topsham, and maybe Eric Picot, will have to go down tomorrow to identify the bodies, the wreckage and the cargo. Then I'll return there on Thursday to hold the inquisition, and take with me some of the sheriff's men to arrest that murderous reeve and a couple of his cronies.'

Old Edwin, the one-eyed potman, shuffled across on his stiff leg, lamed at the battle of Wexford. He held out his pitcher of ale and refilled John's pot. 'Evening, Crowner! Staying the night?' he cackled, his collapsed white eyeball, damaged by a spear point, rolling horribly.

Nesta aimed a kick at his bad leg. 'Get away, you nosy old fool!' she said amiably. Edwin tottered away, chuckling, and she snuggled closer into John's side. 'Have you told your dear brother-in-law about the killings?' she asked.

'Not yet — I'll see him when I go up to Rougemont in the morning,' he replied.

But that was tempting fate, for the coroner and sheriff were to meet long before then, in a drama that was just about to unfold. The door to the street suddenly burst open and a figure appeared, the like of which the inn had

72

never seen before. It was that of a senior cleric, a man of lean and ascetic mien, swathed in a great cloak. He threw back the hood as he stood on the threshold, revealing a white coif, a close-fitting cap tied under his long chin. His sharp grey eyes darted around the smoky room, seeking someone with obvious urgency.

'John de Wolfe! There you are!' The relief in his deep voice was apparent and he strode across the bar, unclasping his cloak as he went to reveal a snowy chasuble with an embroidered edge flowing over the ankle-length alb.

Nesta jerked from under the coroner's arm and stood up quickly. In the years that she had been at the Bush, she had never seen a high-ranking priest in full regalia enter the place. She knew him for John de Alecon, Archdeacon of Exeter and one of the four lieutenants of Bishop Henry Marshall. She also knew that he was uncle to Thomas de Peyne and a firm friend of John: the Archdeacon was faithful to King Richard and, unlike the Bishop and several others of the cathedral hierarchy, had not supported Prince John's abortive rebellion.

'What, in God's name, brings you here, John?' barked the coroner, jumping up to greet him. 'Taverns are not one of your usual haunts!'

The Archdeacon smiled wryly at the mild blasphemy. 'Maybe not altogether in God's name, though everything we do is under him. This is more a criminal matter and one of great urgency.'

De Wolfe waved a hand at the bench he had just vacated. 'Will you not sit down and have something to drink? You look shaken.'

De Alecon looked about the room and at the patrons staring open-mouthed at this unique sight. 'It would not be seemly, I fear. John, you must come with me at once. The daughter of Henry Rifford, the Portreeve, has been assaulted within the cathedral Close.'

There was a deathly hush in the room, as all there heard him. John stared at him for a moment. 'Almighty Christ! How are you involved in this?'

The lean-faced cleric shook his head sadly. 'I was the one who found the poor girl. On my way from Vespers to visit a sick canon at his house. I heard moaning behind a pile of new masonry on the north side of the cathedral. I found this poor young woman lying on the ground there, beaten and obviously ravished.'

'Where is she now?'

'I raised the hue and cry and turned out all

74

the servants and vicars from the Bishop's Palace and the canon's houses, then had her carried to the small infirmary behind the cloisters, where she now lies.'

John was already pulling on his cloak and moving towards the door, when Nesta caught his arm. 'She needs a woman with her — Christina Rifford has no mother, only an old aunt.'

John stopped to listen to the innkeeper: he had learned that she always made good sense. 'So? Will you come?'

'It would be better if you took your wife.'

'She's not at home.'

'Then I'll come — but the girl will have to be examined. That should not be done by any man, not even a leech, especially in these circumstances.'

'So what can we do?' Part of the coroner's duties was the confirmation of rape, but in the three months since he had taken office, thankfully no such crime had come his way until now.

'Dame Madge from Polsloe priory, is the most skilled at problems of childbirth and women's complaints. She should be called, for the sake of the poor girl.'

The Archdeacon had followed this discussion intently. 'It seems the best plan, but the city gates are shut for the night.'

John snorted derisively. 'This concerns a portreeve's daughter! The gate will open at the command of a King's coroner and, no doubt, the sheriff when he hears of it. I'll get word to the castle to send an escort for the lady.'

With that, he stepped into the night, leaving an excited buzz of discussion behind them in the tavern.

4

In which the crowner
meets a nun and an angry man

When the Archdeacon, the coroner and Nesta arrived at the small infirmary alongside the cathedral cloisters, a messenger had already been sent to get the girl's father from his meeting in the Guildhall. He arrived a few minutes after John, who had barely had time to go in with Nesta to see Christina.

The girl was lying curled up on a low bed in the whitewashed cell, her eyes open but staring blankly at the wall. She was shivering violently, and a distraught elderly priest was attempting to soothe her with paternal murmurings. A townswoman who had been passing by when the Archdeacon discovered Christina in the Close had willingly come along as a comforter and was now sitting rather helplessly on a stool at the side of the bed.

Nesta, whose compassion was boundless, went straight to the other side to kneel on the floor, with her face near the girl's. She began talking to the young victim in soft tones, immediately getting some reaction, as Christina's eyes moved to focus on Nesta's face and her hand came out to grip her fingers.

Before de Wolfe had any opportunity to intervene, the door flew open and Henry Rifford erupted into the room. Though John had never had much regard for the portreeve, he now felt very sorry for him in this tragic situation. Normally, the heavily built, almost bald man had a florid complexion, but now his cheeks were dead white, almost grey in colour. Without so much as a glance at the others crowded into the little room, he shot to the bed and put his arms around his only daughter's shoulders. Christina held him around the neck and only one word escaped her lips, 'Father!'

There were no tears, no sobs, only the silent quivering.

Suddenly John felt like an intruder and he motioned the Archdeacon and the priest to come outside, leaving the two women with the father and daughter. 'We must wait until she has settled a little,' he said. 'There is no question of talking to the girl or trying to examine her until her father has calmed her.'

De Alecon grimaced. 'But she seems unnaturally calm now — I suppose that is from the shock of her terror?' He knew nothing of women, being a truly celibate priest, which was something of a rarity.

The door opened and Nesta emerged. 'She would be better returned to her own home, to be among familiar things. This serpent's nest of men, even though they be priests, is the worst place for her at this time.' Her usually cheerful face was drawn and John saw tears in the corners of her eyes.

The old priest, anxious to do something useful away from these women, hobbled off, saying that he would arrange for porters to bring a litter: it would be a short journey to Rifford's house in the High Street as, within the small city, nowhere was more than a few minutes' walk away.

'What about Richard de Revelle?' asked the Archdeacon. 'He is very thick with Rifford. When he learns of this, there will be hangings and ordeals in plenty!'

Any response was cut off by the door being torn open and Henry Rifford appearing before them. His face was now almost purple with rage and he could hardly speak for anger. 'Find me this bastard and I'll kill him with my own hands!' he snarled. Such words from an overweight, middle-aged leather merchant should have been ridiculous, but the heartrending sight of a father in anguish moved both men to genuine pity.

De Alecon laid a hand on Rifford's

shoulder in silent sympathy. 'May God support and comfort you at this time, brother.'

John de Wolfe was more practical in his commiseration. 'A litter has been sent for and we will take her home. The sheriff is being told, and already the castle constable has all his men scouring the streets, looking for this villain.'

'How could this happen in a consecrated place? And what *did* happen?' whispered the father, his rage simmering down to a shaking iciness of spirit.

The Archdeacon explained gently what little he knew, that he had heard sounds of distress, and had found Christina on the ground, almost hidden behind stacks of new stone being used in cathedral repairs. He had run to the nearest canon's house for help and they had brought the girl on a mattress across to the cloister's sick-room. She had not said a word, but from the torn and dishevelled state of her clothing and the bruises on her face and neck, he had assumed reluctantly that the worst had taken place.

'She should not have been out alone at night in the town. I blame myself for laxity in that,' moaned Henry Rifford. 'She should have been with her cousin. That stupid sister of mine should have kept a closer eye on her — and so should I.'

John tried to lighten the load on his conscience a little. 'She is almost a grown woman, Master Rifford. Girls that age are headstrong and unwilling to be cosseted by their elders. She is old enough to be married soon.'

At this, the portreeve groaned and hit his face in his hands. 'Oh, God, married! I had forgotten. What is her fiancé to make of this — and his father, Joseph? Abused and sullied, not two months before the wedding — if now there will be any wedding.'

To do him justice, Rifford failed to think at that moment of the financial loss that might stem from an abandoned union with the rich ship-owning family.

★ ★ ★

By the time that Dame Madge had been fetched from Polsloe, a mile north of the city, Christina had been returned to her home in the high street. Nesta and the Archdeacon had diplomatically left and the sheriff was with the coroner in the house near the East Gate.

Aunt Bernice was distraught with horror and self-recrimination for not having prevented Christina from leaving the house. For a time the old lady was semi-hysterical, but then pulled herself together sufficiently to sit alongside Christina's pallet and try to soothe her with what passed for motherly love.

Henry Rifford had calmed to a cold determination to find whoever had attacked his daughter and have him hanged, preferably after the most hideous tortures. Richard de Revelle seemed to agree with him, but the problem was to establish exactly what had happened and who was the perpetrator.

'I'm not clear what part you have to play in this, John,' said the sheriff aloofly. Matilda's brother was an elegant man, fond of expensive clothes which he wore with a flourish that hinted at his ambitions to be a courtier, rather than the chief law officer and tax collector of a far western county. He had a triangular face, with long brown hair swept back from a smooth forehead, narrow eyebrows and a thin moustache above a small pointed beard.

The current tragedy had temporarily swamped their mutual dislike, but John was determined not to let Richard get the better of him. 'My part is to confirm rape, Richard. If it has occurred then it is serious enough to be a Plea of the Crown, not a matter for the local courts. I must record all the details for the King's judges when they next visit Exeter.

If we find a good suspect, then they will try him.'

The sheriff scowled: it was the same dispute, over and over again. 'If I find a suspect tonight, John, I will hang him tomorrow — that I promise you.'

'And I'll put the noose around his neck myself!' added Rifford, still quivering with emotion.

John glowered at his brother-in-law. 'Let's leave this argument until we set it before Hubert Walter, shall we? There are more pressing matters at this moment.'

They were standing in the main hall of the house, outside the door to the small room used by Christina. This opened and Dame Madge appeared. She beckoned to the coroner, who went in and half closed the door.

The nun from St Katherine's Priory at Polsloe was a forbidding woman, tall and gaunt with a hard, bony face that was at odds with her dedication to healing and the care of the unfortunate. She was the senior of the nine nuns who lived there under the rule of the prioress and, in spite of her stern appearance, was a fount of kindness and compassion. Though she acted as the infirmarer at the priory, dealing with any type of affliction, her main reputation was as a midwife. Her services were often sought by women in Exeter and the nearby villages, especially in difficult births. Now she pulled the coroner aside at the door and spoke to him in a low voice. 'There seems little doubt that she has been violated, Sir John. I have not yet looked at her intimately, but what do you need to be proved for your legal purposes?'

John looked across at the bed, then shut the door firmly on the sheriff, who was trying to eavesdrop. 'We will have to ask her what happened, and if she knows who did this dreadful thing — but I must also have proof that she has indeed been ravished, by confirming a flow of blood from her private parts. That is the law.'

The nun, in her black Benedictine robe topped by a flowing white veil, nodded gravely. 'She will hate all men within sight for some time — perhaps even her father — so it is best if you stay outside and leave her to her aunt and myself. I will inform you of what I find.'

John knew that Dame Madge had forgotten more about female conditions than he was ever likely to know, but he pleaded, 'I must have some material proof of defilement, such as torn and bloodstained clothing.'

'I will see what there is to see,' said the

84

nun, gently pushed him out and closed the door.

In the hall, Henry Rifford's sense of hospitality overcame even his seething anger and distress, and he motioned the coroner and the sheriff to the great fireplace, where they stood and warmed their backs while he fetched some wine and Italian glasses for them. In a stilted imitation of normality, the three men sipped silently for a few moments, until Christina's father suddenly slumped on to a bench and began to sob quietly, his head in his hands. John and Richard de Revelle stood in embarrassment, not knowing what to do or say, until the coroner went across and laid a hand on the leather merchant's shoulder in an attempt to comfort him.

Rifford raised his haggard face. 'If only her mother had lived — she needs a mother at a time like this. My sister is well meaning, but she is a silly old fool. Letting the girl go out alone at night, damn her!'

'Shall I ask my wife to come to sit with her?' asked John, confident that Matilda, for all her many faults, would not hesitate to come to the aid of a family in distress.

Richard felt obliged to match his brother-in-law's offer. 'My lady, Eleanor, too, would undoubtedly be happy to help, Henry, but she is at our manor at Revelstoke, many miles away.'

The portreeve wiped his eyes and gulped his thanks, agreeing that another mature woman might be helpful, after the nun had left. A servant was called and dispatched to Martin's Lane with a message for Matilda.

As he left, two more men appeared on the doorstep, meeting there by chance. One was Ralph Morin, the constable of Rougemont, appointed by the king, for Exeter Castle was held directly by the Crown. Ralph, a large Viking-like man with grey hair and a massive forked beard, was in charge of the garrison and nominally the sheriff's second-in-command as far as the defence of the city was concerned. The other was Hugh de Relaga, the other portreeve, a fat, normally jolly man with a peacock taste for extravagant clothes. Like the Archdeacon, he was a good friend to John de Wolfe, another of the faction faithful to King Richard, grimly opposed to the renegades who had supported his brother. They were the two men elected by the burgesses of Exeter jointly to lead the administration of the city, though now there was talk of adopting the office of mayor, recently introduced in London and Winchester.

De Relaga made straight for his fellow portreeve and grasped his arms, pouring out sympathy and futile offers of help, while the constable reported to the sheriff and coroner. 'The town's sealed as tight as a drum, soldiers on every gate to reinforce the keepers. No one can get out until dawn, so he's bound to be in here somewhere.'

Richard was impatient. 'It's obvious, Ralph, that he must be in the city! But which of the five thousand inhabitants are we seeking?'

John restrained himself from saying that they could discount three thousand women and children. Instead he asked Morin if anything had been found in the cathedral Close. The grey head swung towards him. 'I haven't been told yet exactly where this foul attack took place, other than that it was in the Close. The sergeant took a couple of men through there but saw nothing untoward, only the usual beggars and late stall-holders. They had no news for him.'

Though it was hallowed ground, belonging to the Cathedral and immune from the jurisdiction of the town, the Close was an unlovely and unsavoury area. Everyone in Exeter had to be buried there, like it or not, and was charged for the privilege. The place was a shambles of grave-pits, heaps of earth, old bones and refuse. Hawkers sold their wares, apprentices played ball games and raucous children used it as a playground. Criss-crossed by paths and sewage ditches, the only large open space in Exeter was a place to be avoided by anyone with aesthetic sensibilities. However, although the Close saw frequent fights and hooligan squabbles, John could not recall that it had been the scene of a rape.

'What can we do next, Sheriff?' asked the constable.

'The damned fellow has gone to ground, back to the hole he crawled from. At dawn, search the inns, see if any strangers have blood on them or have anything about them that is suspicious. Keep the guards at the gates and examine every man who leaves town.'

Again John held his tongue at these futile orders, but silently questioned them. 'As yet,' he said, 'we don't know if there was any blood to be smeared on the attacker. I am waiting for Dame Madge to finish her examination.'

The two portreeves came over to them and the next few minutes were occupied with outrage, recrimination and Rifford's fears for his daughter's health, physical and mental — and the almost unthinkable possibility of a bastard pregnancy.

They were interrupted by Dame Madge,

appearing again at the inner door. The coroner went to her, and Richard de Revelle came close behind him. John could think of no reason to deny him being involved, as the chief enforcer of the law in Devon.

'She is easier now, poor girl,' began the nun, in her deep masculine voice. 'Christina is strong and sensible, though it will take her a long time to recover from this experience. She never will get over it completely, I fear.'

Henry Rifford came to stand with them, leaving the constable and Hugh de Relaga to remain discreetly in the background.

'What of her injuries?' asked John directly.

'You had better see some of them yourself, Crowner — those on her neck, arms and face. I think she has been gripped and restrained, rather than beaten. But I fear that she has also been roughly deflowered.'

Her father groaned and pushed past the other three to go to his daughter in the bed beyond.

Dame Madge's cadaverous face turned to John again. 'Her kirtle was soiled with mud and was torn up from the hem, as was the neck of her bodice. But her chemise showed this.' She took a hand from behind her back and held out a rolled-up garment to the coroner. It was of fine linen, thin and supple, the only undergarment that ladies wore under their kirtle, showing only at the neckline and reaching down to the ankles. This one was slightly stained with patches of brown mud and some speckling of blood, with one area of heavier bleeding an inch or so across.

'You said you must have evidence,' said the nun gravely, 'so you had better keep this. The blood came from her womb passage. She was forcibly taken from behind.'

John took the chemise and folded it again so that the soiling would be hidden from her father. 'You said I should see her other injuries?'

The Benedictine nodded and turned back into the room. 'You can talk to her now, the good girl is back to her senses.'

They went to her bedside and Aunt Bernice, still sniffing and snivelling a little, moved back to let John get closer.

He saw some scratches on the girl's cheeks and blue bruises at each side of her throat. The nun slid up Christina's wide sleeves and showed half a dozen purple bruises, the size of coins, on her upper arms.

'You know me, Christina?' John asked gently.

Her face ashen beneath her dark hair, Henry's daughter nodded. 'Sir John, I've seen you in the town. And I've met your wife at the cathedral and at St Olave's.'

'She will be coming in a moment, to keep you company for a while. We have to find out what happened, to bring your attacker to justice.'

'Did you see who it was, Christina?' asked Richard. She knew the sheriff well: he was a frequent visitor to the Rifford house, as her father was one of his cronies.

'No, he came from behind, sir. All the time he was behind — I could see nothing.'

'Tell us what happened, from the beginning,' John prompted.

The young woman, a little colour now returning to her cheeks, put a hand up to her eyes to wipe the moisture that welled from beneath her lids. 'I collected my bracelet from Master Godfrey, at the house next to yours. Then, as I was so near, I thought I would go into the cathedral to make a prayer at the shrine of St Mary, which was my dear mother's name.'

Even in her distress, she was economical with the truth, not mentioning the reason for her sudden need for devotion, but Dame Madge clucked her appreciation of the girl's sanctity.

'I visited the cathedral and made my prayer — there were a few other people and priests in there but it was dark apart from the altar candles. Then I left for home.'

91

John was puzzled. 'But how came you to be on the north side of the Close? That's a long way from the cathedral doors?'

Christina grimaced for her bruised neck ached. 'I used the little door in the base of the North Tower. I know it well, I visit the cathedral often. I prefer it to the small churches of the town.'

John looked at the sheriff, who scowled. They both had good reason to know of that door in the tower, as only a few weeks ago, John had scored heavily over his brother-in-law in the matter of a murderer who had reached sanctuary through it.

'There were great blocks of new stone outside, which I had not seen before. I was picking my way among them when suddenly I was seized from behind. Someone jumped on my back and threw me to the ground.'

The tears began to flow freely for the first time and John wished that Matilda would hurry.

'He grasped my throat, hands coming round my neck from the back. My face was in the mire, I could not scream, for fright and being choked. And it was dark — so dark!' Christina sobbed at the memory indelibly stamped on her mind for the rest of her life.

'Do you need to question her so tonight?' asked the nun sternly.

'One last thing, Christina, it's so important. Did you see or hear anything that might suggest who this attacker was?'

She replied, in abject misery, 'Not a word, not a sound did he make — only heavy breathing. But he was so strong! He tore at my clothing, lifted my kirtle and pulled at my legs. Then . . . the pain . . . '

She dissolved into loud weeping and Dame Madge, using her brawny arms, pushed both the coroner and sheriff towards the door. 'Outside!' she said peremptorily.

When the door was closed on the bedroom, she turned to the law officers. 'She has more bruises on her bosom, where she has been roughly fondled, and others on her thighs, where her legs have been forced apart. And she has bruises elsewhere, where you might imagine, though thankfully, no rips.'

'The blood?' asked the sheriff, insensitively.

'She has lost her maidenhead, of course,' snapped the nun gruffly. 'That is all you will get from her tonight.'

John walked across to the portreeves and gave them an edited version of what he had been told. As he finished, he was glad to see the street door opened by a porter, who ushered in Matilda. Somewhat mystified at the cryptic message she had received, she soon grasped the situation and revelled in the importance of her role, with both the city portreeves and the sheriff involved, even if the latter was her own brother.

Matilda was a stocky, short-necked woman of forty-four, several years older than her husband. Unlike her elegant brother, she had a square face and slightly puffy eyes, though she had had a certain handsomeness in her youth.

A champion snob, she affected French fashions and Lucille did her hair in what John thought was outlandish frizziness, compared to the usual modestly covered hair of Exeter women. But tonight he was glad to see her and piloted her across to Dame Madge, who took her into Christina's room. As she went in, Matilda turned to him and said, 'I'll stay the whole night, John. You must look after yourself at home.'

Cynically, he thought that he would be looked after just the same whether she was at home or not: if it were not for Mary, he'd starve to death. Her promised absence overnight led to another train of thought and, after arranging to meet the sheriff and constable at the castle soon after dawn, he made his way to the lower end of the town, to where the Bush Inn stood in Idle Lane.

5

In which Crowner John
holds an inquest at Torbay

Early next morning John called at the Rifford house on his way up the castle, partly to enquire after Christina and partly to make sure that his wife was still there. Mary would not let on that he had not slept at home that night — and even if Lucille betrayed him, he had weathered worse storms before.

After a rumbustious night in Nesta's bed, he had slept like a log and finally filled up on a great breakfast of eggs, ham, horse-bread and ale. He walked back through the town, his tall, spare figure loping past stall-holders and their customers. He ploughed heedlessly through a herd of goats on their way to slaughter and dodged handcarts filled with vegetables fresh from the countryside — the five town gates were now open. He wondered wryly if the extra guards on duty had been anything but a waste of time: most of them would miss a suspect even if he was shouting, 'Ravisher', at the top of his voice. Ox-carts trundled their huge wheels through the muddy slush as he crossed Southgate Street and the cries of vendors of everything from fresh river-fish to live ducks and bread hot from the oven, rang in his oblivious ears.

On the way to the Riffords, he diverted slightly to have a look in daylight at the scene of last night's crime. He entered the cathedral Close through the Bear Gate and walked around the great west façade to the north side. Here, he found large new blocks of stone, some partly fashioned, others plain cubes, waiting to be hoisted up to the masons on their scaffolding. The building, begun as long ago as 1114 by Bishop Warelwast, was only now in the last stages of construction — indeed, some of the soft stone used eighty years ago already needed replacement.

John found the small door in the base of the North Tower and traced a short route from there to the main path, which ran parallel with the row of canons' houses. He poked about the new masonry, some piled up high above his head. There were several empty spaces, both between each stack and between them and the cathedral wall — plenty of hiding places for a girl to be dragged into and assaulted.

Bending down, he studied the ground but saw nothing except churned mud. He had not expected anything dramatic and the absence of blood was not surprising, given the small quantity shed and the state of the ground.

He soon abandoned the search and strode briskly away, passing his own street door without a glance. He stopped at Godfrey Fitzosbern's house, but decided to leave him until later. Soon he was at Henry Rifford's and was met by Matilda in the main hall. 'The girl is sleeping, thank God,' she informed him. 'I sat with her all night. Her cousin Mary is with her now, and the old aunt has gone to her own bed, so I can leave for a while.'

'Did she say anything more of what happened?'

Matilda clucked her tongue and scowled at him. 'Still the crowner, John? Will you not let it rest for a moment? No, she said nothing, and I did not bring the matter up. She needs peace and forgetfulness for a time, not inquisition.'

As he helped her on with her heavy serge cloak, she commented, 'Where on earth can this Edgar be? You'd think her betrothed would have been around here at the gallop — he lodges only down at Fore Street with the leech Nicholas.'

John had forgotten the fiancé, but now realised that Edgar must have gone with his father, Joseph, down to Torre to identify the wreck and the dead sailors.

When he told Matilda, she exploded. 'You sent word to them yesterday! They must have ridden out before dusk and stayed on the way. The boy will still not know that his fiancée has been deflowered.' In spite of the tragedy, she was excited at all this drama unfolding before her very eyes. 'You must ride and tell him before he returns home, to prepare him for the shock,' she ranted. 'Maybe he will not be so keen on a wedding when he hears this.'

John rubbed the dark stubble on his lean jaw. How was he best to fit together all these tasks? He felt like a juggler at the Martinmas fair, with six balls in the air at once.

He had to have the Topsham people to identify the sailors' bodies, and he had to hold an inquest with them present. In the circumstances, it was a lot to ask them to ride back to Torbay again tomorrow, especially after they learned of the assault on Christina. It would take them the better part of a day's ride, especially with the short hours of December daylight. 'You're right, madam. I must ride down and meet them, to take them back to Torre. I will have to hold the inquest tonight or first thing in the morning, while they are still there — then hurry home to see what has developed with this ravishment.'

John had a few words with the anguished portreeve, then escorted his wife back to Martin's Lane, as she was stridently declaiming that things had come to a pretty pass in Exeter if a good woman couldn't walk the streets in safety. In the busy daylight, she was hardly at any risk — and, John thought bitterly, it would be a brave man who tried anything with Matilda.

After delivering his wife safely to their doorstep he went straight back to Rougemont. Gwyn and his clerk were there, eating and drinking as was usual at that time. Gwyn lived outside the town wall, in a hut at St Sidwell's beyond the East Gate, so had heard nothing of the commotion until he had come into town that morning.

Thomas, even though he lived in the cathedral precinct, had also remained unaware of the assault. However, the efficient grapevine among the castle soldiery had soon brought them up to date and they waited to hear their master's orders.

'First, Thomas, take one of your rolls and enter the facts of the case so far as we know them now. I'll dictate what needs to be said in a moment.' John settled himself on his stool behind the trestle table and poured himself a jar of cider — Nesta's breakfast had filled him and he did not want any bread and cheese. 'Then we have to ride back to Torbay again.'

The little clerk groaned at the effects on his backside of another long ride on his new pony. 'We only came back last evening, Crowner. Why return so soon?'

Gwyn, leaning against the window-ledge, lifted a large foot and pushed the clerk off his stool, the only other furniture in the small room. 'When Sir John says, 'Ride', we ride, you miserable toad!' He looked across at the coroner. 'Is there a connection between these matters?'

'Christina Rifford's husband-to-be is still unaware of her misfortune, as he went with his father and Eric Picot down to Torre to look at those dead seamen. I want to catch them before they return, to tell them of what's happened, and to get this inquest done with at the same time. Joseph of Topsham must bear witness and make presentment of Englishry.'

Gwyn pulled ineffectually at his tangled hair. He had a large face with a massive jaw, balanced by his slightly bulbous nose that bore the marks of old acne. The rest of his face was almost hidden under his rampant moustache. 'What about those murdering villagers?' he demanded.

John took a long swallow of cider. 'They

must be arrested and brought back to the gaol. Go over to Ralph Morin and ask him for a couple of men-at-arms to accompany us — four of us should be more than enough to seize those dogs down there. See if Gabriel can come.'

Gwyn clumped down the stairs of the gate-house, and the coroner prepared to record the rape of the portreeve's daughter. Thomas scrabbled in the shapeless cloth bag that held his writing equipment and came out with parchment, quill and a stone bottle of ink. The parchment was a palimpsest, a piece of sheepskin used several times. The old writing had been painstakingly scraped off and the surface treated with chalk. New parchment and especially the finer vellum, made from young or stillborn lambs, was expensive. Thomas took a pride in both his writing ability and the tools of his trade and settled down happily to scribe the events of the previous night, as recounted by the coroner.

By the time they had finished, Gwyn was back with the news that the castle constable had given him a couple of men, one of them their friend the sergeant.

'Did the sheriff have anything to say about it?' demanded John.

The Cornishman grinned. 'He wasn't

101

there, thank Christ — he's down at the Rifford house.'

John grabbed his sword and buckled it on. 'To the stables then, before he comes back and interferes!'

★ ★ ★

They met Joseph and his party just after midday, on the coastal track where it crossed the estuary of the Teign. Fortunately, it was low tide when they reached the north bank of the river mouth, so that their horses could splash across the shallow water between the sandbanks without having to swim. On the left was the sea, still grey and choppy, and on the right, the wide expanse of sand, mud and marsh that went up for a few miles until the river narrowed near King's Teignton.

As the five riders entered the cold water, Gabriel gave a shout and pointed ahead. 'Four horsemen at the other bank. Are these our men?'

John waved and yelled and the newcomers stopped, letting the coroner's party come up to them.

It was Joseph of Topsham and his companions, who were puzzled to see this unscheduled return of Sir John.

'A sad business, John, losing my men like

that,' said the ship-owner gravely. 'But your message said we would need to return in a day or two for your inquest. Why this sudden rush?'

The coroner felt uneasy about divulging such a delicate matter while still on horseback on the bank of a river in a cold wind. 'There are several important matters to speak about, Joseph, and this is not the place for it. I suggest we ride to my mother's manor, not two miles from here, and talk around a good fire over some food and drink.'

Mystified, Joseph and his companions spoke among themselves for a few minutes. One was Edgar, his son, a tall thin young man with blond hair cut in a deep fringe across his eyes. Eric Picot, the wine merchant, was a dark, handsome man of about thirty-six, thickset and well-dressed. He was French with Breton blood but had lived in Devon for many years, though he still owned vineyards along the Loire. The other man was Leonard, a wizened old fellow who had hardly a word to say. He was the chief clerk to Joseph's several trading ventures.

'Is this really important, Crowner?' asked Picot. 'We all have business awaiting us.'

De Wolfe nodded gravely. 'You will find that it is of very grave importance. Going back to Torre later will save another ride from

Exeter. We can return home first thing in the morning.'

Sensing the coroner's inflexibility, Joseph shrugged philosophically and wheeled his horse around. 'You had better lead the way, John.'

Now on home ground, where he had grown up as a boy and hunted as a youth, John led them inland along the south bank of the estuary. Less than a mile upstream, a narrow side-valley came down to the Teign and they turned into it on a narrow track that wound through the dense woodland that filled the combe. Soon they came to a pleasant dell in the low hills, with crofts and cultivated fields well sheltered from the winds. A stone church sat a little above the village, which boasted a new church hostel, a timber and wattle building providing food and shelter for travellers.

'Welcome to Stoke-in-Teignhead,' called John, reining in his big stallion outside the Church House. 'Eric, Gwyn, Thomas, Leonard and the soldiers can take their ease here for an hour and eat around a good fire, while the rest of us go up to my family's manor.' As he and his party rode away, John could not resist waving a hand around him saying, 'My father, may the Mother of God rest his soul, paid for that church of St Andrew of Bethsaida to be rebuilt in stone, and he endowed the hostel in gratitude for a safe return from the first campaign in Ireland.'

Just outside the centre of the village lay a fortified manor house, a two-storeyed, stone-built building with a steep-pitched stone roof. It was set within a wide bank and ditch, with a wooden stockade along the top. Fertile strip fields lay all around it, and a number of relatively tidy cottages of wattle and thatch, each with a well-kept vegetable garden and a pig, goat or house-cow. Inside the enclosure, there was a barn, several outhouses, stables and kitchens, with a few wooden huts for the servants. The whole place had an air of rural contentment and well-being that was not lost on Joseph of Topsham, who knew a well-run business when he saw one. But his mind was mainly on this unexpected appearance of de Wolfe: he had a bad feeling about what was to come.

John slid from his horse and looked about him with affection and pride. 'This is where I was born — the house was wooden in those days.' Though his brother William lived here and ran the manor, John had a part share of it under his father's will, as did his younger sister Evelyn, who looked after the domestic side with their active mother, who had a life-interest in the manor. But unfortunately, this was not the right day or time for reminiscing about his inheritance. Sad work had to be done.

The manor bailiff bustled up, a cheerful fat Saxon named Alsi, and conducted them to the house, their horses being spirited away for food and water. 'The ladies have gone with Lord William to market in King's Teignton, Sir John, but they will be home before long.'

The coroner was glad of a breathing space before his family arrived, so that he could get the bad news over with.

They climbed to the solar on the upper floor, reached by an outside wooden staircase, which could be thrown down in time of attack for the better defence of the upper storey. Thankfully, this had never been needed since Simon de Wolfe, John's soldier father, had built the new house.

They sat near the smouldering logs in the arched fireplace and Alsi poured wine for the three men. Then he hurried away to organise a meal to be served downstairs in the hall.

Joseph was as perceptive as his wise, patriarchal appearance suggested. He turned immediately to the coroner, whom he had known in the way of business for a number of years. 'Well, John, out with it! You didn't bring us miles off the beaten track just to drink wine and show us your home.'

The coroner looked from father to son and back to the father. Edgar had said hardly a word since they met at the river and looked rather bored. Being dragged from his beloved herbs and poultices to ride for half a day to view drowned corpses did not amuse him, especially as it seemed they had now to ride back to Torre. But the next few minutes were to be the worst so far in his twenty-two years of life.

De Wolfe took a deep breath. 'This is not to do with the loss of your ship nor the death of your men, Joseph,' he began. Slowly and dispassionately, he recounted the events of last night in Exeter, knowing of no easier way to tell them.

Their reactions passed through stunned silence into incredulity, then horror and, finally, unbridled anger. Even John was surprised to see how the languid apothecary's apprentice became almost demented with rage. Though he wore no sword, Edgar whipped his dagger from its sheath and waved it about wildly as he paced the room with jerky, directionless steps. 'I'll kill him, damn him! Whoever it is, I'll kill him! I'll not rest until he's slain!' His rage gradually became mixed with tears. John was not sure whether they were all for Christina or

107

whether some stemmed from self-pity.

His father, red-faced with anger above his grey beard, was less distressed but equally vindictive. After a few futile minutes of rage, Joseph pulled his son to him and threw an arm around his shoulders to console him. He looked past Edgar's head to the coroner. 'What is to be done, John?' he asked, his son's jerking body against his breast. 'How can we return to Torre now? We are needed in Exeter.'

John explained that Dame Madge, Matilda and the other beldames were unanimous in advising that Christina be left in peace without the company of men for a time. 'We have to settle this matter of the boat and its crew, come what may. If we go to Torre now, then that is an end of it as far as you are concerned. Otherwise, the journey will be hanging over you in the days ahead, when you will be most needed in Exeter.'

Joseph nodded, his rage subsiding. 'Edgar and I will walk quietly together outside in the bailey and talk about this. Tell us when you are ready to leave.'

Refusing all offers of food, they went down to the ward around the house and, from an embrasure, John saw them walking slowly and sadly together, talking in low voices.

They were still there some time later, when

the de Wolfe family returned from market. In a covered oxcart, fitted with seats, sat his mother and sister, while alongside them rode his brother William and several manor servants. Though he saw them fairly often, there was always a warm welcome for him at Stoke-in-Teignhead. His mother Enyd was a lady of sixty-three, with red still mixed in her greying hair. She was small, sprightly and pure Celt, her mother being Cornish and her father a small landowner from Gwynllwg[1] in Wales, the same area as Nesta's home. Her daughter Evelyn was ten years younger than John, a spinster who had wanted to be a nun. Her mother had discouraged her as she wanted a companion at home, with her husband and second son always away at the wars. Enyd's main support was William, the elder son, a couple of years older than John. Though tall and dark like his brother — they both took after their father — William was a much milder character, preferring the farm and the manors to campaigning.

After embracing his mother and sister, and grasping William's arm, John brought them up to date on events in Torre and Exeter. The pair from Topsham were still brooding outside and John advised leaving them alone

---

[1] Gwent

with their sorrow and anger for the time being. Now Alsi had the other servants running around with food and drink, all smiling and bobbing their knees at John — many of them had known him since he was a child.

While they were eating, Enyd de Wolfe clucked her dismay over the ravishment and her sympathy for those involved. Her eyebrows lifted a little when John told her of Matilda's Good Samaritan efforts the previous night. She had never shared her late husband's enthusiasm for joining John to the de Revelle family, and her relations with Matilda were as distant as the twenty miles that lay between them.

As usual, William was characteristically intent on practicalities. 'So what happens now, brother? About the ship and the poor young lady?'

John, now warm, well fed and at ease among his own folk, stretched his legs before the fire. 'The dead seamen are the easiest matter — we have a couple of the sheriff's men-at-arms down in the Church House, to help us arrest these thieving murderers. If I can prevent de Revelle from hanging them, they will stand trial when the King's justices next come for the Assize of Gaol Delivery.'

'And the rape?' asked Evelyn, whose long

nose marred an otherwise good-looking face.

The coroner shrugged. 'Where can we start? There are many hundreds of men in the city of Exeter. Christina was acknowledged to be one of the most desirable young women in Devon, so many a lecherous eye must have turned upon the poor girl every day. Unless we have some unexpected good luck, I fail to see how we can find the culprit.'

His mother bobbed her head towards the window opening. 'How is the girl's betrothed taking it?' she asked.

'He is fit to burst every blood vessel in his body. Though he's no fighter, he wants to challenge to the death every possible suspect between here and Winchester, poor fellow.' He rose to his feet. 'We must get on to Torre. There is an inquest to arrange for the morning and the day's passing quickly.' He bent to kiss his mother's brow. 'If I spend much more time on a horse, I swear my backside will fuse to the saddle!'

★ ★ ★

Soon after it was light the next morning, John and the others were assembled on an open space within sight of the sea near the hamlet of Torre. They had spent the night at one of the manors of William de Brewere, the

111

influential lord of these parts. Though he was absent in London, his seneschal readily prepared food and sleeping space for the King's coroner and his party.

The six bodies dug from the sand had had to be kept for viewing at the inquest and the most seemly place for that purpose was the rough buildings that the White Canons had set up on a flat area at the southerly end of the neck of the Tor peninsula, not far from where the wreck and the looting had taken place.

As far as Gwyn was concerned, the holy men were monks, but in fact they were priests, come from the parent Norbetine abbey at Welbeck. They had offered to keep the corpses at the back of their small timber church, next to the wattle and thatch building in which the three of them lived. William de Brewere was negotiating with their abbot in Welbeck for the building of a substantial stone abbey at Torre, and though it was fifteen months before Abbot Adam and six canons were to arrive, these three were the advance party.

When the coroner had arrived at dusk the previous evening, he had given orders for every man and boy over fourteen in the village and surrounding Hundred to be present an hour after dawn. It was difficult to

112

carry out the letter of the law and have every male person present to form the jury, as that would have paralysed the work of several villages. However, this was such a serious matter, compared to the usual accident or sudden death, that Gwyn, Sergeant Gabriel and his men-at-arms went through the village and surrounding hamlets, knocking up each household and ordering them to be present at the inquest.

The rough grass in front of the canons' habitation was soon churned by the feet of several score of reluctant freemen and villeins, backed at a distance by curious wives and girls, who had no legal part to play. Children, dogs and even a goat wandered in and out of the crowd and an enterprising hawker was selling apples.

The reeve Aelfric was there, apprehensive and furtive, as were several others John recognised from the affair on the beach. Even the village priest was present, haggard and yellow-faced.

The salvaged goods from the tithe barn were piled up on two ox-carts at one side, ready to be taken to Exeter. They had been left under the guardianship of William de Brewere's seneschal, when John returned to Exeter after his first visit two days before. He was unsure if the seneschal was party to the

113

theft of the valuable flotsam, but strongly suspected that the bailiff, who was next in command, well knew what was going on and had been hand in glove with his assistant, Aelfric.

The coroner looked around to check that his clerk was ready with quill, ink and parchment to record the inquest. Then he nodded at Gwyn. The Cornishman beat on a wheel of the cart with the flat of his sword to gain attention, before he roared in a thunderous voice, 'All persons who have anything to do before King Richard's coroner for the County of Devon, draw near and give your attendance!'

There was a shuffling and squelching of feet in the mud, as the men of Torre tried to understand the meaning of this new ritual imposed on them by the distant powers in far-off London and Winchester. Few had any idea what an inquest was, but most accepted resignedly that it was yet another way of screwing more money out of an already impoverished population.

Standing apart from the villagers were the men from Topsham and Exeter, the father and son looking grey and downcast, sad enough at the deaths of the men from their ship but even more so about the ravishment of their poor Christina. They were anxious beyond all measure to get back to Exeter to console her and her father. Yet John sensed, through Edgar's simmering anger, an apprehensiveness at both how to handle the crisis and his own feelings about the violation of his future wife, virgin no longer.

There was no chair within miles, so John officiated from a three-legged milking stool brought from the village. Hands on knees, his grey and black-clad figure, with the long jet black hair blowing in the wind, gave him the appearance of some satanic angel of doom come among them. He began in a menacing growl, loud enough for all to hear. 'This inquest is into the circumstances of the death of six men found on Torre beach, and also into the wreck of the vessel of which they were crew,' he began, in a tone redolent of accusation.

The first witness was Joseph of Topsham, who stood forward like an Old Testament figure with his long grey beard and flowing cloak. He swore that the wreck was that of his own ship *Mary of the Sea*. The vessel had been laden with wool on the outward voyage and due to return from Barfleur with a full cargo of dried fruit and wine.

Gwyn handed him the shattered board found on the beach and he confirmed that it was part of the ship's hull, bearing some of the words of its name carved upon it.

'And you have seen the bodies of the six men laid out in the priests' chapel here?' demanded the coroner. 'Are they all members of that ship's crew?'

Joseph nodded sadly. 'They are indeed — and one is missing, a young lad called Hecche. I knew them all, poor souls.'

'And were they all English?' asked de Wolfe.

'Two were Bretons and one an Irishman.'

'But none were Normans?'

The older man shook his head emphatically. 'No, all either Saxons or foreigners.'

At this there was a sigh of relief from the crowd: no Normans meant that at least the murdrum fine, of up to forty marks, had been avoided.

Then Edgar and the wine merchant, Eric Picot, who usually met his cargoes when they arrived at the port on the Exe and knew most of the ship's crew by sight, were able to confirm Joseph's identification of his men. Old Leonard, the silent clerk, produced a parchment copy of the order that the ship's master had taken to Barfleur, listing the goods to be purchased for the return trip.

John led them over to the ox-carts and they formally identified the barrels and boxes by the markings burned into the wood with hot

116

irons as the consignment they had been expecting to arrive at Topsham. 'Much of it is missing, but this would account for about half of the cargo,' said Joseph, laying a hand on one of the wheels of the nearest cart.

'It means a considerable loss to us,' added Eric Picot, brushing back his dark hair as it fell forwards across his forehead.

The coroner looked around at the silent crowd. 'I must assume that almost all the goods that were rescued from the sea are here.' He glared pointedly at the sickly village priest, as if to emphasise that he was well aware that some of the salvage had vanished down the man's gullet. 'But now I will turn to the deaths of these men. Three seemed to have died from drowning.' He named those dug first from the sand, with no injuries. 'These had died from the effects of the shipwreck, casting them into the waters, an Act of God, caused by the storm at sea. But the other three . . . ' He turned a thunderous eye on Aelfric and several of the other village men, who were standing in the front row of the audience, flanked ostentatiously by Sergeant Gabriel and his man-at-arms. 'These three, also named by Joseph of Topsham, carry marks of violence, namely wounds on their heads and other parts, plainly caused by heavy blows from blunt

117

weapons. There were splits on their scalps and severe bruises on their necks. There is no question of them suffering these hurts by the action of the sea. They were done to death by deliberate violence. Then there was an attempt to hide these foul deeds by burying them in the sand.'

After the hermit Wulfstan had been called to testify that he had seen bodies on the beach and casks being concealed, the reeve was thrust forward. He stood before the coroner like a bull waiting for the dogs to bait him, his face showing a mixture of truculence and fear. 'I know nothing about any killings! Those seamen were dead afore I laid eyes on them!' he cried, before John had a chance to challenge him.

Gwyn, standing close behind the reeve, gave him a helpful buffet on the shoulder to remind him of his manners. 'Say 'sir' when you address the crowner!' he demanded.

'You're a liar, Aelfric,' snapped de Wolfe. 'I've seen the injuries with my own eyes. Those men were done to death.'

'Not by me they weren't,' retorted the reeve and got another clout from Gwyn for his pains.

The coroner's black brows came together in an angry scowl. 'Are you trying to tell me that someone else crept into your village, killed them and left you the cargo to steal? You're the village headman, you know everything that goes on in Torre, so don't spin me these lies.'

With a vision of mutilation or the gallows strengthening in his mind, Aelfric cast about wildly for an escape. 'Could have been those people down in Paignton — they're a bad lot and no mistake.'

This was too much for John, who sprang to his feet and bellowed at the hapless reeve, 'Be silent, you evil knave! Don't insult our common sense with such nonsense. You were caught red-handed by the hermit, you had the stolen goods hidden and the bodies cry out that they perished from foul violence. Get back there and wait for the verdict — though there's little doubt what that will be.'

Gwyn jerked Aelfric back to his place at the front of the crowd, before two other men, whom John and Gwyn had picked out as having been on the beach, were interrogated. Their abject denials were treated with similar scorn.

Two other villeins had absconded since the day the corpses had been revealed: one was the man John had seen scuttling away when the second trio had been discovered in the sand. They had probably vanished into the forest to join the bands of roving outlaws, fleeing from justice.

Within a few more minutes, the inquest was over. The jury of villagers were made to file past the six corpses, several of which, in spite of the cold weather, were now beginning to look the worse for wear. John pointed out the injuries on the heads as they shuffled past, and dictated the elements of the inquest to Thomas, who scribbled furiously on his parchment roll to keep up with the coroner's flow of words.

In the background, three White Canons, wearing their small round skull-caps instead of monk's tonsures, stood silently contemplating the evil that men do, more convinced than ever that in this corner of England, which seemed full of sinners, their Premonstratensian order should have a foothold.

Soon the evidence had all been taken and recorded, and the King's coroner delivered his verdict.

'Three men have been done to death, callously and for the venal profit of flotsam washed up from the wreck of the vessel *Mary of the Sea*. The tenants of the manor of Torre had shown great iniquity in stealing the salvaged cargo of the ship, worth at least eighty pounds, according to the merchants here.' He swept a hand across the crowd. 'And for failing to report the wreck and the salvage, as should have been done to the sheriff or the coroner, the village is amerced in the sum of twenty marks, to appear before the King's justices at the next visitation. For attempting to steal the said cargo, the village is amerced in the sum of forty marks.'

A wave of anguish rippled through the crowd at this imposition of a corporate fine, which was huge by the standards of the village's meagre income: a mark was worth over thirteen shillings, two-thirds of a pound. They could not look to their lord for any contribution — he might even impose his own penalties on them at his manorial court when he found out what had happened. Some lords encouraged wreck pillage, and even took part in it as long as they were accorded the lion's share, but de Brewere was too politically ambitious to dirty his hands with petty local corruption.

John had not yet finished. 'Wrecks of the sea and their salvage belong to the Crown and are not for the benefit by theft of those who find them. This remnant of cargo should be forfeit to the royal treasury, but as it so patently belongs to the ship-owner and the consignee of the wine, I will recommend to a later inquest on the goods that they be returned to them in part compensation for the loss of the ship and the rest of the cargo.'

There was more to come. 'For not raising the hue and cry over these bodies and not reporting them to the coroner, the village is further amerced in the sum of ten marks. Maybe this will teach you not to leave it to some poor hermit's conscience to bring it to the attention of the King's officers.'

The coroner paused to draw breath. 'And for the most heinous sin of killing three innocent seamen, who in the hour of need at the foundering of their vessel should have been given Christian succour but who instead were bludgeoned to death to conceal your thieving purposes, your reeve and two freemen are to be arrested and taken to Exeter to await trial, to be kept there at the expense of the village, which is further amerced at twenty marks for condoning these killings and attempting to conceal them and the existence of the valuable salvage.'

There was a groan that almost echoed over the sea, as the village of Torre heard its financial future for years hence being mortgaged to pay these huge fines. True, no money would be paid over until the King's judges heard the case at the General Eyre in Exeter, which might be a couple of years away, so slow was the progress of the royal courts about the country. But the fines would hang over them and the buying in of new cattle and pigs, the expenditure on good corn and other things requiring capital, would now be under a cloud for half a decade ahead, as William de Brewere would still expect the manorial fields to be worked by the villagers as usual.

John's final command, that Aelfric and the other two suspects would be taken under guard to Exeter, had been expected by everyone. They would be imprisoned in the castle gaol to appear before the justices in due course — if they survived more than a few months of incarceration in the foul cells under Rougemont's keep.

The soldiers, aided by Gwyn's huge figure, grabbed the three men and hustled them to the carts, where they were tied on to the tailboards for the slow journey back to Exeter. The reeve's daughter ran forward with screams to hug her father as he was hauled away. Probably this was the last time she would ever see him. Relatives of the other two men also crowded around and the soldiers let them have a few minutes to say their farewells before the cart drivers climbed aboard and flicked their patient oxen into lumbering movement.

The crowd dispersed, grumbling and throwing baleful glances at these officials who had disrupted their simple, but placid lives.

123

To them, a wreck was manna from heaven, goods that could be covertly sold to help village finances, pay the tithes and buy a few more sheep and cattle next spring, perhaps some food, too, if the winter was hard. Starvation hovered over every household after the last salt pork was gone and all the mouldy oats consumed. To them, the death of six sailors was a small price to pay for that: the shipmen would have died anyway, in the next storm, or the one after that.

As they trudged off, despondently wondering who their next reeve would be, John thanked the White Canons for the use of their premises, then collected up his party for the ride back to Exeter. It was not yet half-way through the morning, so they expected to be home well before the December dusk fell.

The sergeant and man-at-arms had gone with the wagons and would not reach the Exe until tomorrow, so it was the coroner and his two men who rode back with Joseph, Edgar, the old clerk and Eric Picot, all in sombre mood. 'God knows what we shall find when we return,' said the merchant from Topsham, as their horses climbed the slope across the neck of Tor headland to reach the coastal track. 'This has been the worst two days of my life.'

But worse was yet to come.

6

In which Crowner John
disputes with the sheriff

That evening, John found his wife in a
strange mood. They ate their evening meal
civilly enough, seated at the long, lonely table
in their hall, with empty benches between
them that should have been filled with sons
and daughters had their marriage not been as
barren in body as in spirit. Mary brought in
hot broth, followed by boiled beef, which was
cheap and plentiful at this time of year: most
cattle had to be killed by December, due to
lack of winter fodder.

At the end of the meal, they took their
mugs of hot wine to the fireside and sat one
each side of the great open hearth. Each had
a monk's chair, almost like a sentry box with
a cowled hood, to keep out the draughts that
blew in through the shuttered window
opening, as well as under the doors.

While they were eating, John had related
the events of his trip to Torbay, the inquest,
the meeting with the Topsham merchant and
his brief visit to Stoke-in-Teignhead. The last

was received with stony silence by Matilda, as her feelings for his family, especially his mother, were as distant as theirs for her. She had always felt that her father had made her marry beneath her, to a minor knight who no longer had family still in Normandy, like the de Revelles.

Now they sat before their fire and she scowled at the crackling logs. 'You're always away, John. What kind of husband neglects his wife so?'

He groaned at the return of the same old topic. 'You know very well that I had to tell Joseph and his son of the tragedy here — you yourself told me to go, yesterday morning.'

'You always have some excuse,' retorted Matilda, illogically. 'No other wife among the leading people of our city is left alone so often to fend for herself.'

John abandoned any attempt to reason with her. 'How is Christina today? You said you had been to the house earlier.'

With a sudden change of mood, she became almost amiable, her interest quickened in the Rifford drama. 'The poor girl is better in herself, in that her pain has subsided and her scratches and bruises are fading already. But her state of mind is delicate. She weeps and laughs by turns, one minute saying that all is well, the next sobbing that she

126

wishes to be dead.'

'It is to be expected, I suppose,' said John mildly, hoping to mollify his wife by agreeing with her.

But she glared at him, her heavy-lidded eyes gimletlike in the square face. 'How would you know what is to be expected? What dealings have you ever had with a ravishment, except perhaps as a perpetrator in one of your soldier campaigns?'

He ignored her attempt to be deliberately offensive and asked, 'Did she say any more about the circumstances of the assault?'

With another mercurial shift of temperament, Matilda lowered her spiced wine to her lap and spoke in a low, almost confidential tone. 'I sat with her this afternoon and for a time she was almost her old self. She related more details of that awful evening.'

John sat forward, hopeful that he would hear something of use to his investigation. 'She has some memory of who attacked her?'

Matilda pursed her lips. 'No, she saw nothing of him. But she told me more details of her visits that evening. She had been to our neighbour to collect some bauble, which that weedy English youth Edgar had bought her.'

Matilda considered all Saxons inferior and Celts, such as the Cornish and Welsh, on a par with farm animals. Part of her antipathy to John's family was that his mother was a Celt. She tried to forget that her husband was only half Norman. 'Christina told me that the two men who work for Fitzosbern, both Saxons, were ogling her continually in a most lewd fashion.' She sniffed in disapproval. 'I can't imagine why he employs such riffraff. Surely there is a better class of silversmith to be had.'

John sat back in disappointment. 'Is that all she had to say? Did she see either of them follow her to the cathedral, for instance?'

Matilda shook her head, the coiled braids of hair in their crespines of gold-thread net bouncing above her ears. 'Is there any need? Obviously one of those foul men was her assailant. She had been in the shop not an hour before and was embarrassed by the suggestive looks and words of these men. One or perhaps even both are surely guilty. How can it be otherwise?'

The crowner sighed: his wife's sense of justice was as arbitrary as her brother's. 'That is pure supposition, without a shred of proof, Matilda. There must be hundreds of men in Exeter who have lusted after Christina — she is an acknowledged beauty. Someone saw her walking alone at night and took the opportunity to satisfy their lust — there is no reason at all to accuse one of those smiths.'

'They are better suspects than any of your anonymous hundreds, John! Can you come up with two better names yet?

He stayed silent, afraid that if he spoke his mind further she would go off into one of her rages or sulks.

'I wonder that Godfrey allowed his men to be so forward with a customer. He should have punished those lechers for so much as casting a bold glance at the girl,' she said self-righteously.

John noticed that Matilda referred to their neighbour by his Christian name. He knew that she fawned upon the fellow because he flirted with her and paid her patently insincere compliments when they met in the street or at some civic function. He himself couldn't stand the fellow, with his dandyish clothing and conceited swagger. 'Christina said nothing else of use, then?'

'I considered that of considerable use, John. I made a point of telling Richard when he called to see me this afternoon. A good job my brother is solicitous over my health and feelings, for my husband certainly is not.'

John chafed inwardly at her words. 'You spun this tittle-tattle to your brother?'

'Of course — and greatly interested he was, too. He said that he will send men to bring the two smiths to Rougemont tomorrow to interrogate them.'

Her husband lost patience. 'I wish you would leave enforcing the law to those whose job it is, Matilda. If Christina had wanted the sheriff to know of this, she would have told him herself.'

Like a spark to dry tinder, that started her off. She raved at her husband, accusing him of being uncaring, ungrateful and half the man her brother was. She upbraided him for a dozen real sins and a dozen imaginary ones, half rising from her chair until her wine spilled over unnoticed.

Mary, who came in to clear the remnants of the meal, tiptoed out again, sorry for the master but unwilling to get embroiled in any partisan role that might cost her her job.

John screwed down his rising anger, in the faint hope that her tantrum would subside as quickly as it had arisen, but now she was in full spate. Eventually, unable to get in a word during her vituperative onslaught, he stood up so suddenly that the cowled chair went over backwards with a crash. 'That's enough, wife!' he roared, so violently that Matilda was stopped in mid-sentence, her mouth remaining open as he loomed over her. 'Rant and shout all you want, woman, but do it alone. I'm going out!' He marched to the door of the vestibule and yanked it open with a screech of its hinges.

As he vanished into the darkness, his wife found her lungs again. 'Go then, damn you, you ungrateful wretch! Go to your squalid alehouse and your Welsh whore!'

She gathered breath for another round of abuse, but he closed the oaken door behind him with a satisfying bang.

In spite of Matilda's words, he did not turn towards the Bush, but decided on a round of investigation concerning Christina's assault. His feet took him only twenty yards from his own dwelling before he made his first call.

Pushing open the door that Christina had entered two nights before, John entered Fitzosbern's shop. The same two workers were there, toiling each evening until the seventh hour rang from the cathedral bell. The older one, Alfred, nervously clambered to his feet, the piece of metal he had been working dropping to his bench with a clang.

'Evening, Sir John. Do you want the master?' His voice was tense, as if he had been expecting a call from the law for some time.

John nodded and swung his head round to look at the younger silversmith, Garth. This brawny fellow stared back at him blankly, no trace of anxiety in his dumb-looking face.

John, who knew almost everyone in the city of Exeter, had always marked down this fellow — whom he often saw in Martin's Lane — as a little retarded, even though it was said that he was an able metal-worker. John contemplated him for a long moment.

'A terrible business, the other night, sir,' quavered Alfred, as if unable to bear the ominous silence. 'The young lady was in here that very evening.'

'Your master, is he in the house?' rumbled John, ignoring the invitation for dialogue.

Without a word, Garth repeated the action he had made for Mistress Rifford: staring at de Wolfe, he swung a great fist backwards to beat a tattoo on the panel behind him.

Without waiting, the coroner pulled aside the heavy woollen drape and stepped through the inner doorway. The back workshop was again almost dark, lit only by the sleeping furnace and the glow of a lamp that came down the stairway at the back.

Though Fitzosbern's house was about the same size as John's, he had given over the whole of the ground floor to his business and lived on the upper floor, made by heavy boards supported on corbels built into the walls, seven feet above the ground.

As John advanced cautiously in the gloom, heavy footsteps clattered on the steps and the light was broken by Fitzosbern coming down to meet him. He held a tallow lamp in his hand and recognised his visitor. 'Mother of God, it's de Wolfe! Come in and welcome. It's many a long year since you stepped into my house.'

John muttered some noncommittal words and followed the silversmith up the stairs.

The solar occupied the whole upper floor and had been divided into two rooms, one of which was a bedroom. They were better furnished than his own: the wealthy guild-master had expensive hangings to brighten the walls, wool rugs on the boards and several chairs and stools around a large table. There was a small fireplace, which seemed to be joined into the chimney of the furnace below, and the place was almost too warm, even for a winter's evening.

'Come in and have some hot spiced wine,' effused Godfrey. Mulled wine seemed to be his first thought when any visitor arrived.

John was suddenly aware of someone else in the room: a head appeared around the side of a highbacked settle near the fire. 'Who is it, Godfrey? Oh, Sir John, it's you!'

It was Fitzosbern's wife, Mabel, a pretty woman ten years younger than her husband. His first wife had died in childbirth six years earlier, the infant still-born. Five years ago, he had married Mabel, the daughter of Henry Knapman, a wealthy tin-miner from Chagford on the edge of Dartmoor. Small, slim and very blonde, she was another lady in Exeter who attracted many looks of admiration and an equal number of lecherous stares.

Though John had never liked her husband, what little he knew of Mabel had left a good impression on him. She was always cheerful, amiable, and yet had that something that made men wonder whether they might have a chance with her, if the circumstances were right. Although he was as fond of the ladies as the next man, he had never contemplated making a play for Mabel, partly because she was almost on his doorstep, too near home for comfort.

Godfrey was already pouring wine and pressing an elegant glass into John's hand, a far cry from the crude mugs he used in his office in the castle.

He settled on a chair near the fire and Mabel resumed her own seat, illuminated by the flames from the logs. He studied her over the rim of his glass, while Godfrey fussed over drinks for his wife and himself. Mabel was dressed stylishly in a pale green silk kirtle, deeply embroidered all around the neck and hem. A green silk cord was wound twice around her waist, and she wore a darker green over-tunic, laced widely open at the front. Her blonde hair was parted in the centre and two long braid hung down over each breast, with green silk tapes plaited into the strands. John could hardly fail to compare her appearance with that of Matilda, who for all Lucille's efforts and her expensive outfits still managed to look clumsy and frumpish.

Fitzosbern brought his glass and sat between them on a padded stool. 'I expect we know what brings you on this nonetheless welcome visit, John — I may call you that, I hope?'

The coroner would prefer that he didn't, but could hardly say so while sitting by the fellow's fire and drinking his wine.

'Is your wife well?' asked Mabel politely.

Her husband broke in effusively, 'Indeed, I hope so. A charming lady, a pillar of Exeter society. I wish we saw more of you both.'

'I am always very busy,' muttered John. 'Away so much I have little time for socialising.' He gave one of his loud throat-clearings which, with his grunts, were always a preamble to serious talking. 'As you suspect, I am looking into the sad episode of Christina Rifford's assault.'

There was a chorus of 'Terrible!' and 'Awful, the poor girl!' from the pair opposite.

'I understand that the last place that she

was known to be was your shop on that evening, Fitzosbern.'

'Call me Godfrey, John, please! Yes, she certainly came here that evening but, from what I hear, it was not her last place of visitation. That was the cathedral, surely.'

John assented reluctantly. He was damned if he was going to call this vain cockerel by his first name, but the investigation must go on. 'True, but so far we have yet to find anyone who remembers her there.' That was mainly because no one had got round to asking, but he was not going to tell Fitzosbern that.

The guild-master ran a hand through his thick curly hair. 'The lovely girl came to the shop some time between the sixth and seventh bell. The smiths were still here, so it could not have been seven. She was here but a few moments, though I pressed her to stay and warm herself with some wine, as you are doing now.'

John noticed Mabel turn her blue eyes on her husband, but she said nothing.

'So she didn't come upstairs, to meet your wife?' he asked deliberately.

It was Fitzosbern's turn to look at his wife now, and he paused momentarily before saying smoothly. 'Mabel was at our house at Dawlish until yesterday. She prefers the sea air to this rather small solar above the workshop, which can sometimes get smoky when the furnace is running hard.'

'So you were alone?'

'Yes, but for those two louts downstairs. They are good smiths, but hardly edifying company.'

John drank down half his wine in one gulp. 'I have to ask this, but certain insinuations have been made. Are those two men, Alfred and Garth, of good reputation?'

The fleshy face of the master silversmith assumed an expression of sudden enlightenment, which John recognised as false.

'Are they suspect of this foulness? Well, as I said they are good at their trade, but I have no means of vouching for their characters. When they leave this shop at seven, they cease to exist as far as I am concerned. I have no means of knowing — or caring — what they get up to in their own time.'

In other words, you bastard, you are throwing them to the wolves, thought John bitterly. He would have stood up for his own men, Gwyn and even the dubious Thomas, against any slurs on their characters.

'Have you any reason to think that they might have had any evil designs on the Rifford girl?'

Godfrey began to leer, then checked himself as he found Mabel watching him intently from her bright blue eyes. He gave a little cough. 'Well, she is an extraordinarily attractive young woman. I suspect that many men in this town have such designs lurking in their imaginations. Alfred and Garth are probably no different.'

'But did you see them do or say anything objectionable or suggestive?'

'No, I did not, John. But I don't watch my servants, my interest is with my customers, especially with a daughter of one of the portreeves.'

After a few more minutes of fruitless questions, the coroner threw down the rest of his drink and rose to leave. Fitzosbern pressed him to stay and have more wine, but John sensed that he would be glad of his departure. Mabel had said not a word more, but he had the feeling that she would have plenty to say to her husband once the street door had closed behind him.

He left the house and walked around the corner of Martin's Lane into the high street and on up to the Rifford house on the other side, towards the castle and the East Gate. Several bells from the many churches rang out for their services at the seventh hour, taking their cue from the deeper toll that issued from the cathedral. The bitter wind had blown up again from the east and there were few people about the darkened streets.

He came to the house on the corner of the lane and rapped on the door. It was opened by old Aunt Bernice who, in a confusedly flustered manner, ushered him inside. Near the fireplace, Henry Rifford was standing, feet apart, almost as if he was guarding the hall. Then John saw the feet and skirts of Christina, who was seated in a large chair. As he advanced across the rush-strewn floor, he was surprised to see the gaunt figure of Dame Madge on a bench opposite the girl.

Christina looked pale but composed and greeted him civilly, but with a wary look in her eyes, which he suspected would be bestowed upon every man for a long time to come.

The usual courtesies were exchanged rather stiffly and, though invited to sit, the coroner remained standing. 'I have no wish to intrude, but I wanted to enquire after you, Mistress Christina, and to hope that you are recovering from your ordeal as well as might be expected,' he said, rather stilted.

She inclined her beautiful head gracefully. 'I improve in body every hour, Sir John,' she said, with the implication that her mind would take a great deal longer to heal.

Dame Madge rose to her feet. 'I, too, called to see if there was anything more I could do for the poor girl, but her bruises are fading quickly. She has a good spirit and is a devout and noble soul. All I can do is pray for her rapid return to full health and happiness.' She walked towards the door, in a stately fashion, like a ship under sail, her white head-rail flowing down over her black habit, a wooden cross flopping against her flat bosom. 'The city gates are long closed, so I will go to St Nicholas's to pray, and beg a bed in their infirmary.' This was a small priory lower down the road not far from the apothecary's shop where Edgar was apprenticed.

Rifford and John thanked her for her continued support and she sailed out into the night, one of Henry's servants accompanying her, to see her safely to the priory.

Henry Rifford, his large face returned to its customary redness, came back to the fire. 'Was there anything in particular you wanted, Crowner, apart from your kind enquiries about my daughter?' He said this in a half-challenging way, as if daring John to intrude further upon their private grief. As one of the bishop's and sheriff's faction, he had opposed John's appointment as coroner but for political rather than personal reasons.

'Much as I dislike disturbing you, I need to discover all I can about this crime, Portreeve. This perpetrator must be caught, not only to avenge your daughter, but to prevent further such evil. If he is not caught, he may well think that he can get away with such an act again. There are many other pretty women at risk in the city, even if none quite so fair as Christina.'

This was quite a speech for the usually taciturn de Wolfe, but it put Rifford in a position where, as a leader of the community, he was unable to resist doing all he could to assist the public good. 'But how can we help? All that can be said has been said. De Revelle has been here three times himself and now favours one of those smiths that work with Godfrey Fitzosbern as the most likely suspect. If I thought that to be true, I would go down there tonight and hack the bastard's head off with a sword.'

Matilda's loose tongue had done its work well, thought John sourly. Once the sheriff got astride a convenient idea, he would ride it into the ground and to hell with justice or common sense. He turned to Christina, who sat apathetically, her hands crossed in her lap, dressed in a dull gown of brown wool, her hair flowing loose and unbraided from under a white linen coif.

'Christina, you have been asked this many times, but do you still have no recollection of anything — anything at all — that might help to identify this man?'

Tears glistened in her eyes, though she made no sound.

'You couldn't sense if he was big and heavy or lean and sinewy?'

'He was so strong, that's all I know.'

John tried another tack. 'You told my wife that in the silversmith's shop the two workers made you feel uncomfortable?'

She nodded, a little more animated now that he had moved from the scene of her shame. 'They stared at me a great deal, but nothing more. I have learned, in the last year or so, how men look at me when they — they — think things,' she faltered.

Her father now indicated that he was nearing the limit of his indulgence and that John should conclude his questioning.

'You saw no one follow you from Martin's Lane to the cathedral?'

'I wasn't looking for anyone. It never occurred to me that anyone would.'

'And in the cathedral? Where did you go? Did you see anyone you knew?'

'I went straight to the altar of Mary, Mother of God, and knelt before it to pray for the soul of my own mother Mary. It stands against the front of the quire-screen, on the left-hand side.' Christina's eyes filled with tears again.

John did not know whether they were for the mother who was not there to comfort her in the hour of her need or for the memory that rapine had been soon to follow. 'Did you see anyone you knew?' persisted the coroner.

'I was there about a quarter of one hour. Several people came to kneel and pray. I knew one or two by sight, but not by name. When I was leaving, I passed a woman, Martha, wife of a wheelwright who lives near my cousin Mary. I spoke a few words with her, then left by the small door.'

There was nothing else to be learned and John took his leave, as Henry Rifford was now increasingly restive.

His next call was at the castle, set on its rise at the north-eastern corner of the sloping city. The man-at-arms at the gate, just below his own office, called out a challenge as he saw a black figure striding up the drawbridge over the inner ditch, but banged the stock of his spear into the ground as a salute when he recognised the King's coroner.

John passed through the narrow rounded archway into the inner bailey and made for the keep, set near the further curtain wall that ran along the low cliff above Northernhay and formed the corner of the city perimeter.

The inner ward was active with people coming and going between the lean-to huts that lined the bank below the walls. Cooking fires were burning, and soldiers and their families relaxed in the evening after a day's work. Chickens perched in bushes and on carts, geese wandered about, and a solitary goat had somehow got himself on to the roof of a low hut to eat the grassy thatch. Horses neighed and oxen lowed in the stables over on the right-hand side, behind the tiny chapel of St Mary. Underfoot, the ground was a morass of hoof-churned mud, refuse and animal droppings, and as the coroner strode across to the building where the sheriff had his town residence, he thought it no wonder that Richard's wife was rarely there.

De Revelle had several manors, one at Revelstoke, another at Tiverton, where his elegant but aloof wife Lady Eleanor spent most of her time, saying that she could not stand the cramped quarters and military squalor of Rougemont.

John reached the wooden ladder that went up to the first floor entrance of the keep, over the semi-subterranean undercroft that housed the castle gaol. There was another prison, a hellhole used for convicts from the burgage court, in the South Gate, but those awaiting trial or convicted by the sheriff's shire court — or by the Royal Justices on their infrequent visits — ended up in equally foul cells under the keep.

At the foot of the steps, another guard, half asleep, roused himself sufficiently to salute the coroner. The security was slack, especially after the town gates closed at nightfall: Exeter had seen no fighting since the siege almost sixty years before, when Baldwin de Redvers, Earl of Devon, had held the castle for Empress Matilda against King Stephen during the civil war. John sometimes thought cynically that Matilda was a name which seemed to suit hard-bitten, aggressive women like the Empress and his own wife.

He climbed to the first floor, most of which was a large hall, deserted at this time of the evening. Another guard drooped by a small door that led to the sheriff's quarters and, with one of his grunts, the coroner stalked past him and entered the inner room. A pair of tallow dips and two candles burned inside, with a moderate fire glowing in the hearth, enough to light up a table where Richard de Revelle was working on some documents.

Unusually for a knight, he was quite literate, which made John secretly jealous. But it was also a measure of Richard's lack of military prowess: he had managed to avoid both the French and Irish wars, as well as the Crusades, being too ambitious in the political arena to risk getting killed or wounded.

The sheriff looked up sharply, his pointed beard jutting aggressively as the coroner pushed open the door and walked in. When he saw who it was, his face changed to the expression that always annoyed John intensely: a faint, pitying smile, as if he was resigned to humouring a slightly backward child.

'Ah, it's our noble coroner! What brings you out on such a cold night, John? You should be at home with your good wife and a jar of ale.'

'Don't patronise me, Richard. There's much work to be done over this ravishment. The girl knows nothing that will help us and I fear this evil man may strike again if he feels he has defeated us.'

The sheriff sighed as he pushed aside his parchments and leaned forward over his table. 'Christina has spoken of the two smiths in Fitzosbern's shop — your own wife told me of her fears of those scum. I will bounce them around in the morning, to see what falls from their lips.' John began arguing with his brother-in-law about the lack of anything resembling evidence, but Richard responded with the same logic as Matilda: he at least had two suspects, however feeble the connection, whereas the coroner had nothing at all. The discussion led nowhere, so John changed direction to report on his visit to Torbay and the arrest of the reeve and other villagers, both for theft of royal flotsam and for the murder of the three sailors.

The sheriff nodded his agreement with the arrests. 'I'll try them next week at the County Court and hang them the next day.'

John shook his head. 'No, Richard, they must await the King's justices, as Hubert Walter has decreed. I have all the details enrolled and will present them at the next assize.'

De Revelle groaned, resting his forehead on his hand in a theatrical gesture of sorrowful resignation. 'Not again, John. I thought we had enough of this last month.'

'Then we will thrash it out with the Justiciar next week,' snapped John stubbornly, unwilling to yield an inch of his coronial powers to the sheriff.

Richard rose from his chair, resplendent in a yellow tunic to his calves, covered by his surcoat of buff linen to knee-level. His narrow face was set in a petulant expression, like a patient but exasperated school-master with a stubborn pupil.

'Hubert Walter arrives after the noon hour on Monday, from Buckfast Abbey. You had better come with Matilda to the Bishop's feast that evening, then we can arrange for a meeting next day to sort out this nonsense of you coroners trying to usurp the sheriff's duties.'

'We have been invited already to the feast,' retorted John, stung again by the other's patronising manner. 'The Archdeacon and Treasurer of the cathedral have already notified us that we should be present as of right.'

After a few more sniping remarks on both sides, John left the sheriff to his business of arranging for the secular part of the Chief Justiciar's visit in three days' time. He marched back through the castle, and this time fulfilled Matilda's allegation by striding down the whole length of High Street, past Carfoix, the crossing of the main roads from the four major gates, and into Fore Street. Half-way down, he turned left into a huddle of small streets and crossed into Idle Lane, where the Bush stood isolated on its patch of rough ground.

He pushed open the door and entered the warm, sweat-and-ale smelling main room. Nesta was not to be seen, but old Edwin, the one-eyed potman, gave him a welcoming wave and limped across to where John slumped on a bench near the fire. 'Evening, Cap'n! We've got a new batch of ale, just racked off today — unless you want cider?'

'A quart of ale, Edwin. And where's the mistress?'

The one eye managed to leer at the coroner. 'Upstairs, Sir John, fixing mattresses for two travellers. She'll be down in a minute or two.'

He lurched off to wash empty ale pots in a leather bucket of dirty water and to refill them with new ale drawn from casks wedged up on a low platform at the rear.

John looked about the long, low room and saw a score or more citizens lolling at other tables, a few whores among them. He knew all the men by sight and most by name, the majority local tradesmen. The few strangers were countrymen, in Exeter to buy and sell livestock or other goods. Several men were foreign, probably German merchants from Cologne or shipmasters from Flanders or Brittany, their vessels tied up at the quay a few hundred yards away. With such a motley collection of virile men in the city, how on earth was he — or Richard — to make any progress in seizing a potential rapist?

'Why so thoughtful, Sir Crowner?'

Nesta dropped down on to the bench alongside him, slipping her arm through his. Her pretty round face, russet hair and shapely body were a tonic to his jaded eyes.

She smiled at him, showing white teeth that were a novelty in women of her age, most of whom had yellowed pegs or blackened stumps. John knew that this was due to the Welsh habit of rubbing the teeth twice a day with the chewed end of a hazel twig.

'Frustration, my dear woman!' he said, dropping his hand to her thigh.

She rolled her eyes in mock ecstasy. 'Frustration at not rolling me in my bed at this very moment, kind sir?' she mocked.

'No, my girl. At getting nowhere with this damned rape.'

She pretended to pout, but could not keep it up for more than a moment. Reaching over for his ale jar, she swallowed a mouthful. 'The gossip says that Godfrey Fitzosbern's smiths are under suspicion.'

The coroner marvelled once again at the rapidity with which rumour travelled in Exeter. He explained that there was no foundation for this idea and told Nesta of his latest quarrel with his wife over the matter.

'Why should the suspicion rest only on Fitzosbern's men?' complained the comely innkeeper. 'I'd far rather suspect Godfrey himself. He's a lecher and ogler of the first water. He's tried it on with me once or twice — and with most of the women in the city who don't have cross-eyes and whiskers.'

John was glad that his mistress's opinion was the same as his own, as regards the master silversmith.

'But surely a substantial citizen like Godfrey, a leading burger and guild-master, would hardly risk everything for two minutes' pleasure with the daughter of a portreeve!' he objected.

Nesta looked at him sternly. 'I know of a King's crowner who regularly beds a common innkeeper! When the sap rises in a man's loins, he is capable of anything.'

John gave her one of his rare grins, a lop-sided lift of his full lips. His hand squeezed her plump leg again, as he leaned over to whisper, 'Are you very busy at the moment, madam? Or can we inspect the upper room of this hostelry to see if the pallets are soft?'

As he followed her up the wide ladder steps in the corner, many pairs of eyes looked knowingly in their direction, but John's thoughts were mainly on the legs of the pert lady ascending in front of him — although a fraction of his mind was mulling over what she had said about Godfrey Fitzosbern.

151

★ ★ ★

At the same time, not far away, others were discussing the silversmith, in a room over Eric Picot's wine store in Priest Street.[1]

Joseph of Topsham, his son Edgar and the wine merchant sat earnestly considering the situation. The rumours about Christina's visit to Fitzosbern had spread within minutes, and it was already well known that the sheriff was going to interrogate the two smiths next morning.

Picot was scornful of the gossip. 'I fail to see why we should suspect those two nonentities,' he exclaimed, standing to pour more good wine into the glass cups of his guests. 'I would a thousand times better suspect their master.'

He was echoing the words of Nesta, but probably a good proportion of Exeter men felt the same, jealous of Godfrey's winning ways with the ladies, which included some of their own wives.

'But there is no shred of evidence — nor can I see how such can be obtained,' objected Joseph, cupping the wine in his hands as he stared moodily into the fire.

'I would kill him with my bare hands if I

---

[1] Now Preston Street

thought he was the one!' snarled Edgar, who since yesterday had turned from an ineffectual youth into a wrathful man, obsessed with hurting whoever had injured him so badly. Though he had not yet admitted it to himself, much of his anger arose from his indecision as to whether he now wanted to marry Christina, who could never come to his bed with her maidenhead intact. He was ashamed at the thought that slid into his mind and used righteous anger to try to block it out.

He and his father had been to see her earlier that evening. The visit had not been a success, as a shutter like a great portcullis seemed to have come down between Christina and Edgar. Though they exchanged courteous words and Edgar made all the right expressions of horror and condolence, they could not embrace or even touch hands. Edgar, sensitive to mood and atmosphere, felt the girl stiffen and tremble when he came near. 'It was almost as if she suspected me of being the ravisher!' he blurted out to his father, after they left the Rifford house.

They made their way to Eric Picot's dwelling, Joseph wanting to unburden himself to a good friend, before going back to sleep in a corner of Edgar's room, in the store of the apothecary's shop. Picot kept his stock of wine in the house in Priest Street, as it was near the quayside, where ships either brought the imported casks direct or lighters rowed them up the river from Topsham. He lived above, in rather Spartan circumstances, as his wife had died five years before and he had reverted to a bachelor existence. However, he also had a new house built on a plot purchased from the manorial lord at Wonford, just outside the city, where he spent some days each week.

'What can we do about this, Father?' demanded Edgar. 'I've a mind to challenge Fitzosbern to deny that he knows anything about this foul assault. Christina was last seen in his shop, getting that damned bracelet. God above, I wish I had never thought to give it to her if this is the ruin it brought upon us!'

'Steady, boy! What earthly good could that do, except to get you into trouble? We have no proof at all that Godfrey knows anything about this.'

Edgar subsided into muttering under his breath, but Picot took up the theme. 'He is an evil man. I know that from the way he treats his wife — he is unfaithful to her at every opportunity. The poor woman made a bad bargain when she married him. He harried his first wife into an early grave.'

Joseph smiled wanly at his friend, because he knew his secret — as did half the city. The attractive wife of the silversmith had been Picot's lover for at least half a year and it was also no secret that she heartily disliked her husband. Edgar, who was as perceptive as his father when he forgot his own self-interest, looked from one to the other. 'It's all right, Father, I know about Eric's affair with Mabel Fitzosbern, you don't have to keep things from me as if I was a child.' Joseph rolled his eyes at Picot. 'It seems common knowledge, Eric, like the crowner and his Welsh doxy. Let's hope that Godfrey isn't aware of it.'

'I don't give a damn if he is. I mean to take her away from him one day,' said the wine merchant stoutly. 'And maybe we can turn this to our advantage, for I can ask Mabel to keep her ears and eyes open for any hint Godfrey might drop about this terrible happening.'

'He's hardly likely to confess to it, least of all to his wife!' objected Joseph.

'But if he does, I'll kill him,' hissed the apothecary's apprentice.

7

In which Crowner John is summoned to a corpse

Next morning, John stood moodily in front of the smouldering fire in the hall. Mary had given him his breakfast, which he ate in solitary state soon after dawn. Then, still in his bed shirt, he went out to the back yard and washed his face and neck in a bucket of water: it was Saturday morning, the day for ablutions. He had the second of his twice-weekly shaves, rubbing his face with soap made from goat's fat and beech ash boiled with soda, then rasped at his black stubble with a special knife, its edge honed to extreme sharpness. It was also the day to change his clothes, and Mary had put out a clean long undershirt and a grey tunic for him which he pulled over his head, after warming them before the fire.

He dragged on his braies, trousers that came to the knee, and then long stockings, over which he wound cross-gartering. His clothes were almost devoid of ornamentation or embroidery, merely a few lines of stitches around the high neck. He was not riding that day, so put on low shoes, pointed but without the extravagant curled tips in the new fashion that dandies like de Revelle and Fitzosbern sported.

'It's cold out, that wind never ceases,' advised Mary, holding out a clean super-tunic in black woollen serge.

'What was she like last night, after I left?' he muttered to his maid and former bed-mate.

Mary's eyes lifted to the small embrasure high above them that communicated with the solar, where Matilda was still in bed. 'She stayed here an hour, poking the fire so hard it almost went out!' she whispered conspiratorially. 'Then she yelled for Lucille and they went up to her solar. She's not moved since.'

John knew that, for he had spent the night on the further edge of their large palliasse, Matilda ignoring him in a pretence of sleep. 'She'll come round, it's not so bad as last month.' Then his wife had barred the solar door against him for several nights, making him sleep on the floor of the hall before the fire.

After dressing, John intended to go up to Rougemont for the eighth bell, to be present when Richard de Revelle interrogated the two silversmiths, as he had threatened the previous evening. But Fate, that unpredictable meddler, took a hand in his plans. She arrived in the form of Gwyn of Polruan who, just as John was taking his cloak from a peg in the vestibule, banged on the outer door and pushed in from the lane outside. The east wind had brought the first flurries of snow and his tattered leather jerkin was spotted with white.

'What's this, man?' demanded John. 'You're usually up in the gate-house at this hour, feeding that great stomach of yours.'

The Cornishman brushed flakes of snow from his wide shoulders. 'More trouble. We've got a body in the city. I don't like the looks of this one.'

Over many years, John had learned to heed Gwyn's warnings. Long before they had become involved in his work as coroner, Gwyn's mixture of common sense and Celtic intuition had so often proved correct, whether it was on the field of battle or lost in some god-forsaken forest or desert.

The coroner hung his cloak back on the peg and motioned Gwyn to come into the hall. He yelled down the passageway for Mary, then led the way to his hearth.

Gwyn, who rarely came to the house, looked about him silently at the large room, the high rafters and the table and chairs. John knew he was comparing this affluence with his own thatched hut of wattle and daub in St Sidwell's, but he felt that Gwyn was not in the slightest envious, only curious as to how the other half lived.

Mary bustled in and nodded pleasantly at the whiskered giant — they always got on well together, both practical, no-nonsense characters. John asked her to bring bread, cheese and ale to compensate Gwyn for his missed breakfast — he seemed unable to survive a morning without a top-up of food and drink.

His officer declined an invitation to sit in his master's house, but stood near the fire to melt the last of the snowflakes. John waited expectantly, knowing that Gwyn would take his time. 'A woman's body, found less than an hour ago, in St Bartholomew's churchyard,' he began. This was one of the many small parish chapels dotted about the city, St Bartholomew's being in the drab quarter between the North and West Gates.

'Who found it?'

'An old crone who sweeps out the chapel. She arrived soon after dawn and saw a pair of feet sticking out from a rubbish pile just inside the gate.'

'Have you been there yourself?'

'I had a quick look, but touched nothing.

The old woman told the priest and he sent word to the castle. I happened to be there when his servant came to the gate-house guard with the message.'

'Does the sheriff know about it yet?'

Gwyn delayed answering as Mary arrived with a wooden platter of food and a jug of ale. She looked enquiringly at John, but he shook his head, having not long had his breakfast.

'I doubt the sheriff knows — he's too busy with the visit of Hubert Walter to bother about a corpse.'

'Any idea who the dead woman might be?'

Gwyn shrugged as he gulped down his food — he knew he would have little time to finish it. 'Most of the body is hidden under old sticks and leaves — the midden is used for ashes from the priest's house fire, as well as trashings from around the churchyard.'

'It has been deliberately hidden, you think?'

Gwyn nodded his great head, his massive jaw champing away. 'Only the feet and lower legs can be seen,' he said, through a mouthful of bread, 'but they are a woman's and the shoes are stylish and of fine leather.'

'Anything else?'

'There's blood under the calves, that I could see.'

John groaned. 'Holy Christ, let it not be another rape — with murder added this time!'

He made for the vestibule and took down his cloak again. Throwing it over his shoulders, he pulled one corner of the square garment through a large bronze ring sewn over his left collarbone, then tied the end in a knot to hold it in place. 'Drink that ale down and bring your cheese in your hand.'

He dived out into the cold morning and strode away, oblivious of the increasing snowflakes that drifted on the wind.

★　★　★

'Did you raise the hue and cry?' John demanded of the parish priest of St Bartholomew.

The portly man nodded impatiently. 'Of course! When the old woman told me, I sent my man off directly to find either you or the sheriff at the castle. Then two of my neighbours alongside the churchyard came out to see what was going on. I told them to knock up all the householders around the chapel and rouse the neighbourhood.'

True enough, a small crowd of people were jostling in the narrow lanes around the small plot that contained the chapel, while Gwyn guarded the rickety gate through the wall that ringed the few square yards of rank grass and bare earth.

St Bartholomew's was built on the edge of the poorest and least savoury part of Exeter. This quarter had long been known as 'Bretayne', probably because the Saxons had pushed out the original Celtic-British inhabitants into this ghetto area, when they invaded the West centuries before.

The church was surrounded by lanes of mean hovels, some wattle, others planked, and some with earthen walls plastered with a slime of horse-dung and lime. Smoke filtered from every one, leaking out from under the eaves of thatch, stone or turf. The inhabitants largely matched their homesteads, a poor ragged lot, who worked as porters, slaughterers, or labourers on the nearby quayside and in woollen mills on the river.

The hue and cry was supposed to flush perpetrators out of hiding and to pursue them until caught, like a fox hunt, but John privately thought it a futile process, unless the crime had been witnessed so that the miscreant could be chased.

'She's been dead a long while,' observed Gwyn, stooping down from inside the gate to tug at one of the still legs protruding from the shrivelled leaves and twigs. The foot was stiff on the ankle and the whole body moved slightly because of the rigor in the whole leg.

'Let's move this stuff,' grated John, and began to push aside the rubbish, which shed grey ashes from the twigs and dry foliage.

Gwyn and the priest's caretaker rapidly shifted the garbage, which included kitchen waste and old floor rushes, revealing the whole length of the pathetic figure. The mantle, a cloak of good-quality brown wool, was thrown right over the body, completely wrapping the head and upper part. Below it, the legs down to the calves were clad in a kirtle of cream linen, and although soiled by the rubbish, it could be seen to be of fine workmanship, with elaborate embroidery around the hem. Woollen stockings ended in delicate shoes of soft leather.

'This is a woman of quality, Gwyn. The noble ladies of Exeter are having a bad week, I fear.'

Gwyn pushed a few over-curious citizens back through the gate and yelled at others to move away.

The coroner stooped at the side of the corpse. 'Let's see what we've got. Unwrap the cloak from her head, but gently.'

The body was lying close against the side of the stone wall and John moved crabwise to the head end, kicking aside more refuse to clear a wider space. Gwyn knelt and carefully pulled out one end of the mantle from under the woman, then drew it right back to expose her upper half.

She lay on her left side as if asleep, the face close to the wall. The coroner gently pulled on her right shoulder and rolled the stiff cadaver on to its back.

They saw a young woman, probably in her early twenties, with a peaceful expression on the even features. The face, eyes wide open, looked up at the grey sky and a few large flakes of snow fell gently on to her brow and cheeks. The hair was dark brown, parted in the centre of the crown, a plait coiled above each ear. She wore no coif or cover-chief on her head and no gorget or wimple around her throat.

John and Gwyn contemplated her for a moment, the gaping crowd behind the wall silent for once. 'Her face seems familiar, but I can't put a name to it,' observed John thoughtfully.

His officer grunted. 'She's out of my league, a real lady by the look of her clothing. What's she doing, alive or dead, in a low district like Bretayne?'

John knelt on the cold ground to get a closer look. 'No marks on her face or neck.

The clothing is not disarrayed, apart from her kirtle being above her ankles.'

Gwyn pointed to its hem. The bottom few inches were bloodstained and blood was mixed with the muddy ashes on the earth below. 'Where's that coming from? Have we got another Christina Rifford? And, if so, why is she dead?'

John shrugged and climbed to his feet. 'We can't leave the poor woman here. Is there room in the church?'

Gwyn looked across at the small chapel, recently rebuilt in stone to replace an older wooden structure. 'I doubt the priest will want a corpse in there, bleeding over his floor — especially as it's Sunday tomorrow and he'll want to hold Mass and other offices. What about St Nicholas Priory?'

John agreed with Gwyn's good advice. The Benedictine monks would undoubtedly show their usual charity, and the little monastery was only a few hundred yards away, towards St Mary Arches.

The rotund local priest was only too glad to get the corpse off his property and snapped orders at his caretaker and three other men who were idling among the gawping onlookers. They went into the church to fetch the bier, which was hanging by ropes in its customary place from the rafters. The four jogged out with the wooden frame and set it on its legs alongside the body. With Gwyn supervising, they lifted the rigid corpse on to it and John threw the cloak over the woman for decency's sake.

Then he stood with Gwyn to look at the ground where the body had lain. A pool of blood, with a thin shiny skin of clot the size of a hand, lay on the hard earth. 'Nothing else — no knife, no weapon, no foot-print!' John commented. 'Yet she was concealed right enough. No highborn lady comes to creep under a midden to die.' He turned to the four men standing expectantly alongside the bier. 'Follow me to St Nicholas's. I'll go ahead and pray that the prior will accommodate us.' He stalked away, leaving Gwyn to potter about the scene and to question the onlookers, before he tried to disperse them — this was an unexpected novelty to lighten their drab existence.

John threaded his way through the stinking alleys between the poverty-stricken dwellings, filled with ragged children, mangy dogs, scuttering rats and trickling sewage. He dodged handcarts filled with firewood, wandering goats and porters bent double under heavy loads. He was greeted respect-fully every few yards by old men tugging their forelocks and housewives and crones bobbing their heads in salute: Sir John de Wolfe had been known to most of the town's population even before he became coroner.

Within a couple of minutes, he reached the priory of Saint Nicholas, a small stone-built range of buildings half-way between the north wall and Fore Street. A tonsured monk in a black habit girded up to his thighs, was scratching with a hoe in a tiny vegetable plot and directed John to the prior's cell. He was a spare, ascetic man with a miserable face, but readily agreed to house the unknown corpse in a store room next to their tiny infirmary.

By then, the bier-carriers had arrived and the frame was set down in the small chamber, which was half-full of bags of grain, old clothes and bedding. Gwyn came in soon afterwards, clutching something in his large hand. 'We have to put a name to this lady as a matter of urgency,' snapped the coroner. 'Surely someone must be missing from home by now?'

His bodyguard nodded, but first thrust his fist under the coroner's nose. His fingers opened and John saw two small, pale, soggy cylinders lying in his palm. They were each about an inch long and as thick as a little finger. Streaked with blood, they looked rather like broken pieces of candle. 'What are they? And where did you find them?'

Gwyn humped his shoulders. 'I don't know what they are, but they were lying in that patch of blood under the corpse.'

The objects meant nothing to John and he turned back to his main problem, that of identity.

'Who might know this lady?' he asked the four carriers, the prior and the other monk with the hoe. None of them seemed to have any inspiration, until the Cornishman suggested Nesta, landlady of the Bush.

The coroner considered this for a moment. It was certainly true that his red-headed mistress was a mine of information on all manner of local gossip — and her common sense and discretion were beyond question. 'Get down to the tavern and ask her to come up,' he said to Gwyn. 'I had better stay here in case our friend the sheriff gets wind of something affecting an aristocratic lady. That would even prise him away from his planning for the Chief Justiciar's visit.'

With a final grunt, Gwyn vanished into the town.

★ ★ ★

The morning was a relatively slack time at the Bush for the Welsh innkeeper and within twenty minutes, she was at St Nicholas's, a green cloak thrown hastily over her aproned figure.

'Great God, Sir Crowner, is there a campaign against the young women of Exeter?' she asked, as soon as she arrived at the store room door. Nesta spoke in Welsh, which both John and Gwyn could readily understand: his mother Enyd had used it with him as a child, and Gwyn's native Cornish was virtually the same language.

'She is no town drab, this one,' John told her, as they entered the temporary mortuary. 'Her clothing is fine and she has the whole aspect of a Norman lady. There is blood upon her, but no obvious wound — and I hesitate to look further at her body at this stage.'

Nesta had seen many a tavern fight and was no stranger to blood and even corpses, but she entered the mortuary with some trepidation. A narrow window-slit threw a dim light from the overcast sky and the monks had lit a few candle-ends to add to the illumination.

John, with Gwyn at his back, walked to the bier, gently steering Nesta by the elbow.

'These are really superb garments,' she explained, a slight quiver in her voice as she approached the still, covered form on the trestle. 'The shoes alone would cost me a week's takings — and that fine wool cloak is more than I am ever likely to have.'

John slowly lifted the mantle and draped it to one side, letting it hang to the floor. Nesta stood breathlessly still, as rigid as the dead woman on the bier. Then she slowly exhaled. 'I know her, John!' Turning to him, she said, 'Surely you must too?'

'The face seems familiar, but I can recall no name.'

The innkeeper looked up at him, her big eyes round in her pleasant features. 'It's Adele, daughter of Reginald de Courcy, of the manor of Shillingford.'

John's bushy eyebrows rose an inch up his forehead. 'Of course! I know Reginald, so I must have seen his daughter with him at some function.'

Nesta looked pityingly at the dead young woman lying still and stiff on her wooden bed. 'Poor woman — she was only twenty years old. And soon to be married, too!'

The coroner's eyebrows could go no higher. 'Good God! Another young woman betrothed, like Christina.'

Nesta knew all the society gossip from overhearing endless conversations at the Bush. 'The wedding was to be at Easter in the cathedral, a grand affair.'

'To whom, for God's sake?'

'Hugh Ferrars, son of Lord Guy Ferrars.'

John whistled. The de Courcys were an affluent family, with several manors in south Devon, but Lord Ferrars was a major landowner in the West Country.

'There'll be the devil to pay over this,' he muttered. Though he was an independent spirit, who offered little deference to anyone but Richard Coeur de Lion, the significance of a sudden and probably criminal death interrupting the union of a de Courcy and a Ferrars struck him forcefully. 'Now we know who she is, we need to know urgently how she came to her death. And who hid her in a rubbish tip.'

Nesta's eyes travelled down the still figure until they reached the skirt of the kirtle. Now that the body was lying on its back, an ominous bloodstain was visible on the fabric between the thighs, as well as at the hem.

'There are no injuries on the head, neck or chest,' offered Gwyn, watching her gaze move over the body.

Nesta turned back to John. 'This seems women's business once again, John. I doubt that even the King's coroner will want to probe the nether parts of a de Courcy lady, especially one who is the fiancée of a Ferrars!'

John agreed fervently with her. Only in

extreme circumstances would a man, other than perhaps a leech, investigate what was patently a lethal condition relating to a woman's anatomy. He looked at Nesta and she returned his gaze. Then, almost as if a spark jumped between them, they both said, 'Dame Madge!' The gaunt nun from Polsloe priory had been such a strength and support over Christina Rifford that she was the obvious person to help them now.

'Do you think this lady may also have been ravished?' asked Gwyn.

Nesta turned up her hands helplessly. 'How can I tell? It's possible, but even if I dare examine her private parts, I am no expert. I'm a tavern-keeper, not a midwife.'

The way ahead seemed inevitable and, within a few minutes, John had dispatched Gwyn to ride the mile to Polsloe to fetch the formidable nun.

Now Nesta decided to make herself scarce. Though she had a thick skin and knew that most of the town were well aware of her relationship with Sir John, she wanted to avoid appearing blatantly with him in public so often that people would think she was trying to displace his wife.

As she prepared to leave, John said that he would have to carry the news to Richard de Revelle. 'This is one case that I don't wish to

172

handle alone — not with de Courcys and Ferrars involved!' he said, with feeling.

They went their various ways, leaving the prior of St Nicholas to lay a flower on the still body of Adele, before kneeling in prayer at the foot of her bier.

8

In which Crowner John
again meets Dame Madge

Unlike the previous evening, the hall of the keep at Rougemont was thronged with people when John arrived there at about the ninth hour of the morning. He had not gone there directly from the priory as, acting on a sensible suggestion from Nesta, he had called at his house in Martin's Lane on the way to the castle. His mistress, ever concerned for his welfare even when it meant improving his relations with his wife, felt that he could use this latest drama to divert Matilda from her current vendetta against him. They were both aware of her obsession with the local aristocracy and the other grand folk of the county. Nesta suspected that news of a sudden, mysterious death of a de Courcy, especially one betrothed to the eldest son of Lord Ferrars, might entice her out of her current evil mood.

She was right. Although John had to summon up the courage to climb the outer stairs to the solar and push his way in, once he had baldly announced the news to his wife, her excitement rapidly banished her sulks. She threw down her needlework and immediately besought him for details. Although John had little real information, he embellished what he had to hold her interest.

Matilda was almost enraptured by the tragedy. 'Adele de Courcy! We met her at the Guildhall two months ago, when the Portreeves were reappointed. You surely must remember her.'

Her husband agreed that he did, but in fact his only memory was of her father, who had become a little too drunk that night, perhaps at the joy of having one of his daughters linked to the rich and powerful Ferrars dynasty. He let Matilda prattle on for a few moments, to consolidate his restoration to favour. She went through the genealogies of the two well-known families and emphasised that the ladies of Exeter had been looking forward to the wedding of the year in the cathedral.

'They'll be greatly disappointed, then,' he said, somewhat unwisely, 'for the poor bride is lying stiff in a store room at St Nicholas's!'

His wife's lips tightened at his earthy dispassion, but the excitement of being the first Exeter lady to know of the matter allowed his stumble to pass. 'A store room! She needs to be moved quickly to some place of honour. They have a town house in Currestreet,[1] surely she should be lying there. Unless they take her to Shillingford.'

This was their manor a few miles to the west, towards Dartmoor. 'Does the family know of her death yet?' gabbled Matilda. 'I am slightly acquainted with her mother — she prays at St Olave's occasionally. Poor woman. She's a dull person who dresses like a haystack but a pleasant soul.'

John backed towards the solar door, Nesta's stratagem successfully accomplished. 'No one knows of her death yet — not even the family. I'm just off to tell Richard. He'll want to know quickly, with all these notables involved.'

He fled while he was still winning and made his way to the castle. The usual crowd of supplicants was milling about, waiting to see the sheriff on one matter or another. Knights hopeful of advancement, merchants with grievances about market competition, applications for fairs and worried-looking clerks clutching sheaves of parchment vied with each other for admission to the sheriff's chamber. In addition, today saw an unusual

---

[1] Now Gandy Lane

number of messengers and servants concerned with the imminent arrival of the Chief Justiciar two days hence. However, John pulled rank as the second royal law officer in the county, and thrust his way through to the harassed guard at Richard's door. The sight of the six-foot black and grey figure bearing down on him, like some great bird of prey, strangled the challenge in the man's throat and the coroner stormed past him without a glance.

Inside, the two window openings were unshuttered to let in both the light and the icy wind. The sheriff sat behind his cluttered table with his cloak wrapped around him, a woollen cap on his head. He was dictating rapidly to a clerk, who feverishly scribbled down a list of guests for next week's feast at Rougemont, in honour of the Archbishop of Canterbury — alias Justiciar Hubert Walter.

Richard's face set into its familiar pose of pained surprise when he saw the coroner, but his voice did not break its pace as he continued his monologue to the scribe. John strode impatiently to the window and gazed down into the inner bailey to pass the time. He saw the usual confusion of a castle ward — oxen trudging through the mire, pulling carts full of vegetables and animal fodder, and a sergeant drilling a squad of soldiers.

Women came in and out of the huts built around the wall embankment, carrying firewood and pots of steaming food or throwing slops on the ground. Some were screaming at their urchins and scooping up naked infants wandering in front of plodding horses, all familiar sights to a man who had spent more than half his life in soldiers' encampments.

De Revelle's voice jerked him out of his reverie. 'Well, John, not another contrary notion about Mistress Rifford, I hope?'

The sarcastic tone brought him round to face the sheriff. This time, he looked forward perversely to shocking Richard out of his sneering condescension. 'Something even more disturbing, Richard. We have a dead woman on our hands.'

'Surely that's no great novelty for a coroner. And why 'we' all of a sudden? I thought you tried to deny my right to dabble in your interests?'

'I think your interests will include this particular lady. It's Reginald de Courcy's daughter — the same Adele who was to wed Guy Ferrars's son.'

De Revelle's mouth opened and then shut with a snap. 'Are you sure?'

The coroner went to the table and leaned his fists on the edge, bringing down his face close to Richard's. 'Never more so. How she died, I don't yet know, but there's blood about her nether parts.'

The sheriff stood up abruptly, half a head shorter than his brother-in-law. 'Oh, good Jesus, not another ravishment! Those knaves of silversmiths, it could still be one of them. When did she die?'

John shrugged. 'She was stiff and cold this morning. Some time during the night or last evening, I suspect. Could be longer, but the body wasn't there last night when the priest's servant tipped rubbish on the spot and saw nothing.'

The sheriff's eyes widened in horror. 'Rubbish? What rubbish?'

Patiently John explained the whole story as far as he knew it.

Richard sat down again with a thud and held his head in his hands. 'Mother of Christ, what's happening in this town? Hubert Walter is almost upon us, we have a portreeve's daughter ravished and a lady of high birth dead in a dung-heap!'

John sat on the stool that the clerk had vacated when he hurried away with his parchments. 'Did you not arrest those smiths this morning, as you threatened?'

Richard raised his head and looked rather sheepish. 'No, I changed my mind. At least, I was going to throw them into the gaol here but Godfrey Fitzosbern came with them to plead for their liberty.'

'I wouldn't have thought that he had much interest in the welfare of his servants.'

'He hasn't — but he said his business would be ruined if I locked up his two best craftsmen before he could find replacements.'

Not for the first time, John realised that the burgesses and merchants of the town had a great deal of power, especially where making or losing money was concerned. Even a sheriff thought twice before antagonising the master of one of the major guilds.

'So what's to be done about this dead lady?' demanded Richard.

'I have sent again for that nun from St Katherine's Priory in Polsloe. She is skilled in examining live women, so I suppose she can apply the same art to a dead one. We must know how she died.'

'Can we be absolutely sure that this is Adele de Courcy? Who identified the body?'

John prevaricated a little as he wanted to avoid any jibes from his brother-in-law, especially if Richard relayed Nesta's involvement back to Matilda. 'Several of the bystanders knew her,' he lied. Then, with a little inspiration gained from a remark by his wife, added, 'It seems that she sometimes worshipped at St Olave's nearby.'

'But she was found at St Bartholomew's in Bretayne, you say. What the devil was a lady doing alone in that cesspit of a place?'

'I suspect the body was dumped there for concealment so it could have been brought from almost anywhere in the city, given a horse, a handcart or even a barrow.'

De Revelle jumped up and yelled at the man-at-arms on his door to send for his horse. 'I must go at once to Reginald de Courcy, whether he be in Currestreet or at his manor. And word will have to be sent to the Ferrars. Hugh, the son, has a lodging in Goldsmith Street, though I know he spends much time in Tiverton or at one of the other many honours his father holds.' As he grabbed a cloak from a curtained recess in the wall, the sheriff groaned in frustration. 'Of all the times for these crimes to happen! The Justiciar is coming — and now my attention is mortgaged by these affairs.' Muttering under his breath, he hurried out, forgetting for once to argue with John about who had primacy of jurisdiction.

★ ★ ★

The coroner was content to leave de Revelle to tour the families — a task the sheriff welcomed, in spite of his protestations, as it raised his profile among influential people in the county. Richard was tarred with the same brush as his sister when it came to currying favour with rich Normans, especially as he needed to restore his credibility after being associated with Prince John's abortive rebellion.

After Richard had gone John left the keep and went up to his cramped chamber above the gatehouse, where Thomas de Peyne was penning some duplicate copies of inquest records.

He rose from his stool deferentially and jerkily crossed himself. 'I wondered where you might have been Crowner — and that hairy ape who makes my life a misery.'

'Sit down again, clerk, and take a fresh roll from your bag. We have a new case to inscribe.' He dictated a short account of the finding of Adele's body, but omitted Nesta's identification — he could insert some other name as official deposer later when many others had confirmed that it was Adele. 'Now come back with me to St Nicholas's. You may have some more scribing to do, if Dame Madge comes up to our expectations.'

When they reached the priory, the snow had increased and a thin powdering of white lay on the roofs and walls. A dappled pony was tied up outside the gate, with a side-saddle girthed to it.

'That was quick, the holy sister must be here already,' said John, marching into the small courtyard and pushing open the store room door.

In the dim light, he saw a woman from a nearby house, who had insisted on chaperoning the female corpse, hovering at the head of the bier. The coroner's officer was deep in conversation with the formidable nun from Polsloe. Both looked up as they entered. At the sight of the still corpse and the tall Benedictine, Thomas's hand automatically strayed to his forehead, shoulders and breast.

After greeting Dame Madge courteously and thanking her for coming again to their aid, John asked her, 'Have you had any chance to examine the lady?'

The long, almost masculine face regarded him steadily. 'I arrived not five minutes ago, Sir John, but already I suspect I know what has happened.' She turned to Gwyn, who again held out his hand to display the two slimy cylinders in his palm. 'Your man found these in her issue of blood. They are pieces of the inner bark of a certain elm tree. When dried, they become shrunken and hard, but swell up greatly when wetted.'

John looked at her without understanding.

What did a lecture on the properties of wood have to do with a suspicious death?

'They are used for procuring a miscarriage, crowner. A length or two of dried elm bark is pushed into the neck of the womb. When moistened by the humours of the body, it swells greatly and forces open the entrance, often leading to dropping of the child.'

John digested this novel piece of information. 'And this is what has happened here?'

A faint smile crossed the gaunt face. 'I am not a soothsayer. I have not yet had time to look. But I see no way in which elm slips would be found in a pool of blood under a dead woman unless that was the most likely explanation.'

Gwyn, deferential to this nun in spite of his usual antipathy to anything religious, asked a very pertinent question. 'You said these things were inserted into the womb. Must that mean by someone else other than the woman?'

Dame Madge considered this for a moment. 'It would be just possible, especially if the woman had some knowledge of midwifery, for her to do it herself — but it would be very unlikely to succeed.'

The coroner took up the questioning. 'Given that the body has been hidden and obviously transported here from somewhere

184

else, we must accept that another person is involved. But why should she die?'

'The flux of blood strongly suggests she bled to death. Though elm slips are moderately safe, I have seen deaths from purulent suppuration of the womb, some days or even weeks after the attempt at miscarriage. But bleeding suggests that the insertion was badly performed and that the hard wood has perforated some internal part. I shall try to discover if this has happened here.'

Gradually John began to assemble in his mind the importance of these facts. It meant that Adele de Courcy, promised to be Devonshire's Bride of the Year, had been already pregnant. Was it by Hugh Ferrars — or, worse, by someone else? 'Will you be able to tell how far gone in pregnancy she was?' he asked the nun.

'Possibly. This method of procuring a miscarriage is unreliable, like all attempts at abortion. But to have any chance of success, it is useless to try before about the fourth month. Later it has more chance of bringing about the desired result, but also more chance of fatal complications.'

She had had enough of talking and now shooed the men out of the room, beckoning the middle-aged neighbour to her as she firmly closed the door on the coroner and his men.

They stood aimlessly outside in the priory yard, imagining what was going on beyond the door.

'Quite a woman, that!' said Gwyn admiringly. 'She should join our crowner's team.'

Thomas saw his chance to goad his ginger colleague. 'Sounds as if you fancy your chances with the lady — she's about your size.'

'I could do worse, if I were not already happily wedded.'

Thomas grinned evilly, his lazy eye swivelling. 'You're twenty years too late — the lady had the sense to take the veil long before she met you!'

Gwyn grabbed the little clerk by the collar of his threadbare surcoat. He lifted him off the ground and shook him. 'Holy Orders didn't stop you feeling the bottoms of the novitiates in Winchester, did it?' he retorted.

John told them impatiently to stop their horseplay — he was too anxious to know what Dame Madge had discovered for he must hold an inquest before the body was taken out of the city to Shillingford, otherwise the jury would have no chance to view it.

After what seemed an age, but was probably only ten minutes, the door opened and the black-gowned figure appeared. She walked to a horse trough standing inside the courtyard gate and washed her hands, both of which were soiled with blood. Wiping them on a linen kerchief she produced from within the folds of her habit, she came over to the coroner. 'It was just as I thought. She was about five months gone with child, I could just feel the enlarged womb in her lower belly. She has bled to death, not suffered suppuration. The neck of the womb is torn and penetrated. Either the elm sticks were inserted with force in the wrong place, or some other instrument was used, maybe after they had proved unsuccessful.'

John and Gwyn heard her in silence, Thomas murmured some unintelligible Latin and, as usual, made the Sign of the Cross.

'Would she have died quickly after the damage to the womb?' asked John.

The nun raised her bony shoulders in a gesture of doubt. 'If you mean quickly in terms of hours rather than days, then yes. It might have been a rapid issue, exsanguinating her within minutes, but there is no way of telling without seeing the amount of blood lost.'

'What we saw at St Bartholomew's must have been merely the last of the flow,' mused the coroner. 'There may have been far more blood at the place she came from originally.'

Dame Madge nodded. 'I can do no more. It is for you to discover who did this thing. I have seen similar cases, but not in a lady such as this, I must admit.'

The prior came up and offered the nun refreshments before she rode her pony back to Polsloe. He invited John to join them, but the coroner decided that he had better get on with his duties. 'I must discover what is to be done with the body — and then arrange the inquest. May we hold it in the courtyard, Prior?'

With some reluctance, the monk agreed, and John sent Gwyn and his clerk to round up as many local witnesses as he could to act as the jury.

* * *

Reginald de Courcy was devastated when the sheriff called upon him at his house in Currestreet, just below the embankment of the outer ward of Rougemont, to bring him the bad news, but an iron will kept him from showing any obvious emotion. He was a thin man, with a grey rim of beard and a matching moustache. Most of his hair was on his face, as he was almost completely bald. He had been a good soldier in his younger days, a faithful supporter of the second King Henry and had fought in France alongside the old monarch. Adele had been a late child of his second marriage; his other family was much older and she had been the apple of his eye.

De Courcy lived most of the time at one of his two manors: his favourite was at Shillingford, and the other at Clyst St George. His wife and three elder daughters rarely came into Exeter, except to visit the markets, for social occasions or sometimes to worship. He kept this modest house for his frequent business visits, as he owned two woollen mills on Exe Island, the reclaimed marshland along the river outside the West Gate. As a burgess, he knew the sheriff well, but this did nothing to lessen the shock of the news.

'I am afraid that you must come down to see your dear daughter's body as soon as possible,' said Richard, with tolerably sincere sympathy for the stricken father.

'Then I must tell Hugh Ferrars and bring him with me. I cannot imagine how he will take the news of the death of his betrothed. It is almost as bad as losing a daughter.' De Courcy's jaw was clenched rigidly between sentences, as if to prevent any sign of emotion escaping him. They strode together the short distance to Goldsmith's Street, which came off the high street near the new Guildhall.

Hugh Ferrars kept two rooms and a squire in a house belonging to a merchant friend of de Courcy's. This was mainly to be within riding distance of Adele at Shillingford, as his family home at Tiverton was too far away for convenience, although he went there for part of each week.

He was a soldier, but one who, so far, had missed all the wars. He had gone to the Crusades but arrived just as King Richard was leaving, after the failure to take Jerusalem, so had come home too. Before that, a campaign in France had ended in a truce within a week of his joining the royal forces, so at the moment he was a knight without a cause. He had decided to get married, to fill in the time before another war came along and to get himself an heir in case he was killed on the field of battle. His father had soon found a suitable match and Hugh was well pleased with Adele, though perhaps he was too self-centred to consider himself in love with her. Still, she was elegant and good-looking, if not a radiant beauty like Christina Rifford.

The news of her death, brought by de Courcy and the sheriff, provoked towering anger. He and his squire were in the yard at the back of the house, practising with sword and shield for a coming tournament. Hugh was a stocky, solid young man, with bulging muscles and generally more brawn than brain. He had flaxen hair and a matching moustache, but no beard. When his prospective father-in-law broke the news, Hugh went berserk, slashing at the fencing with his great blade and yelling a mixture of grief-laden cries and bloodcurdling threats against whoever may have killed her.

After they had calmed him down a little, into a mood of simmering recrimination, the sheriff suggested that his squire ride straight back to Tiverton to fetch his father, Lord Guy Ferrars.

'No need to ride that far, he's in Exeter, thank God. He came today to stay as a guest of the Bishop at his palace as he is to meet with Hubert Walter this week.'

De Revelle knew that the senior Ferrars would be an important figure at any political meeting with the Chief Justiciar, but had not been told that he would be staying with Bishop Marshall. This was another place at which to call, and the two men strode off with Richard to the cathedral, one grim-faced and tense, the younger muttering imprecations against whomever had brought this trouble upon him. In many ways, he was acting just like Edgar of Topsham, who was still marching around in a high temper, obsessed with the idea that Godfrey Fitzosbern was the villain.

The Bishop's Palace, the grandest dwelling in Exeter, was built behind the cathedral, between it and the town wall. With a garden around it, free from ordure and rubbish, it was a pleasant spot that was wasted for most of the time, for Bishop Henry, brother of William, Marshall of England, was rarely in residence. The role of prelate was a part-time job for a politician, the most extreme example Hubert Walter's holding of the See of Canterbury. Today, the Bishop was absent, with Hubert on his way back from Plymouth.

The Archdeacon was in the palace, busy organising the coming week's events with the Precentor and the Treasurer. John de Alecon received the sheriff and his bereaved companions with sympathy, then took them to a guest room to see Hugh's father.

Guy Ferrars was a Norman's Norman, really born a century and a half too late. Large, muscular and arrogant, he still had the mind-set of one of the original conquerors who had come over with William of Normandy. To him, the English were still the defeated enemy after the battle of Hastings, even though he had not been born until eighty years later. He ruled his many manors and a castle with a rod of iron, when he was not abroad fighting either the Irish or Philip of France. John de Wolfe had met him a few times and heartily disliked the man, whose only saving grace in the coroner's eyes was his unswerving loyalty to King Richard.

When he heard of Adele's death, hardly a muscle moved in his florid face, what could be seen of it beneath the large brown moustache and beard. His son, who resembled him in many ways, spat out the news more in anger than sorrow, constantly jerking his sword part-way out of its scabbard and noisily slamming it back.

Lord Ferrars turned stony-faced to Richard de Revelle. 'How did she die, sheriff? She was a healthy young woman.'

'We know little about the tragedy yet. It is less than an hour since the coroner brought me the news. I hurried to see de Courcy and your son, then came here. We are on our way to the place where she lies now, trusting to learn more.'

Guy Ferrars jerked his head in a single nod of understanding and shouted for his own squire to bring his outdoor clothes. 'We will go — and God help him who has brought this about!' he snarled.

9

In which Crowner John
meets an old crone

That Saturday afternoon saw frantic activity among the various participants in this latest tragedy. Reginald de Courcy's seneschal rode off at a gallop to Shillingford to take the sad news to Adele's mother and sisters. He was to bring them back to the house in Exeter, where Adele's body would be taken for the night.

When the Ferrars and de Courcys arrived with the sheriff, John de Wolfe was waiting for them in the small courtyard. With his typical directness, the coroner told them that Adele had died of a miscarriage criminally induced by some unknown person. If a thunderbolt carrying twenty angels had descended just then their shock and incredulity could not have been greater. As John later told Nesta, if the poor girl had been hacked into a hundred pieces or flayed alive, he felt that they would have accepted it with far less dismay than hearing that she had had an abortion.

'She was with child?' bellowed her father. 'My dear Adele?'

'The girl was pregnant?' roared Guy Ferrars.

They both turned to Hugh, whose father gave him a swinging open-handed blow on the side of his head that almost threw him to the ground. As he staggered upright, Reginald de Courcy punched him straight in the face, so that blood spurted from his nose and he reeled backwards again. Both older men seemed more concerned that the young woman had been pregnant than that she was dead.

'You dirty bastard!' raved de Courcy, waving his fists in the air.

Hugh's father was purple with anger. 'You are a Norman, boy! With Norman standards of chivalry. How could you do this to me?'

Before the lad could wipe enough blood from his face to answer, de Courcy rounded ferociously on Guy Ferrars. 'Why could you not control this rutting son of yours, damn you? Could he not wait until Easter to bed the poor girl? Are there not enough whores in the town to satisfy him?'

Lord Ferrars, in an equally towering rage, thrust his face against that of de Courcy and his right hand came up to give him a shove in the shoulder that pushed him against the wall. 'Don't you dare speak to me like that, God blast you!'

There was an ominous rattling of swords in scabbards and both the coroner and the sheriff stepped forward hastily to grab the combatants by the shoulders and pull them apart.

'Now, remember where you are, sirs,' shouted Richard, waving his arm at the priory walls.

'This is not seemly, with the lady lying dead inside,' snapped John harshly, giving Ferrars another pull.

The two men subsided, but stood glaring ferociously at each other, turning only when Hugh spat out enough blood to begin protesting his innocence. 'It was not me, I swear it.' He gagged. 'I never laid a finger on her.'

His father grabbed him by the ear. 'A likely story!'

Hugh desperately rubbed blood off his face with the back of his hand. 'It's not me, Father, I tell you! I swear it was not me!'

Once again his father grabbed him, by the neck of his tunic this time, and thrust his face close to Hugh's. 'You swear that?'

'Of course. I hardly so much as kissed her these last six months. To tell truth, I don't think she cared much for that sort of thing.'

'Are you sure, my son? You swear this on your sword?'

For answer, Hugh immediately drew out three feet of steel from its sheath and holding it aloft like a processional Cross, swore solemnly on his knight's honour that it was not he who had caused Adele to conceive. In the martial ethics that were the religion of the Ferrars, this was more than enough to satisfy his father, who would have slain his son with his own hands if he discovered that he lied in making this solemn oath on his sword.

Guy turned triumphantly to de Courcy. 'Eat your words, sir! You have defamed my family, yet now it seems it was your own daughter that was the wayward one. If it was not my son, then she must have lain with some other man!'

De Courcy, another Norman with the same reverence for such a solemn oath, was deflated. John somehow felt that the dead woman had been forgotten for the moment in this battle of family honours.

Lord Ferrars had not yet finished his tirade. Relentlessly, he went on, 'You would have let my son wed your impure daughter, if this had not happened, sir! Affianced to my son and carrying some other lover's child, eh? Is that the way for a Norman to behave?'

This was too much for de Courcy, who tore

himself out of de Revelle's restraining hands and lunged forward again at Ferrars, trying to drag out his sword at the same time.

'Don't you dare impugn my daughter's honour, Ferrars!' he yelled. 'She was good enough for your son yesterday. Now she lies dead yet you slander her, she who cannot defend herself. If it indeed be true that this son of yours was not the father of this illegitimacy, then she must have been the victim of some ravishment, like that poor daughter of the burgess this week.'

'And how is it that you had not heard of this imagined rape?' snapped Guy, sarcastically.

'She may have been too ashamed or timid to tell us,' said de Courcy, now quite persuaded that his own theory must be true. Hugh Ferrars had recovered his voice, but not his temper.

'The father is of no consequence at the moment,' he shouted. 'She is dead and I am not to wed her. But someone took her life, by the evil of procuring her miscarriage. He deprived me of my betrothed and my honour is at stake. I will seek him out and kill him . . . and then find the father and kill him too!' He whipped out his sword and waved it crazily in the air.

By now a small crowd of bystanders from

the nearby huts had lined up along the low wall of the courtyard and were gazing with bated breath at this unexpected drama that had come to enliven their afternoon.

Gwyn and Thomas watched from the other side of the courtyard, the Cornishman uncertain as to whether he should wade in and knock a few heads together. But his master gave no sign, and the rank of the people involved suggested that he had better keep his fists to himself.

The sheriff, wishing himself a thousand miles away, moved in to attempt peacemaking.

'Sirs, the strain of the moment tells on us all, especially those so close to the dead lady. But we have work to do, if we are to seek the perpetrator of this crime. I need you to look at the corpse and confirm that it is indeed Mistress de Courcy.' Grudgingly, he added, 'And I suppose the crowner needs something similar for his formalities.'

★   ★   ★

In another part of the small city, Edgar was back at work in the shop of Nicholas the apothecary. He had been up to see Christina again and was mortified to find her listless, silent and apparently uninterested in his presence. In spite of Aunt Bernice's feeble attempts to bring them together, the Portreeve's daughter had sat pallidly in her chair by the hall fire, staring at the crackling logs, unresponsive apart from a few murmured monosyllables in answer to his attempts at sympathy.

The skinny young man sat forlornly on a stool near her side, the fringe of his hair hanging lankly down his forehead as he tried helplessly to find something to say that would arouse the smallest spark of animation in her lovely face. Edgar's feelings were ambivalent. One minute he was melting with anguished pity for his intended wife, the next he felt as if he lived in another world from the stranger called Christina. Endlessly, he thrust down the devil's thought that he could now never bring himself to marry her, a woman who had been known, in the Biblical sense, by another man.

After half an hour he gave up and, with a shaming feeling of relief, made some excuse about having to get back to his apprentice-master.

Edgar escaped into the high street and wandered blindly past the Carfoix crossing and into Fore Street, where Nicholas of Bristol had his establishment. As he went, the sense of shame at his own inconstancy gradually faded, to be replaced by growing anger. This always seemed to happen when he left the Rifford house and walked out among other people. His anger was diffuse, directed against the whole masculine world. For all he knew, the next elbow he knocked in the narrow street might be that of Christina's ravisher.

He wanted to find that man and put a sword through his ribs — not only in retribution for the girl's defilement, but in revenge for the way in which his own well-ordered life had been turned upside down. His wedding was now in jeopardy, people's fingers would be pointed at him as the lover of a sullied woman — and his treasured training as an apothecary was disrupted by all these turbulent emotions.

As he hurried along, lurching into passers-by without taking the slightest notice of their protests, he felt for the hilt of his dagger, for he carried no sword. Muttering under his breath, he prayed to all the saints he could remember that they would put the rapist in front of him at that very moment, so that he could inflict unimaginable tortures and wounds upon him with the point of his knife.

As he reached the leech's shop, sanity came upon him abruptly and, with a further flush of shame, he took his hand off his dagger and composed himself. He had realised how ridiculous his behaviour was. It was almost as if the proximity to the apothecary brought him back inside the aura of medical ethics. Edgar was an earnest young man and had read of the Greek Hippocrates, Father of Physicians, who had preached that, to a healer, everything was transcended by the welfare of the patient. Confused, he shook his head, as if throwing off devils, and pushed open the door of the shop.

Inside, the familiar scene and the smell of herbs and potions immediately calmed him. A woman was at the counter with a small boy, purchasing a salve that Nicholas was pressing into a small wooden pot with a bone spatula. 'What do you think of this Master Edgar? Look at the lad's hands.'

Nicholas was a good teacher and shared the experience of every patient with his apprentice. Edgar forgot his troubles for a moment, to immerse himself in clinical diagnosis. A quick glance at the reddened pits in the webs of skin between the child's fingers told him it was scabies.

'Quite right, Edgar. And what will you ask this good lady?' The apprentice turned to the woman, an anxious-looking merchant's wife from Mary Arches Lane. 'Have you other children, mistress?'

'Three more boys and a girl.'

'Then smear the same ointment on their hands, for if they haven't caught it yet they soon will. And keep an eye on the rest of their skin for similar itching marks, though you needn't look above their neck, they never get afflicted in the head.'

As the woman left the shop with her greasy salve, Nicholas beamed at his apprentice's medical acumen. The apothecary was a short man of about forty, rather pasty-faced, with a shock of curly hair, prematurely grey. He had a major affliction in that a palsy of the face had struck him five years ago, leaving him with the left corner of his mouth and left eyelid sagging, the cheek drooping like a wrinkled leather purse. His lips would not quite close and spittle tended to dribble out of the corner of his mouth, which he constantly wiped away with a piece of cloth. Nicholas enquired gravely about the situation in the Rifford family and showed considerable sympathy with Edgar's current mortification.

The young man from Topsham was his only apprentice and Nicholas was a kind and considerate master, which Edgar repaid by being a devoted and hard-working assistant.

They spoke for some time about the awful affair, little knowing of an even more awful business that was taking place only a few hundred yards away at St Nicholas's. Edgar soon got back to work, checking bottles and jars and refilling empty ones from stock.

As he reached up to place pottery jars with Latin names on the shelves that ran all around the walls, the apothecary was chopping herbs with a large knife on a wooden board placed on the counter. They were the last of the season, to be dried for winter use. As he methodically tap-tapped across the board, he chatted to Edgar, to try to divert the younger man's mind from his problems. They discussed the batch of fungi that Nicholas had brought in from the fields around the city that morning, those that were good to eat, that had medicinal properties and those that were poisonous.

'Where did you learn about such things?' asked Edgar curiously.

'From my own master when I was an apprentice in Bristol. He used to send me out into the woods and pastures around the deep gorge above the river, to search for such moulds, and then he would test me on their names and their properties.'

'Is that why you are called Nicholas of

Bristol — because you were apprenticed there?'

The apothecary stopped chopping for a moment to reflect. 'I was only called that after I came to Exeter six years ago. I was born in Bristol and my father was Henry Thatcher, for that was his trade. I was just plain Nicholas there, even when I had my own apothecary's shop near the quayside.'

For a moment, his apprentice was diverted from his troubles. 'So why did you leave Bristol, if it was your birthplace and where you had a business?'

Nicholas seemed rather evasive. 'Trade was not too good — half my customers were sailors or whores who came to have their clap treated. I decided to start afresh somewhere else, before I got a bad reputation as being only a pox-doctor.' He seemed reluctant to pursue his past history and changed the subject.

Their talk ranged from this week's executions at the gallows outside the city to the price of unspun wool, which they used for dressings and padding splints. Edgar was an authority on the wool trade, through his family's business, and explained that this year's poor crop had pushed up the price, especially as the demand in Normandy and Brittany was now greater.

Privately, Nicholas wondered why his apprentice was so keen to pursue the vocation of apothecary, having a ready-made and lucrative trade in the family, which Joseph of Topsham was obviously keen to hand on to his son.

Then the talk was suddenly brought back by Edgar to his own problems. 'Has there been much gossip in the town about Christina?' he asked, rather fiercely.

Nicholas hesitated. 'You know what people are, Edgar. They like to bandy news about, especially bad news. There have been a few customers who enquired after you, knowing that you and the lady were to be married.'

Edgar banged a pot on to a shelf with unnecessary force. 'Were to be married! Perhaps that sums it up, for I am no longer sure that Christina is concerned about a wedding.'

'Oh, come now, boy! It will take weeks for her mind to settle, poor girl. Give her time and I'm sure all will be well again.'

'But I'm not sure that I want to marry her now,' blurted out Edgar. He could talk to his master more easily than to his father about things of the heart.

Nicholas stopped his chopping and looked up at his apprentice, who was now perched on a stool to reach the upper shelves. 'That, too, is understandable, but you must give it time, boy.'

Edgar worried away at the matter, like a dog with a bone. 'Have the gossips suggested any likely culprits for this shameful crime?' he asked, through gritted teeth.

Nicholas considered for a moment. 'Nothing sensible. Only a wild rumour that Godfrey Fitzosbern might know something about it — but that's surely because his was the last place your lady visited before the assault.'

Edgar clattered off the stool and turned, red-faced, to his master. 'Everyone seems to have this idea. There must be fire where there is smoke.'

The apothecary tried to placate his pupil. 'The sheriff took in Fitzosbern's two workmen but they were released within the hour. As our sheriff usually likes to hang the nearest suspect as a matter of convenience, that must mean there is no substance to the gossip.'

'It can also mean that the workmen are innocent and the suspicion falls all the more heavily on their master!' cried Edgar, pacing the narrow space behind the counter. 'All fingers seem to point at that man, especially with the reputation he has for fornication and adultery.'

Nicholas clicked his tongue in warning. 'Be careful what you say, my boy. That man is a bad one to cross. Christ knows that I have no love for him, as he continually blocks my efforts to form a Guild of Apothecaries here in the West — but, even so, I would not dare accuse him of rape without some solid evidence.'

The apprentice seemed unconvinced and fingered his dagger hilt as he paced restlessly up and down the shop, muttering under his breath. 'I will confront him, see if I will, Nicholas! My gut tells me he is the man. I'll have it out with him yet!'

The herb-master sighed at the young man's rapid changes of mood and wondered if there was some calming soporific he could slip into Edgar's broth at the next meal.

★ ★ ★

By early afternoon, there was a temporary lull in the panics of the day and John took the opportunity to visit the Bush. He had been home briefly at midday and eaten a quick meal with Matilda, as part of his campaign for domestic peace. This time Mary had provided pork knuckles with boiled cabbage and carrots, which suited John well, especially as the meat was still freshly killed and not salted as it would be later in the winter. He liked plain food, though Matilda claimed to disdain such 'serf fodder' as she called it, professing to favour fancy cooking, especially from French kitchens. Though born and brought up in Devon, she constantly claimed to pine for her Normandy origins, conveniently ignoring that it was three generations since her forebears had crossed the Channel. The only contact she had ever had with Normandy had been a two-month visit to distant relatives, made some years before.

During the meal, John gave her sparse titbits of information about Adele's death, to keep her mind off her recent feud with him. Matilda relished the scandal concerning the pregnancy and the denials of Hugh that he was the father and avidly anticipated the gossip that would be bandied about among the wives of Exeter.

'Have you any thoughts on who might be the procurer of the miscarriage?' he asked, hoping to get some practical help from among her prurient chatter. 'Does the gossip among the ladies of the city ever suggest a name for such a person?'

His wife bridled at this. 'That's something that I would never lower myself to discuss,' she snapped huffily. 'No doubt there are drabs and old wives, especially down in the slums of Bretayne, who might perform such crimes, but I assure you no lady of quality would know of such things.'

John felt warned off the subject and, fearing that he might set her off on one of her moods, he dropped it. As soon as he could, he left the house, saying that he had to get back to Rougemont to dictate to Thomas de Peyne, but as soon as he reached the high street, he turned left and hurried down to Idle Lane.

Gwyn was in the tavern, filling his capacious stomach with a halfpenny meal and ale. As soon as she could leave her tasks with her cook in the back yard and the girl who put out the pallets and blankets in the dormitory upstairs, Nesta came across and plumped herself down next to them on a bench, to talk to them in Welsh.

'A good thing for trade, this visit of the Justiciar,' she exclaimed, pushing a wisp of auburn hair back under her coif. 'Every penny palliasse and pile of straw upstairs is booked for the next four nights, with people coming to see the great Archbishop!'

'Coming to petition him and beg some favour, more likely,' growled the ever-cynical Gwyn.

The comely innkeeper was anxious to be brought up to date on the day's tragedy, especially as she had played a major role in identifying the victim. John told her the story as far as it was known, and repeated the question he had asked his wife about possible abortionists in the city.

Nesta's pretty face frowned slightly as she concentrated her thoughts. 'I can't say I know of anyone who attacks the womb, so to speak.' She grinned impishly at the coroner. 'I've not yet needed such services, in spite of your endless efforts to get me with child!'

John nipped her thigh with his fingers in retribution. 'Enough of that loose talk, madam. But is there no one who tries to help women who are with child? God knows, there are many poor families with too many little mouths to feed.'

Nesta nodded readily enough. 'Oh, where it comes to old wives' remedies, there are plenty who peddle herbs and magic potions to restore the monthly flow. Useless, most of them, but a few hags have a reputation for success.'

'Such as whom?'

The Welsh woman considered for a moment. 'I should seek out old Bearded Lucy. She is well known for her pills and remedies — the poor come to her when they can't afford a leech.'

'Where can we find her?'

'She lives in a hovel in Frog Lane, on Exe Island. You can't miss her — she has almost as much hair on her face as this great lump of a Cornishman here.'

Gwyn grinned happily, he was almost as fond of Nesta as his master was, and greatly enjoyed her poking fun at him.

John rubbed his dark jowls reflectively. 'Bearded Lucy? Wasn't she in danger of being drowned as a witch some years ago?'

Nesta looked blank — it had been before her time in Exeter — but his officer nodded. 'I remember that. It was soon after we came back from the Irish campaign of 'eighty-five. Some man in the market dropped dead and she brought him back to life some minutes later by beating on his chest and yelling magical spells.'

The coroner gave one of his rare laughs. 'Yes, I recall it now. The man was a member of one of the guilds and he raised a petition among them to have her pardoned, after the Bishop's court convicted her of being in league with the devil.'

John's mistress was not surprised. 'When you see her you might well believe that — and that she might ride the night sky on a broomstick. She is such a hag that the mothers on Exe Island use her to frighten their children when they misbehave.'

De Wolfe stretched out his arms and yawned. 'We shall see for ourselves before long. Gwyn, hurry and shovel the rest of that mutton into your gut. We need a walk down to the river.'

★ ★ ★

Exe Island was formed from the marsh that lay around the western end of the city wall. Exeter came downhill to its river there, but the Exe was no tidy stream running between banks: it was a shifting meander of swamp and mud shoals. The city was at the upper limit of the high tides and this, together with the greatly variable flood that ran down from distant Exmoor, caused the land outside the West Gate to change constantly. For years, efforts had been made to stabilise the area by cutting leats through the marsh to drain it and to persuade the main channel of the river to keep to its bed. An island had been laboriously formed, and a settlement, with fulling mills for the wool trade, had been set up on the extra land.

A precarious footbridge crossed the river to join the road to the west, but only people on foot could use it, all cattle, horses and wagons having to splash across the ford. During the past four years efforts had been made to build a substantial stone bridge. However, the builder Walter Gervase, had run out of money, as the length of the bridge needed proved so expensive. It was against the deserted stonework of this bridge that the coroner and his officer found Frog Lane, the name quite appropriate in this marshy bog. They came out of the West Gate and trudged along a track, still whitened by the light snowfall, until they squelched down a muddy bank to the entrance of an ill-defined lane. This was lined by mean shacks, even worse than those in Bretayne. Wood smoke poured up into the leaden sky from a fire in each hovel. Several dwellings were burned-out shells, testifying to the dangers of open fires in huts built largely of hazel withies woven together and plastered with mud on the outside.

The usual collection of barefoot urchins followed their progress, apparently oblivious to the December cold. Women wrapped in ragged shawls ambled between huts, and men with oat-sacks over their shoulders as makeshift cloaks carried huge bundles of raw wool from the quayside, which lay further downriver, to the fulling mill at the end of the lane.

'Where does Bearded Lucy dwell?' demanded John of the nearest and dirtiest urchin dancing about him.

The boy made a leering grimace and he and his companions all started jigging about with their fingers spread at their foreheads in imitation of hobgoblins. 'Bearded Lucy, Bearded Lucy is a witch!' they all chanted in unison.

Gwyn took a swipe at the leader, but he hopped nimbly out of the way. 'Where is she, boy?' he roared.

One of the lads, less antisocial than the rest, pointed between the two nearest hovels to a hut set back from the lane, sitting alone on a wide expanse of reeds.

The two law officers set off along the side of a stagnant leat that led to it and were soon in wet mud, their feet lifting at every step with a sucking noise.

'By St Peter and St Paul, this must be the worst bloody place for miles around,' muttered de Wolfe, as he felt the water seeping through the seams of his leather shoes.

'Surely a fancy lady like Adele de Courcy would never come down here,' objected Gwyn.

John shrugged. 'Women in dire trouble, like having a full womb and an imminent marriage to someone else, would dare a lot, Gwyn.'

They reached the hut, which was even more dilapidated than the others. It leaned over precariously to one side so that it seemed about to fall into the leat, probably because the marsh had sunk under its flimsy foundations. Smoke filtered out from under the tattered reed thatch, which was patched with clods of turf. There was no door, but a fence hurdle was propped on end to block the entrance. Gwyn heaved it aside and yelled into the smoky interior, 'Anyone there?'

Feet shuffled through the dirty straw on the earth floor and a bowed figure came to the entrance. Though John had seen many strange and misshapen people in his time, this one was unique. Grotesquely ugly to begin with, the hag's face was almost covered with wispy grey hair; only the upper cheeks, nose and forehead were bald. One eye had a red, inflamed lid that pouted outwards, and a slack mouth revealed toothless pink gums. That the person was female was hinted at by the nature of the rags she wore and the dirty close-fitting bonnet tied under her chin.

'Who is it? Why do men come to my dwelling?' she demanded, in a rasping, querulous voice, ending in a fit of coughing, which brought up a bloodstained gobbet that she spat on to the floor.

'I am the King's coroner and this is my

officer. You are the woman they call Bearded Lucy.'

It was a statement, rather than a question, but the old crone nodded. She was bent far worse than Thomas, but probably from the same phthisis of the spine, thought John.

'I need to ask you some questions, woman.'

Lucy cackled. 'Am I accused again of being a witch, sir? I care not. It would be a mercy to be hanged or drowned, anything rather than live like this.'

'I am told that you have been known to help women who are with child and wish to lose their burden?'

She sighed. 'Do you want to come in, sirs? Or will you arrest me out here?'

They declined to go into the hut, having a fair idea of the state of the inside and its various infestations.

John, used to human suffering and despair, yet felt stirrings of sympathy for the old woman, whose mind seemed clear though her body was a wreck. 'We are not here to arrest you, old woman, but I need information about a woman who lies dead in the city.'

He explained about Adele de Courcy and the nun's diagnosis of a bleeding miscarriage. 'Did such a lady ever seek your help?'

Bearded Lucy's dulled eyes rose to meet his and, hardened as he was, he flinched a little and remembered all the tales of witches that his mother had told him as a child. 'Describe her to me,' she demanded.

The coroner did his best and the crone began to nod. 'It must be the same one. Very rarely does any lady of quality come to me. I deal mostly with my neighbours and those from the lower town and the villages nearby. But such a woman visited me a month or two ago.' Another spasm of coughing racked her. Then she said, 'My conscience is clear for I could do nothing for her. She had missed two of her monthly issues and was getting desperate. I did not ask why, though she wore no wedding ring.'

'Did you do any damage to her, old wife?' John demanded.

'No, those days are over for me. But I gave her some herbs, aloes and parsley, and some pessaries of pennyroyal. She gave me sixpence, bless her, then went away.'

Gwyn broke into the inquisition. 'How do you know they did her no harm, then?'

The hag swivelled her bent head and looked up at him obligingly. 'Because she came back. Two weeks ago she returned and said that she was still with child, as my previous potions had not had any effect. They rarely do, for when women miscarry in the early months it is because they would have done so anyway. But sometimes I get the credit for what God performs.'

'She wanted something stronger?'

'She wanted me to interfere with her — the lady knew, as I did, that she had gone too far for any of my witchcraft to have the slightest effect.'

John glared at the old woman. His previous pity had evaporated. 'So what did you do to her?'

'Nothing, sir. Look at this.' She raised her arms and held her hands in front of her. They shook like leaves in the wind. 'And my eyesight is almost gone, I have cataracts in both. What chance is there for me to do anything? I can just manage to find my mouth on the times when I have some food.'

Gwyn murmured to the coroner, 'If it was two weeks ago, it can hardly have been here, if the lady bled yesterday.'

John nodded and turned back to the hag. 'You swear you did nothing?'

'I told her there was nothing I could do and she went away, poor girl.'

John tackled her for a few more minutes, but there seemed nothing more she could or would tell him. He had the tickle of intuition that there was something else she might have said, but all his prising failed to bring it out. When the bearded woman began a prolonged fit of coughing that ended in a trickle of blood at the corner of her loose-lipped mouth, he decided that enough was enough, and they squelched their way back to the relative civilisation within the city wall.

10

In which Crowner John
defends a silversmith

For once, that Saturday evening was peaceful in Martin's Lane. John decided that he had better give the Bush a miss and sit at his own fireside with his wife. The fire crackled cheerfully, thanks to a large supply of beech logs that Mary had piled up at one side of the cavernous hearth.

However, the atmosphere was still hardly jolly as John sat, fidgeting and bored beyond measure. Matilda, determined to play the devoted wife for once, worked with her needle — or, at least, at untangling skeins of silk thread that one of her cronies at St Olave's church had given her for embroidery. De Wolfe hunched in his seat, his body burning on the side facing the fire and shivering on the other, as the inevitable east wind found its way across the stone floor. As well as a chimney, Matilda had insisted on flagstones, considering the usual warmer straw- or rush-strewn floor as low-class.

Outside it was pitch dark, though the sixth

bell had not yet sounded from the cathedral, a few hundred yards away. The snow still came down in irregular flurries, sufficient to whiten the roofs but not enough to settle on the muddied ground.

John had disgorged all his news and had fallen silent for lack of anything else to say. Matilda had heard his account of the unproductive visit to Bearded Lucy with a disdainful sniff, conveying her disapproval of his association with such common people.

To pass the time and relieve his boredom, he took to drinking more than usual. After a quart of ale at their evening meal, he opened a stone flask of Eric Picot's French wine, digging out the wooden stopper with the point of his dagger after peeling off the waxen seal. His wife deigned to take a small cupful, most of which stood untouched alongside her chair, but the coroner attacked the red liquor with morose gusto. Eventually, his tongue loosened a little by the drink, he had the bravado to return to a subject that Matilda had vetoed earlier.

'Are you quite sure that you have never heard of anyone who will procure a miscarriage in this town?'

She raised her broad face to give him a glare of disapproval. 'I told you, John, that kind of matter does not concern me. It is a crime, as well as a sin against the holy teachings,' she proclaimed virtuously.

'But among the ladies' gossip, surely there are whispers now and then of such happenings,' he persisted.

Matilda hesitated. 'Well, some years ago, one of the wives of a rich woolen merchant, who already had six children, fell desperately ill with a purulent fever after dropping a baby at the fourth month. There were rumours that she had deliberately sought damage to herself to get rid of the child, but nothing was definitely known.'

'And who might have done the damage?'

She looked at her husband with pitying contempt at his naïvety. 'How would I know that? She was hardly likely to vouchsafe the details, it was but a rumour. I do know that the leech Nicholas of Bristol treated her almost mortal fever — and did it well, by all accounts, for she survived.'

John stored away this nugget of information and fell to drinking again, as the wind whistled outside and his old hound Brutus crawled surreptitiously nearer to the fire.

★ ★ ★

Elsewhere in the city, the recent crimes against two of its womenfolk were under

223

earnest discussion, the same person figuring largely in their arguments.

'Why did de Revelle release them within the hour?' demanded Edgar of Topsham. 'Someone in that shop knows about the attack on my Christina yet the sheriff has let it go by default.' He was sitting again in Eric Picot's bachelor room above the wine store in Priest Street, with his father and the Breton huddled around the hearth.

'I discount those two smiths,' said Picot. 'Granted, they are unintelligent scum, but all such workmen make eyes and catcalls after pretty girls without having to be ravishers. I still think that their master could tell us a thing or two about what went on that night.'

Edgar muttered incoherently at this, his thin face reddening in the firelight and his hands grasping at his knees, as if in practice for gripping the throat of Christina's assailant.

'We have no proof whatsoever that anyone in that silversmith's place had anything to do with this,' said Joseph reasonably, but his voice had a reluctant note, as if he wished he could say otherwise. He turned to Eric, his friend and trading partner. 'Has Mabel told you anything useful since you spoke to her?' Joseph tactfully avoided any reference as to why or when Picot might have been talking to Fitzosbern's wife.

'She would believe anything of that swine of a husband,' said the wine merchant, with feeling. 'But hard fact is another thing. She says he has made no mention of anything remotely concerning Christina, but he's hardly likely to, is he?'

Edgar scowled. He was almost convinced of the master silversmith's guilt. 'Did she give any account of his movements on Wednesday evening?'

Picot gave a Gallic shrug of doubt. 'He was out from the seventh hour, when his workmen finished their labours. But Mabel says he is out almost every night. He attends many guild meetings and also visits several taverns. She suspects he has at least one other woman somewhere in the town, but certainly he was not at home from the seventh bell until about midnight.'

Joseph stroked his long grey beard. 'That is poor evidence for his wrongdoing, unless we can discover where he was when this awful thing took place. But I see little chance of discovering that.'

The apothecary's apprentice was getting more and more agitated as the conversation went on. 'He is the man — I feel it in my bones! Fitzosbern is well recognised as a

225

philanderer and lecher. The whole town knows it, but most are afraid to say so, because he is a powerful voice in the merchant guilds. Even the sheriff defers to him — look how he let off his two men with hardly a word.' Edgar jumped up and began pacing the room, which was difficult as it was only about three steps each way.

'For God's sake, boy, sit down,' snapped his father. 'There's nothing you can do without further proof.'

'I'll beat it out of him, see if I won't,' said his son wildly. 'I'll challenge him to a trial by battle.'

Eric Picot sighed. 'You can't do that. It's almost impossible, these days. You have to go to five sittings of the county court first, unless the justices of assize declare he has killed one of your kin. And, anyway, Fitzosbern would almost certainly kill you!'

Edgar continued to throw himself about the room for a while, while the two older men talked together. Then he headed for the steps to the ground floor. 'I'm going to visit Christina, to see what she says. I can't sit around like this, doing nothing.' He clattered away, while his father and his friend looked at each other and sighed.

* * *

In Goldsmith Street just off the high street near the Guildhall, Guy Ferrars was also with his son, closeted in the room that Hugh rented from de Courcy's friend. Like the group in Priest Street, they huddled around the fire in a high, draughty room, discussing the tragic events of the day.

'What's to be done, Father? Surely you believe me now that I had no part in getting Adele with child.'

The big warrior-like man asserted sadly. 'I cannot doubt your word, Hugh. But two things must be worked out. Who was the father? And who killed her by clumsy interference?'

Hugh nodded grimly. 'We must know that — and soon! I made no jest when I said that I would have both their lives.'

Lord Ferrars laid a restraining hand on his son's broad shoulder. 'You must be careful, Hugh. We Ferrars have great power in this part of England but we mustn't assume we can ride roughshod over everyone. If we can find the miscreants, it may be better to let the law deal with them. For every high-handed act we make that needs a favour from the law officers, we increase our indebtedness to them. I wish to stay well in credit when it comes to taking favours in this county.'

Hugh scowled. 'But the law can never

touch a man for making a woman pregnant. We would all be at the gallows or in the stocks if that were so!'

'That is true,' his father said, slowly, 'but there are other ways of taking revenge without putting yourself in peril.'

Hugh jumped up and, like the young apothecary on the other side of the city, paced up and down. He had already had a fair amount to drink that evening, and now stopped at his table to swallow the better part of half a pint of mead. His bristly fair hair and short neck seemed to suit his pugnacious nature. 'Father, my honour is in tatters! I was to be married at Easter to a handsome woman of an acceptable family. Now I am not only deprived of a bride but will soon be the laughing-stock of half England for being cuckolded before I even reached the altar.' He slammed his thigh with a sword-hardened hand. 'Somehow I have to get satisfaction for this double insult. I need to kill someone!'

His father's reply was interrupted by a knocking at the street door. Hugh's squire, who lay on a pallet in the vestibule, comforted by a gallon jar of ale, got up to open it and ushered in Reginald de Courcy, swathed in a thick serge cloak peppered with snowflakes.

Their parting that afternoon at St Nicholas's had been anything but amicable and Guy Ferrars and his son looked coldly at their visitor. However, an unexpected olive branch was waved in their faces. 'I come to apologise for my behaviour today,' said de Courcy, in a voice quivering with emotion. 'I was overcome with shock and grief. I think we all may have uttered unfortunate words in the heat of the moment and I, for my part, regret them.'

Guy Ferrars, Norman chivalry soaked into his very bones, could do nothing but gracefully accept the apology. 'We are joined by a common tragedy, de Courcy. Our anger should be directed at whatever villains are responsible, not at each other.'

Reginald bowed his head in agreement. 'That is exactly what my good wife, Eva, told me. She is mortified beyond description by the loss of Adele and I doubt she will ever fully recover. Even the support of our other daughters fails to soften this mortal blow against our family.'

Now that the breach had been healed, each party seemed to vie with the other to be the most magnanimous. De Courcy was divested of his cloak, seated by the fire and pressed to take some wine. They commiserated with each other for a few moments, but the practicalities of what could be done soon surfaced.

'We have a sheriff and a coroner to keep the peace, yet they seem powerless to do anything useful,' complained Hugh, but de Courcy was not ready to blame them yet.

'It has been little more than half a day since they were involved. I doubt we can expect much progress in that time.'

Lord Ferrars was not so charitable. 'They have done exactly nothing, as far as I can see. Probably each dozing by their firesides at this moment.'

'We should take the law into our own hands, as our forebears did,' grated Hugh, his temper rising again. 'Can we not discover who might have violated Adele for a start? That would be one fellow to slay, at least!'

De Courcy said, cautiously, 'The prime villain is he — or she — who caused her death. But it may well be that the man who got her with child was the instigator of the abortion and is more guilty than whoever did the act itself, perhaps some poor drab of a wife in a back lane.'

Guy Ferrars turned this over in his mind. 'Surely there are voices in the town who would tell us who indulges in procuring these miscarriages? I would pay a reward of twenty marks for such news, if it led to the name of the killer.'

'And I would double that, willingly,' said Reginald enthusiastically. The prospect of doing something useful lifted their spirits a little.

'Is there no gossip in the city about it?' demanded Guy Ferrars. 'With less than five thousand souls within the walls, it is usual for everyone to know his neighbour's business.'

De Courcy took a sip of wine and said, thoughtfully, 'The only gossip I hear is about the ravishment of that poor girl of Henry Rifford's. Tongues are wagging that our master silversmith is a possible candidate for that.'

'Why should that be?' enquired Guy Ferrars. 'I thought he was a staunch burgess, a merchant guildmaster.'

'So he is, but he has a bad reputation as a seducer and it was to his shop that the girl went shortly before she was defiled.'

Hugh Ferrars, who had taken again to his restless prowling with a mug of wine in his hand, stopped suddenly. 'Silversmith? Which silversmith might that be?'

De Courcy looked up at the younger man. 'We only have three in Exeter, and one alone produces first-quality work.'

Hugh rushed on impatiently, 'I'm not a city

man, I prefer our country estates. What's his name?'

'Godfrey Fitzosbern, in Martin's Lane.'

There was a bang as Hugh slammed down his mug on the oaken table. 'Fitzosbern! That's the name! Adele was dealing with him over several months. She wanted a whole set of trinkets matched in silver filigree for her nuptial costume — headband, earrings, gorget, bracket and rings!'

Adele's father looked shocked. 'Of course! I was paying for them, I should have remembered. The whole set was delivered and is locked away in my treasure chest at Shillingford.'

Lord Ferrars stood up, his towering height and wide bulk seeming to fill the small room. 'What are you saying, Hugh? What has silversmithing to do with this?'

Hugh beat a fist on the table, making his mead cup jangle. 'The same man, this Fitzosbern! He is suspected of the rape of that girl, who visited his shop the night of her shame. And Adele must have gone to that same shop a dozen times, choosing and fitting those wedding baubles.'

There was a silence as pregnant as the subject of their concern had been. 'But it was many months ago,' objected de Courcy.

'And she was at least four months gone

with child, according to the nun from Polsloe,' retorted Hugh.

'Don't let us go too fast. Probably half the rich ladies in Devon have been to silversmiths for their jewellery. Just visiting a merchant doesn't make him a rapist and a fornicator.'

But Hugh would not be swayed. He had the bit between his teeth and any target for attack was better than none. 'It is a strange coincidence, that the man whom gossip marks out for a rape is the same whom Adele attended many times.'

The older men were far more cautious, but they were by no means dismissive of the possibility. 'He should be put to some questions,' said de Courcy.

'Questions? He should be put to the Ordeal, if not to the sword!' shouted Hugh, as hot-heated as ever. His big head swung from side to side on his thick neck, as if he was seeking some target within the dim corners of the room. In his state of chronic anger, he was desperate for something to hit.

Reginald de Courcy made an unconvincing plea for moderation. 'Come now, we are all romancing, surely? A wild rumour, born of idle gossip about the portreeve's daughter, born out of a man's poor reputation with women. Can we jump to an even wilder surmise that he must also be a murderer?'

Lord Ferrars was silent, at least not disagreeing with the speaker, but reluctant to abandon their only possibility. However tenuous it might be, it was better than nothing in their present state of frustration.

But the younger Hugh was in no mood for moderation. 'I can't stay stifled up in here, forever talking in circles.' He threw more mead into his cup from a jug, splashing half of it on the table, then drained it at a gulp.

At the door, he prodded his squatting squire with a long-toed shoe. 'Come on, we'll walk the town and ease our minds in a tavern or two.'

They pushed out into the lane and made for the high street, finding their way by the dim glow of chestnut roasters, horn lanterns of hawkers' stalls and the glimmer through linen shades over unglazed windows.

★ ★ ★

John de Wolfe slumped in his chair, almost dozing from the effects of red wine and the warmth of the fire on his front. Though it was only the middle of the evening, he was contemplating taking to his bed out of sheer boredom. Matilda had already succumbed and was snoring gently, her head back against her beehive chair, mouth wide open and the embroidery silks forgotten in her lap.

Through eyelids lowered to almost closing, the coroner stared at the fiery patterns made by the glowing logs, trying to decide whether to refill his wine cup or climb the outside stairs to the solar and his bed.

Suddenly, Brutus lifted his head and his ears went back. The big hound had been lying at John's feet, head between his paws, but now he was alert. Sleepily his master caught the movement out of the corner of his eye. 'What is it, old dog?' he murmured.

The mastiff turned his head slightly to one side, listening intently. John sat up and strained his own ears, knowing that despite his age, Brutus still had keen hearing.

There was something outside, some commotion in the lane. Though the house walls were wooden, they were made of a double layer of thick oak and the inside was hung with tapestries, which helped muffle sounds but still some hubbub filtered through. He could hear shouts and raised voices, as Brutus jumped up and loped to the door to sniff at the bottom crack.

John got to his feet and followed the dog. Matilda had not stirred and was still making soft whistling sounds in her throat. Throwing his cloak loosely over his shoulders, the coroner stepped out into the street, looking to his left from where the noise came. The lane was better lit than much of Exeter, as two pitch flares were stuck in rings on the walls of the farrier's diagonally opposite, towards St Martin's church. That light now fell on two struggling figures outside his next-door neighbour's house, the frontage of which was set back a few feet from John's dwelling.

Immediately, he saw that it was a one-sided struggle, as the heavy figure of Godfrey Fitzosbern appeared to be beating the life out of a much slighter man, accompanied by oaths and yelling from them both.

John dodged back into his vestibule to pull his sword from its sheath, then ran back into the street. By the time he returned, a third figure was involved, dragging at Fitzsobern's tunic. Even the dim light was sufficient to show that it was that of a woman.

'What in hell is going on?' roared John, as he ran towards the struggling trio, holding his sword aloft.

When she saw her neighbour approaching, Mabel, for of course it was Godfrey's wife, screamed, 'He'll kill the boy, get him off, for God's sake!' She continued to tug at her husband, but he gave her a swinging back-handed blow that knocked her flying against the doorpost of his shop. He then set to kicking the body on the ground, who

236

huddled up with his arms protectively over his head.

'Stop that, Fitzosbern!' yelled the coroner, grabbing him by the shoulder. His sword was useless — he could hardly run his neighbour through, although he contemplated whacking him with the flat of the blade.

The guild-master was in such a rage that he was oblivious of de Wolfe's presence, almost blue in the face and yelling abuse at the cringing figure lying in the cold mud. John tried to get an arm-lock around his neck to drag him off, but the frenzied assailant twisted away.

Then, abruptly, the battle took another turn as two other figures materialised from the gloom and grabbed Fitzosbern, pulling him away from the man on the ground. But Godfrey pulled an arm free and delivered a ringing punch to the face of one of the new arrivals, sending him staggering. Then there was a metallic scrape as the other fellow pulled out his sword and, an instant later, Fitzosbern was pinioned against his own front wall, with a sharp blade pressed across his neck.

De Wolfe bent down to hoist up the first victim from the snowy mud, just as the man Fitzosbern had punched climbed to his feet and delivered a shin-cracking kick to the merchant's left leg. Fitzosbern roared with pain and the coroner dropped his man back into the mud to leap forward and swing the flat of his sword against the shoulders of the kicker.

'What in Christ's name is going on here?' he bellowed. The other man still had his long blade at Fitzosbern's neck, a thin trickle of blood now running down from a shallow cut across his Adam's apple. Without hesitation, John lifted his huge sword and again brought the flat of it down on the forearm of the assailant, who gave a howl of pain as his weapon clattered down the wall. Fitzosbern slid to the ground and the coroner grabbed the cloaked swordsman. He swung him round to reveal the face of Hugh Ferrars, flushed and obviously drunk.

'You could have cut the man's throat, sir!' he snapped 'Do you to want to hang for it?'

'The bastard deserves it, by all account,' snarled the young man. 'Anyway, I was saving this other fellow's life. Fitzosbern was killing him — who is he, by the way?'

They turned to the groaning figure that John had unceremoniously dropped back into the mire, ignoring both Fitzosbern and Hugh's squire, who was sitting on the ground rubbing his shoulder where the coroner's broadsword had struck him.

'It's Edgar of Topsham, by damnation!' barked Ferrars. They dragged him to his feet and supported him while the apothecary's apprentice gingerly felt his face, ribs and kidneys to see what was damaged.

Now the silversmith himself climbed groggily to his feet and staggered over to him, his temper not improved by the blood running down his neck. 'Arrest them, murderers!' he croaked, clutching John's arm. 'He tried to kill me, the swine — look at this blood!'

The squire had recovered enough to make another lunge at Fitzosbern, but John pushed him away. 'Control this fellow, Ferrars, or I'll have you both in the castle gaol.'

Hugh muttered something at the other man, who seemed even more drunk than his master and the squire backed off a few paces.

The guild-master was still shaking the coroner's arm and demanding that he arrest all three of his antagonists. 'This evil young pup, he began it all!' Godfrey gave the shivering Edgar a hearty push in the chest, but John grabbed his arm and twisted it up behind his back.

'Let's have no more violence from any of you!' he yelled. Suddenly he was aware again of the other person among them, Mabel Fitzosbern, who had come across from her front doorstep, where she had sheltered since her husband had struck her. The light from the farrier's showed that she had a livid bruise down the side of her cheek and her left eye was rapidly closing with purple swelling of the lids. Her linen head-rail had been torn off and her ash-blonde hair was hanging in a tangle across her shoulder. 'He would have killed the boy, if you hadn't appeared,' she hissed, with a venom that surprised de Wolfe, coming from such a pretty and elegant woman. 'It's that damned husband of mine you should arrest, not these men!'

'Hold your tongue, woman! What do you know about it?' yelled Fitzsobern. 'This evil young bastard accused me of raping his girl!'

Mabel put her bruised features close to his and spat in his face. 'And I'd not be surprised if he was right, you swine! I can tell the world a thing or two about you and your habits!' Godfrey raised a hand to strike her again, but de Wolfe grabbed it in a steel-like grip. 'You can't testify to anything about me, you bitch,' yelled Fitzosbern, struggling against the coroner's restraint. 'You are my wife and I command you to get inside that house. I'll deal with you later.'

Now Edgar found his voice for the first time, speaking thickly through bruised lips. 'Coroner, you must arrest this man — or call the sheriff's men if you don't have the power. Look how he used me! He assaulted me and would have killed me if you hadn't come along. And I believe he is a ravisher. My Christina was last in his company.'

Fitzosbern roared again and struggled to get free from John's grasp. Hugh Ferrars, who had managed to keep quiet during these exchanges, launched himself forward to seize the silversmith, but John fended him off with the point of his sword.

'Leave it!' he yelled. 'All calm down, or I'll put the lot of you under the castle keep!'

He became aware of a growing knot of curious onlookers drifting into a semi-circle, attracted from the high street by the shouting and clatter of sword blades.

Hugh Ferrars, rocking slightly on his heels, prodded Fitzosbern in the chest with a thick finger. 'Rapist or not, I want to know what your dealings were with my intended wife. She came to your shop many a time. What was she to you, eh? Come on, damn you, admit how well you knew her!'

His squire had picked up Hugh's fallen sword and handed it to him, and now the baron's son began waving it at Fitzosbern, taking the point perilously near the thin bloody line on his neck.

'Put that away, damn you!' thundered the

241

coroner, clashing his own blade down on Ferrars's weapon. Trying to control four unruly men, two of them tipsy, was proving too much and he wished that he had Gwyn here to bang their heads together.

Mabel came back into the fray, pointing dramatically at her damaged face. 'Look what you did, swine of a husband! You devil, it's not the first time, either. I've had to stay inside my house for days on end until your handiwork healed up and I could go out and pretend to be the loving wife of a respectable burgess!' Godfrey seemed on the point of apoplexy, so great was his rage, but the coroner had his arm twisted up his back to hold him off the others. However, his mouth was still in working order. 'I told you to get inside that house, wife! You'll be sorry for this behaviour,' he screamed, almost beside himself with hatred.

'Not nearly so sorry as you will be, when I've spread your reputation about the town. I've held my peace until now, but enough is enough. I'm leaving you.'

'Good riddance! Go to hell, woman! And take that raddled wine pedlar with you. D'you think I didn't know about your own petty affairs, you fool?'

Mabel ignored this, secretly relieved that it was out in the open at last. But she had not finished with her husband yet. 'What's this Hugh was saying about you and his wife-to be, eh? Another rape, was it, you poxy swine?'

Hugh's eyes swivelled to her. 'Do you know anything of his affairs, madam? Do you know if he had been tumbling my intended wife?'

She looked from one to other. 'I can't say who he tumbled, they came and went so fast. It was too difficult to keep track of his philandering.'

The gathering crowd murmured with delight. This was an unexpected entertainment for a Saturday night and even the cold wind and occasional snowflake did not discourage them from waiting for the next act.

But John had had enough of this public brawl, especially as he spied Matilda coming out of his front door. The noise must have woken her at last, and he knew she would be incensed at such a vulgar fraças taking place outside her house.

'Clear off, all of you. This is no place to hold a private dispute. Ferrars, take this drunken squire and get home to your lodging. Your father would be ashamed of your behaviour in a public place.'

Next he turned to Edgar. 'And you had better mind your tongue, unless you have proof. You cannot go accusing prominent citizens of felony without a shred of evidence. Get back to your lodgings and be glad that I don't have you dragged off to Rougemont for the night.' He looked at the battered face and hunched body. 'And get Nicholas, that leech-master of yours, to put some poultices on your wounds.'

The centre-stage players began to draw apart, but they all had parting shots to cast.

'I'll not enter that house again, he'll kill me next time,' grated Mabel. 'I'll go to my sister's in North Street and beg lodging there.' She glared virulently at her husband. 'Just as well for you that I'm leaving,' she spat. 'You'd likely get my cooking knife between your ribs before very long — or poison in your broth!' She marched off tight-lipped, pushing through the straggling ring of sightseers, cloakless but heedless of the cold in the heat of her fury.

'And if she doesn't slay you, you swine, I will!' slurred Hugh Ferrars, giving his sword a last wave in the air before unsteadily finding the lip of his scabbard to slide it home with a jangling scrape. He thrust his face close to Fitzosbern's to utter a final threat. 'I'll be back to ask those questions, Master Silver-smith. And if I'm not satisfied, I'll kill you.'

He swaggered off, stumbling and pushing the spectators roughly aside, his squire close behind. Edgar limped after them, heading for the shop in Fore Street and some healing potions. Fitzosbern pulled himself away from John's slackening hand and attempted to brush himself down. 'You should have run those louts through — or arrested them! I'll be visiting Richard de Revelle first thing in the morning to demand writs against them all for assault and attempted murder. Just look at my throat!' He lifted his chin to show the line of drying blood across the front of his neck.

John ran a none-too-gentle finger across the mark. 'It's nothing but a scratch. You'll come to no harm.'

Godfrey thrust away his hand impatiently. 'Where's that bloody wife of mine?' he snarled.

'She's gone. I saw her going around the corner into the high street.'

John felt Matilda at his elbow. He knew of her partiality for Godfrey Fitzosbern and her disapproval of Mabel, whom she considered a gold-digging second wife, but the antagonism towards him of the son of Lord Ferrars had made her cautious of offering the silversmith much support.

The small crowd, sensing that the show was over, melted away and the coroner took his wife's arm and steered her towards their own house.

'I should go inside and bar your door, Fitrzsobern,' he advised. 'Let's hope everyone will have a cooler head in the morning.'

11

In which Crowner John
meets an Archbishop

The following day was Sunday, almost a day
of rest for the King's coroner for the county
of Devon.

In the forenoon, Matilda dragged him off
to church, which she did every few weeks. An
enthusiastic worshipper herself, she was ever
nagging John to be more devout. Although
she went often to the great cathedral a few
yards from their house, her favourite haunt
was the tiny church of St Olave's in Fore
Street, strangely dedicated to the first
Christian king of Norway.

Reluctantly, John accompanied her to
Mass, thinking it a prudent move in the
reconciliation plan with his wife. He had no
firm religious instincts. He supposed that he
believed in God — it was almost impossible
not to in the conditioned atmosphere of the
times — but for John, religious belief was just
a part of life, like breathing, eating and
making love. His life-threatening excursions
to the Crusades had had no significant

motive for wishing to rid the Holy Land of the infidels — in fact, he rather admired the Saracens. He went because his king wished to fight there, and loyalty to Richard was more than sufficient reason for him to risk his life — as well as giving him an excuse to be away from Matilda. So he went through the motions at St Olave's, using the time when the priest was mouthing the liturgies and acting out the rituals to think of the various problems thrown up by his current cases.

The Torbay wreck plunder and murders were virtually settled now, with the reeve and two villagers locked up in the gaol of Rougemont Castle. In spite of John's threat to levy the cost on Torre, the sheriff was fretting over the expense of feeding them until the next visit of the judges, which might take months. For this reason, prisoners were often allowed to escape, by the gaolers, who either turned a blind eye or were bribed. This happened even more often in the town gaol in South Gate, where those awaiting trial or already condemned by the burgess's court were incarcerated. The townsfolk had to pay for their lodging there, and it was a standing joke that a steady stream of prisoners got out and vanished into the forests to become outlaws, so relieving some of the tax burden on the citizens of Exeter.

As the priest droned on at the altar, de Wolfe slouched among the congregation, who stood on the bare flagstones for no benches were provided for their ease. His thoughts drifted again to the complexities of the rape, the miscarriage death, and he wondered if Fitzosbern had been to petition the sheriff as he had threatened. If John read Richard de Revelle correctly, he would tread very carefully with the Ferrars, de Courcy, the portreeve and, indeed, Fitzosbern himself, as each had different and varying degrees of power among the hierarchy of the Devon community. The sheriff always tried to come down on the winning side, especially since he had burned his fingers so badly when he had supported Prince John against the King.

The coroner wondered whether there was anything in these almost hysterical accusations against Fitzosbern. Though he disliked the man, he recognised that his feelings were irrelevant in the matter of his guilt: so far there was not a shred of evidence against him, although there had been so much gossip and rumour.

His mind drifted on to another less complicated case. A child had been killed on Friday when a wheel came off the axle of a cart carrying building stone and crushed him.

The jury had declared the offending wheel to be the instrument of death and so was a 'deodand', to be confiscated and sold for the benefit of the child's family. The carter now faced starvation, as he had no usable vehicle to earn his living, but John now decided to let him have his wheel back and pay its value to the family in instalments. Deodand money was supposed to go to the royal treasury, but sympathetic and over-taxed jurymen often voted to have the money paid to the family of the victim.

Having mentally settled that case, John was jogged back to the present by Matilda's elbow and found that the clergyman had stopped droning and the service was over. He walked his wife back to their house, Matilda preening herself before her acquaintances on the arm of her coroner husband. She stopped several times to pass the time of day and indulge in a little gossip. This morning the fraças in Martin's Lane and the break up of the Fitzosbern menage was easily the favourite topic.

As far as John could make out from the snippets he heard, Fitzosbern was already as good as condemned for multiple rape, procuring miscarriages, and murder. Uncomfortable with this exaggerated nonsense, he urged Matilda on. When they got to their door, he said that he must go up to the castle to see her brother about the events of the previous evening. He promised her that he would be back for the midday meal — and promised himself a visit to the Bush that afternoon — then hurried through the town to Rougemont and climbed the stairs inside the gate-house.

Gwyn and Thomas, Sunday notwithstanding, were up in the cramped coroner's chamber, taking their usual morning bread and cheese. John told them of the fight in his lane the previous evening and the whispering campaign in the town against the silversmith. The clerk nodded his bird-like head. 'The same story is all about the Close. The canons and their servants are full of the gossip', he confirmed.

Gwyn swallowed a full pint of ale. 'Do you think there's any truth in it?' he asked.

The coroner shrugged, his favourite form of expression.

Thomas, hunched over his eternal writing, looked up again. 'I saw Fitzosbern and then Henry Rifford hurrying over to the keep not ten minutes ago. Both are chasing the sheriff. No doubt.'

John rose from his stool. 'The portreeve as well? I'd better get across there and see what mischief they're up to.'

Under no circumstances could John de Wolfe ever feel sorry for his brother-in-law, but that morning he came near to it, as he saw the harassment that the sheriff was suffering.

Messengers from the Bishop's palace vied with stewards to bring messages and require replies about the arrangements for the Archbishop's visit the next day. Ralph Morin, the castle constable, waited impatiently to discuss matters of protocol with him in regard to the procession of Hubert Walter into the city — and in the midst of this administrative confusion, two angry men were shouting both at each other and at de Revelle. When John walked into the sheriff's chamber, Fitzosbern and Rifford were almost nose to nose in front of Richard's table. Both were big men and both were red in the face with anger.

'Don't you dare speak to me like that, Rifford! I had enough of such insults last evening, some of them on your family's behalf.'

'Where there's smoke, Fitzosbern, there's fire! Why should there be all this talk of you in the town of a sudden? I want the truth from you, at the end of a sword if needs be.'

Godfrey's swarthy face sneered back at the

252

Portreeve, his dark hair falling across his forehead. 'Is that supposed to be a challenge, sir? You'd regret it! Your days of combat are long past, with years of fat pickings on the council of burgesses putting weight on your belly and flab in your muscles.'

The sheriff, trim in his green tunic and fawn linen surcoat, slammed his hands on his parchment-cluttered table and jumped to his feet. 'Quiet, both of you! Look, I'll give you five minutes to explain what you want with me, then you leave me in peace, understand? Today, of all days, with the Justiciar almost on my doorstep, I can do without this aggravation. Now then, Master Fitzosbern, say your piece.'

The silversmith, in a heavy blue mantle with a foxfur collar thrown back over his shoulders, leaned on the other side of the trestle, his face jutting towards the sheriff. 'I've told you already, I want justice! I was assaulted and defamed last night by no less than three men, outside my own street door!'

'And you half killed young Edgar, son of Joseph, as well as grievously assaulting your own wife, by all accounts,' retorted Henry Rifford, swelling visibly with indignation within his dark red surcoat.

Richard de Revelle held up a warning hand. 'Wait, Henry, you'll have your say in a

253

moment. Now, Fitzosbern, who are you trying to lay charges against?'

'This whipper-snapper Edgar for one, of course! He bangs on my door and attacks me verbally at first, accusing me of ravishing the daughter of Rifford here. Of course, I was devastated on hearing of the foul act, and have every sympathy with the portreeve and his family, but that's no excuse for such baseless accusations against a leading member of the community like me.'

Richard looked increasingly uncomfortable. 'You have to make allowances for the state of mind of the young man, in such circumstances,' he observed mildly.

'Circumstances be damned! What right has anyone to utter such slander? And then for that arrogant swine Hugh Ferrars to make even worse threats and then assault me — attempted murder, see my throat!' He drew back his head and showed the thin, crusted line of blood across his neck, with an angry red margin along it. 'John de Wolfe was there — he probably stopped the drunken oaf from killing me. Your own coroner is witness that Ferrars and his equally drink-sodden squire may well have had my life.'

The sheriff rubbed a hand desperately across his brow. He needed this problem today like he needed an arrow in his back.

'Crowner, can you confirm this story?' he asked wearily.

'There are two sides to every story, Richard,' replied John evenly. 'I was not there at the start and Edgar of Topsham may well have provoked Fitzosbern. But it was Edgar who was in jeopardy when I arrived, for Fitzosbern was in danger of kicking him to death.'

'I was defending myself, the stupid youth assaulted me on my own doorstep when I denied his ridiculous accusations about his betrothed. What would you expect me to do?'

'Not kick him half to death. He is a feeble youth compared to you,' retorted John.

The silversmith glared at him and launched into the second half of his tirade. 'Then these two louts appeared and, without provocation, tried to kill me. Hugh Ferrars tried to hack off my head with his sword.'

John gave a derisive laugh. 'Come, Fitzosbern! They pulled you off the boy to stop you killing him. You punched them manfully and Ferrars held you against the wall by resting his blade against your skin. Don't try to make an assassination out of it.'

Godfrey began to shout denials and de Revelle again had to yell for quiet.

'I've got very little time for this! Lord Ferrars and his son are in a similar position to

255

Henry Rifford here — even worse, as there is a death involved. Now, all our tempers are frayed. I suggest we let them cool off. We have no evidence as yet, though in spite of what you pleaded, Fitzosbern, I am still inclined to take in your two workmen and put them to some stern test to get at the truth.'

The florid Portreeve was far from satisfied at this. 'Why waste time on those two scapegoats, de Revelle? Put this man to the Ordeal — he is far more likely to know the truth of it.'

At that moment, as if to turn the screw on the sheriff's torment, another figure burst into the chamber, pushing aside those others waiting to see de Revelle, and marched up to the central trio at the table. It was Reginald de Courcy, equally as angry as the main characters in the tableau.

'What's all this I hear about you, Fitzosbern?' he shouted, ignoring the sheriff completely. 'The town is buzzing with accusations that you were my daughter's lover and the father of the child that killed her. What have you to say to that? For if it's true, I'm going to kill you, even if I have to hang for it!'

Godfrey Fitzosbern looked as if he was going to explode. 'Mary, Mother of God, has the world gone mad?' he screamed, making a lunge at de Courcy with two clawed hands.

John grabbed him by the shoulders and pulled him back, while two men-at-arms at the end of the table made a rapid move to stand close alongside him, as the silversmith stood quivering with rage.

He swung his head towards the sheriff and, with a supreme effort at self control, said, 'Everyone seems to want to accuse me and to kill me! For God's sake, how often do I have to say that I know nothing of these things?' His voice rose to a crescendo. 'If anyone has any proof, let him provide it — or else keep their mouths closed! Do you hear me Sheriff? Leave me be!' He twisted out of the coroner's grasp and stormed to the door, where he turned to make his last threat. 'Those who defame and assault me, I will appeal in the burgess court, for I see the sheriff's shire court would be disinclined to do anything to give me justice!'

And with that he marched out and slammed the heavy door behind him in a final gesture of angry defiance.

★   ★   ★

That afternoon, John dallied pleasantly with his mistress in the tavern in Idle Lane. After a few mugs of Edwin's ale downstairs, they adjourned to bed in her room which was partitioned off from the general dormitory on the upper floor, where pallets and straw mattresses were rented to guests.

At the same time, another bed in Exeter carried a far less comfortable burden, as Edgar lay aching on his palliasse in the store room of Nicholas's shop in Fore Street. He had stumbled home after his encounter with Fitzosbern the night before and collapsed into the apothecary's arms.

Nicholas, greatly concerned about his apprentice, had cleaned him up, washing away the blood and mud. When stripped, Edgar presented a patchwork of bruises on his face, legs, back and belly, where the muscular silversmith had belaboured and kicked him. Nicholas applied his skills as best he could, with salves and poultices, but he well knew that the only effective healer was time. 'You've got no broken bones or open wounds, thank God,' he announced, after a detailed examination of his battered assistant, 'but you'll ache for a week and be stiff for a fortnight.'

Now, this Sunday afternoon, Edgar, sipping more of a hot concoction designed to dull the pain, told the leech of the suspicions that were going around the town like wildfire about Fitzosbern's involvement in both the ravishing and the fathering of the fatal pregnancy.

'There's no proof of it, though,' said Nicholas, repeating what half the population of Exeter was saying to the other half.

Edgar shook his head over his mug, then winced with the pain of the sudden movement. 'No, but why this sudden surge of suspicion against one man and no other?'

Nicholas looked worried, but had no answer for Edgar. 'You keep clear of him in future, my lad,' he said sternly. 'You're no match for his bullying strength. Fitzosbern's a vindictive person, and he'll appeal you before the courts if you accuse him without proof.'

He patted Edgar gently on the shoulder and pressed him back on to his mattress. 'Get some rest now — let that potion send you to sleep. Tomorrow you may feel well enough to get back to some work in the shop.'

Nicholas left the young man to slumber in the cluttered room, smelling of every spice and herb known to science, and went back into his front shop to clarify some goose-grease for a skin salve.

★ ★ ★

A few miles outside Exeter, Edgar's father was leaning on a wall outside his house in

Topsham, looking past two of his ships moored at the quayside to the muddy banks of the river beyond. The tide was coming in rapidly and down-river, he could see the sails of one of his smaller vessels coming up from the direction of Exmouth, past the treacherous sandbar that projected under water from the tip of Dawlish Warren.

It was the *Berengaria*, named after King Richard's beautiful but childless and now discarded wife, and was bringing more wine and fruit from western Normandy. Alongside him was Eric Picot, for whom some of the cargo was destined. Picot had ridden down from his house in Wonford, just outside the city, to reassure himself of its safe arrival, as the wrecking of the *Mary of the Sea* had been a serious financial loss.

But as they waited, they had other serious matters on their minds. Joseph had heard nothing of his son's escapade with Fitzosbern until Picot had arrived, as he had not been in the city the previous day. Although reassured that Edgar was not badly damaged, he was incensed by the news of Fitzosbern's assault. First he called the boy a fool for his impetuosity, then cursed Fitzosbern for being a cruel and callous bastard. 'What is the truth of all this, Eric?' he asked worriedly. 'Is this bloody silversmith guilty of anything or not?'

Picot scowled across the muddy water. 'He not only assaulted your boy, Joseph, he also attacked his wife in public, when she tried to pull him off Edgar.' His face lightened a little. 'At least the way seems clear for us now. She has broken with him altogether and left his house.' Joseph turned to stare at his friend. 'She is with you?'

Eric sighed. 'We must tread carefully, annullment is a very difficult business. At present she is staying with her sister, but she says she will never go back to Godfrey. She was already at breaking point with his philandering and ill-treatment of her, though he had never struck her so hard nor so openly as last night.'

Joseph stroked his beard and looked down-river again at his approaching vessel. 'What's to be done, Eric? Am I to let his evil attack on my son go unchallenged?'

The wine merchant pulled up the hood of his mantle against the keen sea breeze. 'I should make your great displeasure known to him as soon as you return to Exeter. Keep the pressure on the swine. Perhaps then he will have a seizure, damn him!'

Joseph nodded absently. 'My son is a fool, though a well-meaning one. This defiling of Christina has been a bitter blow for all of us, but naturally mostly for Edgar.'

The tall, bearded man looked down-river again at his ship and his eyes moistened, not from the wind alone. 'He has set his heart on becoming a leech and his apprenticeship ends next month. He was going to marry and take his bride to London, so that he could study at the hospital of St Bartholomew and become a proper physician. Now all is in confusion, he may not marry at all or Christina may not wish to go to London. His world is down about his ears and I can't forecast what his actions will be. God forbid that he does something even more foolish. It would be better if I were to slit Fitzosbern's gizzard myself than that my impetuous son should get hanged for it!'

★ ★ ★

After a frantic Monday morning in both cathedral and castle, the preparations were finally finished for Hubert Walter's progress into Exeter. Ralph Morin, the constable of Rougemont, rode out along the old Roman road to the west with almost the whole of the castle garrison in full battle order, chain mail hauberks with aventails covering their necks, round helmets, shields, swords and lances.

The Chief Justiciar's procession had left the great abbey of Buckfast early that

262

morning, and they met up with it about five miles out of the city. Shortly after noon the sound of trumpets could be heard approaching the river crossing.

The wooden footbridge was of no use to such a mounted multitude, and as Walter Gervase's stone bridge was still only half built, the only way across the Exe was by the ford. Thankfully the river was not in spate and it was not high tide, so an old soldier like Hubert thought nothing of riding his huge warhorse belly deep in the cold water.

With four knights as a vanguard, he came to the city wearing secular garb, rather than his archbishop's mitre. Though he wore no armour, he had a conical helmet with a nasal guard and a yellow surcoat emblazoned with a couchant lion, the same arms on the oval shield that hung at his saddlebow. He carried no lance, but a great sword hung from his baldric, symbolic rather than necessary as he felt sure that no fighting would occur that morning between Buckfast and Exeter.

On each side of him and extending well behind, were lines of Ralph Morin's men-at-arms under the proud captainship of Gabriel. A phalanx of Hubert's own troops followed close behind him, then a mixed collection of nobles, priests, clerks, administrators, judges and other court officials, for Walter was effectively the regent and ruler of England now that the King had left the country, apparently for good.

Behind the riders came curtained wagons carrying the fine ladies and their families, then ox-carts piled with supplies. There were other wagons full of documents, the treasure cart and then a motley collection of nags, mules, donkeys and more carts carrying servants, cooks, falconers, houndsmen and all the rag-bag needed to keep a court on the move. The convoy stretched for a quarter of a mile, ending with a troop of soldiers to protect the rear.

As the Justiciar came up out of the river, a large crowd waited to welcome him at the West Gate, which was hung with banners and flags. Just outside it, the sheriff and coroner waited on their horses with the two Portreeves, Henry Rifford and Hugh de Relaga. Almost all the town's burgesses were there, the only notable absentee being Godfrey Fitzosbern. The Bishop, the canons and numerous other ecclesiastics were waiting for Hubert in the cathedral precinct, partly to emphasise its independence from the secular part of the town.

The advance guard wheeled smartly to the side as they came up to the welcoming party and Hubert Walter rode sedately up to

264

Richard de Revelle and John de Wolfe. There were salutes and greetings all round and the sheriff introduced the Portreeves, who had not met the Justiciar before. Naturally, Richard de Revelle knew him well, as every six months he had to report personally on the state of the county's taxes to Winchester or London. John, of course, was an old crusading comrade, albeit of greatly different rank, but they clasped arms and greeted each other warmly, to the sheriff's ill-concealed displeasure.

The cavalcade set off up the steep slope from the West Gate towards Carfoix, where the four main roads from the gates met in the centre of the town. The streets were lined with most of the population of Exeter, who gave some ragged cheers as the cavalcade passed — though the crushing taxes that the Justiciar had imposed at the King's insistence had markedly blunted Hubert's popularity. The establishment of John's office had been a tax-raising device, and Hubert had plenty more ideas up his sleeve.

The escort delivered him to the Bishop and his clerical entourage, all waiting outside the great West Front of the cathedral, attired in their full ceremonial robes. After being fed and watered in the Bishop's Palace, Hubert would change into his archbishop's regalia, for he was to celebrate a High Mass in the cathedral in the late afternoon, then attend a banquet in the palace that evening.

The sheriff stayed with the Bishop and Justiciar, but when the procession broke up to be housed in various parts of the Close, the castle and elsewhere in the town, John took his horse back to the farrier's stable in Martin's Lane and crossed to his house. Matilda, who had been in the crowd at the West Gate, had also hurried home and intended spending the rest of the day there, for Lucille to primp her hair and her new clothes for the banquet that evening, which would be the high spot of her social calendar.

With a sigh, John ate a meal in solitary state in his hall, then sat by the fire with a quart of ale, before reluctantly deciding to have an unscheduled wash in the back yard and even consider attacking the dark stubble on his chin, in honour of the Chief Justiciar.

12

In which Crowner John
is called out of a banquet

The refectory in the Bishop's palace, between the cathedral and the city wall, was crowded with gaily dressed folk and filled with a hubbub of conversation, laughter and the clatter of dishes. The hall was only large enough to hold a hundred people, so the company was very select. The following evening, there would be room for many more at the banquet at Rougemont, where the sheriff and burgesses were to entertain the Justiciar. Tonight, Hubert was in his archbishop mode, sitting in the centre of the top table between Bishop Marshall and the Archdeacon of Exeter, John de Alecon.

Ranged on either side were the three other archdeacons of the diocese, the Treasurer and the Precentor, then military and civic officials, which included Richard de Revelle and his wife, Lady Eleanor, John de Wolfe and Matilda. The two Portreeves and the castle constable Ralph Morin were next, together with a mixture of county nobility, abbots, canons and burgesses. The other trestles, arranged as spurs from the top table, held as many of the lesser notables, rich merchants, guild officials and minor clergy as had been able to wheedle invitations for themselves.

Matilda was in ecstasy at their favoured position, visible at the top table to all those present, which included some of her women acquaintances. She was too happy even to notice her husband's glumness and boredom, as she sat next to one of the senior canons, Thomas de Boterellis, who was the Precentor responsible for the music and order of services at the cathedral. He was a fat, waxen-faced priest with very small eyes — and no friend of John's, having been on the Bishop's side in his support for Prince John's rising. Across the table, at the end of the nearest spur, Matilda had the priest from St Olave's and the Master of the Guild of Cordwainers, so she could combine religious talk with gossip about the latest fashions in shoemaking.

John was isolated from anyone he knew, other than Matilda, and wished he was within speaking distance of Hubert Walter. Instead, he was seated next to a fat little canon who, with wolfish determination, ate everything that was placed within reach and had no time for conversation.

The coroner looked past his wife to where the two bishops were sitting at the centre of the table. Both had changed out of their elaborate vestments, which they had worn during the Mass, and were now in comparatively plain though rich garments. Each wore an embroidered cream surcoat over an alb and their head-gear was a puffed round cap, with a pair of decorated tails hanging from above the ear to the chest.

John stared at Hubert's strong face, weathered on a dozen battlefields, and compared it with the narrow, long-chinned features of Bishop Henry Marshall, whose face had a curious smooth symmetry as if it was a sculpture. He had no doubt of the Bishop's genuine devotion to the Church, but wondered if the ambitious politician-Archbishop had a similar passion for religion — or whether he took the office of head of the English Church merely as a means to secular power. Hubert Walter had been a senior court official and a baron of the Exchequer since the days of old King Henry, but had never had high office until Richard the Lionheart first made him Bishop of Salisbury, then his lieutenant at the Third Crusade. Hubert's efforts to negotiate the King's release from incarceration in Germany had earned him the twin appointments of Archbishop of Canterbury and Chief Justiciar of England.

John would dearly have liked to talk to him about what happened in the Holy Land when Hubert had remained there in charge of the English army, after John and the King had begun their ill-fated journey home. He hoped there would be time for reminiscing tomorrow, after their meeting to iron out the differences between the sheriff and the coroner over jurisdiction in criminal cases. John looked again around the noisy hall and contrasted the well-dressed and over-fed congregation with most of the population outside, the majority of whom lived in poverty-stricken and squalid conditions, like those in Bretayne — and Bearded Lucy on Exe Island.

The thought of the old crone brought his mind back to the current problems — he still had the nagging feeling that Lucy had been holding something back and he resolved to look into that again in the next day or two. That sent his eyes roving again, to confirm that neither Godfrey Fitzosbern nor his wife Mabel were at the banquet. He presumed that Godfrey was lying low after the events of the last day or two — and presumably Mabel had carried out her threat to leave him.

There had been no sign of Fitzosbern at the cathedral service either, when Hubert Walter celebrated the Mass and then preached a sermon. It must have been a hard decision for the silversmith to shun such an event as this, when he was such a prominent member of the guilds in the city. John had half expected to see him there as an act of defiance against the rumours that beset him.

The evening wore on and John had eaten all he wanted and drunk more than he needed. No one could leave until the Bishop and his chief guest rose from the table, so he was stuck between the strident tones of Matilda and the gargling of the insatiable canon who, deprived of more food, was consuming vast quantities of the Bishop's best wine.

Suddenly, the coroner caught sight of a familiar figure standing just inside the doorway that led from the palace courtyard. For a second he thought the wine was playing tricks with his sight, but it was undoubtedly their maid Mary standing there, her eyes roving the hall. Their gaze met and she waved vigorously, then beckoned urgently.

John, glad of a diversion as long as it didn't mean that his house was on fire, pushed back his chair and struggled along the narrow gap between the seated diners and the wall. Pushing aside a servant balancing four large jars of ale, he reached the doorway. Mary, a blanket enveloping her head and shoulders, pointed a finger towards the outside. 'You'd better come back to Martin's Lane straight away,' she said cryptically. John wondered why she didn't say 'come home', then looked back and saw that the eagle-eyed Matilda had noticed his absence. She grimaced across the hall and beckoned to him pointing with a ferocious scowl at his empty chair then gesturing up the table at the bishops. He ignored her and followed his maid servant out into the cold air of the courtyard. 'What's going on? Not another ravishment or miscarriage?'

Mary grasped his arm in her firm grip. 'No, but I think that Godfrey Fitzosbern has been poisoned.'

★   ★   ★

They hurried across the darkened pathways of the cathedral Close, stumbling over rubbish and heaps of fresh earth from half-dug graves. Gwyn of Polruan and Gabriel, the sergeant-at-arms, were following them. John had known that they had been enjoying the banquet from inside the palace kitchens and had called them out to come with Mary and himself to this new emergency.

As they walked the short distance across to St Martin's Lane, Mary explained what had happened. 'I was carrying logs through the passage into the hall when I heard this noise from the street. I thought it might be another fight next door, as it was the other night, so I went outside to look.'

They reached the gate and passed into the lane, where the farrier's rush lights burned.

'It was Master Godfrey again, but this time he was crawling on the ground outside his door, making a strange croaking noise.'

Now passing John's own house, they came in sight of a small group of people clustered around the open door to the silversmith's shop.

'I went to him, but he was unable to speak, just grasping my skirt and making these strange noises and holding his throat. I ran to the end of the lane and called a man passing on the High Street. He came with me and we dragged Master Godfrey inside his front door out of the cold. Then I ran for you, I didn't know what else to do.'

John pushed past the few onlookers and, Gwyn and Gabriel close behind, led Mary into the shop. Only one of the usual tallow dips was burning, but the occupant was easily located by the rasping noises he made as he breathed. Godfrey Fitzosbern was stretched on his side on the floor, his arms and legs twitching slightly. His eyes were open, but John had the impression, even in the poor light, that they were unseeing.

'What is it, Fitzosbern? What's wrong?' he demanded, kneeling alongside the man. There was no answer and the coroner repeated the words much more loudly. This got some reaction, as the victim turned his head, though his eyes failed to focus. He made some noises in his throat, then slumped back again, unresponsive, apart from spasmodic twitching of his fingers.

'Get me that lamp,' ordered John, and Gabriel reached for the little dish with a floating wick. John held it close to Godfrey's face and saw a clammy pallor, with beads of cold perspiration on the features.

'What's wrong with his neck?' asked the sergeant, pointing to an angry red line of swelling across the throat. This surrounded the slight cut he had received from Hugh Ferrars, but now it was obviously inflamed and going septic.

John tried to communicate again with the sick man, but only incomprehensible gargling noises came back. The twitching began again and the trembling of the fingers was more obvious.

He looked up at Mary, huddled anxiously under her blanket shawl. 'Did he say anything sensible to you?' he asked.

'I could make out only one or two words among the groans and muttering. He said, 'Burning, it's burning', and 'poisoned'.'

John's black eyebrows rose. 'No doubt about him saying poison?'

'It was definite. When he said it, he pointed that shaking hand towards his throat.'

John knew that his maid was a level-headed and reliable woman and he took what she said without question. 'He has this suppuration of the wound in his throat. Maybe the poison from that is sufficient. But we can't leave him here.' He stood up. 'The monks of St Nicholas will be aghast when I take them another patient or corpse within these few days.'

Gabriel had a suggestion. 'I know the prior at St John's and it's nearer than St Nicholas's. Why not take him there? There are three brothers who are skilled in caring for the sick.'

Just within the East Gate was a very small monastic house which had come to be known as St John's Hospital, from the labours of the four celibates who lived there.

'We'd better move him quickly, while he's still alive,' suggested Gwyn. He looked around the room and, with Gabriel's help, lifted the hinges of the inner door from their wrought-iron pintles and laid it flat alongside the twitching silversmith. Two of the onlookers were recruited and Fitzosbern was lifted on to the planks and carried away at a trot, around the corner into the main street and away up to St John's.

De Wolfe sent the remaining bystanders about their business and closed the front door. 'Well done, Mary, you're a good, sensible girl,' he said. 'Now I'd better get back to that bloody banquet or all my good work with Matilda will have been for nothing.'

* * *

Several hours later, he was back inside the silversmith's house with Gwyn. The festivities at the Bishop's Palace were over and, as he had been absent barely a quarter of an hour, Matilda made no great complaint, especially when he regaled her with this new piece of drama from next door.

After seeing her up to the solar and the attentions of Lucille, who would dismantle her finery to allow her to get to bed, he collected Gwyn, who was drinking ale with

Mary in her hut in the back yard. 'Let's see what's been going on in the house next door. Maybe we can tell if he really has been poisoned or whether this is some sickness from that neck wound.'

As they entered the absent Fitzosbern's premises, Gwyn had a question. 'If it is suppuration from that neck wound and he dies, would that not make Hugh Ferrars liable for unlawful killing?'

'It's for a jury to decide, but it seems very likely. Let's not run ahead of ourselves, we must see what's here.'

They looked around the shop, where there was nothing untoward to be found. The workbenches held the usual clutter of tools and metal, and the table that displayed finished wares was bare of anything as the valuable stock was locked up for safety every night.

'There is light upstairs,' observed the Cornishman, putting his head through the now doorless opening to the back workroom. They went through the pungent fumes from the ever-burning furnace, each holding aloft a tallow light, which showed nothing out of the ordinary in the downstairs area. Climbing the wide ladder, John rose into the living space above, which was deserted.

'Does he not have servants?' queried Gwyn.

'The maid went with Mabel when she left him, so the gossip says, and my wife is always abreast of the latest tittle-tattle,' replied the coroner. 'There was a kitchen servant, but God knows where he is. Drinking in some tavern, I expect.'

They looked around the room, holding up their lamps, as only one candle still burned, the stump guttering in a silver candlestick. Another room was partitioned off at the front, in which was a large bed. In the main room, John saw a half-eaten meal on a silver-rimmed wooden platter with a silver chalice alongside. 'What's this? The chair is overturned and there's a soiled knife on the floor.'

Gwyn picked up the platter and looked at it closely. 'Half a roast fowl, much of the leg eaten. Carrots and cabbage with it, some spilled on to the table,' he reported. John, meanwhile, had picked up the elaborate goblet, which looked as if it was better suited to a church altar than a dinner table. It appeared to be half full of red wine, some of which had been splashed on to the table near the base of the chalice. He sniffed at the contents, but could detect nothing unusual. Dipping the tip of a finger into the deep rose-coloured liquid, he gingerly touched it to the end of his tongue, but again could taste nothing but wine.

The coroner thought for a moment, looking around the room. 'We had best keep this food and the wine, to see if some better examination can be made of it,' he decided.

'Did the wine come from there, I wonder?' asked Gwyn, pointing to a small grey-stone jar with a wooden stopper, that stood on a shelf nearby.

John took the flask and removed the bung, sniffing at the contents. He shook it and estimated that it was about half full. 'We'll take this as well — and this.' He picked up a small round wooden box, alongside the wine jar. There was some cabalistic inscription on the lid and inside was a brown fibrous powder that had a faint herbal smell.

Gwyn looked at the specimens they had collected. 'So what do we do with them now?'

'I'll keep them next door until the morning, then I'll take them to an apothecary to see what he makes of them.'

Gwyn's blue eyes looked frankly at his master. 'Not to an apothecary's apprentice?' he asked pointedly.

John sighed. 'I already guess how my brother-in-law's mind will work. If this is a poisoning, then Edgar of Topsham will be the prime suspect, after the threats and attack he has made on Fitzosbern.'

Gwyn gave one of his grunts. 'For once, it is hard to blame the sheriff if he comes to believe that. Edgar is the obvious choice.'

John led the way back to the steps, taking the flask and medicine box, while Gwyn followed with the platter and chalice.

'We had better go up to St John's, to see if we are dealing with a murder or just an attempted one.'

The priory, tucked just inside the massive East Gate, was but a series of rooms attached to a small chapel. Living quarters for the four monks, a tiny refectory and a kitchen were adjunct to several cells and a larger room that acted as the hospital. It was always full of sick people from the poorest section of the town, but Brother Saulf, a Saxon who was the elder monk under the prior, had shifted a patient out of a cell into the main ward so that Fitzosbern could be accommodated.

When the coroner arrived, the silversmith lay on a pallet, deathly pale, still clammy and sweating. As John went into the cell with Saulf, the patient suddenly vomited and retched, a stream of almost clear fluid gushing from his mouth and nose. Saulf knelt to wipe it from his lips and nostrils and tipped the man's head to one side to see if any more could escape. Then, to John's surprise, he picked up a pitcher from the floor and bending Fitzosbern's head back, poured a generous amount of fluid into his mouth.

There was a spluttering and coughing, but the monk clamped the man's jaw shut with his hand so that he was forced to swallow, though he seemed almost to suffocate in the attempt. A moment later, he retched again and more fluid shot from between his lips to join the mess on the floor.

'If it is a poison, then the only hope is to cleanse it from his belly with copious draughts of salt and water,' explained the middle-aged brother, justifying his heroic treatment.

'Do you think he *has* been poisoned?' demanded the coroner.

Saulf looked up from clearing his patient's mouth. 'I cannot tell. It may be some bad food he has eaten or it may be some foul substance that he has been given. The symptoms of so many poisons are the same — collapse, pain in the throat, vomiting and purging.'

'Will he live?'

'That is in God's hands. It's too soon to say. He might be perfectly well in the morning — or he might be dead.'

Gwyn leaned against the door post behind

281

John. 'Has he spoken any sensible words, to say what happened to him?'

'Nothing but groans, apart from a whisper I caught, which sounded like 'burning, burning'.' De Wolfe stood looking down at the victim, who still had trembling of the hands and feet and occasional twitches of the limbs. 'What about that throat wound? He was cut by a sword edge two nights ago, but it was a trivial injury at the time.'

Saulf touched the swollen red line with a finger, expressing several beads of yellow pus. 'It could be the cause of his hoarse attempts to speak and maybe his collapse from purulence in the blood. Yet he has no fever, he is cold and damp. And I fail to see why he trembles and jerks in this way.'

They stayed a few moments longer, but it was obvious that, whether Godfrey lived or died, he was not going to enlighten them that night about what might have happened to him in Martin's Lane.

John thanked the monk and promised to return first thing next morning, leaving the silversmith to the mercies of the brothers and their God.

13

In which Crowner John
meets the Chief Justiciar

The meeting with Hubert Walter was set for the tenth hour on the morning of Tuesday, but John de Wolfe was active about the town before that. In the grey light of a winter dawn, he went first to the hospital of St John to see whether Fitzosbern had survived the night or whether he had a murder on his hands. Brother Saulf was in the cell when he arrived and looked as if he had been there all night. 'He is much better, Crowner, after throwing up most of his guts into a bucket, thanks to the salt-water purges.'

John looked past the monk and saw Godfrey, deathly pale, lying motionless on his side. 'He looks dead to me,' he said dubiously.

'No, he's asleep now — a proper sleep, not the twitching coma you saw last night.'

'Has he spoken at all?'

The Saxon brother shook his head. 'Only the muttered gibberish we heard when he first came here. Let him sleep then we'll see if his senses have returned.'

He shut the door firmly, keeping John and himself outside. 'Do you think he was truly poisoned?' asked John.

'It seems likely, but he might also have had some kind of apoplexy, though I've not seen one quite like this before.'

With that, the coroner had to be satisfied, but at least it looked as if Fitzosbern would live to sin another day. John left the priory and made his way back to his house, where last night he had arranged to meet his two assistants. Matilda was still asleep in the solar and he was happy not to disturb her.

A few moments later, a small procession left Martin's Lane, the coroner striding ahead of Gwyn, who held a wooden tray with the remains of Godfrey's roast fowl and the small box of herbs, all covered with a white cloth. He was followed by Thomas de Peyne, carefully carrying the chalice, still half full of wine, and the stone bottle.

The trio marched out into the high street and down to the crossing at Carfoix, ignoring the curious glances of the stall-holders and shoppers who stood back to make way for them. As John waited for a loaded ox-cart to pass, he looked behind and one of his rare grins spread across his face at the sight of his two companions: his over-sized Cornish henchman, solemnly bearing a cloth-covered tray, and the unfrocked priest, reverently clasping a silver goblet of wine, looked like two acolytes bearing the Sacred Host down the main street of Exeter.

They had not far to go, as on the other side of Fore Street lay the apothecary's shop. As John neared it, the door flew open and three struggling figures erupted on to the roadway.

Two men-at-arms from Rougemont were dragging Edgar of Topsham from the shop, the apprentice yelling at the top of his voice for them to let him go. Behind him, Nicholas of Bristol peered from the doorway, wringing his hands in agitation. When the soldiers saw the King's coroner, they stopped in their tracks, but did not loosen their grip on Edgar. 'Sheriff's orders, Sir John,' said one apologetically.

As soon as he saw the coroner, the captive appealed desperately to him. 'Save me, Sir John, these men are abducting me! Tell them it's a mistake, they must have the wrong man.'

The elder soldier shook his helmeted head. 'We're arresting you, not abducting you. And it's no mistake. The sheriff said Edgar of Topsham — and that's you, son.'

Edgar began to babble protests, but John could do nothing for him at this stage. 'Go quietly, Edgar, it's no use struggling. I'll see what I can do to straighten all this out. And I'll send word to your father so that he can come to see you and the sheriff.'

With this, the apothecary's apprentice had to be content, as John jerked his head at the guards and they marched Edgar away, up the hill towards the castle.

John, followed by his two disciples, crowded Nicholas back into his shop and shut the door. The leech was still twittering with concern at the unceremonious loss of his assistant. 'This is nonsense, what has he done to be treated like that?'

John was patient with him. 'You know full well that he has threatened Godfrey Fitzosbern several times and he attacked him on Saturday.'

The apothecary nodded spasmodically, the corner of his mouth drooping all the more in his agitation. 'He came back on Saturday bruised and battered — that foul man used him atrociously, he could have been killed!'

'Well, Fitzosbern could have been killed last night, by all accounts. He was poisoned and his life hangs in the balance today.'

A little exaggeration never did any harm when you are trying to get co-operation, thought John. 'Naturally, Edgar is the prime suspect — you can't blame the sheriff for wanting to question him.'

Nicholas's jaw dropped, temporarily hiding the slackness of his mouth. 'Poisoned? What has that to do with Edgar?'

John sighed as he began explanations about the silversmith's affliction 'Edgar had promised to kill him and he is almost a fully qualified apothecary, with much knowledge of poisons.'

The leech looked from face to face, as if seeking sanity in a world suddenly gone mad. 'But anyone could put poison in his victuals. Every old wife and village peasant knows of plants and toadstools that have noxious effects.'

John did not reply, but motioned Gwyn and Thomas to put their burdens on the shop counter. 'I want you to examine these, to see if they contain any harmful substance — and if so, what it is,' he announced.

The apothecary stared at the exhibits incredulously. 'But most poisons are undetectable!' he protested. 'There is almost no way in which they can be tested. Our knowledge is hopelessly poor about such things.'

He drew himself up to his full sixty-two inches. 'And not only me. Not an apothecary in England has any better methods.'

The coroner was unmoved. 'Just do your

best, Nicholas. Look, this one might be easier. What do you say about this?' He picked up the small wooden box and handed it to the leech, who glanced at it perfunctorily.

'That's simple. It contains a mixture of ground herbs useful for countering inflammation,' he proclaimed.

Gwyn scowled ferociously at him, his ginger eyebrows dropping towards his equally auburn moustache. 'How can you tell when you've not even opened it yet?'

In spite of his distress, the apothecary could not resist a superior smirk. 'Because it's written on the lid — see?' He pointed to the obscure symbol on the top. 'And I should know what's in it, for I gave it to Fitzosbern only yesterday.'

There was a silence.

'You gave it to him, yesterday?' repeated John slowly.

'Yes, of course. He came in late in the afternoon, complaining of pain in his throat and a fever. I examined him and saw this recent slash on his neck, which was going purulent. I bathed it and put some lotion on it, then gave him these herbs to take thrice a day to try to assuage the sepsis.'

'You gave him the medicament yourself?'

Nicholas nodded. 'Of course. I took it from here.' He turned and pulled out a small wooden drawer from a double row of similar receptacles along the wall behind the counter. Holding it out, they saw that it was half full of a brown powder similar to that in the little box.

'Was Edgar in the shop when Fitzosbern came?' demanded John. The apothecary looked uncomfortable. 'He was, but he turned his back on the silversmith and remained so in the corner of the shop, pretending to work at something.'

'So he had nothing to do with the prescription or the treatment?'

'Nothing! He kept well out of the way, for obvious reasons.'

John digested this. 'Did you leave them alone here at any time?'

The apothecary considered for a moment. 'Only when I had to go into the store room behind the shop to get a supply of these little boxes as we had none left in the shop.'

'Was that for long?'

'Only a few minutes — and I had to get a pan of hot water from the fire in the hut at the back, to bathe his wound.'

A few more questions drew a blank and John had to be satisfied with what he had already learned. Emphasising the need to try to test the food and wine, they left for Rougemont.

At the lower door of the castle gate-house, the coroner gave his officer a last order before going over to the keep. 'I want Bearded Lucy questioned again. I feel that she knows something else, above what she admitted to us last week.'

Gwyn cleared his throat noisily and spat on the ground. 'Can I persuade her a little?' he asked hopefully, scratching his crotch.

'Only with your voice, understand? I don't want her broken in half or anything like that. Take Thomas with you, in case you frighten her to death. Then he can shrive her soul. But get some information from her first!'

He strode away across the inner bailey, his mantle streaming behind him like the plumage of some great black crow.

★ ★ ★

The meeting in Richard de Revelle's chamber had been going on for some time when John arrived, but none of that part concerned him, as they had been discussing county administration and the collection of taxes. When he slipped on to a vacant bench, they were still arguing about the Stannery Towns, the semi-autonomous communities scattered around the edges of Dartmoor, where the tin-miners had ancient rights, including their own courts — and, with the miners of Cornwall, even a form of local parliament.

None of this had any relevance to the coroner, as his jurisdiction was universal. He took the opportunity to study the large group assembled to meet Hubert Walter, who sat at the head of a square of trestle tables, with the sheriff on his right. On his left was John de Alecon, as the Bishop delegated such secular meetings to his staff. The other thirty men were mainly barons and court officials from the western counties and the travelling circus that went around with the Chief Justiciar.

Hubert's lean brown face was following the discussion intently. He owed his power largely to having kept a firm grip on every topic and he had a compendious knowledge of every administrative quirk that the complex government of England and Normandy could devise. Today he wore none of the elaborate finery of the Church or his martial robes, but was dressed in a plain tan surcoat over a tunic of cream linen. His head was bare, unlike many of the others whose more gaudy dress was topped by a colourful assortment of head-gear.

Eventually the discussion reached the matter that had been a source of friction between John and his brother-in-law for almost three months. The Chief Justiciar was well aware of it, for both the sheriff and the coroner had complained to the itinerant justices when they visited Exeter in October, and de Revelle had raised the matter again when he last went to Westminster with his county taxation accounts.

Hubert Walter picked up a vellum roll on which one of his clerks had penned a note as an *aide-mémoire*. 'The problem seems to be this,' he summarised, with the clarity that had helped him reach the highest position in the land. 'The sheriff has long been charged with keeping the King's peace in this county, which in olden days — even before William came from Normandy — included the trial and punishment of criminals. Are we agreed on that?'

There were nods all around and a smirk from Richard de Revelle, who felt that his case was already won.

'But our last King Henry became disenchanted with the integrity of many sheriffs — you will remember the Inquisition of Sheriffs in the sixteenth year of his reign, which effectively dismissed them all for their corrupt behaviour.'

This time it was John's turn to smile and the sheriff's to scowl. Hubert went on with his lecture. 'Then by the Assize of Clarendon and the Assize of Northampton, he set up the visitation of the royal judges, which should come to every county at intervals of a few months, taking over the shire court from the sheriff to try those serious criminal cases which are Pleas of the Crown, not minor local appeals.' He held up his hand. 'I know what you might say, that these courts are irregular and often fail to keep to their timetable, especially in recent times. But judges are few and the distances are great.'

He stopped to drink some wine and water from a glass set before him.

'Anyway, that is the strict law, yet I well know that all over England sheriffs are still holding the Pleas of the Crown, which they should not do.'[1]

One of the barons from East Anglia, a member of the Curia Regis, broke in at this point. 'This is ancient history, Archbishop. What has it to do with these new coroners?'

Hubert did not like being interrupted, but tried to be patient. 'You know well enough that there are two different perambulations of the King's Justices around the country. In the old days, any subject wanting justice from the King had to chase him around England and

---

[1] Yet one of the provisions of Magna Carta, more than a decade later, was that sheriffs and coroners should not try Pleas of the Crown.

France. Old Henry improved that by sending the judges to the people, albeit slowly. The justices, who come, hopefully, several times a year to hold an assize in each county, deal with the serious crimes, but the Justices in Eyre, who come very much more infrequently, investigate all manner of financial and administrative problems in the land. It is those to whom the coroner's efforts are directed, to record every matter that may lead to an addition to the Royal Treasury.'

There was a silence, as not everyone understood his point.

Richard de Revelle spoke cautiously, picking his words with care as he did not wish to sound as if he was ignorant of the law which he was supposed to uphold in the whole of Devon. 'How does this distinguish our roles in prosecuting crime?'

The Justiciar leaned forward with his elbows on the table. 'Anything to do with money is the coroner's preserve — amercements, fines, treasure trove, deodands and, especially, the murdrum fine. This is why the justices at the September Eyre in Kent revived this old Saxon office — *Custos Placitorum Coronae* — Keeper of the Pleas of the Crown.'

Richard de Revelle was growing restless. 'But how do we resolve this nonsense between us, Archbishop?'

Hubert again held up his hand for patience. 'When an obvious killing takes place — let us call it homicide — and there is no doubt about the culprit, for he may be seen committing the crime or caught with blood on his knife, then the dead body is a matter for the coroner, but the criminal is the responsibility of the sheriff. He must arrest him, throw him into gaol and wait the next visit of the Justices in Assize, who will try the case, either by jury or by the ordeal of water or fire. Then, if found guilty, the miscreant can be hanged or mutilated or undergo trial by combat.'

He paused for breath and to check that everyone was paying full attention.

'But if a dead body be found, in any circumstances, where no suspect killer is known, then the coroner must hold his inquest and the village or town must make presentment of Englishry, to prove the victim is not a Norman. If they cannot do this, then the coroner must record the facts for the Justices in Eyre — not the Assize judges — so that when they come in due course, they can decide whether that village shall be amerced for the murdrum fine, however many marks they decide.'

John and Richard eyed each other across

the table, unexpectedly united in scepticism at the smooth explanation.

The coroner was the boldest in speaking first, as he knew Hubert of old. 'That is all very well in theory, Justiciar. It may have worked well enough in old King Henry's time, but since then we all know that the visits of judges to both the Assizes and the General Eyre have become so infrequent that the system cannot work as you suggest.'

De Revelle was emboldened enough by this, to weigh in with his own doubts. 'How can we accommodate all these suspects for so long? The county and the towns have to house and feed them — we will be spending more on building prisons than our taxes will allow!'

The Justiciar tapped his fingers tensely on the table. He did not relish criticism of his administration, yet he knew the dilemma that the law officers found themselves in. 'There are too few judges and too many crimes and civil cases, Richard,' he snapped. 'I appreciate your problem, but we have to live with it, in these times of financial stringency.'

Those were coded words for the profligacy of his monarch in demanding ever-increasing revenue to support his army in France.

John tried to be reasonable and conciliatory, while reserving to himself the duties with which he had been entrusted. 'Where unnatural death is discovered, I must be able to present the matter to the justices, whenever they come. I see the sheriff's point, where obvious homicide exists, that speedy solution is required — but surely, not at the cost of summary justice. The Pleas of the Crown, homicide, rape, arson and the like, are too serious for arbitrary decision at a shire or burgess court. Those places have enough less serious matters to decide, without needing to burden themselves with murder. Surely that must be judges' work?'

The argument went back and forth and no real decision was made, but an uneasy compromise appeared, based on a division between serious crimes where the miscreant was caught red-handed and those deaths where no obvious culprit was in view.

The meeting eventually broke up, with the general unsatisfactory feeling that things would probably continue as they were and that the sheriff and coroner would remain at odds with each other. John remained to join a relatively simple meal with many of those who attended the council and at last had a chance to talk with Hubert Walter. They reminisced about their time in the Holy Land, and the Justiciar also wanted to know the full details of King Richard's capture outside Vienna. Hubert listened with interest, while the sheriff glowered in the background, jealous of John's easy companionship with the man who now ran England. Others broke into the talk and soon they got down to the serious business of eating and drinking.

At the end of the meal, the Archbishop was escorted back to the Bishop's palace and John had a chance to talk to Richard. 'That was of little use in settling our problems, brother-in-law,' he said.

Richard's thin face showed his annoyance. 'We will just have to try to work together, not against each other. If only these damned judges would put on a turn of speed, our job would be easier.'

John was philosophical about it. 'We must stick to the law and not try Pleas of the Crown, however inconvenient it may be. So you carry on hanging your sheep-stealers and let the burgesses hang their coin-clippers, and leave the mystery killings to me and the judges.' Suddenly he changed the subject. 'And what about Godfrey Fitzosbern? He will live, so the brothers at St John's tell me, but you have already arrested Edgar of Topsham. That won't please his father. You'll have Joseph around your ears before the day's out.'

The sheriff banged the nearest table with his fist in frustration. 'What else could I do? The fellow has repeatedly threatened Fitzosbern, he attacked him and now it looks as if he's poisoned him! He must be put to the question, even if it does mean antagonising one of our most prominent merchants.'

'What about Hugh Ferrars, his father, Reginald de Courcy and Henry Rifford?' asked John, pointedly. 'They have all threatened Fitzosbern. Are you going to arrest and torture all of them?'

De Revelle looked pityingly at the coroner. 'Can you really see me trying to throw Lord Ferrars into gaol, eh?'

John nodded, knowingly. 'I see how your mind works, Richard. Start at the weakest and work your way up. I wonder you don't blame the poisoning on Fitzosbern's two workmen.'

The sarcasm was lost on Richard, who for a moment tried to work out some way of incriminating these non-threatening suspects. He gave up and returned to Edgar. 'He will be interrogated as soon as the Justiciar has left tomorrow, I'm too busy until then. If he refuses to confess, then he will be put to the *peine forte et dure* until he does tell us something.'

'Like Alan Fitzhay last month, whom you nearly killed?'

Richard's only response was to walk away, red-faced and angry, leaving John to march back to his chamber in the gate-house.

14

In which Crowner John
interviews an apothecary

Later that Tuesday afternoon, John went down to the Bush for an hour's relaxation. His red-haired mistress was busy with the many guests who filled her upstairs accommodation, these being the lower orders of the Justiciar's entourage, who were distributed around the town. They were all leaving in the morning and Nesta was making sure that she had collected the rent for their bed, food and drink.

While she bustled about with her two serving wenches and Edwin, the old potman, John took his ease by the fire with a jar of ale, gossiping with two old men who had once been in the Irish campaigns. He knew them well, though he had not been across the Irish Sea at the same time. One had been on the first expedition from Pembroke in 1169 and the other had been with Strongbow, the Earl of Clare, in later campaigns. They had plenty of old soldiers' tales to tell and the warmth of the big room and Nesta's best ale induced a rare sense of well-being in the coroner that he never experienced at home.

Outside, the snow had gone, but the sky was dark and cloudy. There were gusts of wind and fitful showers of cold rain, which made the inside of the Bush a good place to be. He saw no chance of bedding Nesta today, but he was philosophical about that as later he had to go home and dress up to take Matilda to the final banquet for Hubert Walter at Rougemont, another event that was improving her state of mind to a point almost approaching benevolence. He feared that the anti-climax of sinking back into humdrum routine later in the week would set her off into her usual cantankerous mood.

Eventually, Nesta found a few moments to come and sit close to him on his bench, the two old soldiers tactfully moving off in search of Edwin for refills. She pressed her soft hip against him and laid her head against his shoulder. 'Thank God the Archbishop of Canterbury doesn't come to Exeter too often,' she said. 'Though the money is welcome, the work is just too much, without an able man about the house.' She looked up at him mischievously. 'Any chance of you changing the post of King's crowner for tavern-keeper, John?'

He put an arm around her shoulders and

squeezed her to him. 'Don't tempt me, lady. The way these deaths and assaults are piling up, I might consider it. Rather than lose you, I'd certainly leave home — but as for being an innkeeper, I might drink all the profits.'

They flirted and joked for a few moments, until a yell from upstairs brought Nesta to her feet to scream back at one of her maids, who was complaining that one of their lodgers was lying dead drunk and vomiting on one of their palliasses. 'I'd better go and put the silly fool to rights!' she snapped, and ran off to settle the girl's problems.

Almost immediately, the door to Idle Lane opened and Gwyn and Thomas came in, looking damp and cold from the inclement weather outside. The little ex-priest, dressed in a frayed brown cloak, went off to order some food from Edwin, while Gwyn came and sat in the place just warmed by Nesta's bottom.

'Did you find Bearded Lucy?' demanded the coroner.

The Cornishman held out his hands towards the fire and rubbed them together vigorously. 'We did indeed — and she improved on what she told us last time.'

'You didn't do her any damage, I hope?' asked John, knowing of Gwyn's frequent over-enthusiasm.

'No, I didn't lay a finger on her. Didn't want to catch her lice, for one thing.'

'But he threatened to push her hut into the leat if she didn't talk,' said Thomas, who had appeared with two wooden dishes of pork leg and bread. Edwin hobbled up behind with a quart of ale for Gwyn and a smaller jar of cider for Thomas, who claimed that ale tasted like donkey's water.

Thomas sat at the end of the bench while Gwyn told his tale. 'The old hag stuck to her story at first, that she had sent Adele de Courcy away the second time, when the pills she gave her didn't cause a miscarriage.' He tore a piece of pork from the bone and spoke through a mouthful of meat. 'I persuaded her a bit then, suggesting she might like to spend a week or two in the South Gate gaol before being tried as a witch and burned at the stake. That didn't seem to worry her too much.' He washed down the pig meat with a great swig of ale. 'Then I punched my fist through the front wall of her miserable dwelling, probably frightening the rats inside. When I suggested that a good push would probably send it all floating down the Exe, she decided to talk.'

John was used to Gwyn building up his story to a satisfactory climax and avoided the temptation to hurry him. 'So eventually, with

304

bad grace and many vile words about my character, she admitted that she had directed Mistress de Courcy to someone who might help her more directly in getting rid of the unwanted burden in her belly.'

'And who was that?' asked John, sensing that the dénouement had arrived.

'Our favourite leech, Nicholas. It seems that he had a reputation for helping such ladies in Bristol some years ago, but one almost died and the Guild of Apothecaries there forbade him from practising his trade.'

John turned this over in his mind with interest. Nicholas might then have been the cause of Adele de Courcy's death, though it would be almost impossible to prove without his confession. If he had introduced the slippery elm into the neck of her womb, then undoubtedly, according to Dame Madge, the fatal bleeding had been a direct consequence. 'Drink up and eat your food. We've another call to make at the leech's shop.'

While they were hurriedly finishing their refreshment, John went to the foot of the ladder to the upper floor and called for Nesta. She came down and he related what Gwyn had told her. 'Have you ever heard of Nicholas of Bristol being involved in performing miscarriages?' he asked her.

She shook her head. 'No, but I suspect that

any leech might help a woman out on occasions, either for money or for pity. So it doesn't surprise me.'

He kissed her, and then hustled his two assistants out into the lane. They made their way through the narrow streets with their jumble of wooden and stone houses and crossed the road leading down to the West Gate to reach the leech's shop.

A man with a huge abscess on his face, which closed one eye and puffed up the whole of his cheek, was buying a pot of salve as they entered. 'Give that one more day and I'll lance it for you,' ordered the apothecary, as the man, groaning with pain, felt his way to the door. When it had shut behind him, Nicholas produced the tray with the platter of food, the wine flask and the silver chalice from Fitzosbern's house and placed them on his counter. Then he went into his store room behind and returned with two small wooden cages, one containing a brown rat, the other, a cat, which he also put on the bench.

John, who had come mainly to accuse him of manslaughter, was momentarily non-plussed. 'What's all this?' he demanded.

Nicholas wiped saliva from the sagging corner of his mouth with a rag. 'My examination for poison, as you requested, Crowner. I find no evidence at all. Look at these.' He poked a finger between the withies that formed the bars of the cat's cage. The scrawny tabby looked at him fearfully. 'I gave it a large piece of the fowl from the platter and then forced down more than an egg-cupful of the wine.' He turned to prod the smaller box containing the rat, which sat unconcernedly preening its whiskers. 'The same for this, though it was more difficult to get wine down its throat.'

Gwyn looked at the two animals. 'You mean they suffered no ill-effects?'

'Nothing, they seemed glad of the sustenance.'

The quick-witted Thomas questioned the results. 'How long ago did they eat the food — and how do we know that such beasts are as susceptible to poison as men?'

The apothecary lifted the two cages back to the floor behind the counter. 'I gave it to them within an hour of your coming this morning, so they consumed it at least six hours ago. Ample time for it to affect such small animals. As to the effects on humans, there is only one way to test.' He grabbed the chalice from the tray and before they could protest, drained the wine that had half-filled the goblet. 'There! If I collapse and die, then you know that I was wrong.' The trio was silent for a moment. Thomas crossed himself and watched Nicholas intently, as if to detect the first sign of his dropping into a twitching coma.

'So what was wrong with Godfrey Fitzosbern?' grated the coroner.

Nicholas shrugged. 'Either he had some poison from elsewhere, maybe other rotten food, or his affliction was an Act of God, an apoplexy or some other natural disease. It can happen.'

This was what Brother Saulf had said, John recalled, even though he considered it unusual. 'Fitzosbern may tell us himself soon, he seems to be recovering his senses,' he said somberly. 'Now then, Nicholas of Bristol, I have another serious matter to put to you.'

* * *

'Of course, he flatly denied it, it's to be expected.' John was telling Matilda of the events of the day, as they got ready for the banquet at Exeter Castle. Once again, his wife had been attended for half the day by the ferret-faced Lucille and was now arrayed in a new kirtle of yellow silk, the round neck revealing a chemise of white lawn. Huge sleeves, tight at the armpit and bell-shaped at the wrist, had tippets hanging almost to the ground. Tonight Matilda wore a white linen wimple at her throat, which framed her face under a cover-chief. This was a large head veil held around her forehead by a barbette, a linen band made popular by the old queen, Eleanor of Aquitaine.

'Did you arrest him?' she demanded, her attention torn between the latest scandal in the town and the need to titivate herself for the great occasion at Rougement.

'I'll talk to your brother about it in the morning. He's set on squeezing a confession from Edgar, but maybe it's the apprentice's master who needs a little persuading.'

'Is there any other evidence apart from that old crone's allegation that he may have tried to get rid of Adele's baby?'

John was reluctantly struggling into a tunic of dark red worsted, which had fitted him two years ago but was now dangerously tight around the belly. 'After I accused him, I got Gwyn of Polruan and my clerk to search his shop. That was a hellish task, as any apothecary's is a mass of bottles, boxes, drawers, vials and strange bits of apparatus.'

'Did they find anything?'

'In one of the little drawers there was a supply of those slips of elm bark, in a dry state. The same that Dame Madge explained were meant to swell and open up the neck of the womb.'

'What did the leech have to say to that?'

'He seemed unconcerned. Claimed that every apothecary would have such devices, because they were used for treating severe costiveness of the bowels. He says they are pushed up the fundament to help open the obstructed gut.'

Matilda looked faintly disgusted. 'I've never heard of that. You'd better check with some other leech that he's not just making some excuse.'

John had already thought of that, but he meekly thanked her for her good advice. She was in an excellent mood, having both the invitation to the banquet and plenty of material to gossip about with her wag-tongue friends at St Olave's.

The celebration at the Shire Hall in the inner ward of Rougemont went according to plan and Sheriff Richard was relieved that his lengthy preparations had led to a crisis-free event. The food was good and plentiful, the drink was copious and the general atmosphere was cordial. Musicians and mummers came to entertain the guests after the food had been cleared away, and at midnight the party was still in full swing.

People were moving around from bench to bench and table to table, so John had a chance to speak again to Hubert Walter, albeit briefly. The sheriff was attending on Bishop Marshall, so Hubert could speak frankly to de Wolfe. 'This problem with de Revelle is by no means unique. Several coroners and sheriffs are at odds with each other for the same reasons,' he confided. 'All I can suggest is that you tread carefully and let him have sufficient cases to soothe his pride.'

John nodded as he bent over the Justiciar at his place at the top table. 'I will do my best, but it can be difficult when he always takes the easiest road to settling a crime. We have such a situation in Exeter at this very moment.' He briefly outlined the rape, abortion and suspected poisoning, which de Revelle was trying to clear up by summary trial and wringing confessions by torture. 'These should be brought before the King's justices, but God knows when they will arrive next in Devon,' he concluded.

The Justiciar promised to do what he could to speed up the perambulation of the assize, but John suspected that he was pessimistic about much improvement.

The night wore on and John was glad that no one came to drag him out again to some mortal emergency. In the early hours, the guests streamed away in various stages of intoxication and Matilda took John's arm to be led back to Martin's Lane, for once happy with her lot.

Her husband, equally glad of her good mood, looked forward to a busy day ahead, wondering what fresh problems it would bring.

★　★　★

The first arose an hour after dawn, when the coroner went up to the sheriff's chamber to discuss the most recent developments in the Fitzosbern intrigue. He had called at St John's on the way and found that the silversmith was now almost fully recovered, though he was still very weak, had palpitations of the heart and strange tinglings in his feet and hands. He could speak now, but he had nothing much to say. All he could recollect was eating his meal, prepared as usual by his back yard cook. He had difficulty swallowing, as his infected throat wound was becoming more painful, but he managed to get down some of the roast fowl. Within a few minutes, he felt a numbness and tingling in his mouth and throat, which spread as a burning feeling in his belly. Then his heart began to flutter, his fingers felt numb, and he started to sweat and feel faint. That was all he remembered until he woke in the priory.

Brother Saulf stopped any further questioning at that point, but said that perhaps by the evening or next morning Fitzosbern might be well enough to be taken home on a litter to his own bed.

Now John was back in the castle keep, trying to catch Richard during his last hectic hours before Hubert Walter's procession went on its way, back to London via Southampton and Winchester. A solid phalanx of clerks and soldiers was clustered into the sheriff's chamber and even the coroner failed to push his way inside.

As he waited in the main hall of the keep for the crowd to thin, a tall figure shoved its way towards him, manhandling aside anyone who stood in his way. It was Joseph of Topsham, followed by Eric Picot, and both were in a state of agitation.

'What in Christ's name is going on, de Wolfe?' bellowed the usually serene shipowner. 'You sent me word about my son last evening and I came as soon as the town gates were opened. Is it true that this madman of a sheriff has arrested him on suspicion of murder?'

John explained what had happened and that he was there now to talk to Richard de Revelle about the matter. Fitzosbern was rapidly recovering and there was no real proof that he had been poisoned, according to the apothecary, although the symptoms and circumstances certainly pointed to it.

The thin, grey-bearded merchant grabbed John's arm. 'I must see Edgar! His mother is beside herself with worry. You are the crowner, you can take me to him. He is down below us, I suppose, in that hellhole they call a prison.'

John sensed that Joseph was in no mood to be challenged and, as one of the most powerful of the trading class in the area, he deserved attention. With a glance at the throng still milling around the door to the sheriff's office, he led the way outside and went down the wooden staircase to the ground. A few yards away were stone steps leading down into the undercroft of the keep, which was partly below ground level.

'What happened to that bloody man Fitzosbern?' asked Eric Picot as they went. 'We only have half a story.'

John told them all he knew, leaving out the allegation against the apothecary himself concerning Adele de Courcy.

'I wish whatever it was had killed the bastard, whether it be food, poison or apoplexy,' snarled the wine merchant, with a viciousness that surprised the coroner.

John stopped at the arched entrance to the

cavernous basement and looked at Picot. 'Where was Mabel Fitzosbern when he was taken ill?' he asked sternly.

The dark-haired merchant laughed easily. 'Nowhere near her husband, if that's what you're thinking. Though she had good cause to kill the swine, after all the suffering he's caused her, but she was far away.'

'I heard she went to her sister's house in the town?'

'Only for a night and a day. Then I took her back to my house at Wonford, well outside the city, where she could be rid of him. Her maid and my sister are with her, so she's well chaperoned,' he added pointedly.

John, who was quite indifferent to the morality of Mabel leaving her husband to stay with Picot, turned and went into the gloomy undercroft. The main area was empty, the damp floor of beaten earth glistening under the light of a few pitch torches burning in iron rings fixed to the walls. The further part was walled off and a low arch with a gate of metal bars guarded the entrance to the castle gaol. John loped up to the barrier and rattled the bars violently to attract the attention of the gaoler. 'Where are you, Stigand, you fat bastard?'

There was a clinking of keys and mumbling, then a dirty, grossly obese man

315

dressed in a ragged smock shuffled up to the other side of the gate, peering through at the new arrivals. 'Who's there?' he demanded.

'It's the coroner — or are you too drunk to see straight?' snapped John. Stigand, a Saxon who previously had been a slaughterman in the Shambles, was not one of his favourite people. 'Let us in, I want to talk to Edgar of Topsham.'

Grumbling under his breath, the gaoler unlocked the gate and pulled it open with a screech of rusted hinges. Wheezing with the effort of moving his ponderous body, he tramped back up the dark passage beyond the gate. 'He's there, on the left,' he grunted, waving his bunch of keys to one side.

Off the passage, half a dozen narrower gates led into tiny cells. At the further end was a larger cage, with about a dozen wretches penned in together. John recognised the reeve and two men from Torre, who stared at him with undiluted hatred.

He waved at the cell on their left. 'Open it up, damn you!' he commanded, and slowly the gaoler unlocked and pulled back the gate. Inside, Edgar sat dejectedly on a stone slab that served as a bed, below a narrow slit that admitted a sliver of daylight on to the filthy straw on the floor. The only other furniture was a leather bucket.

The apprentice jumped up and ran to embrace his father, then clasped the arm of Eric Picot, whom he looked on as an uncle. There was a torrent of speech between them all, with Edgar loudly declaiming his innocence and the other two denouncing both Richard de Revelle and Fitzosbern.

When the hubbub died down a little, the coroner managed to get in a few words. 'Did you have anything to do with poisoning Fitzosbern, if that was the cause of his collapse?' he demanded.

Edgar, already dirty and dishevelled from his hours in prison, was hotly indignant. 'Of course not, Sir John! I wish him dead, I admit, but I would try to kill him openly in a fair fight, not by poison, which is against my apothecary's oath.'

There was more in the same vein and John could not but be impressed by the lanky apprentice's sincerity. Then, rather to the coroner's surprise, there was a clanking of a sword scabbard in the passage and Sergeant Gabriel escorted the sheriff into the cell. 'I heard you were here. I came to see that no impropriety takes place,' snapped Richard imperiously.

That made little impression on Joseph of Topsham, who stepped up to de Revelle and prodded him in the chest. 'What nonsense is

317

this, Richard? You have no right even to accuse my son, let alone drag him off to gaol like a common criminal. Where is your proof?'

The sheriff deflated a little, as the ship-owner from Topsham was a powerful man in the merchant community. But he tried to bluster on for a while. 'He attacked Fitzosbern the other night and has threatened to kill him. Being a puny youth, he could not do it face to face so he used his leech's art to dispose of him by stealth.'

Joseph pushed his grey beard almost into Richard's face. 'Rubbish! That's pure speculation, to make your task easier. Tell him, John, what the apothecary found.'

De Wolfe explained, not without some satisfaction, that Nicholas had tested the food and wine on animals, had even drunk the rest of the wine himself, all with no ill-effects. 'Both he and Brother Saulf at St John's Hospital say that it could have been some natural apoplexy,' he concluded.

Richard coloured and huffed and puffed, but then John motioned him outside the cell and took him by the arm to the other side of the dank passage. 'There is something else, brother-in-law, that they had better not know yet. I now have reason to believe that Nicholas of Bristol is the one who procured the fatal miscarriage on Adele de Courcy. If he committed the one crime, maybe he is a better suspect for the other.' He did not believe this for a moment, but he saw no reason not to use it temporarily to take the pressure off Edgar.

The sheriff stared at John, who could almost hear the wheels going round in his head, as he set this information against the other powerful factions involved, such as the Ferrars and de Courcy. 'This must be pursued with vigour,' he muttered.

They went back to the cell and immediately Joseph went on the attack again. 'Unless you release my son, and certainly lift any evil threat of torturing a false confession from him, I will seek out the King, wherever he is. I shall use one of my own ships to go straight to France to petition him — and I will refuse you all my taxes and stop my ships from exporting the wool from Devon, even if it ruins me. It will certainly ruin you, when you have to account to the Westminster Exchequer for the collapse of the county revenues! And I shall seek out the Chief Justiciar to tell him what I have done.'

Richard knew that the senior trader was in deadly earnest. Not only would the taxes collapse if the main cross-channel transport was withdrawn, but Richard would personally lose money as, like John de Wolfe and many others, he had a considerable private stake in the wool-export business, which was the backbone of the local economy. He put the best face on it that he could.

'This claim of the apothecary, together with other information I have just been told, allows me to be lenient for the moment. You may take your son, but he must not leave Exeter until this matter is finally settled.'

He turned on his heel and marched stiffly away, his pointed beard jutting out like the prow of a ship. As Gabriel followed him, he risked giving John a slow wink.

★　★　★

When the last of the Justiciar's rearguard had vanished over the brow of Magdalen Street, the eastward road out of the city, Exeter seemed to breathe a collective sigh of relief, as life got back to normal. The sheriff and his constable had gone off with half the castle garrison to escort the long cavalcade as far as Honiton, but would be back by nightfall.

In the meantime, the coroner had an unusual function to perform that afternoon, a first for him. The remnants of the cargo of the ship *Mary of the Sea* had been trundled by wagon from Torre and were stored in a warehouse on the quayside, outside the Water Gate.

As coroner, he was also Commissioner of Wrecks and his duty was to view the remains of the stricken vessel, which he had done at Torbay, even though only a few planks were to be seen. Then he had to claim any salvage for the Crown, make a valuation and get a jury to decide where the proceeds were to go — though John had already made up his mind to return it to the obvious owners.

'What about the killing of those sailors?' asked Gwyn, as they strode down from the Bush to the quayside, Thomas limping along beside them on his short legs.

'That forms no part of this enquiry,' replied John. 'That was homicide and as the perpetrators are well-known, I suppose I must let the sheriff have his way, as they are already in his gaol. My only dealings with them will be to record their hanging and confiscate their property, they being felons.'

He was still uneasy about this as, originally, the miscreants from Torre were to be kept in the gaol until the Justices of Assize trundled back to Exeter. Only because of his half-promise to Hubert Walter to try to placate the sheriff was he willing to turn the criminals over to de Revelle. He consoled himself with the certainty that, whatever judicial process was applied, they would inevitably hang.

They reached the quayside and went to inspect the goods. The casks of wine and dried fruit, about forty-three in number, were stacked in a large thatched shed near the tidal landing stage slightly downstream from Exe Island. The port of Exeter was losing out to Topsham in volume of business: it was so far upstream where the river was shallower that it could only be reached by small ships at high tide. Much of the merchandise now came up from Topsham, after being off-loaded from the seagoing vessels into barges.

Gwyn had cajoled a few dozen locals to act as jury although, strictly speaking, they should have been from Torre and district where the wreck had occurred. The only other interested parties were Joseph of Topsham and Eric Picot, who were the sole original consignees of the goods aboard the ill-fated ship.

The proceedings were short and uncomplicated. Gwyn herded the mystified jurors into the shed, where they stood next to the goods under discussion. These were piled at one end, the rest of the large hut being filled with bales of wool, finished worsted cloth and sacks of grain waiting for shipment out of the Exe. Joseph and Eric stood a little away from the common folk, each with some tally sticks in their hands. Neither could read nor write, but they were accustomed to keeping an accurate check on their stock by means of notched sticks, just as a manor reeve would keep tally of all the produce of his village. As a further check, old Leonard, the clerk from Topsham, was also there with written lists of what should have come over from Normandy. De Wolfe wasted no time in getting down to business. 'All wrecks of the sea within the waters of England belong to King Richard,' he stated, in a loud voice. 'The wreck itself, if it has any value — and certainly any salvaged fittings or cargo — must be listed and valued. Then a decision is made by the coroner and his jury as to its disposal. Legally, the value should go to the royal treasury, to help the Exchequer of the Realm.'

He looked sternly at the vacant faces of the jurymen, most of them from nearby Bretayne and along the lower streets near the church of All Hallows-on-the-Walls. Bemused, they waited patiently to be told what to do.

'The vessel was completely destroyed in the gale, so there is no need to consider it further. However, much of the cargo was washed ashore, and it lies behind you.' He waved his hand at the pile of casks, and the jurymen dutifully craned their necks to look at it. 'All that remains is to prove its origin and, although all the crew perished, that can still be done easily.' He motioned politely for Joseph to step forward. Gwyn lugged the splintered length of ship's timber from a corner and displayed the crude lettering carved into it.

'Joseph of Topsham, do you recognise this plank?'

The grey beard wagged as he nodded. 'I do indeed. It is from my own vessel, *Mary of the Sea*, which was sailing from Barfleur in Normandy to Topsham.'

'And was that some of the cargo she carried?' asked John, again waving a finger.

'It was, some of it my own goods being imported. The rest belongs to Eric Picot here.'

'How much was there?'

Both merchants consulted their tally sticks again.

'I had forty-six casks and ten crates of dried fruit ordered from my suppliers in Cotentin. Only twenty-two seem to have survived,' said Joseph.

The coroner turned to Picot, and gestured for him to speak. 'Like Joseph, my imports of wine come regularly from across the Channel. This shipment would have been' — he looked down again at his tally — 'sixty barrels, of which only twenty-one are here.'

John rubbed his chin. 'So even if the goods are returned to you, you will both have lost over half your investment?'

The two traders concurred glumly. 'It will put up the price of fruit and wine this winter, I fear,' said Joseph. 'We have to make good the loss somehow.'

'And if the salvage goes to the Crown?'

Picot rolled up his eyes in his handsome dark face. 'It may not ruin me, but the loss of profit on even the twenty-two remaining casks will prevent me from being able to purchase a full cargo again for a long time.'

Joseph echoed his sentiments and John turned to the jury. 'The issue seems a matter of natural justice. These two honest merchants had goods on their way to harbour, when an Act of God, a gale, threw their ship and its cargo on to the rocks. More than half was destroyed and the rest washed ashore. My opinion, which I commend to you, is that the casks have never left the ownership of Joseph and Eric. Even the thieving antics of the villagers of Torre were but an illegal and temporary diversion.' He paused to marshal his thoughts. 'It would be different if unknown goods from an unknown wreck were scattered along the coastline. Then the crown could legitimately claim them. But here we have a known ship, every dead crewman named and the cargo patently identified. How can it be other than their property, as it never left their ownership?' He glared along the sheepish line of jurors. 'What say you?' he demanded, fixing his eye on a large man at the end of the front row.

The impromptu foreman shuffled to his feet awkwardly and gave a quick look along the line and over his shoulder at his fellows. Without waiting for a response, he said, 'We agree, Crowner.'

Before there could be any discussion or second thoughts, Gwyn herded out the jurors like a sheepdog behind a flock. Joseph and Eric came over to thank John for his efficiency and they, too, left the warehouse, after making arrangements with the custodian for the goods to be collected later. They walked back to the town gate with John, Gwyn and the coroner's clerk following behind.

The conversation moved to other matters. 'Edgar told me that he had been discussing the awful events of last week with Christina,' began Joseph. 'She is much recovered in her mind, thank God, being a resilient young woman. He suggested to her that she might still be able to recognise her assailant by voice or some mannerism, if she confronted him.'

John looked doubtful. 'She has always steadfastly denied any clue as to who the villain might have been.'

The ship-owner sighed. 'I know, and probably that is the case. But Edgar is desperate to make some breakthrough in this tragedy, both for her sake and to lift this suspicion off his own shoulders about attempting to kill Fitzosbern.'

'So what does he propose?' asked Picot, as they climbed Rack Lane to Southgate Street.

'That Christina confronts Godfrey Fitzosbern, to see if the meeting triggers off any memory.'

'He may not agree to that,' objected Eric.

'Agree be damned!' retorted Joseph. 'He must be made to agree. As a law officer, you surely have that power, de Wolfe?'

John considered the proposition for a moment. 'I don't know if I have or not,' he said frankly. 'But, by the same token, neither does Fitzosbern know so I could bluff my way to doing it.'

'What about the sheriff's approval?' asked Eric.

'To hell with him. He does his best to shelter the man because of his prominence in the guild and among the burgesses,' replied John. 'I don't see that he's in a position either to offer or refuse his consent.'

As they left to go to their various dwellings, it was agreed that John would call upon the Riffords and get Henry's approval to take Christina to Martin's Lane, when Fitzosbern had returned home from St John's Hospital.

It was now late afternoon and the light was beginning to fail below heavy rain clouds. John went home and consolidated his good standing with his wife, who showed no signs of descent from the euphoria of the past few days' high social activity. They had a meal and sat before the fire, while he regaled her with the events of the day. The last item was the business with Christina Rifford, which rather cooled Matilda's good spirits.

'I think you have all used poor Master Godfrey badly,' she said, reluctant to abandon her championship of a man who at least pretended to fancy her from time to time.

'He used his own wife more than badly,' ventured John. 'She has left him for good after the assault, according to Picot the wine merchant. I saw him give her a blow that would have felled an ox.'

Matilda clucked her tongue. 'He had been provoked more than a little. That silly apothecary's lad challenging him on his own doorstep — and the Ferrars son, grand though the family may be, had no right to attack him like that. Then he gets poisoned, no doubt by that idiot from Topsham — it's just too much.'

John tried to placate her. 'Well, perhaps if Christina says that he has no resemblance at all to her attacker, then he should be restored to favour.'

His wife seemed to approve this tactic. 'Then bring her here to me. You cannot march the poor girl up to his front door yourself. Arrange a time with Master Godfrey, fetch the young woman here and I will support her when you confront the pair of them.'

On that co-operative note, John slumped deeper into his chair and, one hand fondling Brutus's ears, dozed in front of the fire, ignoring the wind that rattled the shutters and blew cold about his feet.

15

In which Crowner John
hears a confession

As the coroner expected, Godfrey Fitzosbern
was inflamed beyond measure with the
proposition that Christina be brought to
confront him, but after some reasoned
argument, his mood subsided to grudging
acceptance.

John had left his own house after one of
Mary's substantial breakfasts and went next
door. The silversmith was not in his shop,
only the two workers, who looked furtive
and subdued when they saw the law officer.
The old man who had been looking after
the house since Mabel had left with the
maid took the coroner upstairs to
Fitzosbern's living quarters, where he found
the guild-master still in his night-tunic,
sitting slumped on the edge of his bed.

He looked pale and ill, a shadow of his
usual self — no longer the bouncy,
well-dressed man-about-town, who always
had a smile and a smooth word for the ladies.
John noticed that his hands had a marked

tremor when he held them out.

He began by enquiring after his health since leaving St John's, which set Godfrey into indignant ranting. 'I'm sick, de Wolfe, damned sick! Poisoned by that bloody madman son of Joseph. When I'm recovered, I'm going to bring an appeal against him for attempted murder.'

'But the apothecary said that there was no poison in that food and wine.'

'Nonsense! Of course I was poisoned! Within minutes of taking them, my mouth began to burn, my throat was tight, my belly was in spasm and my heart was thumping like a lunatic drummer.'

John shrugged. 'There was no sign of poison. Nicholas of Bristol showed me a rat and a cat that had been fed with them. They suffered no harm at all.'

Fitzosbern sat on his bed, his head in his hands. 'Did he give them any of that herb powder? It was either that or the wine.'

'Why not the food? That fowl may have been corrupt before it was cooked.'

'It was never in the apothecary's shop where that crazy boy could contaminate it.'

John pricked up his ears. 'So are you saying that the wine came from there?'

'Of course it did! Nicholas gave me the powder for my neck wound and said to wash each dose down with this special wine, which had a medicament in it to enhance the goodness of the herbs.'

John wondered why Nicholas had not mentioned the wine — though if it was innocent of any toxin, it did not matter.

Godfrey looked up at him. 'Did you come here only to enquire after my health?'

When the coroner explained the proposal to bring Christina to confront him, the expected violent objections materialised. It took a long time for him to convince Fitzosbern that the only way to lift the cloud of suspicion was to show that the girl had no recollection of his being the assailant. If he was innocent, as he steadfastly maintained, then it could only be to his benefit.

Eventually, Godfrey reluctantly agreed, on condition that no one else from the Rifford family was present, and no one from the Topsham family either. They arranged for her to come at the twelfth hour and John left, casting a last suspicious look at Alfred and Garth as he went out through the hot and smoky workshop, where the smelting hearth was now in full spate.

His next call was at the Rifford house, where he explained the arrangements to Henry and Christina. Old Aunt Bernice would take her to Matilda, and John and his wife would lead her next door. Edgar was at the house, and both he and Christina's father were reluctant to be left out of the deputation to Martin's Lane, but John insisted that Fitzosbern would not cooperate if they came.

The coroner went from there to his chamber in Rougemont Castle and listened to Gwyn and Thomas as they told him of a few new cases that needed his attention. The rest of the morning was spent in viewing the body of a boy who had fallen into a mill-race down near the river, and was recovered drowned on the downstream side of the woollen mill.

When John returned home, he was chagrined to find his brother-in-law there, with Matilda and Christina. The sheriff had somehow heard of the identity venture and had marched down to protest, still in his role of protector of the guild-master. 'By what authority do you think you can do this?' he demanded, standing in John's hall with his smart green cloak draped over one shoulder, to show off his yellow surcoat.

'Because I am enjoined to record the Pleas of the Crown, Richard, and rape is undoubtedly a crime serious enough to be brought before the King's Justices, not the shire court. So I am perfectly entitled to pursue my investigations, to be enrolled for the royal judges, when they come.'

As this was the deal proposed by Hubert Walter only the day before, de Revelle could hardly prohibit it, but his face conveyed the bad grace with which he gave in to the coroner. 'Let's get on with the farce, then. Fitzosbern is threatening to appeal everyone who is against him, for assault, attempted murder and God knows what!'

Matilda and Christina sat near the fire, listening to this exchange with concern. 'If this will cause Edgar and my father more trouble then perhaps I should not go through with it,' said the girl tremulously.

John held up his hand. 'It is part of my enquiry. No harm will come of it.' He turned to the sheriff, partly with the intent of diverting his antagonism. 'My officer discovered yesterday that Adele de Courcy had been recommended to the apothecary Nicholas as someone who might rid her of the child. He denies it, of course, but we found elm slips in his shop, which he claims were for another purpose.'

The sheriff's eyes lit up, he was certainly diverted by the news. It gave him a possible route to get back in favour with the de Courcys, and especially the Ferrars clan, who were accusing him of being ineffectual in finding the truth about Adele's death. 'Was there any clue as to the identity of the father?' he demanded.

'No, not a word. And we have no proof that Nicholas *was* involved, only that the old hag the woman first consulted told her to try Nicholas as a last resort.'

The cathedral bell boomed out the noonday hour from across the Close and they moved out of the coroner's house to visit the silversmith. Once again, the two craftsmen almost cowered behind their work-benches as the sheriff and coroner strode past them, half convinced that they had come to rearrest them. But the party walked on into the back room, still filled with heat and the acrid fumes from the furnace that glowed red on one side.

'Come up, if you must,' said a voice from the stairs at the back. The lower half of Fitzosbern, now dressed in a sombre tunic, could be seen going back up to his living chamber. They all followed, Matilda solicitously supporting the anxious figure of Christina. Upstairs, the silversmith stood defiantly in the centre of the room, his back against his dining table.

'What do you want of me? Let us get this nonsense over as quickly as possible to avoid embarrassing these ladies more than necessary,' he snapped. Though he was still pale and had trembling fingers, he looked better than he had a few hours earlier.

'This is the crowner's idea, Fitzosbern, not mine,' said Richard de Revelle, immediately backing out of any responsibility that might rebound on him.

John took the arm of the beautiful brunette and led her forward to face Fitzosbern. 'Take your time, Christina. Look at this man from various angles. Listen to his voice, shut your eyes, and see if any memories come back to you.'

The guild-master snorted in disbelief. 'What nonsense this is, de Wolfe! She has seen me around the town for most of her life — and recently she has been to my shop half a dozen times. We have stood together and touched hands while I fitted her bracelet. How in God's name can she not recognise me?'

Privately, John had sympathy with his views, as this was not like picking out a stranger from a crowd. But he wanted to settle her recollections once and for all, to satisfy Joseph, Edgar and Henry Rifford.

At a sign from the coroner, Godfrey turned himself through a full circle, a sneer of contempt on his face at these antics. Then Christina walked round him, and did it again with her eyes shut.

'Say nothing now, my girl. We will discuss it outside,' commanded John.

Suddenly, Christina burst into tears and sank to her knees in abject distress. Matilda rushed to her and pulled her up, her arms around her, cooing into her ear. She gave a nasty look to her husband and even her brother, as representing everything masculine who battened upon poor women, then guided the sobbing girl to the stairs and took her back next door.

John was strangely touched by his wife's tenderness, something she had never showed him in the slightest degree. As the unexpected motherliness suddenly blossomed in the hard-faced woman, he wondered what she might have been like if they had had children.

'Have you finished this stupid game?' demanded Fitzosbern dropping heavily on to a bench.

'Let's hope this is the end of the matter,' said Richard, in a placatory tone. 'I think I have some other avenues to follow in this matter.'

John had no idea what he meant by that, but they followed the women back to the house next door where they found Christina, red-eyed and sniffing, slumped on a settle near the great fireplace, with Matilda still comforting her.

'I hope you're satisfied, upsetting the poor girl like this,' she grated. 'All to no purpose, I'll be bound.'

John went over to Christina and looked down at her. 'Well, any impressions at all, Mistress Rifford?' he asked gently. She sniffed and dabbed at her nose with a kerchief pulled from the wide sleeve of her red surcoat. 'It is as he said — I know him so well, especially from visiting his shop, as I did on the night . . . the night it happened.'

John was disappointed, but not in the least surprised. 'So there was nothing at all?'

'No, not really,' Christina answered, so slowly that the keen ear of the coroner picked up a small element of doubt.

'Wait a moment — are you sure there was nothing?'

The girl looked up at him, her lovely face framed in the white linen circle of her gorget and headband. 'I told you before, I saw no one, he was behind me. But just now, something . . . not a sight, it was when my eyes were shut.' She shook her head in despair. 'Maybe it was imagination.'

'What, Christina? What was it?' he asked urgently.

'A smell — no, not even a smell. A

sensation in my nose. I don't know what it was, I can't tell. But something reminded me — and upset me.'

She promptly burst into tears again and the newly discovered maternal spirit in Matilda fiercely drove the two men away.

★ ★ ★

The fortnightly shire court was due to be held on the next day, Friday, and John spent the early part of the afternoon in his cramped office, getting Thomas to go through the cases that were due to be heard. Though presided over by the sheriff, except when the King's Justices were in town, the coroner was entitled — and usually obliged — to be present for a variety of reasons, either financial or administrative.

As his reading ability was still negligible, he depended on Thomas to record all matters as they came up, then to relay them back to him in the court. As the crook-backed little clerk droned through the list of fines, amercements, attachments, securities to attend trial and other odd jobs that came to the coroner, Gwyn stood at the window opening, carefully touching up the edges of their swords on the soft sandstone of the sill. He regretted the rarity of chances to use his own weapon, these days, compared to when he and Sir John had so often been in the thick of fighting, but he kept his blade sharp in the hope that some unexpected combat might come along.

A few moments later, while the coroner and his clerk still worked their way through the court list, Gwyn's rhythmical honing was interrupted by the sound of shouting down below. From the narrow window slit, when the shutters were fully open, a view could just be glimpsed of a few yards of the road leading up to the steep drawbridge below. The yells of protest and the deeper answering commands of soldiers drew his eye to a tight group of people who rapidly passed his narrow line of vision.

The Cornishman, his unruly hair looking like a hayrick in a gale, turned to the coroner. 'That's odd. Gabriel and a couple of his men have just brought in those two men from Fitzosbern's workshop — and I'm sure that young Edgar and his apothecary master were with them.'

De Wolfe looked up quickly. 'Brought in? You mean they were under guard?'

'Looked like it, especially from the noise they were making.'

John got to his feet and picked up his mantle from where it lay across the table.

'What's that bloody man up to now? Maybe that's what he meant this morning when he said something about following other avenues.' He slung the cloak over his shoulders and made for the stairs. 'You'd better come with me, Gwyn — and you can check through the rest of those tasks for tomorrow, Thomas. I must go to see what new mischief the sheriff is planning.'

They tracked the prisoners to the under-croft of the keep and found them herded together in the cold and dismal area outside the gateway to the gaol. The place always reminded John of a cave in which he had once hidden during a French campaign, with a musty smell of old dampness, and water slithering down green walls. At the back of the low hall, under one of the arches of the vaulting, the obese gaoler, Stigand, was stoking a small fire with logs.

The sergeant-at-arms was in charge of the party, looking slightly awkward as he knew of the difference in views between sheriff and coroner over this affair. 'Sir Richard himself sent the orders to bring them in, Crowner not more than an hour ago,' he said apologetically.

Of the four detainees, the only one to be voluble was Edgar of Topsham, whose voice Gwyn now recognised as that of the protester

341

he had heard from the window. Struggling vainly in the grip of a soldier, his dishevelled fair hair fell even more into his eyes than usual. 'He promised my father that this was all over!' he shouted at John. 'This is the second time that the sheriff has dragged me here. What does he hope to gain from it?'

There was a new voice from behind them, as Richard de Revelle had come in unnoticed, together with Ralph Morin, the castle constable. 'I hope to gain the truth at last for my patience has run out with these milk-and-water methods.' He turned to the coroner. 'The failure of Mistress Rifford to give any credence to these unjust accusations against Godfrey Fitzosbern, and that news you gave me about this apothecary here, make me determined to resort to more effective methods.'

The words sounded ominous in the dank, echoing vault.

'I fail to see what you hope to achieve, when there is no useful evidence from anywhere,' retorted John, who had a good idea what the sheriff was planning.

'I hope to gain confessions Crowner! Your methods of seeking a solution to these crimes that have plagued Exeter this past week and more have led nowhere. So now let me try my way, if you please.'

He turned imperiously towards the two workers from the silversmith's shop, who stood cringing behind the apothecary and his apprentice. Their forebodings of this morning, when the law officers came into their workshop, seemed to have come true with awful rapidity. 'Alfred and Garth, I seem to remember you are called that,' he began menacingly, 'I suspect you, either one or both, of being the ravisher of Christina Rifford. Will you now confess to that crime, eh?'

Both broke out into a cacophony of denial, Alfred falling to his knees on the cold slime of the floor, pleading with his hands outstretched. The sheriff impatiently gestured to the guards and they silenced the two men, dragging the older one to his feet and giving the boorish Garth a clout over the head to close his mouth.

'Right, we'll see if we can loosen your tongues in a little while. First, I want to deal with you, Edgar of Topsham.'

At a sign from Morin, Gabriel pushed forward the young apprentice to stand right before de Revelle. He began his usual loud protests, but the sheriff slapped him across the face with a gloved hand. 'Be silent when I speak to you, boy. Your father is not here now to threaten me.'

John, silently observing his brother-in-law's tactics, felt that he was building up trouble for himself, unless he knew something of which John was unaware — which he doubted.

'I am sure that our master silversmith was poisoned, whatever the leech here says, and I'll question that opinion very soon. It's thanks to our good brothers at St John's that he failed to die — but attempted murder carries the same penalty as one that is successful.' He leaned forward to put his face close to Edgar's — the young man was as tall as the sheriff and their noses almost touched. 'I think that you gave that poison to Fitzosbern — you, the one who repeatedly threatened him, publicly said you wished him dead and who attacked him on his own doorstep.' His voice rose to a crescendo, reverberating from the uncaring stone walls. 'Who else is a better candidate for murder, eh?'

Edgar flew off into his usual denials, this time tinged with terror as he saw the way things were going. But the soldier behind him gave him a kick in the back of the knees that sent him sprawling before the sheriff.

Richard stepped back a pace and looked down at the young man. 'If you refuse to confess, then the law approves a process called *peine forte et dure* to encourage the memory — and no one need be a scholar to know what those words mean.'

Edgar, on his hands and knees in the mire, looked up in unbelieving horror. 'You cannot torture me — my father will petition the King, he told you so himself.'

'The King is over the seas. It would take your father months to get there and find him — if he ever returned, as his ships seem prone to sink. And we are here today. I do not have months to spare.'

John felt it was time to intervene. 'Attempted murder is a Plea of the Crown, like rape. You cannot take it upon yourself to deal with the matter in this summary fashion.'

Richard sneered at this. 'Wrong, Sir Crowner! Fitzosbern has appealed Edgar for attempting to kill him and it will be heard in the shire court tomorrow. No jury of presentment has sent the matter for trial by the King's Justices, so the Crown has no say in the issue. And today I am not trying the case by the Ordeal, I am merely seeking evidence in the form of a confession by the accepted means of *peine forte et dure*. So you have nothing to do with it, John, until you attend his trial by battle or declare him an outlaw if he

345

should escape.' He stood back triumphantly.

John chewed over the words in his mind but could find no valid objection in law, much as the Crown authorities disliked the King's courts being bypassed by these residual old laws.

De Revelle waved a hand in the direction of Stigand and his fire. 'Take him over there. That offensive old swine should soon have his branding irons hot enough for his purpose.'

Now screaming, rather than objecting, Edgar was dragged by two soldiers across to the archway, where the flabby gaoler was wheezing with the effort of thrusting some heavy iron rods into the red heart of the fire.

The sheriff sauntered over, leaving the two silver-workers trembling with awful anticipation of their own fate as they stood between their own guards. Nicholas of Bristol, who had not uttered a word since being brought in, stood pale-faced but impassive as he watched what was going on around him, his mouth hanging grotesquely as spittle leaked out unheeded.

At the fire, Ralph Morin was speaking in a low voice to Gabriel, his sergeant, then went to talk quietly to the sheriff, who shook his head impatiently. Like John de Wolfe, Morin thought this afternoon's adventure ill-advised — not because they had any particular aversion to torture, which had been an accepted method of law enforcement for centuries, but because he thought that it was a mistake to use it against the son of such an influential person as Joseph of Topsham.

Gabriel, acting on his commander's instructions, stepped up to Edgar and, with a single movement, ripped his tunic from neck to waist and pulled the torn cloth from his shoulders.

Now shrieking and twisting in the grip of two soldiers, who impassively held him by each arm, Edgar was pushed nearer the fire, as Stigand pulled out an iron and examined the red-hot cross-piece at the tip with professional interest. He spat upon it and heard the sharp sizzle with apparent approval.

'I ask you again, and for the last time, Edgar of Topsham,' intoned the sheriff, 'do you confess to poisoning Godfrey Fitzos-bern?'

'Jesus Christ help me! How can I confess to something that never happened?' screamed the young man, as the repulsive-looking gaoler, satisfied with the heat of his iron, advanced on with the glowing cross aimed at his left breast.

'We have plenty of irons — and a good fire,' observed Richard, casually.

The branding iron was close enough for the

few hairs on the young man's chest to begin shrivelling, when a shout came from behind. 'Stop that! It was not him. He knows nothing of it.'

Stigand hesitated and the sheriff motioned him to go back. Everyone turned and looked back towards the entrance, where Nicholas of Bristol stood between his two captors.

'Let Edgar go free. I will confess to the poison — and much more besides.'

* * *

In the approaching dusk, John walked with Nesta along the top of the city wall, between the towers of the South Gate and the Water Gate. She had wanted some air after a heavy day in the tavern and they strolled along the rampart behind the battlements like a pair of young lovers, she holding his arm. The weather had improved and, though cold, there were breaks in the cloud towards the west, where the setting sun threw a pallid pinkness over the countryside. Nesta had a green scarf wrapped over her head and a thick dun woollen cape down to her feet. 'They'll hang him, of course?' she asked, as they stopped to look at the sunset.

'Most likely — or perhaps instead they will use combat or the ordeal. Someone will have his life, one way or the other,' agreed John, slipping his arm around her. 'But it's a strange situation, and depends on what happens with Fitzosbern.'

They stood silently for a moment, looking down on the vegetable gardens inside the wall, which belonged to the houses in Rock Lane. To their right loomed the huge mass of the cathedral, and elsewhere within the walls, tightly packed houses of all shapes and sizes threw up smoke into the evening sky, punctuated by the towers of the fourteen churches.

'I don't understand all this, John,' she said, at length.

He began to explain the complexities of the day. 'Allegedly the silversmith was going to appeal Edgar for attempted murder, according to de Revelle, though I don't know whether to believe him. Then, when Edgar was about to have a false confession burned out of him, Nicholas couldn't bear it and confessed himself.'

Nesta squeezed his arm. 'He must have been very fond of the lad, to give his life for him.'

'I think many apprentices brew up a father-feeling in their masters. Anyway, the bloody sheriff couldn't lose — he says he knew that Nicholas would confess before

Edgar was tortured, but again I don't believe him. I think he was just lucky, for if he had branded Edgar, Joseph would have gone berserk and caused much trouble for de Revelle.' He paused and hugged her tightly. 'If the apothecary had stayed silent, Edgar would have made a false confession and been convicted. Now the sheriff has Nicholas instead, but I don't think he cares who it is, as long as he has someone.'

They turned and looked over the new battlements, away from the city to the south and east. Almost thirty feet up, they could see for several miles across country, their eyes following the diverging roads to Topsham and Honiton. Just below them were hedged fields going down into the little valley of the Shitbrook, named since Saxon times for the town's effluent that escaped under the wall into the stream.

'What exactly did Nicholas confess to, John?' asked Nesta.

'He said that he had put extract of wolfsbane, sometimes called monkshood, in the wine he gave Fitzosbern. It should have killed him, but presumably he didn't swallow enough.'

John's mistress shivered a little, he wasn't sure if from the cold or the thought of being poisoned.

'So his so-called test for poison was false?'

John gave a lop-sided grin. 'The jest was on me, my love. Only a fool like me would take a suspected poison to the poisoner for analysis!'

'He never gave the cat or rat any of it, then,' she said.

'No, and his dramatic gesture of drinking the suspect wine was play-acting. He'd naturally emptied the poisoned chalice and refilled it with good liquor.'

'But he couldn't have known that the silversmith was going to come to his shop that day,' she objected.

'It must have been an opportunity taken on the spur of the moment. He hated the man and here was a chance to dispatch him. It could have been attributed to the effects of his neck wound, in which case the blame would have fallen on Hugh Ferrars. I'm sure the last thing Nicholas contemplated was that his apprentice would be accused.'

They walked on further towards the mass of the South Gate, above fields of Southern-hay.

'And you said that he did it because Fitzosbern was virtually blackmailing him?'

A gust of wind moaned from the east and John pulled his black leather hood more tightly on to his head. The long point at the back balanced his great hooked nose and made him look more than ever like some great bird of prey.

'It was like this. Nicholas claims that Fitzosbern was the father of Adele's child. She had been seduced by him when she visited to order her wedding jewels. Nicholas says that he boasted that Adele wasn't at all keen on Hugh Ferrars, it was to be a marriage of convenience forced on her by her father.'

'A seduction by Fitzosbern of one of his lady customers — that surely must have a counterpart with poor Christina?' said Nesta worriedly.

The coroner shrugged. 'That's another matter. God knows, there'll be trouble in plenty when the first part becomes known to the Ferrars family and de Courcy — whether it's true or not!'

They reached the mass of red masonry that was the side of the South Gate, under which was the town gaol run by the burgesses. Instead of going down the steps to the ground, John and Nesta turned and strolled slowly back the way they had come.

'I still don't follow why Nicholas wanted to kill Fitzosbern. He seems such a weedy, inoffensive man, a bit like his apprentice.'

'When Adele came, at Bearded Lucy's suggestion, to see Nicholas, he refused to

352

consider interfering with her womb. He told her he had had terrible trouble in the past because of that and had sworn never to help women again.'

'So what happened?'

'Adele went in desperation to Fitzosbern, saying that if she had the child — or even when her swelling was noticed, as it soon must be — there would be a scandal that would undoubtedly swallow him up as well. It would probably cost him his life, if she knew the Ferrars, she said. So he came to Nicholas and threatened him with exposure and ruin if he refused to procure Adele's miscarriage.' Nesta stopped and turned against John, burrowing under his cloak to cling tightly to him, her head against his chest. 'How could he ruin him?' she asked, her voice muffled as she cuddled up to him.

'Nicholas had for a long time been trying to advance himself in the Guild of Apothecaries, but Fitzosbern, as a senior guild-master in Devon, had been opposing him. He even tried to get him thrown out of the guild, which would mean he could no longer stay in business.'

She raised her pretty round face, but still clung to him. It was a welcome change to get away from the tavern and have him to herself. Dallying with a fellow in the twilight made her remember the carefree days of her youth, even though, that was little more than a decade ago. She spun out the time by keeping the story going, though, as an ardent if discreet busybody, she was keen to hear it anyway.

John pulled her tightly to him and carried on with the tale. 'In looking into Nicholas's worthiness for being a guild member, Fitzosbern sought opinions from other masters all over the West Country. He found that the leech had been forced to leave Bristol some years ago, because he was under suspicion for being an abortionist.'

'Nicholas admitted all this?' Nesta sounded incredulous.

'He had no choice, once he was launched on his confession. He knew he was doomed so he seemed ready to expurgate himself. Fitzosbern discovered that he had run away from Bristol, evading appeals from damaged women and their families — and the indignation of his fellow apothecaries. He lay low for a year or two, then appeared here in Exeter.'

The Welsh woman shivered again and they began walking back towards the steps near the Water Gate. 'So unless Nicholas did the deed for Adele, Godfrey threatened to expose his past sins in Bristol?' she observed.

'Yes, he had little choice. Though with those elm slips in his shop, I wonder if he is as innocent as he makes out. Maybe he helps other women in Exeter, too. Anyway, the attempt went horribly wrong and she died, which gave Fitzosbern an even greater hold over him.'

'What actually happened to poor Adele?'

'He wasn't very forthcoming on that, but it seems there was massive bleeding almost straight away. She had come to his shop after he had sent Edgar home for the night. He emphasised that, to keep the lad in the clear, and I believe him.'

'So how did the body get to St Bartholomew's churchyard?'

As they started down the steep steps, John going in front in case she slipped on the uneven stones, he replied, 'The lady died of a bloody flux within the hour, he said. He waited until after midnight, then took his pony from the stall in his garden and draped the body over its back, covered with a blanket. He led it through the small lanes in Bretayne where few people are likely to ask questions, then slid it off behind the wall of St Bartholomew's.'

They walked silently between two garden

plots into Priest Street and then into Idle Lane, where the timber and thatch inn stood to welcome them.

'What happened to Edgar after all today's excitement?' she asked, as they stopped at the tavern door.

'He was released and went home to his father. He was desolate at the thought of Nicholas never leaving gaol, except to go to his death.'

'And Fitzosbern? What of him now?'

John followed Nesta into the warmth of the inn and helped her off with her cloak. 'I'm not sure if he has committed any offence at all. Maybe inciting Nicholas to induce a miscarriage is a crime, but he can deny that if he wishes. There's no proof apart from the leech's word.'

'The sheriff doesn't seem much bothered about proof, it seems,' observed Nesta, with bitter sarcasm. She led the way to a table near the fire and motioned to Edwin to bring some ale. A few regular patrons were in the tavern, but after the bustle of the Archbishop's visitation, it was quiet at this early hour of the evening.

They sat talking for a while, the locals already aware of the day's drama concerning the best-known leech in town — John often marvelled at the speed with which news travelled in Exeter.

As it grew dark, he rose reluctantly to his feet, his head almost brushing the rough-hewn beams that supported the upper floor. 'I'd better be on my way, Nesta,' he said, in the mixture of Cornish and Welsh which they used together when alone. 'Mary is cooking boiled beef tonight and my dear wife will be agog to hear the latest scandal straight from the horse's mouth.'

She saw him to the door, where he kissed her goodbye and set off in the gloom for Martin's Lane and married bliss.

16

In which Crowner John
unsheaths his sword

The break in the clouds that John and Nesta
had seen from the town wall had rapidly
widened and, by mid-evening, there was a
clear sky and a biting frost, unusually severe
for the eleventh day of December. The wind
had dropped and the sky was a brilliant mass
of stars, with a half-moon just rising in the
east.

Like most of the folk of Exeter, John was
indoors, glad of hot food, mulled wine and a
good fire. Both he and Matilda wore woollen
tabards over their surcoats and thick stockings with their soft house shoes. With no glass
in any window in the city, they depended on
linen screens and shutters to keep out the
wind and rain, but the all-pervading cold
required heavy clothing and a good stock of
fire wood.

The boiled beef, with turnips and cabbage
had been good: Mary was as efficient in the
kitchen hut as she was in other things. Over
the meal, John had told Matilda all the details

of the afternoon with some relish, enjoying the chance to demolish the reputation of their next-door neighbour whom his wife had always championed. Even now she fought a rearguard action on his behalf, but without much conviction.

'At least, this nonsense about Fitzosbern being the attacker of Christina Rifford is banished — the girl recollected nothing to his discredit. As to the fathering of Adele's child, these are only the allegations of that murderous apothecary,' she objected.

She was silent for a moment, a sobering thought having struck her. 'To think that I visited him last month when I had that pustule on my eyelid — he could have poisoned me, for all I knew.'

John pushed aside his empty platter and laid his dagger on the scrubbed table. 'Nicholas would have no reason to lie — his confession means the end of him, so what could he gain by distorting the truth?'

She grumbled under her breath, but had no answer for this.

They moved to the fire and sat eating a couple of hard apples each, which served as dessert. John had some of Picot's wine warming by the fire and he poured Matilda a liberal draught, using a thick wine-glass, one of a pair he had looted in France some years before. Usually they used pewter or pottery cups, but tonight he felt like celebrating with the luxury of glass. It was true that the breakthrough over the death of Adele de Courcy had been made by the sheriff, against John's better judgement, but he consoled himself with the thought that the result had been quite unexpected by de Revelle, in spite of his claims that he had tricked Nicholas into confessing.

'What will happen next, John?' asked Matilda, her curiosity overcoming her pique at having her flirtatious neighbour discredited.

He looked at the leaping flames through the cloudy glass above the wine. 'I strongly suspect that the Ferrars and Reginald de Courcy will dictate that. When they hear of Nicholas's revelations, our silversmith will be in great trouble. I think Nicholas is safer in the castle gaol than Fitzosbern is in his own house.'

'They wouldn't harm him there, surely. That attack by Hugh Ferrars was on the spur of the moment, when he was deep in drink.'

'He's often deep in drink, so I've heard. But you're probably right. They may appeal him together with Nicholas for conspiring to procure a miscarriage, leading to manslaughter.'

'Could you be involved in this, as crowner?'

'Yes, I'm supposed to be present at all appeals — but if my inquest jury made a presentment of homicide, then it should go before the King's Justices when they come.'

Matilda groaned. 'Oh, we're back to that old business. I thought Hubert Walter had settled this dispute between you.'

'He couldn't, not if his damned Assizes don't appear often enough.'

Suddenly, their fireside chat came to an abrupt end. With an awful feeling of familiarity, John heard a commotion in the lane outside. Simultaneously, Brutus, who had been eating supper scraps in the back yard, dashed through the passage, barking furiously.

John leaped up and hurried to the vestibule, where Mary had run through to grab the big hound by the collar. 'There's a riot in the lane!' she announced. 'Men with torches.'

John grabbed his round helmet from a bench and slammed it on his head. He hauled his sword out of its scabbard, which was hanging on the wall, and pulled open the front door. As he expected, the rumpus was coming from his left, where the silversmith's shop lay. Bobbing flares added to the light from the farrier's torches, carried by half a dozen men who were crowding around Fitzosbern's door, shouting for him to come out, with oaths and some of the foulest language even John had ever heard.

As he ran along to the shop, he saw one man kicking lustily at the front door, though it was far too sturdy to be shifted, having been built to protect a valuable stock of silver. 'Stop that, damn you!' he yelled. 'I command you to stop, in the name of the King. This is a riotous assembly!'

It was the first thing he could think of. On reflection later, he was not sure if a coroner could prohibit a breach of the King's peace but, as he was the most senior law officer in the county after the sheriff, it seemed a reasonable thing to do in an emergency.

He reached Fitzsobern's door and pushed aside the fellow who was battering upon it, whom he recognised as Hugh Ferrars's squire, the one he had clouted on this same spot a few nights earlier.

As his eyes became accustomed to the dimmer light, after staring into his own fire, he saw that Hugh was in the forefront of the group, with his father behind him. He was more surprised to see Reginald de Courcy, too, alongside Hugh, with two others who were presumably squires or friends of the older men.

'Get out of the way, de Wolfe,' snapped de Courcy. 'This is none of your business.'

Hugh's squire attempted to push John aside, but the coroner gave him a punch in the belly that doubled him up in pain. 'For the love of Mary, what do you all think you're doing?' he roared. 'This is a civilised country, and there is a shire court tomorrow morning. If you have accusations or appeals, take them there.'

Hugh Ferrars moved forward to stand right against the coroner. He had been drinking, but did not appear out of control. 'We have heard what the leech said, Sir John,' he shouted thickly. 'This bastard in here was the one who seduced my woman. He's cuckolded me to make me the laughing stock of the county.' Even in the turmoil of the moment, John noticed that his only concern seemed to be the loss of his own pride, not the death of his fiancée.

Now de Courcy elbowed his way to the coroner. 'I want to hear this Fitzosbern admit or deny his guilt, Crowner. If he admits it, I will kill him. If he denies it, he can fight me any way he wishes — and if he wins, he was innocent.'

John glowered at the angry group, whose mood was getting nastier by the minute. 'You cannot settle matters like this. Go to the sheriff. It is his responsibility to mete out justice in Devon, not yours.'

'He favours Fitzosbern too much — he has shown that all week.'

This new voice, deep and authoritative, came from Guy Ferrars, standing behind the others.

John, standing higher than the others from his position on the doorstep, as well as from his own stature, lifted his long sword in the air. 'Lord Ferrars, you, above all others here, must know this is sheer foolishness. Tell your son and your friends to go home — or at least go up to Rougemont to petition Richard de Revelle.'

Ferrars shook his head. 'We want to see this villain and hear what he has to say from his own lips. It's a wonder that Henry Rifford is not here with us. He must have similar scores to settle with the evil bastard.'

Exasperated beyond measure, John yelled at the top of his voice, 'I tell you again, you cannot profit by this. For God's sake come to your senses and go away! If he is in there, he will not come out. And this door is too stout for you to break down.'

'Then we'll fire his house!' yelled another young man, who seemed to be a more drunken companion of Hugh Ferrars's. He waved his flaming rush torch, as if to throw it

364

at the closed shutters of the shop.

'I'll smash the bloody door for you,' yelled the squire John had punched. He rushed at the coroner, his sword pointing at John's heart. The coroner parried it with a clash of metal on metal, the man's blade sliding harmlessly down to strike the hilt-guard. Simultaneously, John lifted a foot and kicked him as hard as he could in the groin. Though he had only a house shoe on his foot, the squire screamed as the blow crushed his testicle and he fell back doubled up in pain.

'Stop this, I command you!' John bellowed. 'You'll hang for attacking the King's officer.'

He swung around just in time. The man who had been standing with de Courcy, a hulking fellow wearing a shoulder cape with a hood, lunged forward with a long dagger and struck at him. John twisted to avoid the thrust, but heard the blade rip through the cloth of his tabard and felt the prick as it nicked his side just above the waist.

With a roar, all the fighting reflexes learned in twenty years of battle sprang into action. This was no time for parleying or mediation, his life was now in danger.

As the man stumbled past him with the momentum of the dagger blow, John whirled round and, using the massive broadsword with two hands, whistled it in an arc through the air to land squarely on the back of his assailant's neck.

Gwyn's honing of his blade on the window-ledge of the gate-house must have been very effective, as the spine was cut clean through and only the windpipe and skin on the front prevented the head from parting company from his body. The man fell to the floor jerking spasmodically, a torrent of blood from the big neck arteries jetting on to the mud below the doorstep.

There was a sudden silence in the lane. Nothing could have been more effective in quelling the small mob than the sight of a man spilling his life blood into the mire.

De Courcy, presumably the victim's master, bent down and rolled the body on to its back. 'You are bleeding, Crowner,' said Guy Ferrars, in a subdued tone.

John, who had stood immobile since striking the mortal blow, looked down at his left side and saw a growing stain of blood spread across his tabard. He pulled it aside and put a finger into a small hole in his tunic, ripping the linen widely apart. 'It's nothing but a scratch,' he grated, looking at a one-inch slash in his skin, just above belt level. A few inches nearer the mid-line, and the dagger would have killed him. He stepped down from the doorstep, walked a few paces towards his house, then turned to face the silent throng. 'There'll be no inquest on this one, I assure you, for there's no other coroner but me. But I doubt anyone will contest that it was a justifiable homicide.' He held his side to reduce the bleeding until Mary could tie some rags around it. 'I advise you all to disperse quietly. Go home — or if you still feel strongly about Fitzosbern, then go to the castle and have it out with de Revelle. There's nothing here for you.'

He turned and walked away, leaving the group of protesters to pick up their dead and decide what to do next.

★ ★ ★

Unusually for her, the sheriff's wife was in residence at Rougemont that night.

Eleanor de Revelle detested the bare, draughty quarters used by Richard in the keep, merely a pair of rooms joined to the chamber where he carried on all his business. They had manors elsewhere in Devon and the aloof lady far preferred country comfort there to the Spartan facilities of the castle at Exeter. But this weekend the visit of Hubert Walter had demanded that she be at her husband's side, so she had grudgingly suffered several nights of discomfort in a bed that, she strongly suspected, was often occupied in her absence by other women.

This night, she was huddled under three woollen blankets and a bearskin, only her thin nose poking out into the cold, damp air of the lofty circular bedchamber. Richard was lying on his back beside her, snoring gently, after having lain on her and performed his husbandly duty some time before. To her, it was a sexual assault more than making love, but she had the impression that he did it more from a sense of duty than to satisfy his lust. He lived in Exeter most of the time, coming back to Tiverton never more than once a week, an arrangement which suited her well. It seemed to suit Richard also, as being the best way to manage a marriage that had certainly been one of political and financial convenience.

They had gone to bed early, as after a good meal, there had been little left to occupy them. Conversation was even scarcer in this household than in the coroner's. It was still a couple of hours before midnight and a shaft of light struck through a crack between the shutters from a moon now high in the icy heavens.

Almost asleep at last, Lady Eleanor heard, with annoyance, a tentative tapping on the door. She tried to ignore it, but it came again, this time more insistent. Her husband's snores never broke their rhythms, so with some satisfaction — and far more force than was needed — she nudged him in the ribs with a bony elbow. It took a couple more jabs to wake him, but eventually she got him sufficiently out of his stupor to call a testy 'What is it?' to whoever was knocking.

His manservant, a dried-up old Fleming who had been with him for years, put his head tentatively around the door, a flickering candle in his hand. He had more than once interrupted de Revelle in amorous acrobatics in that bed, and was always cautious of entering, even though he knew it was m'lady who was there tonight.

'There are men who say they must see you on a matter of greatest urgency,' he announced.

'Is there a rebellion in the county? Has the King returned?'

The old man looked confused. 'No, sir. Not that I know of.'

'Then tell them to go to hell or come back in the morning.'

'One is Lord Guy Ferrars, sir. And the other Sir Reginald de Courcy.'

At these words Richard shot out of bed. 'Sit them in my chamber, give them wine. I'll be there in a moment.'

The Fleming shuffled out, leaving the candle-holder on a shelf. When his wife turned her head, she saw Richard struggling to get a tunic over his night-shirt, then sitting on the low mattress to pull on tight breeches and shoes.

'What's going on?' she demanded.

'God knows — but if it's Ferrars and de Courcy together, it'll concern that dead woman of theirs.'

The sheriff reached his office in record time to find the two Ferrars, de Courcy and Hugh's squire standing stiffly around the fireplace, where the old servant was trying to stir some life into the smouldering logs.

'De Revelle, you have to do something about this situation,' snapped Lord Ferrars, with no greeting or preamble.

The sheriff needed no guesses as to what situation he meant. 'But what more can I do? We have the man who caused the death of your daughter, Reginald.'

The group moved toward the sheriff almost threateningly. 'He was but a tool, some wretched leech!' snarled de Courcy. 'We know now that he was forced into it by that swine Fitzosbern. He is the one we want for retribution.'

Hugh Ferrars threw up his arms dramatically. 'She's dead — my Adele is dead! That bastard took her flesh and then her soul!' His voice was thick and he swayed a little, obviously from more mead and cider taken since he had left Martin's Lane.

His father pushed him aside impatiently, the squire steadying the younger man while Guy Ferrars returned to the attack. 'We'll not rest until he is brought to justice one way or the other. De Courcy is bringing an appeal against him for conspiracy at your court in the morning. And Hugh and I are demanding that he be brought before a jury to present him before the King's Justices at the next Assize.'

'But you can't do both!' protested Richard.

Ferrars jabbed his fists on to his sword belt and stared pugnaciously at the sheriff. 'Where does it say that two different persons cannot bring different charges, eh?'

De Revelle was silent. He didn't know the answer to that.

'Your coroner suggested that we come to you. He said I should bring an appeal of homicide against Fitzosbern, though I don't want money compensation, I want his life.'

Richard silently cursed his brother-in-law for sending this bunch of troublemakers to him, whom he could not send packing, but to whom he must pay every deference if he wanted to keep his job.

'You've seen John de Wolfe tonight?' he asked

'More than seen him, we've fought him,' muttered Hugh Ferrars. 'And he beheaded de Courcy's bailiff for our trouble.'

Richard sat down heavily behind his desk. This was getting too much for a man dragged from his sleep not five minutes ago.

The story was told and they came round again to their ultimatum. 'I want Fitzosbern arrested and put in your gaol to be brought to the shire court on my appeal,' demanded de Courcy.

'And I want him arrested on a Plea of the Crown to stand trial before the judges. He can choose combat or be hanged, I don't care which,' said Guy Ferrars, almost in a shout.

'That would need presentment from a coroner's jury,' objected Richard.

'What's the problem? The inquest de Wolfe held was only provisional. He didn't know then how she died, nor who did it. So he can open his inquest again and the jury can commit that swine to the justices.'

Hugh staggered away from the support of his squire. 'Cut the bastard's throat, I say! Quicker and surer than all this lawyers' talk.'

His father ignored him. 'I want him arrested, de Revelle. I don't want any argument, if you want to stay sheriff of this county.'

De Courcy nodded vigorously. 'At the very least, he must be brought before the court and made to account for his involvement. Tomorrow will be as good a time as any.'

Guy Ferrars agreed. 'So we want him arrested tonight.'

De Revelle stared. 'Tonight? Impossible!'

'Why not? It's long before midnight. Does the administration of this county not function in the dark?' asked de Courcy sarcastically.

The sheriff pleaded for good sense. 'What earthly good will it do to turn out guards, get them down there and drag him back at this hour? There's nowhere he can go in a closed city. And why should he? He knows nothing of your desires to get him locked up. The morning will do just as well.'

They argued for a while, suspecting that the sheriff still desired to protect the master silversmith. Eventually they conceded that a few hours would make no difference to the outcome, once Richard had promised to send down men-at-arms at first light to bring Fitzosbern up to the shire court, which began its session at the ninth hour.

With a sigh of relief, de Revelle watched the two noblemen leave his chamber, the squire half dragging the drunken son behind

373

them. He stumbled back into the bedroom and hauled off his outer clothes again, cursing Fitzosbern, his brother-in-law and everyone else involved in the affair.

He rolled shivering into bed and grabbed his wife for a little warmth. 'God, woman,' he muttered, 'your feet are as cold as your heart.'

17

In which Crowner John
takes a dying declaration

The Shire Hall stood in the inner ward of Rougemont, a plain building with a stone-slated roof. It was a large hall, like a barn, with a wide door on one side. The interior was bare, apart from a raised wooden platform across one end. On this were a few benches and stools for the officials, clerks and other functionaries and observers who came to the sessions. When the King's Justices came, the place was spruced up a little, with high-backed chairs for the judges and some banners and hangings on the wall above the dais.

The witnesses, jurors, accused, guards and sightseers had to mill about on the floor of beaten earth and this morning they were there in their usual abundance, restive at the delay in the start of the proceedings.

Usually Gabriel, the sergeant-at-arms would march across from the keep ahead of Ralph Morin, the constable, followed by the sheriff and the coroner, with a priest and a few clerks at the tail end. But this morning there was still no sign of them long after the distant cathedral bell had tolled nine.

They were in the keep, arguing heatedly with some other citizens.

'So where is he, de Revelle? Your promises are worthless!' declaimed Lord Ferrars, red in the face as he strode up and down in frustration.

'We demanded last night that you arrest him there and then. Now the devil has flown!' shouted Reginald de Courcy.

Richard tried to stem the growing storm. 'He may be here somewhere in the city — because he was not at his house, it doesn't mean that he's absconded,' he pleaded. Then he turned on the castle constable, in a typical attempt to shift the blame. 'This is your responsibility, Morin, it was you who sent men to arrest Fitzosbern.'

The big constable, an impressive figure with his forked grey beard and huge moustache, was not one to be browbeaten by his immediate senior. 'I did exactly as you commanded, sheriff,' he said evenly. 'At dawn, you asked me to send guards to arrest him. That was the first I heard of the matter. That he was not there is no fault of mine nor of my men.'

De Revelle turned on the sergeant as an

alternative target. 'Why could you not find the silversmith, eh? Did you look well enough?'

Gabriel stood at attention and replied, stolidly, 'The door was locked, sir. We hammered on it and eventually the old cook-servant came. He said no one was there. Both the craftsmen were in your gaol and the old man said that his master went out early last evening.'

'Where was he going?'

'He said he didn't know and that it wasn't his place to ask. His master was heavily cloaked and carried a large bag, which he thought was one in which he kept money and some silver.'

'There was no one else in the house?' demanded Ferrars.

'Not a soul, sir. The old man said that the maidservant of the departed wife had come earlier to collect some clothing for her mistress. His master was angry with her, but eventually let her take what she wanted.'

'You searched the house?'

Gabriel nodded. 'From top to bottom — and the yard, the sheds, the pigsty, the kitchen. We couldn't have missed as much as a mouse.'

De Courcy glared at the sheriff. 'You see? He must have got wind of the rumours. God knows, there were plenty blowing around the town yesterday. The whole of Exeter must have known what that leech confessed to.'

'Everyone in Devon must know by now that the bastard seduced my woman,' blurted out Hugh Ferrars, still obsessed with his loss of face over his fiancée's infidelity.

John had remained silent throughout the tirade that had erupted when the complainants found that Fitzosbern was not at the court, but now he spoke out in his usual practical fashion. 'What's to be done? That's the thing. Has he left the town since the gates were opened at first light?'

Ralph Morin rocked his great head from side to side. 'Very unlikely. As soon as the sergeant reported him missing, I sent his men around the walls to question the gate-keepers. No one had seen Fitzosbern leave. He's a well-known man and I doubt he'd have slipped through unless he was disguised. There's a man-at-arms now with the watchmen at every gate to look out for him.'

'And his two horses are still in the livery stables,' added Gabriel.

Guy Ferrars wagged a finger at the sheriff. 'You'd better find him, de Revelle. This virtually confirms his guilt, if he has taken fright and tried to escape.'

'Maybe he has sought sanctuary in one of

the churches,' suggested de Courcy. 'There are enough of them, God knows.'

The priest on today's court duty interjected solemnly, 'It would have been reported to the Archdeacon if anyone had taken refuge. Unless it's happened in the last hour or so, there is no news of a sanctuary seeker.'

Richard turned again to the constable. 'Morin, turn out every man you can spare from the garrison. They are to search every corner of the town to find this man.'

Ralph sighed under his breath, but saluted the sheriff and strode out to do his bidding.

'There's nothing we can do without a defendant, thanks to you, de Revelle,' snarled Guy Ferrars. 'We may as well go and join in the search, if he is still in the city. It's a small enough area within the walls — he must be here somewhere.'

Angrily, he turned on his heel and marched out, his son and de Courcy following, leaving the mortified sheriff to get on with the remnants of his court.

★ ★ ★

It was neither men-at-arms nor watchmen who eventually found Fitzosbern, but a small boy and his dog. Between the east end of the cathedral and the town wall, recent excavations had been made to improve the water supply that had long benefited the church authorities. More than twenty years ago, the Chapter had caused a lead pipe to be laid from St Sidwell's, half a mile beyond the East Gate. According to an ancient legend, Sidwell was a noble virgin who had been martyred just outside the city by having her head lopped off with a scythe. Where she fell, a spring of pure water issued forth and it was this that the cathedral used for their supply. It came in a deep trench around the town wall through Southernhay and burrowed beneath it half-way between the East and South Gates, the nearest point to the cathedral Close. It ended in St Peter's Fountain near the west front of the cathedral, from where a branch pipe went across to St Nicholas Priory, which took a third of the water. The townsfolk of Exeter got none of this, relying on wells in their gardens and water-sellers who came around with carts and donkeys carrying casks from outside wells and the river.

Due to new building and disturbances of the ground within the city wall, the soft lead pipe in its trench was frequently damaged, so the Chapter had recently built a stone-lined passage just below ground to protect it and make it accessible for repairs. This ran for a hundred paces from the inner face of the wall, with a small access door built in a low archway at its foot.

Just before noon, when the shire court had finished its session, a ragged eight-year-old urchin from a porter's family in Milk Lane was playing with a mongrel. He was throwing a rolled-up piece of rag in lieu of a ball for the dog to chase and bring back to lay at his feet.

One chance throw sent it to fall within the archway to the aqueduct. This time the animal failed to return, but set up an incessant barking, its muzzle pointing into the archway. The lad ran up and was surprised to see the wooden door ajar — usually when he played there, it was tightly closed.

He pushed the dog aside, then walked down the four steep steps to see the body of a man a few yards up the low tunnel. It was slumped on the narrow floor, the head propped against the wall, the face covered in dried blood. The urchin, young as he was, felt sure that the man was dead.

He had seen dead men before and was more intrigued than frightened. Stepping down on to the new stones of the culvert floor he went up to the body when, to his surprise, the man groaned and partially opened one eye between swollen, bruised lids.

He muttered something unintelligible, then the eye closed and he seemed dead again.

The lad turned and ran out of the arch, ball and dog forgotten. He streaked across the open ground to the nearest garden, where a man was hoeing end-of-season weeds from his vegetable patch. This belonged to the last house in Canon's Row, the northern limit of the Close, where the prebendaries lived. The boy grabbed the arm of the man and pulled him, babbling excitedly about a wounded man near the town wall. The gardener, a young vicar choral, one of the junior priests who carried out most of the canons' duties in the cathedral, tried to shake the lad off, but soon realised that he was in earnest.

He followed the boy across the wasteland, still with his hoe in his hand and the mongrel barking happily about their feet. One look into the water conduit was sufficient for him to see the seriousness of the situation. He bent low and moved up to the injured man. 'I think he's dead, boy,' he said, after putting a hand on the victim's chest and looking into his face in the dim light.

'He moved and made a noise just now,' offered the lad.

The vicar waited a moment, but saw no movement. He was a nervous young fellow and did not wish to get mixed up in what looked like homicide.

'I must get help — raise the alarm,' he exclaimed, and ignoring the boy, ran back to Canon's Row. He had a vague idea of the law and knew that when a crime was discovered the First Finder — which was now himself — had to raise the hue and cry. He was from a village near Torrington and knew that in the countryside the person to be notified was the manor reeve or bailiff but here, in the big city, he was not sure as to what should be done.

He solved the problem by hammering on the doors of the last four canons' houses, in all of which lived assistant priests and servants. Soon men were running out of the doorways until a dozen or more were crowding around the vicar, who still brandished his muddy hoe.

When he told them of the emergency, they streamed across the rough grass towards the culvert arch and confirmed that there appeared to be a bloody corpse down in the tunnel.

The urchin, determined not to be left out of the drama, yelled that the man was alive a few minutes ago and had made a noise. One of the older servants from the second house slipped a hand under the victim's blood-stained mantle. 'He's still warm, for sure.'

There was a pause. 'But I can't feel his heart beating.'

There was an agitated debate about moving the presumed cadaver. Most of the crowd advised against it until someone in authority came along.

'Who do we call?' asked the First Finder, anxious not to be fined for failing to carry out the correct procedure.

'Ask Thomas de Peyne,' suggested one man. 'He's the coroner's clerk. He lodges in the third house from the other end of the row. He'll be back from the shire court for his dinner by now.' A servant boy was dispatched at a run to fetch him and, a few moments later, Thomas came at a fast limp down Canon's Row to see what was going on. Rather self-importantly, he passed through the crowd, who stood aside deferentially to let him get to the arch. He clambered awkwardly down the steps, his lame leg hindering him, then moved up the passage more easily. The victim's face was unrecognisable, due to the caked blood smeared all over it and the swelling and bruising of both eyes, nose and lips.

'Give me a cloth, someone,' he commanded, feeling an unusual sense of superiority as a representative of the law.

A man up above grabbed the rag the dog

had been chasing and dipped it in a puddle of muddy rain-water, before passing it down to the coroner's clerk. Thomas used it to rub away some of the blood from the face and immediately, in spite of the swelling, recognised the victim. 'It's Godfrey Fitzosbern, the master silversmith!' he called back to those clustered on the steps under the little arch. 'He's been murdered!' he added dramatically.

As if to contradict him, the corpse groaned again. One arm twitched and moved slightly across the body.

'I told you so!' yelled the urchin triumphantly, from where he crouched at the foot of the steps.

There was consternation among the onlookers.

'What shall we do?' worried the First Finder. 'He's so badly injured that if we move him, he may die — and then we will get into trouble with the sheriff and the coroner.'

There was a chorus of agreement. 'Let him be, until the law officers come. Let them take the responsibility.'

Thomas was also unsure what to do. His quick brain ran through the options and decided that even though the man was not yet dead he was almost certainly going to die, so they may as well call the coroner first.

'Send across at once to Martin's Lane for

Sir John de Wolfe,' he ordered imperiously. It was not often that he had the chance to be the centre of attention and his ego blossomed, repressed as it had been since he was disgraced in Winchester.

Fitzosbern seemed to have relapsed into his death-like state and Thomas crouched anxiously at his side while they waited for the coroner to appear. He had a sympathetic nature, born of suffering his own disabilities, and he hoped that the silversmith would survive — or if he didn't, that he would die without further pain.

Within ten minutes, a scattering of the murmuring crowd around the arch and heavy feet on the steps told of Sir John's arrival together with Gwyn, who had been eating with Mary in the back yard kitchen.

Thomas moved further up the conduit beyond the injured victim, to make room for the two large men. 'He groaned and moved a little a few minutes ago,' he reported, 'but he's said nothing sensible.'

John took the dirty wet cloth and wiped the silversmith's mouth clear of blood and mucus. As he did so, the tongue came out and feebly licked at the moisture. 'Get me some water,' yelled John. Although a pipe lay only inches away there was no means of getting into it, so someone had to sprint to the nearest house to get a jugful. Meanwhile, John was continuing to clean the rest of the face and speaking loudly into Fitzosbern's ear in an attempt to get a response. When the water came, he held it to the man's lips and though most dribbled down on to his chin and chest, some entered his mouth, where it provoked a fit of spluttering.

'He's choking,' observed Gwyn dispassionately, as he crouched on his haunches at the wounded man's side.

The second attempt at drinking was more successful and Godfrey managed to gulp some water between coughing spasms. Then he said his first coherent word. 'More!'

His right eye opened, the left being completely closed by its puffed-up lid. He stared blearily at the coroner. 'De Wolfe!' he whispered.

'Who did this to you?'

Fitzosbern managed a miniscule shake of his head. 'Didn't see — dark. Where is this place?'

He drank again as John told him he was in the cathedral culvert.

'Not here . . . not hit here. Can't remember . . .'

John turned to Gwyn and Thomas. 'Let's try to sit him up, his neck is bent, no wonder he chokes when he tries to drink.'

They attempted to lift him to set his back against the wall, but Fitzosbern let out a strangled croak of agony. 'My chest — oh, Christ!' A moment later, he gagged and a massive flow of blood erupted from his mouth, landing on his cloak, the remains dribbling down his chin and neck. 'He's punctured a lung, his ribs must be broken,' diagnosed John, from his long experience of battle casualties.

'He'll not survive this,' muttered Gwyn.

John bent closer to the silversmith, whose only good eye had closed again. His breathing bubbled weakly through the blood in his windpipe, and when Gwyn felt the pulse in his neck, it was thready and irregular. 'He's going, I reckon,' he said gravely.

Thomas began crossing himself and muttering the Last Rites in Latin over the moribund figure.

The coroner bent close again. 'Fitzosbern, you are dying, man. Do you understand?' The one eye opened and there was a weak nod. 'You cannot say who attacked you?' Again the head moved sideways and back for an inch. 'In the certain knowledge that you will not recover, have you any confession to make? There is a priest here, who can give you absolution.' He thought it kinder not to mention that the priest had been unfrocked.

Godfrey's mouth worked, but almost no sound came out. John bent closer, but could not understand any of the words. He tried a different method. 'Listen to me. Were you the cause of Adele de Courcy being with child?' There was a weak nod. 'And did you force Nicholas of Bristol to procure a miscarriage?' Another nod.

The one visible eye rolled up, showing only the white between the slit in the lids. 'Hurry up, he's going,' warned Gwyn.

'And did you, Godfrey Fitzosbern, ravish Christina Rifford?

The eye rolled down, there was a jerk of the body and a sibilant croak, louder than before. 'No, never!'

At that, another gout of blood rolled from between his lips and, with a great sigh, the master silversmith went limp and his head fell limply on to his chest.

'He's gone, God rest his soul,' whispered Thomas, who all this time had been intoning the Office for the Dying and passing his hand endlessly between his forehead, chest and shoulders.

The coroner settled back on his heels in the narrow passage and looked at his officer. 'Well, Gwyn, who did it?' he asked.

18

In which Crowner John
examines some wounds

For want of a better place, the body of
Fitzosbern was taken to Martin's Lane and
laid on the floor of his back workshop. The
furnace was cold in the deserted house. The
two workers were in the castle gaol, Mabel
had eloped and the cook-servant had
returned to his son's home in St Sidwell's, as
he no longer had an employer.

An hour or so after Godfrey had died, John
de Wolfe, his brother-in-law Richard de
Revelle and Ralph Morin stood over the
body, with Gwyn, Thomas and several
soldiers in the background. 'He confessed,
you say?' asked the sheriff, greatly relieved
that Fitzosbern had solved several of his
problems by dying. He no longer had to try
to protect the leading guild-master and the
pressure from the Ferrars and de Courcy was
now off, as their prime suspect had been
satisfactorily dispatched.

'He made sufficient agreement to my
questions, in the presence of witnesses and in

the knowledge that he was beyond hope of recovery, so that makes it a valid dying declaration,' said John carefully.

De Revelle frowned as he sensed the coroner's caution. 'The questions were what?'

'Was he the father of Adele's child and did he insist on the abortion. He agreed to both.'

The sharp eyes of the sheriff locked with John's. 'What else?'

'He denied raping Christina Rifford.'

De Revelle thought for a moment, then shrugged. That was a lesser worry to him, as Henry Rifford, though he was a Portreeve, was not in the same power class as those campaigning over Adele's death.

'You will hold your inquest on him, I suppose?' he asked loftily.

'Later this afternoon. The jury will almost all be vicars, choristers and servants from the canons' houses. We know we have a Norman corpse, so no presentment is involved.'

The sheriff had a sudden thought. 'The death was not on Church ground, was it?'

'No. Although the water conduit belongs to the Chapter, the land is just outside the cathedral precinct, so belongs to the town.' Neither man was sure whether to be relieved or sorry that, if any culprit were found, the case would not be handled under ecclesiastical law.

Richard de Revelle left them to their examination of the corpse and returned to Rougemont with his soldiers. Gwyn undressed the body, so that they could better see his wounds. 'He has a crushed face, for a start,' said the Cornishman, feeling the crackle of shattered bone under the left cheek, the skin of which was purple and swollen. 'The left ear is torn and there are lacerations and bruises all across the left side of the scalp.'

When they stripped off the tunic and undershirt, they found the chest covered in bruises, mostly of a long rectangular shape. 'These marks with sharp edges look like blows from a post or stake,' mused John. 'Some of those on the head have the same shape, about an inch and a half wide.'

Gwyn pressed the left side of the chest with his big hand. The ribs indented along a line running up to the front of the armpit and blood-stained froth issued from the dead lips. 'His chest is stove in, as if someone has stamped on him.'

Thomas, squeamish about such bloody matters, had gone to the bag that had been alongside the body and was searching inside it. 'Money, both silver and gold — and some solid silver cups and ornaments,' he reported, marvelling at the wealth that lay under his fingers. At twopence a day salary, this was more than he would earn in several lifetimes.

John looked over at the valuables his clerk was displaying. 'Make a full inventory of that, Thomas. An inquest will have to decide later on whether it is forfeit to the Crown because of his possible felony in conspiring to procure a fatal miscarriage or whether it should go to his relatives. Mabel is still his wife.'

Gywn looked at the Fitzosbern treasure with indifference. 'All it does is prove that the attack on him wasn't robbery. That narrows the field quite a bit.'

They turned the body over and saw a number of shallow parallel scratches over the shoulders and on the buttocks. There were further similar red lines on the backs of the thighs and calves, all running in the long axis of the body.

'Let's see those garments again,' growled John.

Gywn took them from the pile on the floor and they spread them out on the floor of the front shop, where the light was better.

'Yes, there's dirt and tearing in the same direction on the back of the tunic,' the coroner pointed out. 'Especially on the breeches and hose.'

Gwyn threw the clothing back into a heap. 'So he's been dragged over rough ground?'

John nodded. 'That's what he meant when he said, 'Not here'. Though he lost his memory after being struck on the head, he knew he'd never been in the pipe passage, so the attack must have been elsewhere.'

Thomas had been listening in fascination, eager to be a part of the big men's discussion. His nimble brain thought of something. 'Would he have bled from those wounds?' he asked.

Gwyn looked at him as if a cat had suddenly developed speech. 'Of course, you fool! Cuts on the scalp ooze blood like the very devil.'

'Then would not the assailant himself be blood-soiled?' suggested the clerk.

Gwyn looked at his master. 'Maybe, I suppose. Or maybe not.'

The hawk face of the coroner looked dubious. 'These wounds have been made by some kind of club, even if it be a fence-post or a length of firewood. If held at arm's length, the splashing of blood might not be sufficient to reach the attacker.'

Thomas was not yet ready to abandon his theory. 'But if he then had to manhandle and drag the victim a long way, he might well get bloodstained.'

Gwyn reached out grabbed the priest by the neck of his brown smock and shook him.

'Well done, little scribbler! Now all you have to do is to go around Devon and find someone who has blood on their clothing. Maybe you should try in the Shambles, to see if a slaughterman is the culprit!'

Deflated, Thomas went back to the treasure bag in a sulk.

John was not quite so dismissive as his officer. 'If this is not robbery with violence, then we have only about five suspects who would wish to see Fitzosbern dead. So perhaps we need not look at the whole of Devon to see if we can find bloodstains.'

Thomas came back with a rush, eager to justify his suggestion. 'I'll seek out servants in each household, Sir John. I can get into places unobserved, as no one cares about me. I can see if there is any suspicion of blood at each place.'

John gave one of his rare, rationed smiles at the clerk's enthusiasm. 'Very well, Thomas, you do that — but only after you've listed those valuables and after you've recorded the inquest on your rolls.'

19

In which Crowner John
holds another inquest

The gaol in Rougemont was full, the filthy cells all occupied. The gross custodian, Stigand, was panting more than usual, as he staggered up and down the arched passage under the keep, doling out stale bread and water and collecting the stinking leather buckets that were the only sanitation.

In the early afternoon, there was a diversion, as the castle constable came down with the sheriff, the coroner and a priest from the cathedral to put the two silversmiths to the test. Torture was an accepted way of extracting confessions, just as a conviction for a crime led either to hanging, combat or the Ordeal.

Gwyn of Polruan and Thomas came with John de Wolfe, the former merely as a spectator but the clerk was there to record the event for the coroner's rolls, in case the matter ever came before the King's Justices.

The two suspects were dragged out of their cells by two men-at-arms, as the wheezing

Stigand would have been hard-pressed to drag out even a sheep. Dirty and dishevelled, they were a pathetic sight, though the younger Garth had a certain sullen defiance about him that was in marked contrast to Alfred's abject terror.

Rusty shackles rattled at their wrists and ankles, far different from the elegant silver bracelets they were capable of making. They were hauled across the muddy floor, their reluctant feet skidding in the slime.

'Which one do we do first, sir?' whined the gaoler, hardened by years of service into a callous indifference to the suffering he witnessed or inflicted almost every day.

Richard de Revelle flicked a bored finger towards the older workman. 'To save my time, take him. He'll break far faster.' Babbling with fear, Alfred fell to the ground, in attempted supplication to the sheriff, who pointedly turned his back on the man as the soldiers dragged him across to an alcove on the further wall.

'It's obvious that poor Godfrey Fitzosbern's denial of this ravishment was true, so it must be one of these knaves,' he declaimed to John.

His brother-in-law scowled at the lack of logic in Richard's words. 'Why 'poor' Godfrey, all of a sudden?' he demanded. 'He confessed to conspiring to a fatal miscarriage.'

The sheriff clucked his tongue reprovingly. 'Is that such a crime, eh? Who of us can honestly deny a little adultery now and then? Not you for sure, John. And what might you do if your pretty innkeeper got with child — or that comely merchant's wife down in Dawlish?'

The coroner's face darkened at this: although his liaison with Nesta was almost public property, he thought that he had been more discreet about his occasional dalliance with Hilda down at the coast. How the hell did Richard know of it? Though John could easily even up the score, as only last month he had caught the sheriff in bed with a whore.

The screaming behind them reached a crescendo and they turned to watch Alfred being laid out for the *peine forte et dure*. This took place in a shallow bay in the stone wall, arched over by vaulting. The alcove was about eight feet wide and a stout hook was embedded just above floor level into the supporting pillar at each end.

The men-at-arms held the victim on the ground, wriggling like an eel, while Stigand managed to bend himself enough to drop the ankle shackles over one hook. With much puffing and blowing, he then hooked the wrist chains over the other, so that Alfred was stretched across the mouth of the alcove, lying on his back. The party of observers moved slowly up to the weeping, wailing and terrified man, and stood looking down at him dispassionately.

Privately John thought this process a piece of useless witchcraft, like the Ordeal, but it was approved by Church and State alike. The fact that confessions extracted under the duress of exquisite pain were as often false as they were true seemed no hindrance to their effectiveness in improving the conviction rate.

Richard de Revelle took a step nearer, the hem of his long green tunic almost brushing the craftsman's chest.

The priest from the cathedral chanted something incomprehensible under his breath and made the sign of the Cross in the air. Thomas de Peyne followed suit, three times in rapid succession, almost dropping his precious writing bag into the mud.

'Alfred, son of Osulf, do you confess to the carnal assault and defilement of Christina Rifford?' asked the sheriff, almost conversationally.

The man stopped his tumble of beseeching, pleading words long enough to deny it. 'No, sir, of course not, sir! I never so much as touched the good lady, as God is my judge!'

'He's not your judge here, my man. I am your judge today.'

Both the canon and the Coroner looked sharply at Richard, for different reasons. He was claiming precedence over both the Almighty and the Royal Justices, but they decided to stay silent.

'I did nothing, sir. How can I confess to something that never happened?' Alfred's voice cracked with hysterical fear, but the sheriff stepped back and motioned for the soldiers to commence.

At the foot of each green-slimed pillar lay a pile of thick metal plates, roughly rectangular in shape and red with rust.

'If you persist in your innocence, then we must jog your memory,' said de Revelle, nodding at Ralph Morin, whose opinion of this process was similar to John's. Many fighting men were uneasy with these cold-blooded antics in hidden dungeons. However, he had no choice but to motion to one of his soldiers, who bent and lifted one of the iron slabs, weighing about fifteen pounds.

'Place the first one on his breast,' commanded the sheriff. The plate was lowered on to Alfred's chest, resting from his collarbones down to his belly. Though uncomfortable, there was no perceptible

400

effect and the older man kept up his noisy protestations of innocence and his entreaties for mercy.

'Another!' ordered de Revelle, and the other man-at-arms moved to obey.

'If this fellow confesses, what will you do with the other?' asked John, with a trace of sarcasm.

'Give him the same treatment, of course,' snapped the sheriff. 'No doubt they were both in it together.'

When the second iron was lowered on to his chest, the skinny Saxon gasped and his exhortations stopped as he made the effort to breathe against the weight of thirty pounds pressing down on his breast-bone. As the third slab was balanced on the others, he became dark in the face and his lips had a bluish tinge as he wheezily tried to get air into his lungs.

Stigand, his drooping belly hanging down over his wide belt, stood with hands on hips, watching the process with an expert eye. 'This one will not last a quarter of the hour, sheriff,' he said critically. 'He's skinny and his ribs will crack under the next plate, mark my words.'

Ralph Morin held up his hand to stop the next slab being laid. 'Best get him to confess while he's still conscious or you'll just have a corpse and nothing to write on the crowner's rolls,' he advised.

Richard stood at the head of the failing Alfred. 'Well, man? Are you ready to confess?'

Spots of blood were breaking out in the whites of the man's eyes and his purplish tongue was swelling between blackening lips. Unable to speak for lack of breath, he nodded feebly.

Triumphantly, the sheriff turned to his brother-in-law. 'See? He admits it! This method is far better than all your snooping and poking about with your poxy parchments, John.'

There was a sudden jangling of chains behind them as a scuffle began between the remaining guard and Garth, who was as massively built as Ralph Morin.

They swung round to see the younger smith dragging the man-at-arms towards the alcove. The other soldiers ran to seize him, but he shouted, 'Let the old man up! He did nothing. It was me! Let my friend go — it was me, I tell you.' His big face was deadly pale, as pale as it would be at the end of the rope that he must know would now be his inevitable fate.

The faces of the onlookers reflected their varying reactions to this sudden development. The sheriff wore a self-satisfied smirk, the coroner seemed unconvinced and Stigand looked disappointed.

'Do you know what you're saying, boy?' John rasped. 'You are not just moved by pity for your fellow worker?'

Garth's expression was now impassive and resigned. 'It was me all right. That girl preyed on my mind ever since she came to the master's shop some weeks past.'

'So how did it come about, then?' demanded John, still not sure of the truth of the younger man's confession.

'The young woman left our shop just before we closed. I was burned up with desire for her, so I followed her to the cathedral. At first I had no intent to have my way with her, only to look at her from a distance, to see that face, those full lips. But the way her hips swayed, the curve of her breast — I lost my senses. When she left through the little side door, I followed — and outside, in the darkness, my wits gave way altogether . . . '

The passion in his voice as he relived those moments, convinced John, but as Alfred seemed now on the verge of death, the constable interrupted to send one of his men to displace the iron plates, while they settled this new twist in the story.

'So were you in it as well, you evil swine? I suppose this Alfred took his turn with the poor girl, eh? They're both in it, didn't I say as much, John?' cried Richard de Revelle, self-satisfaction oozing from every pore.

'Not as well, I tell you,' shouted the deep voice of Garth. 'It was me on my own, see. Not him. The old man is past ravishing, though his eyes still fancy a pretty woman.'

Richard drew on his soft leather gloves nonchalantly. 'Perhaps, but I'll hang both of you next week, just to make sure, I can't believe any of the lies that you rabble give me.'

This was too much for the coroner, even though he was used to the sheriff's arbitrary sense of justice. He drew him aside and muttered, close to his face, 'You have no authority to hang them, Richard. Rape is a Plea of the Crown, you know that well enough. I let you waste time with this charade here to get your confessions, but they must be tested before the King's court.'

Richard waved a hand dismissively at the coroner. 'The shire court has been good enough for centuries and it's the same gallows at the end of it. Why are you so obdurate, John?'

'Because the King's law is the law. The families have the right to speak and to choose either compensation or death.'

Ralph Morin came across to interrupt.

404

'What are we to do with these men? The older one is surviving though he'll not get his breath back inside an hour. Are we to press the younger one?'

De Revelle was annoyed at the coroner's interference, but could hardly torture a confession from a man who had already proclaimed his guilt. He waved a hand at Stigand, who still stood by his fire with the branding iron in his hand, looking vaguely disappointed at the turn of events. 'Take both of these vermin back to their cells. I'll decide later what's to be done with them.'

The guards led the two men away, Alfred still gasping for breath and the doomed Garth stolidly silent. As they passed close to where Gwyn was standing, his bulbous nose wrinkled and he sniffed noisily. He moved to the coroner's side and murmured into his ear in Cornish-Welsh, to keep it confidential, 'That smell on them. It's surely the acrid fumes from that silver furnace hanging about their clothing.'

John looked at his officer blankly. 'What's that supposed to mean?'

'Remember when Christina Rifford confronted Fitzosbern, she hesitated about some familiar smell in connection with her ravisher. Maybe Fitzosbern had that same stink upon him as those men have, from living near that furnace — but it came from Garth, not Fitzosbern.'

The coroner nodded. 'You may be right, Gwyn. I'll ask her when we next meet. It might explain her uncertainty, which worried me at the time. Though, with Garth's confession, we have all we need — assuming it's true,' he added cynically.

Gwyn pulled the end of his luxuriant moustache as an aid to thought. 'I reckon it's true enough. No young man would falsely let himself in for the gallowstree, even to save a friend.'

With the sheriff glaring at them suspiciously for speaking in a tongue incomprehensible to him, the group broke up and made their way into the castle courtyard. Ralph Morin asked John what would happen next about Fitzosbern's death. 'An inquest first, in two hour's time. Though that will not take us very far in discovering who beat him to death,' replied John. 'My clerk Thomas is looking into it now,' he went on, as they strode over the frost-hardened mud towards the gate-house. 'Fitzosbern's injuries bled a great deal and we need to look at certain persons and places to see if fresh stains can be found.'

They parted inside the arch of the main gate, and the coroner and his henchman climbed to the cramped chamber high above the guard-room. Here de Wolfe was surprised to find Eric Picot waiting for him, muffled in a long, dark green cloak, the hood thrown back to reveal a rich red lining.

John pulled off his own cloak and sat behind his trestle table, motioning the wine merchant to the only other stool, while Gwyn hauled himself up on to his favourite perch on the window-sill.

John looked expectantly at Picot who, his swarthy face set in a troubled frown, began hesitantly, 'I wanted to tell you something before the inquest begins on Godfrey Fitzosbern. For me to say it openly at the inquisition may cause an injustice — and might also expose me to anger and perhaps even violence.'

John sat hunched behind his table with arms outstretched to grasp its edges, a puzzled look on his dark face. 'Why should this be, Eric?'

The other man continued to look uneasy. 'What I want to say may lead to suspicion of certain persons. That may be quite false, but they will still blame me for it, whether it be true or not.'

The coroner looked past the Breton to catch Gwyn's eye, but his officer merely raised his bushy eyebrows and lifted his shoulders.

John returned his gaze to Picot. 'You'd better tell me what you know and then I'll judge what to do about it,' he suggested.

Picot hunched forward on his stool, hitched his cloak up on his shoulders, then pulled off the close-fitting felt cap that covered his curly black hair. 'Last night I decided to call on Fitzosbern, now that he was recovered from his poisoning or whatever it was. About three hours before midnight I went to his house, next to yours.'

'And why did you do that? You are hardly friend enough to enquire after his health.'

'I went to plead with him to release his wife.'

John frowned his deep frown, the old crusading scar on his forehead whitening as the skin furrowed. 'Release her? What do you mean?'

'Not to oppose us pursuing an annulment that would allow Mabel and me to marry. She had left home for ever and was living at my home in Wonford, but we needed her freedom to become man and wife.'

'A difficult ambition, Eric. Most marriages offer freedom only when one partner enters the grave,' said John sonorously.

Gwyn thought that he spoke with too much

feeling to make it a casual observation, and Matilda's face swam briefly into his mind.

'I know it's difficult, John. An expensive process, with appeals to the King, to Canterbury and perhaps even to Rome. But it was the only route open to us.'

'Until today, with Godfrey's death,' commented the coroner with no apparent irony.

The wine merchant shrugged resignedly. 'I didn't even contemplate that last night when I stood before his house. But, in any event, I got no answer there. I banged on his door endlessly and waited for a long time, but there was no response, no light behind the shutters. So I went away, despondent.'

The coroner waited expectantly until Picot continued. 'I left Martin's Lane, walked towards the cathedral and entered the Close. The moon was out and there was more light from those flares outside the farrier's.'

John interrupted, 'You were going home, across the West Front of the cathedral, then through the lanes to Southgate Street?'

'Yes, but as I crossed the Close, I saw two men in the distance, in front of the canons' houses. By then, I had turned down the path in front of the great doors of the cathedral and they were going back towards Martin's Lane.'

He paused, then launched himself into the

most difficult part of his story. 'They didn't see me, I'm sure. I always worry about footpads at night, so I stood still behind a great pile of earth from a newly opened grave until they passed, looking over my shoulder at them.'

'And who were they?'

'Undoubtedly one of the men was Reginald de Courcy — and the other the younger Ferrars, the one they call Hugh.'

There was a pregnant silence in the chamber.

'You are sure of this, Eric?'

The dark head nodded emphatically.

'As I said, there was a clear moon — and as they passed near your house, the yellow light from the farrier's torches fell upon them. I have no doubt who they were.' He rubbed a hand over his face in agitation. 'As to why they were there, I have no comment. They may well have had legitimate business, but the fact is that they were hurrying at night from the place where the injured man was found next morning.'

Picot shifted uneasily on his stool. 'That's all I have to tell you, but de Courcy and Ferrars, even if they have nothing to hide, would be ill-disposed towards me if they knew I had told you about this.'

The coroner pondered a moment, 'At the

inquest, I can ask them about their movements last night. If they admit being in Canon's Row at that time, there is no problem. If they deny it, then it's their word against yours. Two of them to your one. And they might demand to know who challenges their denial.'

Gwyn rose from his seat at the window to ask a question. 'Can anyone else back up your claim?'

'I saw no one else at that moment. There was a beggar and a drunk further on, towards Bear Gate, but they would be no help as witnesses, even if they could be found.'

John stood up. 'I'll do my best to keep your name out of this, but I can't promise it, Eric. It depends on what happens at the inquest. You'll be there, no doubt?'

The wine merchant nodded unhappily. 'This has released Mabel and we should be overjoyed, but we wouldn't have had it happen in this unfortunate way, even though he made her life a misery these past few years.' He replaced his cap and made his way out, promising to be back at the Shire Hall for the inquisition.

After he had gone, Gwyn pulled out the pitcher, which he had replenished that morning, and they sat for a time over a contemplative quart of ale.

'What about Picot's claim, Gwyn?' asked John.

The Cornishman sucked the ale from the whiskers around his mouth before replying. 'Firstly, is it true? If not, why should he come to tell us a string of lies? And if is true, were Ferrars and de Courcy walking the city at night in innocence or with malice?'

John nodded agreement. 'So what do we do next?' he asked rhetorically, as although he always valued his henchman's unfailing common sense, the responsibility was his alone. He carried on, musingly. 'The errand Thomas has undertaken includes the city households of the Ferrars and de Courcys. I doubt we need visit their habitations outside Exeter, as any signs of what happened last night must still be within the walls. So let's wait until our ferrety little clerk returns from his adventures — hopefully with some intelligence for us.'

* * *

Late that afternoon, the Shire Hall was again in use, this time for an inquest rather than a trial.

The coroner occupied the centre chair on the dais, but Sheriff de Revelle sat alongside in a nonchalant posture that was aimed at suggesting that he who was presiding and that John de Wolfe was merely an underling.

Thomas de Peyne squatted on a stool slightly behind his master, quill and ink at the ready. Near him were Archdeacon John de Alecon and Thomas de Boterellis. On the floor below the platform, Gwyn of Polruan ambled about, shepherding the witnesses, the jury and the motley crowd of spectators that milled about the back of the hall. A more macabre duty was to guard the body of the dead man, which lay under a sheet on planks laid on trestles, immediately below John's chair. The jury were legally obliged to view the body, as was the coroner, to examine the wounds visible on the corpse.

Gwyn now called out his summary demand to the effect that all those who had any business before the King's coroner for the County of Devon, should 'draw near and give their attendance'. Among those who were giving their attendance were Reginald de Courcy, Hugh Ferrars and his father, Joseph and Edgar of Topsham and Henry Rifford, the Portreeve. Eric Picot stood unobtrusively at the side of the hall, but Mabel, the dead man's widow, was not to be seen.

These major players were standing at the front, just below the dais, and to their right stood some twenty jurors, those who may have had some personal knowledge of the affair. Most were in clerical garb, comprising several of the junior residents of the canons' houses in the cathedral Close. The large contingent of vicars and choristers explained the presence of the Archdeacon and the Precentor, who were there jealously to guard their ecclesiastical rights against the secular authorities.

For the first part the inquest followed its usual course. The small boy who had found the mortally injured Fitzosbern was considered too immature to be called, though he stood at the side of the hall in fascination, his mother's hand grasping him firmly by the collar. The dog still played around his feet. The young vicar told of his first view of the dying man, after which he virtuously described his attempts to raise the hue and cry by rousing most of the occupants of Canon's Row.

The coroner himself then took up the story. 'I was summoned myself at that point and can state that the injured man was alive when I saw him, but died shortly afterwards. I took a dying deposition from him about certain matters, but he was unable to say who had attacked him.'

At this a murmuring went around the hall. Everyone was well aware from local gossip that Fitzosbern had confessed to being Adele de Courcy's lover and the instigator of her miscarriage. They knew equally well that he had denied ravishing Christina Rifford and that Garth, the silversmith's man, had confessed to that particular crime, but John felt it no part of his inquest to go into those matters.

'The identity of the cadaver as being Godfrey Fitzosbern is well known and no presentment of Englishry is necessary. The question of a murdrum fine will have to be left to the King's Justices, unless a culprit is discovered in the meantime.'

The coroner stood up and hovered at the edge of the dais, the sheriff looking up at him, half amused. 'The jury will now examine the body, as the law demands.' John stepped down to the floor of beaten earth and advanced towards the crude bier, where Gwyn preceded him to whip off the sheet and expose the body down as far as the belly, leaving the lower part of the cloth in place for decency's sake.

Thomas humped his stool nearer to the edge of the dais and hunched over his parchment, ready to write down the proceedings.

Hesitantly, the score of junior priests, servants and choristers formed a circle around the bier, as John began to point out the injuries. Fitzosbern lay with his head on a block of wood, face puffy, eyes almost closed by swollen bruises. Purple-red discolouration covered all the left side of his face, with some straight lines of contusion running down the cheek.

John prodded each injury with a long forefinger, in the manner of a pedagogue giving an anatomy lecture. 'He has been sorely beaten on the face with some long object, maybe a stave or fence-post. See these splits in the skin.' He poked a fingernail into a long gaping wound running diagonally up the left side of Fitzosbern's forehead into the thick dark hair. The pallid vicars gaped at the sight and one chorister left the back row to go outside to vomit. 'On the left side of the neck, there are several of these long straight bruises, but also some small round marks, perhaps from knuckle blows.'

John then turned his attention to the chest, where mottled areas of blue and red bruises showed some lines across the skin. 'As well as these marks from a rod-like weapon, there are these crescents and large marks over the ribs. I suggest to you that they are from heavy kicks.'

'What really killed him, Crowner?' ventured a more robust juror, a servant from a prebendary's house.

For answer, John pressed a strong hand downwards over the breastbone, showing how the front of the chest caved in. This was accompanied by a gurgling from the dead man's throat and a crackling of bone upon bone as the broken rib-ends ground together. Another juror slipped outside to be sick, as John explained that stamping and kicking had crushed the front of the chest.

As the crowd stood in silent awe, he dictated a short account to Thomas, then climbed back on to the platform, as Gwyn drew the sheet discreetly up over Godfrey's face.

'So there is no doubt how he died,' continued the coroner. 'The question is, who caused him to die? Has anyone any information to give me?' He scowled around the hall, almost as if to challenge anyone to offer information.

There was a silence, broken only by feet shuffling on the rough floor.

'Did anyone see anything untoward in the cathedral precincts last night?' he demanded. Strictly speaking, the whole area around the cathedral, apart from the paths, was outside the jurisdiction of the town, coming under ecclesiastical law — but John de Alecon had told him that the bishop had waived any right to challenge the coroner's warrant where deaths were concerned. There was no answer to his question, neither from Picot nor from the two men he had named.

Never one to mince words, John stared down at Reginald de Courcy and Hugh Ferrars, who stood side by side in the front row. 'I have had a report that you two gentlemen were abroad in that area last night. Is that true?'

Hugh Ferrars jumped as if stuck in the backside with a pike. 'What? Do you know what you are saying, Crowner?'

De Wolfe gazed at him steadily. 'I know what I am saying, sir.'

Hugh looked as if he was about to have a stroke. 'Tell me what bastard spun you that tale!' he yelled.

His father was also stung into instant response. 'De Wolfe, are you mad? What nonsense is this?' His face went puce, and both father and son marched up to the foot of the dais and confronted the coroner and the sheriff.

Amid the sudden hubbub in the hall, de Courcy added his voice in loud yells of protest and angry denial, as he joined the others below the edge of the platform.

Richard de Revelle, to whom this was equally a surprise, jumped to his feet and

418

rounded on the coroner. 'You can't accuse people in public, man!' he hissed. 'Who gave you this scurrilous slander?'

John suffered the clamour for a moment, then threw up his hands and yelled, in a voice that could have been heard in St Sidwell's, 'Be silent, all of you!'

His outburst was so dramatic that there was momentary silence, into which he snapped out an explanation. 'I accused no one. But information came my way which I cannot ignore. I asked a simple question, which requires a simple answer. Were you, Reginald de Courcy, and you, Hugh Ferrars, walking in the cathedral Close late last evening?'

Red in the face, the younger Ferrars glared up at him and shouted above the returning babble of voices, 'No, I bloody well was not, Sir Crowner! You are too fond of baseless accusations. By Christ and Mary, Mother of God, and St Peter — and any number of damned saints you like — I was drinking in half the inns in Exeter last night — and none of those lie in the cathedral Close!'

There was a ripple of ribald laughter at this sally, but John was not amused. 'And, no doubt, you conveniently walked half the town doing it, eh?'

'With a dozen witnesses who caroused with

419

me to prove it,' retorted Hugh angrily.

His father pointed a quivering forefinger at the coroner. 'You'll regret this, de Wolfe. Your mouth will be the ruin of you.'

John ignored the threat and turned his gaze on de Courcy, who was similarly flushed with anger. 'Do you say the same, Sir Reginald? I ask only for a yea or nay, there's no accusation involved, at this stage.'

De Courcy was almost livid with fury. 'To settle this once and for all, hear this, Crowner.' He pulled out his dagger from the sheath on his belt and waved it aloft. Gwyn started forward, thinking he was about to plunge it into the coroner, but instead he grasped it by the blade and held it high above him. 'By this Sign of the Cross, I swear once — and once only — that I spent the whole evening by my own fireside until I took to my bed.' He lowered the knife and slid it back into its sheath, then turned on his heel and walked out, his brown surcoat pressed close to his body by the cold wind as he left by the open archway.

As if to emphasise their contempt, the two Ferrars followed him out without a glance at the coroner, stalking away in high dudgeon.

With a poisonous look at his brother-in-law, the sheriff stepped down from the platform and hurried after them.

The rest of the inquest was an anti-climax after the drama. Inevitably the jury returned a verdict of murder by persons unknown and everyone drifted off, including Godfrey Fitzosbern, who was trundled on a handcart across to St John's Hospital, to await burial in the cathedral Close, where he had met his death.

20

In which Crowner John
discovers the truth

Next morning, the coroner sat, somewhat despondently, in his Spartan chamber within Rougemont Castle. He felt that nothing had been achieved by yesterday's inquest, apart from further antagonism between himself, the Ferrars, de Courcy and the sheriff. 'I suppose we'll have that bunch back this morning, spitting venom at me for daring to ask where they were the night before last,' he grumbled to Gwyn. They were waiting for Thomas to report on his search around the town for bloodstains and more servants' gossip, which might give them a lead to Fitzosbern's killer.

Reluctantly John pulled out the latest Latin lesson given him by his cathedral tutor and half-heartedly began to study it on the table. Gwyn sat quietly on the window-ledge, staring absently at the floor, his brow wrinkled in thought. His unusual silence soon unnerved his master. 'Are you sick, man? You're not even drinking ale!'

'I was thinking about Reginald de Courcy.'

John was immediately attentive. When Gwyn had some deep thoughts, they were always worth considering. 'What about him?'

'He was one of those named by Eric Picot, but he couldn't have struck those blows.'

The coroner threw down his Latin roll and leaned back on his stool. 'Come, Gwyn, what's on that great mind of yours?'

'All the injuries on Fitzosbern were on the left side, both face, neck and chest. If struck by someone in front of him, which he must have been, then de Courcy is exonerated.'

The coroner stared hard at his henchman. Gwyn never said anything without a good reason. 'Why do you claim that, man?'

'When he took that oath in the court yesterday, did you notice that he held up his dagger with the left hand? I watched him thereafter and he is undoubtedly left-handed. Even his dagger sheath is on his right hip, instead of on the usual left. And no left-handed man could have caused those injuries from the front.'

John mused over this for a moment and could find no fault in Gwyn's argument. 'Right, I give you that he never struck the blows. But he could have gripped Fitzosbern for another to strike him, or otherwise been in conspiracy with Ferrars to kill the man.'

Gwyn shrugged his massive shoulders.

'True, but at least it's a bit of knowledge we didn't have before.'

The conversation was ended by the uneven tip-tap of a lame leg climbing the stairs, then Thomas pushed his way through the hessian hanging over the doorway. His pinched face had a gleam of suppressed excitement, the little dark eyes glittering with pride.

'Here comes the gnome of Winchester!' teased Gwyn rudely. 'What news from the gutters?'

The clerk was too pleased with himself to rise to the bait. 'Blood, Crowner. I've found blood!' he declared proudly.

With a peremptory jerk of his finger, John got the little ex-priest to sit on the stool before him and tell his story. 'What blood and where?' he demanded.

Agog with self-importance, Thomas de Peyne described his adventures of the previous afternoon and early that morning.

'I went to de Courcy's dwelling in Currestreet. There was a chestnut-seller outside and I waited there as an excuse, eating from a halfpenny sack for some time, watching the house door.' He produced a big hessian bag of cold roasted nuts, which Gwyn immediately began to peel and chew. 'Eventually, a serving-maid opened the door to brush out old rushes and I spun her a tale that I had a message for her master from the sheriff. I knew he was not in, but persuaded the girl to allow me inside to wait for him, chancing that he wouldn't return and catch me there.'

John gave one of his rare grins at the deviousness of the crooked clerk. 'And you found nothing?'

Thomas looked piqued at the anticipation of his tale. 'No, I had no chance to get beyond the porch and outer hall, but slipped through into the yard to tell the maid and the cook that I could wait no longer. But I had time to examine all the clothing that hung on hooks and the shoes and boots that lay on the floor. There was nothing to be seen. Of course, what may have been near the hearth or in the solar, I had no opportunity to view.'

Gwyn and the coroner exchanged glances and the Cornishman spat out some chestnut shell before speaking. 'As we thought, he could not have struck the blows.'

Thomas looked puzzled at this obscure comment, but plunged on with the best part of his story. 'This morning, I went to the younger Ferrars's lodgings in Goldsmith Street. He has only one room and the vestibule there, where he and his squire live when he is in the city. It was easier, for he has no house servants, the squire carrying out any menial tasks. They seem to eat and drink — mainly drink — entirely in the town, not at home.'

'Get to the bloody point, man,' growled Gwyn.

Thomas made a rude gesture at him and poked out his tongue. 'There are other men lodging there, some using the upper room and others the back yard, so there was considerable coming and going. I followed one man through the front door, which wagged back and forth as often as a Cornishman's mouth.' He dodged a chestnut thrown by Gwyn. 'I stood inside the vestibule, where there was a rude pallet for the squire's bed and much clothing, boots and armour. There was so much that it must have belonged to both Ferrars and his henchman.' He drew breath to prepare for the climax of his story. 'I took the chance that no one was at home, as they seem to spend half their time jousting and the other half in the taverns. I searched among the clothing. There, on the side of a surcoat I have seen Ferrars wearing, were many spots of fresh blood.' He ended on this triumphant note and looked expectantly at his master.

'Where was this garment?' asked John, sceptically.

'Hanging on a peg on the left-hand side,

just within the street door. There were a few drops of blood on the floor beneath, which must have dripped off the hem.'

Gwyn pulled hard at his moustache. 'You said that Hugh Ferrars is often away at sword practice and horse-jousting. The blood could have come from that.'

'He would never wear a fine linen surcoat to go fighting,' objected Thomas, annoyed that his great discovery was not being received with due acclamation. 'He would have worn a hauberk or at least a leather cuirass.'

'What colour was this coat?'

'A pale dun — a greyish-brown.'

'Not the best colour for showing up blood spots,' objected Gwyn, but Thomas ignored him.

'Do you recall what Hugh Ferrars was wearing in the shire hall yesterday?' asked John, looking from Thomas to Gwyn. Neither could remember, and the coroner himself could not call it to mind.

Thomas was eager to consolidate his great discovery. 'But you have a report that he was seen near the place of the assault — and he has blood on his clothing! What more do you want?'

John stood up abruptly. 'No good debating upon it — we could do that until next

Michaelmas. Let's go to see Thomas's blood spots.'

★ ★ ★

Goldsmith Street was a turning off high street, running northwards, with All Hallows Church at the near end and St Paul's further along. Just past the entrance from the High Street were several shop-houses with heavy shutters and thick doors. These were the establishments of the gold-workers, the rest of the lane being dwelling-houses. Some were old and wooden, with thatched roofs. More recent ones were built either of plastered wattle in timbered frames or solid masonry.

The wind had dropped overnight, and when the coroner's trio entered the street, the atmosphere was heavy with smoke from a thousand hearth fires in the city. The fumes seemed particularly heavy in that canyon-like lane, as the smoke seeped from under the eaves of the older houses and from the few chimney-stacks of the newer dwellings.

Hugh Ferrars had his lodging half-way down on the left, the ground floor of a narrow timber building with a stone-tiled roof. It had a solar that extended right across the upper part, where other young men lodged. At street level, it was similar to John's own house, with a small entrance vestibule where his squire slept, with a passage running back to the yard behind. Another door led into the hall, a single large room whose ceiling was low and heavy-beamed, because of the presence of the upper chamber.

The street door was shut, but opened when the iron latch was raised. Gwyn stuck his head inside and called out in his bull-like voice. An answering challenge came from the hall and the squire appeared, a tankard in his hand. Behind him Hugh Ferrars, flushed of face, grasped an even larger quart jug. They moved forward into the vestibule and saw John de Wolfe behind his officer.

'Ha, you've come to grovel your apologies, I trust,' grated Ferrars, his voice already unsteady with drink. 'My father is seeking a meeting with Hubert Walter when he goes to Winchester next week, to indict you for your behaviour. You'll regret crossing our family, Crowner.'

John ignored this and turned his attention to the clothes hanging in disorder on the left-hand wall of the vestibule, in line with the low, narrow passage that went through to the rear of the house. Thomas pointed to a dull tan linen surcoat that hung on the wooden peg nearest to the front door.

'What the devil are you up to now, damn

you?' snarled Ferrars, his thick neck reddening with anger as he swayed forward from the hall door.

'Is this your garment?' snapped John, pointing at the super-tunic. It was an open-fronted robe of midthigh length, with short sleeves reaching to the elbow, for wearing over the tunic, a tube-like gown coming to the knees.

Surprise dulled Hugh's aggression. 'Mine? Of course it's mine. Why in God's name do you want to know?'

John bent to lift up the hem of the coat. 'Because of these blood spots, Hugh Ferrars. Can you explain their presence?'

The young man stumbled quickly across the small room and peered at his property. The garment was hanging from its neckband on the peg and on the left side was a spatter of blood, and runnels streaking down to the embroidered hem. On the line of flagstones that crossed the earthen floor to run down the passageway were a few splashes of dried blood.

'Well, what have you to say?' demanded John.

Ferociously, Hugh grabbed the surcoat from the peg and held it up to stare at it as if he had never seen it before. Ale sloshed from his pot as he twisted the coat this way and that to inspect it from every side.

'I know nothing of this, the devil damn it! What game are you playing now, Crowner?' he shouted. Then he rounded on his squire, standing bemused in the background. 'Roland, what do you know of this? Have you been using my clothes?'

As the squire made protestations of innocence and ignorance, John fixed the younger Ferrars with a cold eye. 'When did you last wear this? And I ask you again, where were you the night before last? Were you in the cathedral precinct at any time, eh?'

For a moment, John thought that the young man was going to strike him and his hand went automatically to the hilt of his dagger.

But Hugh settled for a stream of abuse and threats of dire retribution when his father heard of this latest defamation. The coroner waited patiently for this storm of drink-laden invective to die down, then took the coat from Hugh's hand. He pointed to the blood spots, splashed thinly over an area twice the size of a spread hand. 'Look at these, Ferrars, will you?' he asked calmly. 'You are a fighting man, you know blood when you see it. Do you deny that this garment, hanging in your hall, which you readily admit belongs to you, has blood upon it?'

This cold, direct questioning rapidly sobered Hugh's temper. Grudgingly he admitted that the spots could be nothing but blood. 'But as God is my judge, I know nothing of it. I have not worn that coat for at least three days. As you see, I have plenty of others to choose from.' He swept a hand expansively around the vestibule, where every peg had several garments hung upon it and where many more were thrown across stools and even on Roland's tumbled bed.

Gwyn muttered something into the coroner's ear, using their Celtic patois. John turned back to Hugh Ferrars. 'Would you put that ale jar down there for me?' he asked, pointing to the ledge running around the wooden walls.

Mystified, but now deflated by the finding of blood on his clothes, Ferrars dumped the rough pottery mug on the ledge.

'I see you wear your dagger on your left hip?' said John.

Hugh stared at him as if he had gone out of his mind.

'Of course I do — as do you! Why, for Lord Christ's sake?'

John ignored this and puzzled the man even more by asking him to pick up his ale jar again. Rolling his eyes in exasperation, Hugh did so, and Gwyn and John confirmed that he used his right hand.

'Have you finished your mummers' play-acting?' demanded Hugh, his truculence returning.

Suddenly, the case that the coroner and his officer were building up against Hugh Ferrars began to crumble, thanks to the inquisitive and nimble mind of their little clerk. This time it was Thomas who came to whisper into John's ear and, under the uncomprehending gaze of the tenant and his squire, the coroner's team turned their attention to the wall and the street door.

'Gwyn, hang this surcoat on the peg, just as it was,' ordered de Wolfe.

When this was done, Thomas pointed a thin finger at the wooden planks of the wall immediately to the side of the coat. Though hard to see on the dark, weathered timber, a few spots of blood had dried at the same height as those on the gown. Some were elongated, almost fish-shaped, lying horizontally on the planks.

The clerk now pointed down at the blood spots on the grey stones of the floor. 'Some are also spear-shaped. They could not have dripped from the coat but have struck at an angle,' he observed. 'Now open the street door,' advised Thomas, who seemed now as keen to destroy his own theory as he had been, originally to propose it.

It had been closed after they entered, but when it was fully opened, the door swung back against the left-hand wall, its free edge reaching within a few inches of the clothes on their pegs. 'See there, at the same level,' squeaked the clerk.

John looked and saw more small elongated splashes of dark blood dried on the rough black wood.

'Blood has been thrown in through the open door,' rumbled Gwyn. It was now obvious that the blood on the surcoat had got there while it was hanging on its peg, the spray being confined to the side facing the doorway.

'And some has missed the coat and spattered on to the wall, the floor and the edge of the open door,' concluded Thomas. He was now unsure whether to be complacent about his latest discovery or mortified that his original finding of the blood was now discredited as proof of Ferrars's guilt.

Hugh and Roland had been watching the others in total bewilderment, but now the significance dawned upon them. 'I have been falsely accused, then!' ranted Ferrars. 'Not only have you repeatedly slandered my good name, but I have been the victim of a foul plot against me!'

De Wolfe turned and bent from his greater height until his hooked nose almost touched the red face of the young man. 'Listen, sir! You should be grateful for your good fortune. I had information that you were seen in the vicinity of the killing of Fitzosbern at about the right time. Then your bloodstained clothing is found in your own dwelling! Can you deny that those facts should lead to suspicion?'

'False — all false!' snapped Hugh, but the logic penetrated even his fuddled and outraged mind.

'Maybe, but you should be grateful to this astute clerk of mine, for he has removed you from suspicion. It is now obvious that someone has tried to mislead us and plant a false trail to your door.'

He paused and drew back from breathing into Ferrars's face. 'This also involved Reginald de Courcy, but we have eliminated him by other means.'

He turned back to the line of garments and angrily tore the surcoat from its peg and threw it on the ground. 'I should get this to your washerwoman as soon as you can and give thanks to God for the sharp eyes of Thomas de Peyne.'

His fuming anger drilled into Hugh Ferrars's brain and blew away the remnants of his indignation.

'Who did this to me, Sir John?' he muttered.

The coroner hoisted his grey cloak over his hunched shoulders as he prepared to leave. 'I think a certain wine merchant needs to be questioned about that, young man.' He swung out of the house and walked rapidly away, with his clerk and officer hurrying after him, leaving two bemused but now very sober young men staring after them.

★ ★ ★

Ten minutes later, they were in Priest Street, at the lower end of town. This ran down from Southgate Street, past the entrance to Idle Lane, where the Bush tavern stood. The wine merchant's premises were near the lower end, not far from the town wall. They hammered on the door, but there was no response and their shouting through the crack of the shutters was met with stony silence.

Gwyn's yelling and kicking at the stout oak door soon attracted a group of idle onlookers, mostly old men and children. The noise also brought a junior priest from next door, a teacher from the cathedral school, who was home with an attack of the colic. Pale and clutching his stomach, he spared a few minutes from sitting in the privy in the back yard to tell them that he had seen Eric Picot leaving the house soon after dawn.

'Can this door be forced?' demanded John of his henchman.

Gwyn shook his head, the unruly hair flying wildly. 'Not without an iron bar or baulk of timber to smash the lock. I suppose it's meant to keep thieves from his valuable wines.'

The coroner glowered at the young clergyman. 'Has Picot no manservant or worker in the wine shop?'

'He usually has, but no one has been here today.' He was about to add something but, hit again by belly cramps, he turned and stumbled off to his earth closet, leaving the trio to stare in frustration at the closed building.

'If he's not here, why do we need to get inside?' asked Thomas reasonably.

John, in a bad temper, scowled at him. 'Because I can think of nothing else to do at the moment. If the man's gone, we can't question him, so the next best thing is to search his dwelling.'

'I'll get myself around to the back lane,' grunted Gwyn. 'There may be some better chance of entering there.' He vanished down the narrow passage between the house and the next building, which was a barn or storehouse.

A few moments later there was a series of distant crashes from the rear and soon the front door opened from inside. Gwyn stood there, a large axe in his hand.

'This was in the woodshed, and the back door was not so tough as this one,' he announced, with smug satisfaction.

He stood aside as the coroner pushed past into the deserted house.

* * *

Almost an hour later, they were assembled in the Bush, just around the corner.

'He's gone for good, that's for certain.' Gwyn was stating the obvious, but there was nothing else to be done or said for the moment. Thomas had been dispatched to Rougemont to inform the sheriff of the recent developments and to raise men-at-arms to form a search party.

They waited in the warmth of the tavern, sitting before a glowing fire and sustaining themselves with pots of Nesta's best ale. She sat on a bench between John and Gwyn, with old Edwin hovering nearby to eavesdrop under the pretext of refilling their jugs.

'So what *did* you find in his house?' asked

the Welsh woman.

'Very little, except the damned furniture!' growled the coroner. 'It was obvious that he had been preparing to leave for good. All his clothes had gone, his treasure chest was wide open and empty, not so much as a penny piece left anywhere.'

'There was some wine downstairs, but not much,' added Gwyn. 'He lost a lot in the wreck of the *Mary of the Sea* so he had little stock to abandon.'

De Wolfe rummaged in a pocket inside his mantle, which was thrown over the end of the bench. 'He did leave this on his midden behind the house though, which proves his guilt beyond doubt.' He held up a small stone winebottle, pulled out the wooden stopper and up-ended the neck on to his finger-tip.

He held it out to Nesta, who saw thick red blood on his skin. 'Probably from a fowl or a pig. Maybe from his back yard or the Shambles but, wherever it came from, no one can tell it from human.' She took it from him gingerly and looked into the open end, which was rimmed with dried blood. 'So he threw the blood from this in through the open door over the clothing, to make it look as if Hugh Ferrars became soiled when he attacked Fitzosbern?'

John nodded as he took back the bottle and

439

stowed it away again in his cloak. 'If our crafty little clerk hadn't spotted the blood splashes on the door and wall, we might well have been taken in by it.' He felt a hot flush rise in his neck. 'God forbid that I should even imagine the uproar if I had arrested Hugh. His father and half the court in Winchester would have fallen on me like a ton of quarry stone!'

The red-headed innkeeper pressed closer against him, enjoying the solid warmth of his firm body. 'What's to be done next, then?' she asked.

'Find the fellow, wherever he is. Long gone from the city, that's for sure,' growled John. 'When Ralph Morin comes down from Rougemont with his search party, we'll ride out to Wonford to see if he's there.'

Gwyn gulped the last of his ale and looked around hopefully for Edwin to give him a refill. 'He'll be leagues away by the time we get there but God knows where. He could be half-way to Salisbury by now — or to Plymouth or Bristol.'

Nesta got up to throw a couple more logs on the fire. The hearth was set out from the wall on a platform of flat stones. There was no chimney, but the bone-dry wood burnt with almost no smoke and what there was found its way through the shutters of the windows and the cracks between the planks of the floor above. As she sat down again alongside John, she added a woman's comment. 'Eric will not leave without Mabel Fitzosbern, after all the trouble he's gone to, to get her. If she's to travel with him, that will slow him down. She's no horsewoman, for sure.'

This made the coroner jump up, impatient to give chase to the fugitive. 'Where the hell is Thomas? He's had time to get to the castle and back on his hands and knees.'

Gwyn settled back calmly to enjoy his new mug of ale. 'He'll have got there fast enough, no doubt. But perhaps he's run foul of the sheriff. Gabriel couldn't raise a band of soldiers on his own account — he'll at least have to get Ralph Morin's approval.'

As if to prove his words, there was a clatter of hoofs and shouts from outside. The door flew open and John groaned as he saw the crowd that burst in, all in riding gear. First came Richard de Revelle, then his castle constable, but behind them streamed in Reginald de Courcy, Guy Ferrars and his son Hugh.

'A fine situation this!' shouted John's brother-in-law. 'You defame these honourable men for the third time, then find that some other rogue is the culprit!'

'And let the swine slip through your fingers at the last moment,' snapped Lord Ferrars.

John stood four-square before them, his hands on his hips in an attitude of defiance. He learned later that the Ferrars and de Courcy had been with the sheriff when Thomas's message had arrived. They were at the castle to complain about John's allegations and to demand that the Justiciar dismiss him from the coronership. Now he was in no mood to defer to them or anyone else.

'Listen, Hugh Ferrars, if it hadn't been for my clerk, the King's Justices would soon be measuring your neck for a rope collar. Let's not start throwing blame about — none of us has come out of this affair very well.'

Ralph Morin, the only one wearing a chain mail hauberk, made known his own disapproval of any recriminations. 'If we don't get to our horses soon, we'll never catch the man. I've had your steed brought down from the stables, John, and your man's mare. They're outside.'

They jostled out into Idle Lane, where they saw Gabriel and four soldiers alongside their horses, holding the reins of the other seven. Lurking at the rear was Thomas, sitting side-saddle on his little pony. The sky was a pale, cold blue, but a wind from the north-west had suddenly started to moan through the city lanes.

Within minutes, they were all mounted and streamed away from the inn. Nesta, Edwin and a knot of curious customers watched them turn up Priest Street, with the Nordic figure of the castle constable leading the squad, the clerk trotting in the rear.

John rode alongside his brother-in-law, as they clattered towards the South Gate. 'Picot told me that he had established his ladylove in his house in Wonford,' he shouted, above the thud of hoofs. 'We must try there first.'

De Revelle looked his usual elegant self as he sat erect on his gleaming bay horse, his wolf-skin cloak flowing down across its rump. 'He'll not be there, John, you can depend on it. But someone may know which road he took.'

They passed under the looming arch of the gate, the side of which housed the town prison, then went out to where the track split into Holloway and Magdalen Street. They took the latter and put on speed, changing from a trot to a canter as they went past the gallows, now deserted apart from a couple of rotting corpses hanging in their rusting gibbets, which creaked eerily in the rising wind. Thomas was left behind as the big horses charged away up the frost-hardened

443

road, but his tough Exmoor pony always got there in the end.

The hamlet of Wonford was just over a mile outside the city walls and within a few minutes the pursuers had reached it, turning left off the main track, the old Roman road to Honiton and the east. One of the men-at-arms was from the village and knew the place that the wine merchant owned. It was a small but solid house of stone, with a newly thatched roof, nestling behind a wooden palisade. Although Wonford was part of a manor holding, Picot's dwelling had been built on a small plot of land he had purchased from the manorial lord and took no part in the feudal economy of the village.

The gate in the stockade was closed but unbarred. Gabriel dismounted to open it then led the horsemen through.

Inside, the compound was deserted and the two wooden outbuildings were silent, no smoke filtering from their eaves. A few moments' reconnaissance by the sergeant and several of his men proved that no one was there, not even a cook or stable-boy. The stalls in the horse-shed were empty and the saddles were gone. The door was locked, and the house seemed devoid of any life.

'They've flown, right enough,' growled

Ralph Morin. 'But where the hell are the servants?'

John swung around in his saddle to speak to Gwyn, who rode behind. 'Get into the village and see what's happened here.'

The Cornishman, wrapped in his tattered brown cloak with a pointed hood covering most of his unruly ginger hair, wheeled his mare around and clattered out of the gate.

Within minutes he was back with his news. 'The cook and the washerwoman are in their cottages. Their master was here soon after dawn and told them he had to go to France on urgent business. He paid them their wages and told them to go home until they were needed again. Then he left with the two ladies, one of them his sister, and all their horses loaded down with bags.'

'The servants will never hear from him again, that's for sure!' snapped de Revelle. He glared at the coroner. 'You've lost him, John.'

De Wolfe returned his look calmly. 'If we're talking about losing people, what about you letting Fitzosbern slip through your fingers?'

Lord Ferrars for once joined in on John's side. 'Yes, if you'd arrested the silversmith that night, as I'd demanded, he would not have been murdered. He'd have lived to be killed by Hugh in combat — or hanged. And this Picot wouldn't need to be escaping now!'

445

Once again, the taciturn constable of Rougemont reminded them of time-wasting. 'If he's going to France, he may well be trying to sail from Topsham. That's the nearest port and he's got Joseph's ships to use there.'

They all turned their horses and sallied out through the gate into the road. They wheeled again, turning away from Exeter to pass through the village to rejoin the road that followed the river down from Holloway towards Topsham.

Just as they vanished around a bend, Thomas clip-clopped into sight and resignedly carried on in their wake. The wind gusted at his back and he turned to look at the sky. The pale winter blue was now being encroached on by an enormous mass of blue-black cloud that was creeping up over the northern horizon. He shivered and pulled his thin mantle more closely around his bent shoulders, as the pony ambled after the distant band of horsemen.

Topsham was another three miles further on, and some twenty minutes later the pursuers trotted into the single street that ran parallel to the river until it reached the small quayside. Here there was a long thatched warehouse, belonging to Joseph, and a variety of huts and sheds close to the water's edge.

The stone wharf was quite short, sufficient

to moor two vessels, but on each side the sloping mud of the Exe was used to load and unload other smaller vessels at low tide. A hundred yards away, on the other side of the river, miles of mud flat and reed bed stretched up and down the estuary, with the low hills at Exminster and Powderham far away on the other side.

Ralph Morin reined in near the edge of the quay and looked down at a stubby vessel tied up to two tree-stump bollards set in the wharf. A man and a boy sat on the deck repairing sails and it was obvious that this ship was going nowhere in the near future. The constable swung back to Richard de Revelle and the coroner, the rest of the party clustered behind them. 'If they left from here, then they've long gone,' he called.

Gwyn looked at the river. The muddy water was swirling downstream, though the level was high and two small boats upstream from the quay were afloat pulling strongly at their moorings. 'It's an hour or so past the top of the tide,' he pronounced. Then he dragged on his mare's reins and pulled her round to canter to the further end of the wharf. He stopped and held a hand above his eyes to shield them from the winter sun that was low in the south, directly over the river mouth. 'There's a vessel making down-stream, on the ebb tide. She's got full sail on and, with this rising wind, she'll be out of the river in less than an hour.'

The wind was indeed rising with a vengeance, whipping the surface of the river into steep wavelets and whistling across the bare quayside, whirling old leaves and rubbish into the water.

John walked his horse to the edge of the quay and shouted down at the pair working on the ship's deck. 'What vessel is that down-river?' he demanded, in English.

The older man, a grey-bearded sailor, stared up blankly, then looked at the teenager. The boy shouted back at the coroners, 'He speaks only Breton, sir. That other boat is the *Saint Non*.'

John immediately changed to western Welsh, which was virtually the same as Breton. 'Where is she bound for, then?'

The grey-beard, happy with the change of tongue, called against the whistle of the wind, 'She's taking wool to St Malo, sir. Though the master was far from happy to set sail with this coming!' He looked up and pointed heavenwards with his sail-maker's needle. Everyone within earshot followed his gaze and saw that the ominous bank of steel-blue cloud had now reached zenith and the northern horizon was virtually black. The gusting wind was now throwing down a few slivers of sleet.

'Did he have any passengers, my man?' called the sheriff, not wishing to be outdone by his brother-in-law in this chase.

As he spoke no Celtic, the boy had to answer. 'Yes sir, the wine-master and two ladies. That's why Matthew, the ship-master, was persuaded to sail.'

'What d'you mean, 'persuaded'?' yelled de Revelle.

The boy spoke rapidly to the old man, who leered and tapped the side of his nose significantly. The boy turned back to the sheriff. 'Money, sir! The wine merchant offered the ship-master more money. He said it was urgent he got across the Channel without delay.'

Richard de Revelle swung away and confronted the other mounted men. 'He's aboard that vessel, damn him. Can we do anything about it?' He sounded furious, baulked of his prey at the last moment.

Everyone looked at Gwyn, the only one among them with experience of the sea. He shot another look down-river, where the *Saint Non* was dwindling in size with every passing moment. He shook his head. 'Not a chance, unless someone can persuade her master to anchor before he reaches the mouth of the river.'

'Any hope of a fast horseman catching her up before she reaches the open sea?' snapped the coroner.

Again Gwyn pulled a doubtful face. 'This wind is dead astern and is sending her scudding down at a fair old rate — and the ebb tide is helping her on. Though these merchant vessels are ungainly old tubs, in these conditions she'll be moving as fast as a cantering horse.'

The sheriff looked desperately after the distant ship. 'But perhaps not a galloping horse! Morin, send your best rider down the riverbank, try to get within hailing distance of that vessel and tell her to stop. Now, d'you hear?' he roared. 'I don't care if the horse is flogged to death. Stop that ship!'

The constable of Rougemont, though muttering under his breath at what he felt was a futile gesture, decided to try himself, rather than delegate to a soldier. He dug his spurs into his big roan stallion and shot off down the track that ran along the east side of the river, towards distant Exmouth. Within minutes, he had vanished among the scrubby bushes and stunted trees that lined the road.

As he left, Thomas de Peyne jogged up on his pony and joined the band on the quayside, in time to hear Gwyn grumbling, 'It's useless. He'll never get the master to heave to, even if he were to get within earshot.'

Ferrars, as eager as the sheriff to get Eric Picot in his clutches, tried to be optimistic. 'The river mouth is very narrow, the channel between Dawlish Warren and the Exmouth side can be no more than a few hundred paces wide.'

A great sand bar, most of it overgrown with grass and scrub, stretched far out from the western lip of the river mouth, leaving the Exe to squeeze its way against the opposite bank through a narrow passage.

Gwyn was unimpressed. 'Even if the constable can attract their attention, he'll never be heard across the water in this wind. And anyway, maybe the master wouldn't want to heave to. It would be very dangerous over the bar on an ebb tide, in this rising gale.'

'Especially if he's being paid a handsome sum to keep going,' added the coroner, cynically.

For lack of anything else to do, the band of mounted men moved to the further end of the quay and grouped together in the lee of the warehouse, where there was some shelter from the merciless wind and the increasing flurries of sleet. From here they could see the white sail of *Saint Non* as she was driven

451

down the estuary, now fully three miles away. Although, as Gwyn had pointed out, she was a short, stumpy cargo vessel with a single mast, she was indeed fairly ripping through the water, bow-down from the pressure of the high wind against her sails.

Reginald de Courcy sat his horse and watched the diminishing vessel with mixed feelings. 'Much as I should regret the escape of a cunning felon, I have to say that I must give him some thanks for ridding the world of that evil bastard who caused the death of my daughter,' he said, half to himself.

Alongside him, Hugh Ferrars, sober for once, muttered a grudging agreement. 'Maybe he did us a service, though I would liked to have run Fitzosbern through in combat, after the swine was brought to justice.'

As they sat staring downstream, the sky darkening perceptibly as the huge black cloud-bank moved menacingly further south, a new voice was heard coming towards them.

From across the track to the village street came a tall figure, the bottom of his hooded cloak whipping around his legs in the wind as he walked across to them from his house. It was Joseph of Topsham, who had just been told of their arrival. 'In the name of the Holy Mother, what's going on?' he cried, as he

452

went to the coroner's stirrup.

John explained what had happened, and that they had been trying to arrest Eric Picot, Joseph's friend and partner. The coroner had a fleeting suspicion that the old merchant might have been a party to the crime, but dismissed it rapidly, knowing of Joseph's piety and straight-dealing.

The old trader was ashen-faced with shock and disbelief. He grasped the edge of John's saddle and hung on to support himself, almost in tears. 'I can't believe it! He came this morning, he had arranged days ago to take passage on my *Saint Non*, leaving on this tide. He said he wanted to take Mabel over to meet his family at his vineyard in the Loire — his sister was coming to chaperone them.'

John looked down-river again and at the distant white blur that was the vessel. 'It looks as if he's had his wish, Joseph.'

They waited another half-hour until the sails of the *Saint Non* were only occasionally visible between the squalls of sleet and rain that hurtled down the Exe valley with increasing fury.

'No chance at all of Ralph Morin getting anywhere within hailing distance of her now,' declared Gwyn, with some self-satisfaction at having his nautical prophesies vindicated.

John stared into the distance until his eyes

hurt, his hawk-like head poked forward under his hood as if to gain even a few inches on the fleeing ship. 'I wish I had some magic device for looking through to see things nearer,' he fantasised. 'Then I could see Picot's face over the stern of that boat to see if he is regretful, or triumphant at giving us the slip.' He sighed and swung Bran around to follow the others as they thrust their way through the gale back to Exeter, the wind stinging their eyes until their noses ran.

That night, the worst storm for forty years swept Normandy and the West Country, tearing off a thousand roofs and bringing down the tower of St Clement's church in Exeter.

Next day, both shores of the Channel were littered with the planks of wrecked ships and the corpses of their mariners.

THE END

We do hope that you have enjoyed reading this large print book.

Did you know that all of our titles are available for purchase?

We publish a wide range of high quality large print books including:
Romances, Mysteries, Classics, General Fiction, Non Fiction and Westerns.

Special interest titles available in large print are:
The Little Oxford Dictionary
Music Book
Song Book
Hymn Book
Service Book

Also available from us courtesy of Oxford University Press:
Young Readers' Dictionary
(large print edition)
Young Readers' Thesaurus
(large print edition)

For further information or a free brochure, please contact us at:
Ulverscroft Large Print Books Ltd.,
The Green, Bradgate Road, Anstey,
Leicester, LE7 7FU, England.
Tel: (00 44) 0116 236 4325
Fax: (00 44) 0116 234 0205

STRANGER IN THE PLACE

Anne Doughty

Elizabeth Stewart, a Belfast student and only daughter of hardline Protestant parents, sets out on a study visit to the remote west coast of Ireland. Delighted as she is by the beauty of her new surroundings and the small community which welcomes her, she soon discovers she has more to learn than the details of the old country way of life. She comes to reappraise so much that is slighted and dismissed by her family — not least in regard to herself. But it is her relationship with a much older, Catholic man, Patrick Delargy, which compels her to decide what kind of life she really wants.